The *Poet* of *Tolstoy Park*

BALLANTINE BOOKS

NEW YORK

The *Poet* of *Tolstoy* Park

a novel

SONNY BREWER

A Ballantine Book
Published by The Random House Publishing Group

ISBN 0-345-47631-X

Map illustration by Sonny Brewer

Manufactured in the United States of America

TEXT DESIGN BY DANCING BEARS DESIGN

THIS BOOK IS DEDICATED TO
FOUR PEOPLE WHO PROVE TO ME
THAT GETTING OLD DOES NOT MEAN WINDING DOWN:

Helen "Nannie" Prados LIVED ON HER OWN UNTIL NINETY-TWO,
AND READS TWO BOOKS A WEEK AT NINETY-THREE;

Windy Johnston, AT EIGHTY, WAS STILL TEACHING KIDS
TO WINDSURF DOWN AT THE FAIRHOPE YACHT CLUB;

Ray Parmley HAS LIVED FOR TWENTY-FIVE YEARS
ON HIS FORTY-TWO-FOOT SLOOP,
AND SAILED IT TO CUBA IN HIS EIGHTIES;

AND Mama—Nylene Estes—GOD BLESS HER,
LIVED THROUGH A STROKE THE DOCTORS SAID SHE WOULDN'T
AND IS STILL STRONG AS A HORSE AT SEVENTY-THREE.

After the heyoka ceremony I came to live here where I am now between Wounded Knee Creek and Grass Creek. Others came too and we made these little gray houses of logs that you see, and they are square. It is a bad way to live, for there can be no power in a square.

You have noticed that everything an Indian does is in a circle. And that is because the Power of the World always works in a circle, and everything tries to be round. . . .

The sky is round and I have heard that the earth is round like a ball. And so are all the stars. The wind in its greatest power whirls.

Birds make their nests in a circle, for theirs is the same religion as ours. . . . The life of a man is a circle from childhood to childhood, and so it is in everything where power moves. . . .

But the Waischus [white men] have put us in these square boxes. Our power is gone and we are dying, for the Power is not in us any more. . . . Well, it is as it is. We are prisoners of war while we are waiting here. But there is another world.

—BLACK ELK, HOLY MAN
OF THE OGLALA SIOUX,
FROM *Black Elk Speaks*
BY JOHN G. NEIHARDT

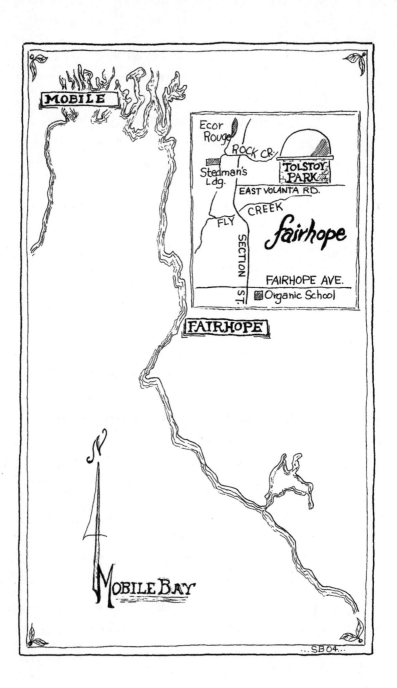

MOBILE

Ecor
Rouge

ROCK CR.

Stedman's
Ldg.

TOLSTOY
PARK

EAST VOLANTA RD.

CREEK

FLY

fairhope

SECTION ST.

FAIRHOPE AVE.

Organic School

FAIRHOPE

N

MOBILE BAY

..SB 04..

ACKNOWLEDGMENTS

Some years ago I met a South Carolina writer, Tommy Hays, who assured me there's no good excuse for not writing, if you want to write. He had a wife and two children and a full-time job and two novels to his credit. In fact, he made me a promise: in his novel *The Family Way*, he inscribed it to me, "It won't be too long before you find the time to write. . . ." I had been lamenting the lack of time to get a book done, what with having a family and a bookstore and—back of the wrist to my forehead—*all that I do, there just weren't enough hours to go around.*

Of course, there are. Read author-bio sketches and sooner than later you'll come across a story of how a certain book was written under some pretty tough circumstances and tight constraints on time. On the other hand, some writers get help from the good people around them who want to enable the writer's craft. That's what happened at my house. My wife Diana, my sons John Luke and Dylan, and my daughter Emily consented to a broader margin of time in my company with them so I could get the work done on *The Poet of Tolstoy Park*. Diana was supportive above and beyond the call of duty and deserves a medal.

Bookseller Martin Lanaux read the manuscript pages as I completed them and pushed the story along in his good-natured way. He collected old photographs and anecdotes of Henry Stuart, kept tabs on my progress, and catalogued odd coincidences that made me believe we were on the right track. Jim Gilbert took the reins of my bookstore, Over the Transom Books, and kept it from going under, and kept the roads hot between the bookshop and the copy center.

And speaking of bookstores and booksellers, John Evans, my dear friend and owner of Jackson, Mississippi's Lemuria Books, is the

Godfather of Southern Lit with a heart and head for books that is legendary.

Mac Walcott was there for me and for Over the Transom like the Patron Saint of the Difficult Cause of Independent Booksellers, underwriting space in my workdays so I could get this book out. Cindy in Mac's office stood by me at the overnight mailbox, and cranked out some copies of the chapters for early readings. Smokey Davis bet on this book, too, and caught errors in the manuscript; our backstory proves busted publishing partnerships cannot undo friendship.

Mary Lois Timbes and Cathy Donelson and Butch Sheldon provided research materials. Wade Baldwin opened a door on the past upstairs at the hardware store. Artist Bruce Larsen did a sculpture of Henry Stuart for Tolstoy Park, and loaned his sons Brock and Dane to help my boys John Luke and Dylan clean up the hut where Henry lived. The artist Nall gave me wrought-iron fencing to decorate the grounds at the hut. And, Ken Neimeyer, bless him, had the heart to instruct the bulldozers to work around Henry's hut, and granted me a nine-year lease to the place so I could restore it. Maria Rosso made curtains so I could have some privacy while completing the book on the premises in Henry's hut. Her husband, Chris John, photographed me inside for the back flap of the dust jacket, and recorded images of the construction progress.

My writer pals Rick Bragg, William Gay, Tom Franklin, Bev Marshall, and Joe Formichella offered me their friendship and words of encouragement. It kept me going back to the computer to write another paragraph, and another, until there were pages and chapters.

My great pal Kyle Jennings and his sweet wife Jill Connor Browne bid me set out on this adventure to find a New York publisher. My friends at MacAdam/Cage Publishing in San Francisco, publisher David Poindexter, and editor Pat Walsh gave me the initial shove from their familiar shores that brought this book to a berth in Ballantine's good harbor. My agent-navigator, Amy Rennert, plotted my course and saved me from certain grounding and loss. The best editor in the world, Maureen O'Neal, and her super assistant Johanna Bowman captained this novel into Bristol fashion. Dorothy Smith in

San Francisco hoisted brilliant colors over Henry Stuart's story with a poetic cover design. And before I finish this metaphor, a takeoff on the Breton sailor's prayer seems appropriate: "Lord, be good to me. My book is so small and thy sea of readers so wide." (And keep a watchful eye on the doings of my buddy Steve Wallace, whom I owe Big Time for his support and secondhand knowledge of train lore.)

And good old Cormac, my dog, lay so patiently near my desk re-minding me that, like Kerouac's cat, there is, finally, nothing so great about human endeavor or failings that should disturb our rest.

The *Poet* of *Tolstoy Park*

PROLOGUE

Clarence Darrow stopped on the path. He thought he heard footsteps in the scattering of leaves on the forest floor. He'd made his way along here, under these tall pines and bent magnolias, beside the thick trunks of occasional live oaks, and had never met another person walking here. Not even the man to whose house he was going. House—such as it was: round and domed at the roof, heavy, of castle-looking blocks with ivy and honeysuckle partly obscuring the lower walls. And today, when the lawyer would arrive there, it would feel like a castle, offering him rest and haven. The threats had come before, but never bearing such—what would one say?—*promise,* and the crunching of the leaves behind him was more likely the imaginings of an overactive mind, and a mind become less certain of the outcome of the fights he chose so carefully. Still, he knew that this man, the castle-keeper and lord of these woods, bewhiskered and barefoot old Henry Stuart, would put a proper lens to this thing.

Darrow's address was being well publicized in the Fairhope and Mobile newspapers. Even the upstate paper in Birmingham carried announcements of the Chicago lawyer's upcoming talk: "The Inequities of Race in the U.S. Judicial System." The note Darrow had found this morning nailed to his door at the Colonial Inn overlooking Mobile Bay replicated the tone and intent of the other threats. "Take your lessons in nigger loving back up North, or we'll ship you home in a trunk." Some from the courthouse in Mobile had begun to express concern that his lecture there could cause a backlash in the city. There was fear for his welfare, and Clarence was taking the possibility of violence seriously.

He stopped and put his hand on a tree, leaning forward slightly. He perspired under his shirt, and tiny beads of sweat shone on his forehead. The bark cut into the soft flesh in the palm of his hand, and an ant crawled onto his finger. He did not recall becoming so winded trekking up this little knoll the other three times he'd paid a visit to the "hermit of the Montrose woods." But, he thought, as he waited for his breathing to settle, that had been a year and a half ago now. Could time have gone by that quickly? Darrow had an idea that this speeding up of time as his hair grew thinner and became more silver at the temples was a consequence of the pro rata portion of his life being considered. A year to a child of seven is one seventh of the time and experience of its entire life; a year to a seventy-year-old man is one-seventieth of the scope of his existence on this planet. He'd have to take this up with Henry, who loved to joust about with "notions," as he called them, to chase high ideas across an afternoon and into the evening and up to the yawning of a late night. Such was the nature of the affection Darrow had developed for Henry James Stuart since their first meeting after his lecture in Fairhope to raise money for the school there. Henry, a stranger then, had brought for him a small handwoven rug, exquisite, the supple yarn virtually alive with color. Clarence had been reluctant to believe the rug was the work of the old man presenting it to him.

And this notepaper folded into Darrow's shirt pocket, the scrawl of ink upon it so filled with hatred that the lawyer believed a blood-hound could smell it, would provoke just what Clarence needed from his friend. Henry would take the note in his hand, his hand that shook a little more than the last time they'd sat together in Tolstoy Park, what Henry called his ten acres of Alabama, and he would read it. He would continue looking at the page for long moments. He'd refold it slowly, and hand it back, and let the same hand travel to his chest and the white beard curling at his open shirt collar there. He would twist the long, soft hairs around his index finger, and pinch the tuft thoughtfully. Then would come what Darrow so longed for at this moment: starting in his eyes with a small spark, intelligent and rascally at the same time, the warmth of a smile would spread across his Indian-looking cheeks and catch the corners of his mouth and pull them up just so. And he would say, "Well." He would turn his face and lock eyes with Clarence and nod gently, un-blinking. "Let's talk about this."

Henry walked out of the doctor's office and the drumming rain that had begun to fall went straight through his thin white hair, wetting his head and sending a chill down his back. Instead of putting on his hat, he placed the flat of his palm on his forehead and stroked the dampness accruing there. He sat down on the edge of the porch, quickly soaking the seat of his pants.

He rubbed his hands together and massaged the pain in his knuckles, then lifted his left foot and took hold of the heel of his boot and tugged it off. He straightened his back, took a breath, and in a moment crossed his right leg over stiffly and removed the other boot. Henry decided, because it was his option to do so, that he would abandon his boots. He paired them up evenly there on the boards.

Henry could not remember when last he had walked barefoot in the rain, mud squishing up between his toes. He believed it was Black Elk, or maybe Chief Seattle, who had said that the man who always wears his moccasins thinks the earth is covered with leather. Henry looked at his boots and wondered how long they would sit before someone took them. They were good Wellingtons and not badly worn, and he thought someone would be surprised to find a pair of boots on the porch at Dr. Belton's place.

Henry planted his palms on his knees, caressed the wet brown twill trousers, and from those points levered himself to standing. He would let his feet know that this piece of earth was covered with mud, and thought perhaps they'd enjoy knowing that.

He tilted his face downward and was lifting his rumpled and sweat-stained felt hat when he heard his name called and, looking up, saw a horse and wagon drawing near the plank sidewalk in front of which he stood. Twenty years earlier in Nampa, Idaho, the first automobile had been delivered on a flat train car. Now in 1925 the tables were turned and only a few stubborn sorts still went about in horse-drawn carriages or wagons. This driver was among them. He sat alone on the buckboard seat, the long leather reins drawn tight in his gloved hand, making to stop his dappled gray Appaloosa. With his left hand the driver pulled back hard on the brake shaft.

"Whoa! Whoa back there, Bo," the driver said.

The horse slowed his walk, its hooves sucking at the muddy street, but did not come to a stop until the wagon was dead even with Henry. This side street was one of four remaining unoiled or unpaved streets in Nampa, and some of Dr. Belton's patients said perhaps the dust and mud was unsanitary, but the doctor disagreed. He did not like automobiles himself, and he owned the entire block, so the town council took their pavement and their oiling elsewhere for the time being. That kept at least some of the cars away, and the smell of oil out of the air.

"How do, Brother Webb?" Henry nodded to the man in the wagon, then raised his arm, hat in hand, and slowly wiped the top of his head with his shirtsleeve, depositing his hat there before dropping his hand to his side. His arms hung straight, his fingers loose.

"Did you pray up this rain, Will?" Henry was making small talk, postponing for a moment at least what was coming. But the Reverend William Webb had been dealing with people of all stripes for forty years, and Henry knew this preacher's practiced eye would discern that the news from the doctor was bad. Like as not, Henry's two boys had made such a prediction to the preacher man. Both his sons went to this preacher's church, Harvey, the oldest, a regular. We might as well go ahead and get on down to the quick on this one, Henry thought.

"Henry," the preacher said, rain dripping from the brim of his hat, "Thomas and Harvey have been telling me something's bad wrong with you. Said you've been coughing and spitting up blood and you were coming in to see the doctor this morning. I watched you go in there, and I've been lying in wait like a highwayman for you to come out. Now, I—"

"Dr. Belton said it's consumption, Will," Henry said evenly. "Tuberculosis. He's given me a year to live. Maybe not that long. Maybe a little more." Henry stood, like a patient man in line at a bank, his arms at his side. He was a tall man, just at six feet, and medium-built, his shoulders still square and his spine still straight. Nothing about him projected grave illness, and he could have passed for a man of fifty, though he was sixty-seven. His clear blue eyes locked on the dark eyes of the preacher, darker still under the soaked brim of his hat.

William Webb shook his head, then bent his face downward. When Will looked up, he said, "I am sorry, Henry. This is a hard one, my friend." The preacher wrapped the reins around the brake, slid across the wet seat, taking hold of the seat back to help steady his rise. "If you'll let me, I'll pray with you, Henry. Just a brief word with the Lord." A big redbone hound bellied out from underneath the porch, startling the horse into a quick forward step, snatching the wagon. The preacher lurched and fell back, sitting down hard on the wagon seat. "Aw, Bo, damn your hide!"

Henry smiled. "Keep your seat, Reverend." He watched the old hound trot across the street, going diagonally toward the alley that would take him behind the Melton Hotel, and perhaps a scrap of bread raked off a breakfast plate. The morning fell darker, and there was a low roll of thunder toward the hills east of town, and the rain fell harder. Henry turned his collar up. "I'll let you know when I need a prayer lifted on my behalf, though I do appreciate your intent, Brother Webb."

"Can I at least give you a ride back out to your place? This muck'll ruin your boots." The preacher let his eyes travel slowly down to Henry's long bare feet. "Well, that is, when you put your boots back on. I've got to go in that direction, Henry, and I'd not think a thing of carting you to your front gate."

"But it's to the Pearly Gates you truly want to cart me. I have known you for too long, Will. You'll never give up. You would talk all the way and make half a dozen altar calls."

"I expect there'd not be time for half a dozen entreaties meaningful enough to rescue that starving soul of yours." Preacher Webb propped a booted foot on the buckboard's dash, caught the wet and wilted brim of his hat and tilted it back a bit for a better look at Henry James Stuart. "I worry about you, Henry, staying away from the church like we've got out a quarantine sign. Both your sons come as often as we open the doors. Don't you think Molly would want you in the church with her boys?"

Henry braced his shoulders and closed his hands, though not tight into fists. "Molly did want me to go to church. With her. And I went, glad to go for the pleasure it seemed to give to her. But, Will, Molly is dead three years now, and—"

"And you have not darkened the door of my church one time since she passed, Henry."

"Nor shall I, Will. We don't really have to talk about this again, do we?"

"But do you not fear for your soul now that you'll soon face the Almighty?" The preacher sat straighter, still holding up the brim of his hat.

"My face has never turned away from God, nor my ear ever inclined away from his counsel. You do not stand between me and my creator, Will Webb. It seems a prideful thing to suggest, and a touch arrogant."

Preacher Webb took his foot from the dash and banged it down on the puddled floorboard, leaning forward to unwrap the reins. "And you are the stubbornest man in all of Idaho, Henry. My prayer is that you get a chance to argue your name onto Heaven's roll, for you could argue the horns off a goat." The rain quickly eased and almost stopped, and both men looked briefly toward the sky, as if to find the cause of the lull.

"Since you have got it going this morning, Will, let me argue with you for half a minute," Henry said, drawing his bushy white eyebrows together in a frown. "Let me tell you how I believe that all the names of all the people in all the ages are written forever on that roll you speak of. How I believe that when our Maker claims what is his at the birth of a child and duly records it in his Book of Life, that little one becomes a divine property that neither foe nor force nor deed can steal."

Henry lifted his hands, a questioning gesture. "Can't you get your preacher's heart to believe that what was ever once God's is always God's? It's simple to me. There is nothing that can oppose the creative force of the universe. There is nowhere to get to, Will, if you never truly left. It's because you and others of your ilk cannot even approach such an idea that I have no need of what you're selling at the churchhouse, Will."

"This is your 'Everybody Gets Back to Heaven' sermon. I've heard it before, Henry." The reverend held the reins one in each hand, and was bent forward slightly with his forearms resting on his heavy thighs. "Come on, Henry. What a load of bull. I don't know how they graduated you from Mount Union. Must've been an off year for them in their divinity department to turn you loose among good Baptists."

Henry shook his head, but smiled. He had first laid out his theology to Will Webb on one of their fishing afternoons down at a favorite spot on Lake Lowell. It was after Aldus Sansing, a man well known to Henry, had been cut down with a double-barreled shotgun during a robbery and had died without officially "coming to the Lord" on a Sunday morning. Aldus never went there. Not for weddings and not for funerals.

His murderer was soon caught, and while he waited in jail to be hanged, he found his salvation, presided over and attested to by Reverend Orlen Estes. A grammar-schooler, thought Henry, could see something wrong with the killer getting his writ to enter Heaven while a good man had been murdered and tossed to Hell.

Ruminating upon that, in a moment's insight, Henry had come to believe that if indeed there was a "next step" after this trail is quit, then all and everyone is privileged to walk that walk. Henry believed he saw clearly the advance of all things. He knew that a boy who takes early to drinking and carousing is not left in some box marked 1907, but gets himself along to 1915 and a box labeled "Loving Husband/Good Father." But then he might run off with the neighbor's wife the next year. And that was that. And it did not matter a whit, for all manner of things would in time be set right.

And Henry was at ease with his belief, but Henry's first son Harvey had told him to his face that he was hell-bound. Neither he nor his friend Will Webb could cotton to a simple line that all persons would perfect the soul awarded them, even if it takes eons. Neither could seem to comprehend the absence of a devil that could actually oppose and defeat the maker of the universe. For Henry, the debate was ended. And now, it seemed, he'd be the first of the three to discover the truth of his religion. And that was well enough for Henry, who in apprehending the mix of sadness and exasperation on Will's face found his thoughts turning to Tolstoy. Henry had been reading and rereading the novels of Tolstoy since he was in his twenties, and had long studied his nonfiction. Henry knew that Tolstoy was a deeply spiritual man, and yet was excommunicated and therefore buried without the help of the Russian Orthodox Church. Some in Tolstoy's church, certainly his family and friends, must have been nonplussed by his disdain for organized religion.

The Reverend William Webb slid back across the wagon's board seat, making a swipe at the spot he'd just vacated. "Here, then. Put your boots back on, Henry, and hop up here and let me give you a ride home. Come on now, before this rain takes up again. I'll not preach a word in the direction of your black heart." The preacher gave an exaggerated wink. "While we're riding you can tell me about this consumption, or what have you, that's fool enough to think it can kill you." Will paused, removed his wet right glove to accept the hand of his friend and help him onto the wagon seat, then said, "It's not catching, I guess. Consumption, I mean."

That got another smile out of Henry. He shook his head. "It's not the contagious strain of the illness." Henry motioned with his hand to the preacher. "I'll walk, Will. And without my fine boots. It will be excellent practice for those long barefoot walks up in the clouds. But I do thank you for the kindness of your offer."

"Now who is the arrogant one? Where do you come by the certainty that it'll not be red-hot coals you'll be treading upon, Henry? Down there!" And Will Webb gave a thumbs-down toward the ground. Both men fell into laughter for a brief moment until Henry gave a deep raspy cough and turned to take from his unbuttoned shirt pocket a clean fold of handkerchief and coughed into that, putting it into his trousers back pocket when normal breathing had come again to him. Unguarded, muscles in the preacher's face now sagged downward around his eyes and mouth and the sadness was plain to see. "I am mighty sorry, Henry. Mighty sorry." Will shifted both reins to his left hand and held his open right palm out toward his friend. "May the peace of the Lord be with you, Henry."

Henry drew a finger to his hat. Will gestured a final time to the seat beside him. Henry shook his head no. Will nodded and slapped the reins. Bo pulled the wagon into the sloppy, gray-mudded street, and Henry saw Will draw himself down against the cold rain.

Henry spoke into the soft sigh of the morning. "And also with you, Brother Webb."

· TWO ·

John McAlister's daughter Ruth had returned his boots, but Henry walked barefoot more and more often, particularly on the longer trips to town. A chill September wind snapped at the trees, tore loose the first crisp yellow leaves, and invited sweaters and heavier sleeves down from the closet shelves, but the sun would not be intimidated and shone brightly upon the ground. Henry's toes and the balls of his feet found the warmth there in the soil, and the fire in the earth coursed up his calves and thighs into his belly and settled in his chest, warming his breathing, relaxing the muscles of his shoulders and neck so that he did not withdraw into his collar from the whistling wind.

In all his years here in Idaho, the cold seasons of late autumn and winter, often stretching into delayed springs, had not suited Henry well. And now he would choose someplace warm to die. The doctor said it would probably bring him more comfort toward the end.

For two weeks now the brochures Henry had written away for had come to the Nampa post office. Towns and counties in Southern California were therein wrapped in words so picturable and well chosen, so vivid and sensual, that it seemed to Henry as he had read them that he could practically feel the climate. It had been only a month since Dr. Belton had told him about the consumption, but he did not wish to drag out his departure and was set upon moving before winter. Henry had thought the right place to go was San Diego. But today he was looking for another letter, the third such posting from Peter Stedman in Fairhope, Alabama, a town a dozen miles as the laughing gull would fly across the bay from the port city of Mobile. Henry was now all but decided on moving to Alabama.

Will Webb had suggested to Henry that he take a look at a move to the high bluffs along the Eastern Shore of Mobile Bay, saying that one of his congregants, who had come back to Idaho from a visit with relatives in a coastal Alabama town founded only thirty or so years earlier, was "just crazy" for this little town he had found. Will had produced for Henry an illustrated brochure "setting forth the advantages of Fairhope" given him by this church member, and in it one Peter Stedman compared the town and bayside area to a utopia: "Dear Friends, you will find here in the single-tax colony of Fairhope and its environs nothing less than an idyllic and beautiful spot of Heaven, embroidered into a rich cultural and recreational tapestry to rival our large cities up East."

Henry doubted the veracity of the pitch, but sufficient curiosity was stirred in him, especially regarding the reference to Fairhope as a single-tax colony, to prompt a letter of further inquiry to Mr. Stedman, who immediately responded.

Henry's letter from Peter Stedman had arrived and Henry stood in the post office and opened it, Jeremiah in his cage shuffling mail into boxes, humming off-key. Henry began reading, his eyes moving quickly down the page. His heart began to beat faster as he followed Peter Stedman's lines about how the town had been founded in 1894 by freethinking followers of the economist/philosopher Henry George. Leo Tolstoy, Henry knew, had been an admirer of this man's beliefs about land and wealth. Henry recalled Tolstoy introducing his readers to Henry George's ideas, calling Henry George by name in his novels. And here was this Fairhope, incorporated some sixteen years before Tolstoy's death. Under other circumstances, the great Russian man of letters himself might have liked to visit this place! Stedman's letter told Henry, too, that one E. B. Gaston had recruited some twenty-eight men, women, and children in Iowa to join him in the purchase of a tract of land where they would found, with "a fair hope of success," a reform community to stand against what they believed was America's wildly competitive society of rampant monopoly capitalism and land speculation.

Henry thanked Jeremiah, whose face appeared behind the bars at the mail counter, and who, letters flowering from both hands, said, "Mr. Henry, it is my pleasure to be of service." Henry had not waited for Jeremiah to say more, quickly going out the door of the post office, still holding the letter from Fairhope in his hand, the pages flapping with the long arcs of Henry's swinging arms. He banged open the front door of his home and charged into his study, fairly tossing the letter onto his desk as he passed it. He went directly to the bookcase where his Tolstoy volumes were neatly arranged and took down *Resurrection*. In five minutes he had found in that novel a reference to Henry George.

In Book II, Chapter I, this: "Nekhlyudov knew all this when, as a university student, he had confessed and preached the doctrines of Henry George and, on the basis of that teaching, had given to the peasants the land inherited from his father."

And soon in Chapter VI: "Henry George's fundamental position recurred vividly to Nekhlyudov's mind. He remembered how he had once been carried away by it, and he was surprised that he could have forgotten it. 'The earth cannot be anyone's property; it cannot be bought or sold any more than water, air, or sunshine. All have an equal right to the advantages it gives to men.'"

Chapter IX found Tolstoy's character continuing: "Nekhlyudov was encouraged by this, and began to explain Henry George's single-tax system.

" 'The earth is no man's; it is God's,' he began."

There was more in *Resurrection,* and then, within an hour, Henry was into Tolstoy's diaries, and found this:

April 2, 1906. "People talk and argue about Henry George's system. It isn't the system which is valuable (although not only do I not know a better one, but I can't imagine one), but what is valuable is the fact that the system establishes an attitude to land which is universal and the same for everybody. Let them find a better one if they can."

Henry closed the Tolstoy, stacked the book on the others and pushed them all away from the center of his desk, and turned back to the letter, meaning to take up where he'd quit reading when he bolted from the post office. He blinked several times until he relocated his spot on the second page.

After a rocky start, according to Stedman, the little colony had attracted numerous hardworking settlers from various parts of the country. The natural beauty of the location together with cooperative development, nurtured a kind of democratic communalism that appealed to intellectuals and mavericks, artists and writers and craftspeople, and a reasonable share of crazies. The literature also boasted that several famous visitors, including Upton Sinclair, Sherwood Anderson, Mrs. Henry Ford, and Clarence Darrow, had come to see what Fairhope was all about.

Henry returned the letter to its envelope and slipped it into his shirt pocket. He had felt a little chill on his outing to the post office, especially on the way back home, and he went to the hall tree and took down from the brass hook his heavy woolen vest. He slipped it on, and briefly considered his boots standing there beside the hall tree, but thought, no, and walked to his front door and outside to go find his friend Will.

Henry found him in his church office, bent over his desk preparing a sermon for Sunday, a Bible and concordance and paper open beside an oil lamp, its wick holding a small yellow flame behind a smoky glass chimney. Before Will could rise to greet him or even re-move the spectacles from his nose, Henry told Will about the Henry George/Leo Tolstoy connection of the Alabama town. Then Henry stopped abruptly and asked the preacher if he'd known of it all along, aware of Henry's affection for Tolstoy. Will laughed loudly. "I know less about nuances in the Gospels than I should, Henry. The prospect of my ferreting out such obscure details about your Russian is a fan-tasy of a higher order than walking on water."

"Well, then it's Providence that you bring this to me, Will." Henry rapped his knuckles on Will's desk. "If Clarence Darrow and Upton Sinclair are curious about the goings-on in this Fairhope, then so am I." He walked behind Will's desk and clapped him on the shoulder. "I do believe, Will," Henry had said to his friend, "that you have helped me to discover the right place to live until I die."

"And better than that," Preacher Webb said, "I know a good place where you can live after you die." His broad smile revealed good white teeth, but his eyes revealed the melancholy of a man soon to lose a friend.

"But how could I rest if you also plan to reside there, Will?" Henry patted Will on the back and asked him to walk with him. "I will write back to Peter Stedman and ask him to act as my agent in the purchase of a small piece of land near this Fairhope." Will told Henry he'd make the walk to the post office with him. "Just stop back by in a bit when you've got your letter ready to go. The walk'll do me good."

In quick succession, two more letters had been exchanged be-tween Henry and Stedman. Ten days earlier, Peter Stedman had writ-ten to say he had found some property that Henry might like. Now Henry was waiting on a letter that he hoped would quote a final price on a ten-acre parcel of land on the highest hill along the eastern crescent of Mobile Bay. Stedman had written that it lay about a mile inland from the bay, part of a place called Montrose that was a good hour's walk north of the town of Fairhope. Upon the ten acres, "high and dry in the piney woods," were a small barn and an outhouse, which had survived Union troop burnings fifty years earlier, and a

deep well with sweet cold water. It sounded good, and Henry had decided he would, if the price was right, buy the land.

Henry could have asked Stedman to petition on his behalf for a
leasehold on Colony property in the town of Fairhope, but this notion he declined, for he had his misgivings as to the administration
of a good idea institutionalized. Henry had read of how Tolstoy's passion became the Tolstoyan Movement. But in the quarter-century
since around 1900 when the first communal farming colonies had
been attempted by Tolstoy's disciples, Henry had not read of a single
success. On the other hand, the Sioux and Pawnee, Cheyenne and
Pueblo—indeed, all the Indian tribes Henry had ever read of—had
found a working proposition in communal living, and he wondered
what was the component of *civilization* that was our hindrance.

Perhaps, he thought, it was working first with the aggregate rather
than the individual that was the problem, an individual who wants
to emend first the group rather than the member who is himself.
Henry believed strongly that only *self*-perfection improves mankind.
He'd not have much time in Alabama, according to Dr. Belton, and
he'd spend it settling the dust in his own soul, on his own. He'd not
ever been much for joining groups.

Still, this single-tax colony was intriguing and the connection,
albeit a loose one, to Leo Tolstoy was exciting. Learning of it and ob-
serving its dynamics could be enough to at least provide some distraction to Henry and keep him from ruminating incessantly upon
his hour of death. It was not a thing Henry feared. Dying was an absolutely provocative proposition, however, that could draw the mind
into too much debate about it. He did not want to follow the path of
so many poets and writers and philosophers who chased after the
mystery of death in line after line after line to come out by the same
door by which they'd entered: in the dark about what dying really
means.

Henry had been intrigued by Tolstoy's obsession with death. As a
young man, Tolstoy had mostly feared and loathed the proposition
that a thing of awesome and beautiful possibility, our very lives, should
come to such a mean and horrendous end in a last rattling, gasping

breath. While Henry was certainly melancholic about dying, his own regard for life's end bore an equal measure of intense curiosity. It was Henry's nature to be curious about the workings of things, even the end of the working of his own body. And it would suit his curiosity well to share company with men and women whose bent for curiosity bade them settle in this Fairhope, wondering if the little colony would bring them a better life. There would certainly be interesting souls down in Alabama with whom to while away some moments chasing high ideas about living and dying.

Henry mounted the steps onto the board sidewalk, bound for the Nampa post office. He walked past two storefronts and was certain that eyes within were following him, that those within were whispering: Would Henry really leave town? Would a father leave his sons and go off down South to die alone?

Henry turned the knob and pushed open the post office door, and it swung on squeaky, rusting hinges. A yellow square of sunlight fell through the single front window and lay upon the darkly varnished plank floor. Dust motes moved on air currents like tiny insects in the light. Jeremiah was leaning his elbows on the gray marble counter at the mail window with the letter that Henry was hoping for held high between his thumb and forefinger. Jeremiah did not alter his position except to push the green visor over his eyes upward and higher onto his brow.

"This'll be what you're wanting here, Mr. Stuart," Jeremiah said. He stood up, seeming to adapt his bearing to the importance of the moment.

"You know, Mr. Stuart, all the town knows of your plan to choose a place and just go there." Jeremiah handed over the letter to Henry. "If you are not aware, sir, I must say from what I hear, folks sure are enjoying a vicarious sense of adventure. Everybody is just so intrigued that you seem set upon heading off for the Deep South."

Henry nodded, but was so excited to find out what Stedman would report that he only nodded, finally muttering yes as he opened the letter. Henry removed the single page and read to its bottom.

"One hundred and fifty dollars is the asking price for the ten acres of Alabama land, Jeremiah," Henry said, dropping his hands, the letter in one and the envelope in the other. "And I, being of sound mind"—Henry feigned an idiot's vacant stare—"shall buy it!"

Jeremiah bounced on his toes and clapped his hands twice. "Mr. Henry, it sounds like a bargain at twice the price!"

Henry was grateful that Jeremiah did not encumber his prospective departure from Nampa with the heaviness in his eyes that so many others could not seem to conceal. "Well, Jeremiah, I must go and pack," Henry said with a broad smile, then, aware of the duplicity of the moment, said, "People are right, Jeremiah. It is an adventure. And the prospect of moving onto a small square of land beside a lovely bay in Alabama is just the thing to get this old man's blood coursing bright red and warm again. Though some don't understand, I expect."

"No, some do not understand, Mr. Stuart," said Jeremiah, his eyes conveying to Henry that he was not among that group. "But I tell you this, sir, to all who'll listen, I try to get them to see it better. Now, the bare feet—I don't know if I can stop that talk."

"But for your tireless attempts, dear Jeremiah, I do thank you," said Henry, smiling, extending his hand through the mail cage bars. Jeremiah took Henry's hand and returned a strong squeeze. Then Henry retrieved his hand, and after stuffing the letter into his shirt pocket, grabbed the bars like a man in jail. "Now I'm going to make my break!" Henry said, looking left and right, then turned and quickstepped from the post office. Outside, he hopped down from the walk and made for the center of the street, the cool pavement greeting each footfall. He strode with purpose, and did not this day think of how his feet preferred the soil or flat stone pavers to bricks or cement or asphalt. He would go right away and get one hundred and fifty dollars cash from the bank and wire it directly to Mr. Peter Stedman and trust him to complete immediately the land purchase transaction.

Turning onto the hard-packed dirt street and easier walking at the edge of town where Dr. Belton's clinic was, Henry soon walked past the doctor's office. He slowed, then stopped, and considered the closed door. He stood still and looked down the street to where it left the town limits and disappeared across low rolling hills east toward the Salmon River Mountains, and farther beyond them to where the purple Rocky Mountain barrier would rise abruptly. Henry bent his neck, bringing his chin toward his chest, where he rested it and gazed at his bare feet, pale with heavy blue veins seeking his toes. He straightened, squared his shoulders, and even jutted his chin forward, striking out now with a different purpose: Henry would go into the clinic and take his seat and wait for a turn to see Dr. Belton. He would ask him to describe the changes the disease would bring to his body, when he might look for the worst of them.

Henry wanted to know how he would die.

· THREE ·

As Henry drew near to his home, his head was abuzz with the catalogue of symptoms Dr. Belton had recited, the physiology of the impairment of his body's organs and systems. Henry angled across the street to where the white picket fence began at the corner of his well-kept yard and took in a small 300-by-300-foot lot from his thirty-six acres that rolled away into pasture and scattered trees behind, over hills and into hollows, cut across on the northwestern corner by Gentry Creek's clear and cold shallow burble.

Henry raised his right hand to touch the boards' sharpened pickets and walked some distance allowing the long fingers of his opened palm to slap-pat, slap-pat, from one whitewashed board to the next, as a child might. He stopped near the gate and looked at his home set well back from the street. The green of the grass was mostly gone now. Close around his house was a yellow-gold moat of flowers in autumn bloom. Small, clipped evergreen shrubs reached outward like arms down either side of the broad cobbled walk, delineating that space with undulations of soft green. Molly had wanted a pretty yard, and Henry had given Molly a pretty yard, though on some days he felt from the effort that he himself had become planted, rooted. Before he met his Molly, Henry had traveled and lived in many parts of the country, holding down a variety of jobs, just for the experience of the work. He was a seminarian who would rather run plumbing to a hotel boiler, as he had done in Washington, D.C. He had operated a telegraph machine for his father. Then he became a husband and a father and a professor. Henry taught young men and women who wanted to be teachers until he retired when his home was paid for.

"This I'll give to you, Harvey," Henry said aloud to himself, pushing back the strands of white hair fallen over his ear. "And most of the land to you, Thomas." Harvey was the older son by two years, and about to marry, his wife-to-be already working beside him in his fledgling Stuart Mercantile. Thomas was a sensible boy and working hard, a foreman at Frank McGuffy's sawmill, but not yet of a mind to marry, nor had he taken a woman for more than frivolous company.

Henry went inside to the kitchen, where he put on a kettle of water for tea. He took down from the cupboard a teacup and saucer of the plain white hardier china that Molly had liked to call her everyday dishes. He removed the silver tea thimble from the drawer and filled it with aromatic and smoothly cut brown leaves. He closed the tiny lid and draped it inside the empty cup, dangling its dainty chain outside the rim.

While he waited for the water to boil and whistle, Henry went into his study and looked within a section of mahogany bookshelves behind his desk, to the right of his degree from Mount Union College, class of 1888. He read his name upon the framed certificate and felt a brief flush of nostalgia. He wondered which of his things Harvey would put into the attic, and how soon. Presently Henry was reminded of what he'd come looking for, and he spied it then, one shelf up, a book bound in jade-green cloth with gilt typography on the spine. It was a new volume of poetry, 1923, out not quite two years,

Sonnets to Orpheus, from the German Rainer Maria Rilke. He took it down and turned to the table of contents.

He closed the book on his index finger and walked over into the light beaming downward through the tall, curtainless window. Standing there, Henry opened the book and traced the numbered poems down the page with his finger until he came to XIII, and beside it the poem's first line: "Be ahead of all parting . . ." He opened the book to page 43, the entire brief poem laid out there, then moved his eyes to the top line and, when his breathing had moved deep into his chest and seemed calm and steady, began reading aloud:

> *Be ahead of all parting, as though it already were*
> *   behind you, like the winter that has just gone by.*
> *For among these winters there is one so endlessly winter*
> *   that only by wintering through it will your heart survive.*
> *Be forever dead in Eurydice—more gladly arise*
> *   into the seamless life proclaimed in your song.*
> *Here, in the realm of decline, among momentary days,*
> *   be the crystal cup that shattered even as it rang.*
> *Be—and yet know the great void where all things begin,*
> *   the infinite source of your own most intense vibration,*
> *   so that, this once, you may give it your perfect assent.*
> *To all that is used-up, and to all the muffled and dumb*
> *   creatures in the world's full reserve, the unsayable sums,*
> *   joyfully add yourself, and cancel the count.*

The teakettle whistled into the quiet of the house, and Henry took the small book into the kitchen with him and put it on the table while he prepared his cup of tea. While he stirred in a teaspoonful of sugar and considered Rilke's line "to all that is used-up," there came a knock on the back door. Henry looked up and saw through the door's window glass Will Webb standing there.

He set down his cup, distracted from his visitor for a moment by the heady steam rising and curling upward like tendrils from the tiny cup. They seemed to rise in slow motion, almost as if they would at any moment gather themselves into . . . into what? A script, some revelation in ghost writing? Some elucidation of how one might serenely add, as the poet suggested, one's own name to the roll call of the soon dead? Before Henry could invite him in, Preacher Webb opened the back door and came in.

"Got another one of those?" Will asked, gesturing toward the cup on the table.

"It'll just take a minute. Have a seat, Will."

Will drew into the room, and Henry could smell the wind-fixed scent of earth and stone, grass and trees, attending his friend. The essence of the out-of-doors had swirled in upon the chilled air following Will as he sat down and removed his hat.

While Henry busied himself making another cup of tea, Will took the volume of poetry from the table and began leafing through it, too rapidly, Henry noted, to be reading or taking notice of any lines.

Henry gave Will a saucer and a cup of tea, prepared as he liked it without sugar or cream. Will blew across the top of the cup, and as he inhaled, took a loud sip before setting the cup down in its saucer on the table. Henry took the book again and opened it slowly. He wanted to share his thoughts on the poem with Will, aware that his visitor turned frequently to lines in his Bible for comfort and advice, knowing that Will must often read those lines aloud to others.

"May I read something to you, Will?"

"Of course."

Then Henry read Rilke's poem, each line and phrase slowly, some words with a pause, to the preacher. "Does that speak to you at all, Will?" A small cough rasped at Henry, and he excused himself and turned away from the table, holding his handkerchief to his mouth.

In a moment, when Henry breathed normally, Will spoke. "Some phrases rang, yes." Will sipped his tea, holding the small cup between his big hands. " 'Know the great void where all things begin,' that is the business of my working life. And that we must give that void our assent—well, my friend, it's my constant exhortation."

"Yes, well, there's much to find in this poem, I think, and they do say that we see what we look for." Henry was staring out the window toward the hazy distant hills.

"And you, Henry, what are you looking for in there?" Will pointed at the little green book.

"Oh, I understood this poet's advice as though I'd written it myself when first I read it, soon after Molly's death. I found it remarkable how the poet had strung words together so beautifully articulating the manner in which I found my way through the loss of my wife." Both men lifted their cups and drank. Will was waiting for Henry to speak again.

"Here is this German, Will," Henry said, "predicting that ahead of us all is some experience so benumbing, such an endless winter, that our only chance of getting through it is to have already partaken of it in thought, to descend into the brutality of that winter in willing reverie." Henry gently shook his head, his blue eyes telegraphing sadness.

"Oddly, before Molly died," Henry continued, "indeed, before anyone knew she was ill, early one morning I walked in brown study all the way to Gentry Creek and back wondering just what I'd do if Molly died before me. I got ahead of her parting from me, Will."

"So somehow," Will asked, "after you had first gone there in your mind, becoming widowed from Molly did not turn into a harsh winter of despair?"

"Precisely, Will," Henry said, becoming more animated. "It did not and could not obviate my sense of loss, but it did diminish the depth of my grief." Henry put down his teacup and placed his hand flat on the table with a resolute and authoritative smack. "So now I must visit my own death in meditation and thoughtfulness. 'Be ahead of all parting'—even my own. That way, by God, Will, I may approach it with some familiarity and without fear."

Will let a long moment of silence stretch into the warmth of the well-lighted kitchen. "Are you afraid, Henry?" Will got up and went across the room to straighten a framed, creweled *Welcome to Molly's Kitchen*. He stood back to gauge the accuracy of his leveling. Satisfied, he returned to his chair at the round oak table.

"No." Henry rose from his chair and moved near the kitchen counter and turned, leaning against it. "But I harbor a notion, Will, that fear might come to me down in Alabama as my time to die draws nearer and the pain increases, as Dr. Belton told me it must. Hard pain might compromise my rational mind and allow the fear to creep in."

Henry stared at a spot on the floor. Will looked in the direction of the wall hanging he had adjusted. For a full minute the room was silent except for the ticking of the huge clock on the mantel above the fireplace. Then Will said, "If you *believe* actively imagining your final days can give you strength"—Will's voice was soft—"then let's set to it, Henry. What can I do?"

Like grain pouring from an open bin, talk between the two men came easily; ideas were planted, extirpated, disagreements never becoming personal even if at times Henry's and Will's voices were raised and their heart rates quickened. Together, over two more cups of tea each, Henry and Will explicated the Rilke poem, gleaning from the lines advice a man could use: Henry must let his life ring as long as he held any piece of it; Henry must give his consent to what he faced; Henry must cease tabulating inequity where none existed; Henry must allow the occasional freak intrusion of joy into this reckoning down in Alabama.

Henry drank the last swallow of his tea, now cool, thinking that even on a third cup it still had a bright good taste. He lifted a napkin to the corner of his mouth. "I'll travel with only a few possessions, but this volume will go with me. And I will take the Russian," Henry said, speaking of Leo Tolstoy, "for whither I go"—he smiled at Will as he spoke in the silence within his kitchen—"thou, Leo, also goest, making my path before me in that great southern wilderness."

"Would you stand over there, a bit away from me, Henry? I don't want to be charred when the lightning comes to strike your blasphemous head," said Will, and though a smile played on his face, his voice had a definite scolding quality. "You know his church had excommunicated him. Tolstoy died a heretic."

"How would you know such gossip about Tolstoy?" Henry shook his finger at Will. "This much is true, Will, Leo Tolstoy died with a mind unshackled by dogma," Henry said, and got up and walked to the windowed back door, its blue gingham curtains drawn back with big looping ribbons just as Molly had fixed them so many years ago. Looking out at the season's last vestiges of his carefully tended garden, he placed his forehead to the glass, the breath from his nostrils blooming frost on the pane. *This is not supposed to be an easy passage,* he reminded himself.

Casting about for some reconciliation of illness and justice, he thought, oddly, that he was glad his working life was finished and there was not a class of college students to tell that he'd not continue his teaching through to the end of the term. His plants in the yard, the flowers and shrubs, some fruit trees, a grape arbor, objects of his care and keeping, they would seek of him no apology, require of him no reason for his absence. These green and growing things would face whatever was their fate without Henry James Stuart and without complaint.

Then Henry straightened his head, his eyes lighting up like shattered blue ice. "A sketchbook," he said.

"What?" asked Will.

"I must take to Alabama a sketchbook. That new leather-bound, shirt-pocket-size volume of blank pages Thomas gave to me on my birthday. I'll stop in those foreign woods and put down my knees upon the soil and carefully, precisely draw with a pencil this and that leaf and branch and berry and stalk I don't recognize."

Henry told Will that from a book in the library in the town of Fairhope he would identify the species he'd drawn and make brief notes on the page with his drawing. Henry marched right past his visitor, back into his study, and opened his center desk drawer and found there the sketch diary. He smacked it against his palm. This and some good pencils, he thought, will brighten a portion of my hours while getting to know my new home on that faraway hill.

· FOUR ·

Peter Stedman wrote to Henry to say that the land purchase had been closed, the deed prepared, and as soon as it was signed and returned to him, the papers would be duly recorded in the probate court of Baldwin County, in the Great State of Alabama.

"And now that you, sir, are practically a landowner," the surveyor continued in his letter, "how may I serve you further?"

Henry sat in his swiveling desk chair and folded the letter from Stedman carefully. Taking out pen and paper, he wrote back that he would waste no time in taking possession of his property, and that it would be of great service to him and counted a true act of kindness if Stedman would consent to do two things: meet him at the train station on his day of arrival in Mobile and transport him to Montrose; and acquire with money wired to him right away a list of supplies including:

- a hundred board feet of one-by-six pine lumber
- a bucket of white paint and a bucket of black paint
- a small, medium, and large paintbrush, and mineral spirits
- ten pounds of twelve-penny nails
- a hammer and saw and carpenter's ruler
- an axe
- fifty feet of half-inch cotton rope and a ball of twine
- a rick of split stovewood
- a small cast-iron stove and flue pipe
- a lantern and coal oil fuel
- matches
- two woolen blankets and a wood and canvas cot

- five yards of heavy canvas, scissors, and needles and thread
- three drinking cups and three plates
- a small and large boiling pan and a kettle
- a two-gallon bucket
- three each knives, forks, and spoons
- tea, cornmeal, rice and oats and flour, sugar, honey, salt and peppercorns

"I would not, Mr. Stedman, burden you," wrote Henry, dipping his pen into the inkwell after each several words, "had I a means of transportation for bringing these items to my property. I will pay you a fee for your time. If you are agreeable, then, and will gather these things together for me and put them into the barn, you will have done a great deal to ensure my comfort there. I will take shelter in the barn until I have decided what to do next."

Henry put down his pen and swiveled his chair for a view out the window of his study. The thin trees scattered here and there on the land rolling away toward the smoky foothills were stripped of their leaves, and the sparse grass was the color of wheat at harvest. Perhaps, thought Henry, I shall set to work right away and construct a small cabin with plenty of windows and tight against the elements, as winter will be coming on. Henry had never before lived or traveled in the Deep South and wondered about winters on the Gulf Coast. He was sure such a cabin as he might build would not have to be as rugged as one in Idaho. Well, he thought, we'll see. Henry spun his chair, bent to his pen and paper, and closed his letter, writing, "I will send more than enough money, based upon Nampa prices, to purchase my list of goods. Again, Mr. Stedman, I thank you, and will be pleased to repay your kindness."

Henry reviewed his list before sealing the letter and was satisfied that the supplies would meet his immediate needs, and even, he thought, with a little hopeful anticipation, the extra dishes would accommodate the needs of a visitor, should someone come calling.

The act of ordering supplies for his new home made it seem all the more real to him, and Henry decided he would make a list of his belongings, his medicines and toiletries, clothing, all that he would take with him from Nampa to Montrose—indeed, to give consideration to the actual luggage he would take along. Henry was quickly settled on the premise of less and fewer things. He would travel light.

The previous summer, Henry had attended a guest lecture at a Nez Percé community lodge, where Black Elk, a medicine man of the Oglala Sioux nation and a devout and vocal convert to Catholicism, had spoken to a small audience on a Saturday evening. He talked about his new church, about finding that the Great Spirit taught the same things to white men as had been handed down to him to teach his people.

Black Elk had spoken of the giving-away ceremonies practiced by his people in the springtime: extra pemmican, extra furs, extra horses—these were not hoarded but were given to those who had none or not enough. The joy of giving is more full when the gift is finer, Black Elk said. This is because each thing owned takes a measure of spirit from the owner. And more spirit is paid out into finer things. To make a gift of these things, the more prized things, Black Elk continued, returns a fuller measure of spirit and power to the giver's body.

Henry looked around his study, at the hundreds of books lining the shelves, at the small bronze bust of Leo Tolstoy and another of William Shakespeare serving as bookends for his four-volume *Diary of Samuel Pepys*. All his books, all his mementos and curios kept close like friends in this favorite room, these things he would give to Thomas, a rough-and-tumble sort who did not shy away from whiskey and fighting and who loved the ladies, but who also loved books.

Henry had once visited Thomas at the sawmill during his lunch break and found his son sitting in the sun on a board between two sawhorses with his lunch pail beside him and a book open in his hand. Henry also knew Thomas to frequently scribble in a small journal. It pleased Henry that he would make this gift to Thomas, the entire contents of his study. The bequest of the homeplace to

Harvey satisfied Henry as an amply fair exchange. Given to Harvey, these books would sooner rather than later, Henry believed, be stored away and forgotten. In Thomas's hands, the books would continue to breathe out their fiery ideas and ignite responsive thinking. Henry, on the other hand, would shed belongings and conjure strong medicine for his spirit. At the notion, he placed his hands together as in prayer and smiled to think that Black Elk, the Catholic, might appreciate the Christian gesture.

Thomas was much more the sentimentalist, but practical-minded enough, Henry knew, to acquire a place for keeping these books and tokens and talismans of a father's life. Then someday, and perhaps soon, Thomas would construct his own home and begin a family. Henry forced from his mind the quick longing that sprang up there like a well-watered seedling in the sun's full light when he thought of grandchildren. He pushed out of his head the maudlin reckoning that those unborn children, who were the very source of his longing, must undeniably follow him back into that void from which they had not yet even emerged. Let life come, he thought, here to this place. Wherever the soul finally arrives, it always floats in the one same river into which it first tumbled.

Henry addressed his letter to Peter Stedman and moved it to the corner of his desk pad. He opened the top right drawer, took out a lined notebook, and began making for himself another list of the items he would take from his home. Travel light, he reminded himself: two pair of pants, one denim and one brown twill—this would give him a clean change of clothes while the other was being washed and dried—four shirts, two summer weight and two winter weight; a set of suspenders; and four handkerchiefs. Enough, but not more than enough. No shoes or boots. No hats. His concession to luxury was two dark woolen vests, favorites for years.

He would also take the big sweater Molly had knitted for him. It was much too large and hung on his shoulders like a heavy robe. Molly had been embarrassed by the sweater's huge dimensions, and it had taken him many tries to convince Molly that he was not just being nice to her, that he really did love the sweater. "A man could live in a sweater like that," Henry had told her. But that had not been the right thing to say; she wanted him to speak of its loveliness, and she had cried. Henry said no more about it. He wore it, however, each time a sweater was called for. He never wore any other sweater. One cold day when Henry was working in his woodshop, the sweater billowing around him as he rocked back and forth planing a piece of oak, the shavings caught on the fuzzy sleeves, Molly had walked up behind him and turned him around into a soft hug. When she stepped back, she brushed gently at the curled wood shavings on the sleeves, adjusted the sweater's shoulder seams higher on Henry's shoulders, patted his cheek, and left him alone. Not a word had been spoken, but the issue of the sweater was ended forever.

Henry continued to work on his list of things to take with him on the train until it was finished except for the books he would take. He would make those choices last, at the moment he placed the books into his canvas book bag. He was putting away his notebook and pen when the sound of heavy footfalls on the porch floor echoed throughout the house. He had forgotten, padding about barefoot now for almost three weeks, how loudly rang the leather heels and toes of a man's boots. Before he could rise from his desk, Henry's older son called into the silent spaces. "Father?"

Henry sat back down, turned in his chair, and looked out his study window. He did not answer. "Father, are you here?" Harvey drew nearer, ahead of the thump of his boots on the plank floors, muted when he crossed a carpet.

"Come in, Harvey," Henry said without turning from his view out the window. "I'm in the library."

"Father, there you are." Harvey unbuttoned his light coat and sat down in the leather wingback chair opposite his father's huge desk. He waited for his father to turn his chair and face him. Henry slowly turned and gripped the armrests of his chair, making to rise.

"No, please don't get up. I've only a minute." Harvey crossed his legs and looked down at his boot. "Did Brother Webb speak with you?"

Henry relaxed into his chair. He knew where this speech was

going. "I have seen him in passing, and we have exchanged greetings. But more? No, we've not had a conversation. Should I expect a visit from my friend?"

"I don't think he can face you, Father. So I've come to tell you that we don't like this idea of yours." Harvey rested his elbows on the chair arms and brought his hands together in front of his chest, templing his fingers. "You have gone so fast. One minute we are reconciling your departure to California, the next you are buying land and leaving for Alabama. In California, at least, we could occasionally visit, but in Alabama? My God, Father, we will lose all contact with you."

Henry smiled at that. "But unless you plan to cross the River Styx with me, my son, that is inevitable. Is it not?"

"Must you make of this such histrionics, Father? Please! Listen to reason."

"I think, Harvey, that it's your reason you would have me hear. Thomas has said only that he wishes he could come with me. And it was your very own minister who apprised me of the advantages of living in Alabama."

"And I," Harvey said, arching his eyebrows, "have withheld my full tithe from his basket two Sunday mornings now because of such foolish counsel." Harvey uncrossed his leg and thumped his boot down loudly. "And Thomas has been absent from worship services two of the last three Sundays. When I have worked so hard to get him into the church. Now, it seems he will use your leaving Nampa as all the reason he needs to abandon his faith."

"Or perhaps he will grow into his own understanding of the spiritual mysteries," Henry said, taking up a pencil from his desk, momentarily caught by its lightness, quickly juxtaposing that to its power for assembling words into thoughts. "Will Webb does not hold title to what is true, Harvey. Surely you see that. Nor does it travel as if by conduit through his building. Will knows these things and will admit the same when pressed."

"This much is true, Father," Harvey said, leaning forward in his chair, nodding, and opening his eyes wide. "A dying man's deed to ten acres of Alabama land is a ticket to folly." Harvey rose, faced his father, and began buttoning his coat. "Who will be there when the consumption racks your body with coughing? Who will wipe a cool cloth across your brow when the fevers burn you under your covers, Father? When you are too fatigued to get out of bed for a glass of water, who will bring it to you? I cannot but think this decision of yours is some morbid imitation of your Tolstoy's foolish nighttime flight."

Henry's clear blue eyes became quickly filled with tears. He blinked, his eyelashes brushed the tears, and they rolled down his cheeks. Henry rose from his chair, and Harvey thought his father would come to him and take his hands or seek an embrace. But Henry walked to the window and stood in the warm yellow cloak of the sun falling there, as he had done so many times before, usually with a book in his hand held to catch the beneficial light. Henry clasped his hands behind himself, his feet wide and well planted, and looked in profile as a general might in forethought of coming battle.

"Harvey, pray tell who"—Henry turned to face his son—"who will return those moments to me when I was here in this house and a well man, and I longed in great health for your voice and your company, when I hoped that you and Thomas might come by and allow me to fix you a cup of tea. But not once since your mother died has such occurred. From what am I flying? Is it flight to leave what is not there?"

Harvey let his eyes fall to the floor and fidgeted like a schoolboy awaiting permission from the headmaster to take his leave. For once it seemed Harvey had nothing to say. Henry said, his head lifted and his voice full, "You will be surprised, I believe, at the measure of relief accorded you and Thomas by my absence."

Harvey lifted his eyes, clearing his throat to speak, but Henry cut him off. "There is nothing you or Will Webb can say to influence me to alter my plans. I have made my choice." Henry stepped to his desk and lifted the letter to Peter Stedman. "My plans are in motion. I will be leaving within the week. I will sit down tonight and write clear instructions for the disposition of my things, and on the day after to-morrow, if you will, I'll ask you and Thomas to gather with me here in this study. I'll read my letter to you both, and I will ask Will to be present. I want to be sure my wishes are clearly understood."

"Father, I—"

Henry sat down in his chair and gazed intently upon the face of his son. Henry's face was now relaxed. "You must forgive me, Harvey. I know well, full and certain, that you are unconditional in your loving regard for me. What I as your father have shared with you and Thomas does not stand on the frailty of a cup of tea sipped in my kitchen. This is a hard time for us both, but it is good for me to go."

Henry waited for Harvey to meet his eyes, to offer some concurrence in the strength of their familial ties. Harvey did not look at his father, only said, still looking down at his chest, buttoning his coat up to his collar and brushing the wrinkles from it, tugging down on the coat's hem, "Yes, well, I will be here—say, six o'clock Wednesday evening?" And still without meeting his father's eyes or waiting for an answer, Harvey walked briskly out of the study, closing the front door gently and quietly.

· FIVE ·

You may open Mr. Stedman's letters to me, Jeremiah," Henry said, smiling as he spoke to the postal clerk. "I always tell you anyway what he has to say."

Jeremiah had drawn up as near as he could to the bars on his teller's cage as Henry prepared to open this latest envelope from Fairhope.

"Oh, no! Never, sir. I could not do that," said Jeremiah, shaking his head and fanning the warm flush rising in his cheeks with his open palm. Jeremiah peered left and right, straining to see from behind his counter into the outer room of the small post office. "But I don't mind hearing," he said, lowering his voice, "what the Alabama man has written us this time." He snickered and, Henry thought, was delighted to permit himself the use of the plural pronoun.

"Let's see." Henry's eyes scanned the lines on the unfolded page. "He tells me that he cannot meet me at the train station in Mobile and drive me to my property in Montrose, that transit by motorcar from the western to the eastern shore of Mobile Bay involves a large arc to the north, a crossing up above the river delta there, a drive of several hours." Henry read further. "He tells me that I can take the steamer *Bay Queen* from the foot of Government Street in Mobile to the end of Fairhope's quarter-mile-long municipal pier, that he will drive me from there. And Mr. Stedman has included a postcard photograph of the pier." Henry studied the postcard, then handed it over to Jeremiah.

"Ooh, it's lovely," Jeremiah said. "Just look at all those sailboats and swimmers and people out for a stroll on the pier. All those men sporting their dandy white straw hats. And ladies with parasols! Heavens. Do you suppose I could stow away in your steamer trunk, Mr. Stuart?" Jeremiah chuckled.

"If I were traveling with such a trunk, Jeremiah," Henry said in all earnestness, "you would be most welcome to nestle down inside. But a book satchel in my left hand," Henry said, lifting first his left hand, curled into a fist, then his right, "and a fat suitcase in my right. Weight an old man can handle. That's all I'm taking, Jeremiah. Now, my friend, you are welcome to come and visit me whenever you will."

Both men at the same time lifted their eyes to meet each other's, as if simultaneously they apprehended the unlikelihood of sufficient time remaining for Henry to welcome even a single visitor from Idaho.

Silence hung overlong in the tiny post office until Henry announced that he would be going and told Jeremiah he expected there would not be more than one, maybe two remaining letters from Peter Stedman. "I'll be leaving next week, on Thursday in the early morning. But I will come each morning to see if Mr. Stedman has anything to add in the way of last-minute advice for this unenlightened traveler."

As Henry was about to turn and leave, Jeremiah disappeared from view at his teller's cage and, with a rattling of keys, opened the wooden door to its side, stepping into the outer post office. He extended his hand to Henry. "Are they ready for you down there, Mr. Henry?" Jeremiah glanced at Henry's bare feet, looking to the door for a moment's release from embarrassment before gazing back at Henry.

Henry smiled, and gripped Jeremiah's hand. "Yes, here. Read the rest of the letter. Please," he said, passing the envelope to the other man, who took it and regarded it briefly. "And thank you for your concern, Jeremiah." Henry shifted his gaze from Jeremiah to look through the window down the street past the buildings lining the street. "Perhaps the greater question is, am I truly ready for Alabama?"

Henry knew that they both knew "Alabama" was to be interpreted not as the state bounded by lines on a map, but as the state of readiness for the eventuality Dr. Belton had promised his patient. Henry felt that Jeremiah joined him in his uncertainty as to how the lines should be drawn and labeled to lead a traveler from here to there.

· SIX ·

Do I have to take my shoes off to join father and son for this little hike?" Will Webb asked Henry, who was pulling shut his back door. Henry stopped to cough quietly into a folded handkerchief, then joined Thomas and the preacher underneath the apple tree a few yards past where the sharply drawn shadow of the house cut across the dry ground. Henry turned up his collar and stepped barefooted into the glare of sunshine. The September morning's frost was disappearing, but still lay in the shadows. A brisk breeze lifted a sharp yet pleasant odor of woodsmoke. Dry leaves skittered past, swirling and flying over the ground at their feet.

"Man, don't you want to put some shoes on those feet?" Will asked, shaking his head. "You're giving me a chill just looking at your skinny toes."

"Actually, Will," said Henry, "I've learned that if I keep my neck warm, I hardly notice the weather down at my feet."

"Well, maybe if I can keep my eyes off your feet, I can keep my neck warm."

The three men were now walking abreast of each other. They went in silence. Only the scrunch of the brown grass beneath their feet, when it could be heard over the wind, announced their small parade.

"Damn this!" Thomas suddenly said. "How in the hell," Thomas continued, shoving both hands into his pockets, looking first at his father, then at the preacher, "can a doctor know a man's got a year to live? Is there a timer in there someplace"—he pointed toward Henry's chest—"that he can read and from that make his computations? He might just be banging a bull in the butt with a bass fiddle."

"Now, Thomas," Will began, "don't you expect it's something doctors are taught? It seems reasonable to assume—"

"I spoke at length to Dr. Belton about this illness, Thomas," Henry cut in, drawing up ahead of the two men and turning to walk backward a step. He stopped, facing his son. "I wanted to know where and by what means one contracts consumption, this tuberculosis. A dozen things, and I asked him how he could be sure the disease has progressed to the point that it will kill me. He was quite specific—coolly clinical, I might add—about the symptoms." Henry gestured toward the pasture out beyond a brambly hedge they were coming near to. He still held his handkerchief in his hand.

"And . . ." Thomas said, waiting for his father to continue.

"And?" Henry answered.

"And how does old Belton know how much time you've got left?" Thomas asked.

"Basically, it's because I'm coughing blood that he can make his prediction of how much time I have left." Thomas and Will allowed Henry to set the pace and followed just behind him, the two of them walking abreast on the easily rolling meadowland of short grasses. In the distance, low mountains rolled away toward higher peaks spiking upward into thin white clouds skating across the blue sky. "Dr. Belton showed me a passage in one of his medical texts from which he drew his conclusions."

"Conclusions?" Thomas was agitated, and his voice rose. "But, Father, who is doing the concluding? It's your end, not his, of which he speaks so glibly."

"I'm not sure, Thomas," said the preacher, "that you can assume Dr. Belton is being slick with Henry."

"What point are you making, Thomas?" Henry caught his hands behind his back, his left fist resting in the closed palm of his right hand, a corner of white handkerchief protruding there. Thomas and Will overtook Henry, one to either side of him, Thomas on the right, and the three of them fanned out and walked together like this, their pace slow. Just ahead of them a covey of quail erupted into the afternoon air. The drumming of quails' wings startled the trio, and they each laughed at their exaggerated reactions.

"My point is simple," said Thomas, who had picked up a knobby stick and was whacking it against his pants leg, or sometimes into the grass like a scythe, as he walked and continued speaking. "Who says you've got to believe the doctor's decree? Is there not some weight given in your own mind, Father, to the possibility that this doctor might be plainly wrong? I should think there's something to be gained from resolute steadfastness on your part to resist the illness."

Will looked from Thomas to Henry, absentmindedly nodding assent to the possibility Thomas had raised. "Well?" Will said when some steps had been taken without an answer from Henry.

"Of course"—Henry had to speak above the breeze that had freshened in their faces, and his tone conveyed annoyance to his friend and son—"you may both rest assured that I will not open my shirt and expose my breast to the Reaper's blade. I'm a bit disappointed and find it audacious for either of you to assume otherwise."

Henry slowed his pace, then put both hands out to his side, which Will and Thomas read to mean for them to stop. They stopped walking and Henry stepped up and turned to face them. "I have begun to actually feel the tuberculosis in my body, and I know that according to its common name, it wishes to consume me. I don't feel as strong as I felt even last week. All of that to remind you both that any display of bravado has an inherent opportunity for a balancing measure of hubris."

Then Henry laid his hand on Thomas's shoulder as he turned and began again moving slowly in the direction of a stand of thin willows at a bend in Gentry Creek. Thomas walked close by his father, clearly enjoying the weight of the hand on his shoulder. Once Thomas raised his own hand across to touch his father's fingers, brushing them so lightly that Henry thought perhaps he had not even done so.

"Thomas, you and Will both know that we take a step nearer death with every tick of the clock. Of that there can be no denial." Henry motioned to a scattering of gray boulders, like small round bales of hay in a field. He asked them to sit with him, and in a moment said, "Chief Seattle asked how the Big Bellies in Washington could offer the Indians a deed to their lands. 'How can we take title to our mother?' And I can see," Henry said, patting his chest, "how our very bodies are not ours to own. Believing that makes it easier, according to my own devices, to give up my body." Will and Thomas were staring out across the hills rising on the other side of the creek. "I need for you both to believe that I'm not afraid to die. For me, this is a Sioux warrior's good day to die."

The small party sat in silence on the rocks at the edge of Gentry Creek, and soon Thomas stood up and walked over and put his hand on his father's shoulder. He pointed with his other hand to a small flat boulder embedded in the creek bank. "Harvey and I used to sit there," he said, "and dry in the sun after we'd swum the afternoon away." Thomas took off his hat and the wind fretted his curly black hair. Eyes blue like Henry's gazed toward the creek. A good-looking boy, Henry thought, and put his palm onto the small of Thomas's back. Thomas put on his hat and bent over to pick up a smooth gray stone the size of a hen's egg. He held it in his fist, his arm hanging down like a baseball pitcher awaiting the right signal from his catcher. Thomas broke his stare at some unknown spot on the flowing creek to look directly at his father.

"And you need to know, Father, that I am not afraid to let you die," Thomas said, and fired the rock into a shallow spot where the fast current rolled the water around a piece of broken log protruding from the opposite bank. The sun caught the spray of water droplets and created a diamond-like dazzle in the air where the stone entered the creek with a *choog*ing splash. "If you allow both Will and Harvey and me a measure of disappointment at your going." Thomas put his hands on his hips and met his father's gaze. Will was now on the rock beside Henry.

"A fair enough trade, don't you think, old man?" Will asked.

Henry nodded and smiled. "Fair enough, indeed." And after a moment, when the only sound in the air was the chortle of the creek and the whisper of the wind in the willows, Henry said, "Thank you, my son."

· SEVEN ·

The leather-and-canvas satchel that Henry put into service as a book bag for his trip to Alabama looked almost as fresh as it had when Molly had given it to him twenty years earlier. Henry knelt on his front porch and unbuckled it. He would add to its inventory this one last book that he had in his hand: a palm-size red leather book published in London by Walter Scott Limited on good Japan paper, two short works in one volume by Count Leo Tolstoy. Of the two titles contained in the small book—*What Men*

Live By and *What Shall It Profit a Man?*—Henry preferred *What Men Live By.*

He'd bought the book new, what, more than twenty years ago? Must have been in 1901 or 1902, some time during the first three years into his first teaching job. And though its price then had seemed expensive to him, he had been excited to find it in the tiny shop of M. Lanaux, Bookseller. When the proprietor rang up the sale and offered to wrap it in brown paper, Henry declined, preferring instead to keep it in his hand. He read three pages as he walked home along the sidewalk before bumping into a lady, causing her to drop her basket of fresh bread and pastries and give Henry a good tongue-lashing.

Now, these many years later, there was some wear at the top of the little book's spine and a slight loss of luster on the gilt title, and the hinges were beginning to loosen. But the gold was still bright on the edges of the book block and Tolstoy's words still bathed his mind with light. Henry found there such painful devotion to his quest for understanding the human condition, such passion in offering solutions to our predicament. Henry turned the book over in his hand, then placed it into the satchel atop his Russian-language copy of Tolstoy's *A Calendar of Wisdom,* the work of the author's last years. He closed and buckled the satchel.

The previous evening Henry had given Will his first English translation of Tolstoy's *War and Peace,* a six-volume set presented to Henry by his mother upon his graduation from Mount Union. Henry had known that his mother would be casting about for a special graduation gift and had told her straightaway that he coveted this entire work since the publication of its first English translation in 1886. Two years later they were his. And now, after forty years in his library, these, his precious books, would find a spot on the shelves of the Reverend William Webb.

"Maybe I'll discover what you see in this man's writing that so infatuates you," Will had said by way of letting Henry know the books of the novel would be read and not merely displayed. "Though I'm not entirely sure I want to let the notorious Russian into my home." Henry's later acquisition, the twenty-eight-volume *Complete Works of Tolstoy,* he had given to Thomas.

"Well, mine is not an infatuation with *War and Peace,* Brother Webb," said Henry. "I actually prefer his nonfiction and *Resurrection—*"

"Scant chance of that unless you've been holding out on me, Henry," interrupted Will, a grin upon his face.

"I was about to say, 'of his novels.' Do you not listen to your sermons on manners, Preacher?" Henry shook his finger at his friend. "I was also about to say that if you ask Thomas to allow you to borrow some of the other works of Tolstoy you will perhaps discern more clearly my love for the Russian. Did you know that the count, in his diary, said that the socialists will never destroy poverty and injustice and the inequality of talents? The most intelligent and the strongest will always make use of the most stupid and the weakest. Justice and the equality of goods, he said, can never be attained by anything less than Christianity, by renouncing the self and recognizing the meaning of one's life to be in the service of others."

"I did not know Tolstoy said that." Will's expression revealed his genuine surprise, and Henry so enjoyed this small surge of appreciation for Tolstoy that he would not add that Tolstoy did not endorse the church at all. He let the opportunity pass and instead told Will that his favorite work by Leo Tolstoy was also the author's own favorite everyday reading, *A Calendar of Wisdom,* a gathering of wise sayings from the world's sacred texts, her greatest poets and writers and thinkers, arranged under 365 headings, one for each day in a year. "It's a book on a par with the Bible, Will, for inspiration and nourishment of the soul."

"And you expect me, Henry, to ever—ever in this life—join you in that appraisal?" Will was scowling.

"No, Preacher. Not unless you learn to speak Russian. It hasn't yet been translated."

"Well then, that saves me the worry, doesn't it?" Then Will realized that his friend had just revealed something he never knew or would ever have guessed. He asked, without disguising his incredulity, "You speak Russian?"

"I do. I wanted to be able to read Tolstoy in his mother tongue." Henry raised his eyebrows, like a request for concurrence. "In the manner of your reference to Greek and Aramaic in your Bible studies."

"So this is something you picked up in Moscow?" Will began grinning. "Moscow, Idaho?" And Will had a good laugh at his joke.

Henry also smiled and said, "No. I learned it back in my college days. But I have visited many times with Widow Ilyich across town for the pleasure of discourse with her in Russian."

And the two men continued their talking into the evening, sharing tea and cold biscuits, Henry taking down this and that book from his shelves to show passages to Will. When Will was going out into the dark of a late night, at the door Henry said, "These hours have passed too quickly, my friend." Will only nodded and placed his hand on Henry's shoulder, his brown eyes shining assent, then shook Henry's hand and said good night.

This morning the sky was cloudless and bright blue; the air was still and dry and a touch cold from the night's low in the thirties. A north wind had swept all the haze from the valley, and the hills rose up in an undulating and multicolored embrace of the homes and buildings of Nampa. Henry stood on the porch and with his toe slid the book satchel snugly up beside a large, sturdy brown leather suitcase with brass corners and hardware, another gift from Molly on the occasion of his promotion to full professor at Lewiston Normal School. She had imagined that Henry would be called upon to travel and lecture, so she bought for him a five-piece set of luggage and the satchel. Molly had clapped her hands together and bounced on her toes as he'd opened the shipping cartons. Henry knew Molly would be pleased to see two of the bags finally getting some use.

Henry cupped his hand over his eyes and looked down the road toward town. He could see no car coming, but there on the road were a pair of small rabbits ready to spring into the long brown grass. Henry wondered, but could not remember, did rabbits mate for life? Had he not also given Will his eleventh edition of the *Encyclopaedia Britannica,* he'd go inside to his study and look the matter up. But Will had boxed up the reference books on the spot and taken the soft tan leather volumes with him, not waiting to come back this morning to cart them home. Henry decided he would ask Will to research the question and compose an answer to him in a letter to Alabama. Something in Henry's memory made him believe rabbits chose life mates, but truly, he could not say for certain.

It was troubling to Henry when his mind these days failed to set quickly before him whatever fact or verse or date or name for which he went gleaning. And the failure to recall a name, this was worst of all. Would this TB working to kill him consume more of his memory before it took him? That was one thing Dr. Belton had not included in his enumeration of symptoms. Another item he would like to look up.

It was plain to Henry that he would miss his books a great deal, that he had not yet fully incorporated Black Elk's teaching, for he felt no real infusion of power from giving away his belongings. Henry did feel something akin to growing relief last night as this and that of his things were disposed of right down the list. Still, the distribution of his books at this moment felt only like a loss. One of his first pathways through the woods of Baldwin County would be to the town library. At least, though, he would there be a borrower and not a buyer.

Henry looked once more down the road, then moved toward the end of the porch and sat down in a rocker. Actually, he sat in a rocking chair that he himself had built. Henry rubbed his hands along the armrests, pushing slowly back, recalling how he had announced to Molly that he would build for himself an heirloom to commemorate his retirement from teaching, a fine ash chair with a nice rounded bottom and two long and slowly curving rockers underneath, well made so they met the floor like things alive, whispering secrets, not mechanically grinding down the wood.

Henry had imagined, when he had begun its construction, that there would be lazy afternoons spent reading on the porch until twilight, with Molly seated nearby. They would talk and perhaps read passages to each other, and he would arise and go quietly inside to prepare some tea. Maybe she would bring out a plate of scones she'd made the evening before. They'd close their books and watch the silent red setting of the sun behind the hills. Then Molly would rise and pat the back of his hand and say it was time for them to go inside. Henry would nod and tell her he would be right in, and she would kiss the top of his head lightly before going in to warm up the kitchen with some supper for them.

And they had done just that.

The rocking chair had for seasons of afternoons and evenings, of days cycling from short to long and back around to short, for many years embraced him in its easy rhythm. He had gone to his rocker only a few times since Molly had died, and he noted with interest that, while he had thought to build the chair for himself, in truth it had been for the two of them, though Molly had not once sat in it.

Henry had also stuffed into his suitcase a small rug he had woven for Molly, soft and thick for her to stand on at the kitchen sink. It was brightly colored, among the prettiest and most festive of the many rugs Henry had woven since retiring. He had woven this rug of vividly dyed fibers to match his Molly's love of washing dishes. She said it was a spiritually uplifting task to clean the plates and bowls and cups from which her family took sustenance, almost as fulfilling, she had said, as preparing the meals themselves. And she loved the view out the window above the sink, the birds and rabbits and flowers, and trees bending in the wind. Henry had constructed a window box for Molly, and she kept it planted with flowers whose blooms were in season. This rug of Molly's Henry would not lay on the floor, but rather hang on the wall of whatever dwelling he occupied in Alabama. When he looked at it, he would allow it to animate his spirit as Molly's window box had hers.

The satchel and suitcase were packed and ready to go beside him there on the front porch. These two Henry had chosen from among Molly's gift set. Thomas, who should be along any minute, had been happy to accept the other four cases at last night's parlor meeting for the distribution of Henry's things, and as Will had done with his books, Thomas had also taken the luggage off with him.

"I suppose," Harvey had groused to his brother, folding his arms across his chest when Henry had given Thomas the luggage items, "that you have a number of excursions planned during the next few months." Henry had not yet made the bequest of his real property, wherein Harvey would get the house and six well-kept acres. So far the evening's best prizes had gone to Thomas and Will, and Harvey sulked a bit, looking about the room, feigning disinterest as the short list was read aloud.

"I don't intend any drama for your sakes," Henry had said to the three men gathered in his study, "for disposing of these 'trivances of mine. This ceremony is an indulgence for me, if you don't mind." Then Henry had explained to his listeners that a giver retrieves spirit in the act of passing his things on to others. Henry told them that he wanted to briefly call each thing's history to his mind by naming it, that by so doing he'd fully derive its return of power to himself. Harvey had rolled his eyes, Will had shaken his head, and Thomas had lifted his shoulders slightly and nodded almost imperceptibly, then turned his head and smiled at the other two men seated on either side of him.

Then Harvey had sat bolt upright, planting both feet on the floor and gripping his knees, when Henry said he'd give the house and six acres to him. Harvey disallowed himself the luxury of a smile, but quickly said, "Thank you, Father. I shall take proper care of your home."

"And let us then," Henry smiled and said, "properly think of it from now on as your home, Harvey." Then Henry allowed that he meant for Thomas to have the remaining thirty-three acres. Thomas then got up and crossed the floor, circling behind Henry's desk, and tugged his father up from his swivel chair and wrapped his arms tightly around him. Thomas made no effort to conceal his crying, and with grief's tautness binding him to the moment said, "I bloody well hate this! Is there somewhere I can redeem this gift of land in exchange for the life of my father?" And then Thomas asked to be excused, saying that he'd return before eight in the morning to take Henry to the newly opened Union Pacific train station in Boise. Thomas left the room quickly and noisily.

"Well, at any rate, we're almost finished with this," Henry said

when the mental echo of Thomas's leaving had had time to abate. He
sat forward in his chair and propped his elbows on the desk, then
crossed his forearms. His eyes were locked on the wooden desktop as
if contemplating a matter of grave importance. He inhaled deeply
and slowly lifted his gaze to meet the eyes of first Will, then Harvey.

Henry cleared his throat and spoke. "There is one other possession that I must dispose of, and that is my money. What I am about
to tell you both has been set down in my own hand and delivered to
the lawyer Hollon on Front Street. My decision is my own and will
be protected by the courts, if ever the need arises." Harvey looked at
Will as if to determine whether he knew what was afoot here, and
Will lifted his eyebrows and puckered his lips, a signal that he did
not know.

Henry continued without moving or blinking. "I have wired some
money, enough to meet my needs for several months and then a little more, to a bank in Fairhope. The rest, after deducting expenses
for title transfer of my property here, and such incidentals as may
arise, is to be given to William Webb."

"Now, see here, Henry. You're clearly out of your head!" Will
stood from his chair. Harvey looked at Will, then at his father, waiting, Henry knew, to hear the end of this bit of news. "You won't even
look in the direction of my church on Sunday morning. So what—"

"I did not leave my money to your church, Will. I left it to you.
And not a great deal, mind you, an amount that would keep me here
living as I do for another ten years or so. At any rate, you may use it
as you see fit. There are no stipulations at all."

"Henry."

"Brother Webb," Harvey said, still seated, now templing his fingers. "It's clear that my father has thought this through. I have not
the slightest objection, nor would Thomas, I'm sure." What more
might have been said was truncated by Henry's slap to his desk before standing and speaking, clear and strong.

"So let's all take our leave and see each other at the post office in the
morning." And that was that. Harvey shook hands with the preacher
and his father, bidding them both good night. Will only embraced

Henry and thanked him, saying his money would be available to several in the community through his church.

"As you wish, dear friend." Henry said to Will that he was tired and would now retire for the evening, expecting a good night's rest before beginning his travel tomorrow. "I will see you, then, at Jeremiah's post office."

According to Will's wishes, at the Nampa post office Henry would stand on the porch and say good-bye to any who wished to see him off to Alabama. Will and Dr. Belton had organized a notification of all the town's citizens.

But this morning as Henry sat rocking, listening to the purr of the rockers on the tight tongue-and-groove boards of his gray-painted porch floor, he began to wish he had declined the farewell event at the post office. He was suddenly filled with distaste for staging his departure, for making of it something of a spectacle, like a public hanging. Henry's grasp tightened on the armrests as he lifted his eyes to follow the movement of a hawk wheeling on an updraft against the fierce bright sky. He suppressed a cough, the spasm in his chest rising to close his throat, and the hawk loosed a skree that raked through Henry like one of its razored talons.

He stilled the chair and parted his lips slightly and took in a breath. He drew in another, letting the exhalation rise gently from his lungs like the scent from a blood-red rose until the thump of blood in his veins became a slight tapping and the muscles in his neck unwound and his face inclined forward and down as in prayer. "I will not go before the town," Henry said softly as if to Thomas, "to make theater of my leaving. This little drama is mine alone." And he closed his eyes and waited for his son to come.

Henry fumbled with the broad leather strap of his book satchel, adjusting it where it crossed his chest and pressed against his shirt pocket and the folded surveyor's map of his ten acres in Montrose. He could not, just yet, lift his face to behold the trio who stood in this railway station before him in awkward silence. Their muteness was juxtaposed to the hubbub of voices and calls and whistles from passengers and those come to deliver travelers to the transcontinental train from Boise to points south and east, the powerful hiss of ready steam from the piston valves of the brass-appointed massive ebony-black engine, the thump and bump of luggage and the little thunder of steel-wheeled carts across the platform planking.

Henry's suitcase was itself secured in the luggage compartment of the Union Pacific's *Twilight Limited*. The attendant would soon call out his plaintive "All aboard!" Henry stood on the platform, his eyes contemplating the toes of his boots, the polished sheen Harvey had found in the old reddish-brown leather, how shining them last evening must have lent authority to Harvey's insistence this morning that they be worn: "There now," he'd said when he handed them to Henry. "They look good as new. Not a passenger will fail to notice their soft patina."

"Did you take up these boots and shine them yourself?" Henry had asked Harvey.

"Yes, Father. I thought perhaps . . ." But Harvey had not completed his sentence and offered his palm in a gesture that translated as: "But of course I could be wrong."

"You thought that I should need them for my train ride. And so I do. It's kind of you." Henry leaned forward to pat Thomas's shoulder. "And kind of you, Thomas, to give me a new hat. It's a good hat, and comfortable. Thank you." Then Henry had turned himself sideways to face Harvey, who had sat straight-backed beside him on the car seat as they rolled out of Nampa, the sun out the passenger-side window mounting higher into the soft purple sky. Henry had ridden several of the miles to the station this morning wiggling his toes in his boots. He had peered at the back of Will's head, surprised at the abundance of curled gray hairs tickling the preacher's sharp white collar, the unruly mane blown about by the rush of air into the open window beside him. His eyes had traveled to Thomas in the driver's seat, the knot of muscled jaw beneath Thomas's clean-shaven cheek, his well-shaped ear, a Roman nose and strong brow in silhouette, both hands locked on the big steering wheel. And he had stolen glances at Harvey, almost at Henry's elbow on the rear seat beside him, looking out his rolled-up window.

Henry stood on the station platform fixing in his mind more of the memory of their car ride here to the new train station in Boise, some twenty-five miles. The sweet smell of new boot polish had stayed strong in the swirl of air in the car during the entire trip. The miles had scrolled slowly past the car's windows while the four men inside had maintained a flat silence, punctuated only now and again by some dry observation of the terrain or sky, an animal perhaps. Once Thomas had swerved to avoid a gray tumbleweed as it rolled like a playful cougar onto the roadway, and he said, "I suppose I could stop and put that escaped bush into the car with us to enliven things a bit."

Immediately the mood had changed. Henry smiled, and when Will had turned in his seat to fix his own schoolboy grin upon Henry, they had both fallen into a fit of laughing. At first the dismay on Harvey's face looked frozen there until Thomas leaned forward and slapped the dashboard, letting go a deep "haw-haw-haw" and stealing a quick look over his shoulder at his brother. Harvey had looked at Henry, who had his hand over his mouth, half laughing and half coughing, and then Harvey had broken into a titter. There followed a collective and audible exhalation, a sigh that flowed into easy conversation among the men, sustained until their arrival at the train station.

Then, just as abruptly, a heavy silence poured over them. Twenty minutes at the station now, the spell had held. Henry and Will and Harvey and Thomas circled there together on the boarding ramp near enough, one to the other, to reach out and grasp the shoulder of each or any of the others, but this did not happen. Each man was an island, and together they were an island, shrouded in calm and mystery and set in the station's frantic and confused sea. An on-looker would wonder and speculate. What story bound these four men together in their collective solemnity? For though they were certainly members of the same party, none would look at the other. That Henry would probably never lay eyes on his sons or his friend again and would in minutes step up onto this train and ride off into a morning's eternity stole completely from him, and from his companions, the gift of language. There was simply nothing more to say.

It was not lost on Henry how Oscar Wilde had written in *De Profundis* of the separation of himself from his children, how it was a "source of infinite distress, of infinite pain, of grief without end or limit. . . . Those lovely links with humanity are broken. We are doomed to be solitary while our sons still live." And yet while Wilde believed such reunion with Vyvyan and Cyril would "bring balm to [his] bruised heart, and peace to [his] soul in pain," Henry sensed a certain curious and incongruous relief, a vexing desire for estrange-ment from Harvey and Thomas. In his mind's eye he saw a lion killing the cubs within a usurped pride for the sake of the continua-tion of its own lineage, and Henry saw his lineage extending into realms of the soul rather than the corporeal. But he could not pre-vent a darkness of shame and guilt from passing over him. Henry would seek such relief from that shadow as might reasonably be at-tained without hardening his heart.

Maybe, and this was easier for Henry to understand, his need to be parted from his sons had more to do with wishing for them some distance from the pain of watching him die. This would be difficult, for his purpose was to die in peace. How could it be that he wished he were already on the train and rolling eastward and away from here? He rifled through the mental files of his seminary days. There must be some secret to be gleaned from reflection on the way of Jesus when someone said to him that his mother and brother were outside and wanted to talk to him. But Jesus had responded with a question: "Who is my mother? And who are my brethren?" Henry asked of himself in that moment, *Indeed, who is the father and who the sons?*

And Henry drew a deep breath, and it was answered in his lungs with a fierce objection. The intake of cool air fanned like a blacksmith's bellows the banked coals smoldering in his chest. Like biting down on a toothache, Henry held the fiery breath as if to draw from it the will to speak his peace.

"If you," Henry began, raising his eyes and looking first to Harvey, then Thomas and Will, "the three of you who mean most to me, if you will grant me your continuing love and hold me steadfast in your prayers, then you will have bestowed upon me all that any man could hope for on the occasion of a last good-bye."

They shook their heads, blinked, chanced glances at each other and made as if to offer simultaneously some objection, to say that it was not so. But Henry put his folded handkerchief to his mouth and with his other hand waved off any attempted denial. He turned his head and coughed quietly. When his breath was again even, Henry said, "I don't remember, Harvey, Thomas, when first I knew that I did not belong to my parents." He shook his head. "It does not seem to have been an epiphany, more like a slow dawning, and perhaps through a shrouded mist at that, but I know it was enlivening." Henry nodded and a smile teased the corners of his mouth. "Even thrilling."

And then he told his sons of his, a young man's, growing awareness that there was no intercessor, no bargainer, who stood between God and himself. "In fact, there is no one who has the right to review your comprehension of the Creative Principle."

Harvey shifted nervously. "Father, must we do this theology now? You know that I for one do not—"

"Harvey, Henry is going to make some point," Will said, arching his eyebrows in Henry's direction as if seeking validation. "Right, old man? Some gem of wisdom for these boys to remember you by?" Will grinned.

Thomas moved his weight from one foot to the other, a scowl fixed on his face. "I'm with Harvey, Dad. May we please not try to put a face on this? It is what it is, and a damned sorry thing at that. No one has yet convinced me of the good doctor's sense in sending a sick man thousands of miles from his family. What in hell is its benefit?"

"Its worth, Thomas, is to provide help in dispelling the illusion that you belong to me." Henry straightened his back, squared his shoulders, held his head erect, all of a purpose to cast off sadness, claiming authority. "Or that I belong to you." There, he had said it. Perhaps he was not sure that he believed it, but it was spoken. And it was not a "face" he'd put on his leaving. It was *permission* that he had claimed. "We do not owe each other the keeping of some artificial proximity because of our common family name. Love is what we share. And love does not dissipate across distance, falter through the passing of time. It will not succumb to your anger at my leaving."

Henry stepped close to his sons, offering a hand to them both. Will glanced away. Thomas took his father's hand. When Harvey made no move to take the other hand, Thomas glared so hard at him that it must have struck him like a blow, and Harvey grasped his father's hand. Henry slowly took in their faces, then smiled and said, "You will each have this image of me standing fully dressed on my feet—in these boots, for God's sake, Harvey. Speaking clearly, my eyes hard open. That, in love, you may keep. And so shall I, my sons, keep you in love fully formed and as near as my thoughts."

A bright red rubber ball, fat and lively, bounced against Henry's thigh, and what more he might have thought to add to his homily was lost in the ensuing clamor of a girl and boy chasing it. Neither child comprehended the violation of close space with strangers as they skipped right into the middle of the men. They were dressed in matching blue-striped fabric, he in knee pants, she in a lace-edged dress. Both wore shiny black shoes with hard heels that rat-a-tat-tatted on the platform's gray-enameled boards as they danced after the ball. Henry let go his sons' hands and in two light steps, with a quick bow and a catlike crosswise slap of his right hand, captured the ball.

"Aha!" cried Henry. "Sayeth Sir Gilbert, 'Roll on, thou ball, roll on. Through pathless realms of space, Roll on!' And so it shall, irrespective of our little drama."

"Now! By God!" Thomas cried. "That's the image I want. Not another word. Nothing else!" And Thomas caught his father in his arms even as Henry made to toss the ball to the boy, who was clearly not at all sure he would regain his toy. Henry flicked the ball away to the child and returned his son's strong embrace.

When Thomas pulled back, he was crying. He spun around, but made no move to trot away across the platform. Harvey extended one hand to his father and clapped him on the shoulder with the other. Harvey then put his arm across Thomas's shoulder and with a low word bade him follow. The two young men looked together at their father and held him in their gaze with palpable intensity. Then they turned, and with that, his sons were gone from him for good.

"All aboard!" the attendant cried out in a voice something more of a question than a command. He was a bespectacled skinny man with freckles and straw-colored hair poking out from underneath his cap, who stood on a nearby train car's boarding step, leaning outward holding to a short vertical handrail affixed to the exterior of the car at shoulder height. He cast a pleading look at Henry. With a nod, Will Webb pointed Henry to the train car door and put a hand on Henry's shoulder as they fell into step moving toward the train. Henry took hold of the satchel strap and held onto it as a soldier might hold his weapon at rest.

"You have a four-day train ride's worth of reading in that bag of yours?" Will clasped Henry's shoulder more tightly.

"I have a lifetime's reading in my little Tolstoy volumes alone,"

Henry said, and winked at Will when he added, "and there is not a pun there intended. Who knows? Perhaps Thomas is right and Dr. Belton is wrong. Perhaps I will have time before I die for many books."

"And if you live in spite of the good doctor's promise," Will asked, "you'll be a good boy and come straight home?"

Like a brace of cold water in the face after a morning's shave, Henry knew that he did not want at any time to return to Idaho. Out of the dimness of his earlier uncertain desire to leave, this reckoning had sprung now fully formed. For a moment Henry considered Tolstoy's flight from his home, when at last as an old man he'd found the resolve and will to synthesize the results of his long analysis of the human condition, and left behind his family for an ascetic's wandering. That Tolstoy died not a month later was of no consequence to the fact of his leaving, nor did an arbitrary count of days diminish the beauty of this monk's pilgrimage. Simply, and finally, he had walked out. Henry, however, had secured a writ from the doctor, like a schoolchild, to excuse his own pending absence. Certainly lacking the courage of Tolstoy. Nor would he tell his friend the truth, since it would be hurtful to him. So Henry shook off the reverie and quipped, "Will, I never was a good schoolboy. You know that!" But Will was not paying attention, having now laid his arm across Henry's shoulder for the last few steps on the platform.

"This is hard, Henry. Let it be so, okay? And don't try to talk me out of it." Henry drew up and turned to face Will, who tugged his hand loose from the satchel strap and took the other hand as well and lifted them to his face and kissed the ridge of knuckles on each of Henry's hands. When Will took half a step back, still holding Henry's hands, his eyes were red-rimmed and wet. The moment moved into Henry's heart and bound his chest and throat tightly. But Henry did not weep. He swept Will into a broad hug and squeezed him fiercely.

Up ahead the engine revved and a steam valve belched a cloud, subsiding into a deep hissing sigh. There was a clank in the long drive-wheel arms, and the train shuddered and the attendant called again, speaking only to Henry, "All aboard, sir," and disappeared from view into the train car.

"I will miss you, dear Henry," Will said, tears breaking free, rolling onto his cheeks.

Henry replaced his hand on the strap of his book bag, nodded to Will and, fixing Will with his eyes, said, "Yes. And I you, my brother." And Henry boarded the train.

· N I N E ·

The Union Pacific *Twilight Limited* clackety-clacked, steaming away from the setting sun on a promise to meet again at dawn, swaying on the silver rails as if a mother's hand had hold of the passenger coach in which Henry rested his forehead against the cold glass window. The painted sands and menacing mountains of the western landscape, its inscrutable devil rock spires, its scrubby pines and thin brown grasses, its horizon-to-horizon sky, seemed carted off like abandoned set props in a madly paced theatrical dreamscape, and replaced with a verdant rolling tableau that was shook out like a tablecloth over the Mississippi River plains. He could feel all over the eager trembling of the train. His head buzzed against the glass. His feet tingled in his boots, heel and sole light on the gray-painted metal floor. Henry felt he might be shaken down into the very blackness that founded the soil itself.

"You all right, mister?" the attendant asked, leaning slightly toward Henry from his stance in the carpeted aisle of the coach, his hands dutifully at his sides. He was a square-built black man with a bushy salt-and-pepper goatee. Henry tilted his head upright and wiped his mouth again, crumpling the white cloth in his hand, then bringing it down to rest on his knee. Feeling the wheeze still in his chest, hearing the thin whistle as he inhaled, he declined to speak and only nodded. As if to ensure that his passenger was okay, the attendant stood by. In a moment, Henry asked, "Can you tell me where we are on our route?"

"We just come through Osceola and got Memphis coming up"— the attendant tugged his watch chain, fishing from a vest pocket at midriff his gold Waltham pocket watch—"in a hour and thirty-six minutes."

"That precisely?"

"On the money. This engineer, Mr. Royce, he never late half a minute." The attendant asked Henry where he was bound.

"I'll depart the train in Mobile, Alabama," Henry said.

"We roll into the station there tomorrow afternoon at three twenty-four. I got a extra shift, so I be rolling into the GM&O terminal right with you." The attendant checked his watch as though confirming in advance tomorrow's arrival. "You going home, sir?"

"In fact, yes, I am going home." Henry let his eyes slip past the dark-skinned man, his eyes a deep and liquid brown like sorghum molasses, to rest on a section of the coach ceiling, but seeing nothing there, or even focusing there. He thought of how his friend Will often preached funerals for those *gone home.* In several seconds he looked back at the attendant. "I've just bought some land there, but it is home that I am going to." Henry patted his shirt pocket, lifted its flap, reached his fingers into the pocket, and withdrew a folded map. "May I show you here on this plat?" He unfolded the lightly soiled page, fifteen inches by fifteen inches, and flattened the paper across his lap with tender caresses. The attendant removed his hat and leaned closer.

"Sit with me, please." Henry slid over nearer the window to make as much room on the seat as he could.

"Well, sir, I . . ." With a look left and right, the attendant sat gingerly on the edge of the seat beside Henry.

"See, this long wavy north-south line, that is the shoreline of the bay." Henry bent his neck and shoulders a bit, inclining himself closer to the map, pointing with his index finger, following the vertical mark that represented where the land met the water. "And here, this is Rock Creek, and just south of it, right here you see, is Fly Creek. Now, between the two and eastward, not quite a mile, here," and Henry tapped the page where a dotted line made a rectangle there, "that is the ten acres to which I have a deed."

"I bet it look pretty down there." The attendant looked fixedly upon the map, as though seeing into a hole in time and space where the landscape of Henry's new home was revealed to him as through a window. "You got family, peoples there?" The attendant was easing himself up from the seat beside Henry, replacing his cap, now watching Henry and not looking at the map.

"I have neither family nor acquaintances there." Henry became more animated, as if in anticipation of his arrival tomorrow. "It will be an adventure for me." Henry returned the map to his shirt pocket, smoothed down the pocket flap, and found a smile for the attendant, who paused, assuming an almost cautious demeanor, and asked, "You left somebody back where you come from?"

Henry looked back toward the window and saw nothing within nor beyond the descending darkness outside the glass. His own face was reflected there and stared back at him, and from underneath shaggy white eyebrows his own eyes fiercely sought an answer to the question about who'd been left behind, the "somebody."

"I'm sorry, I haven't taken notice of your badge. What is your name?" Henry leaned forward in his seat for a better view of the attendant's uniform front, and the big man presented his chest. "Lawrence, sir. Name of Lawrence Washington. From Memphis, Tennessee. Been riding these trains now thirteen years."

"And I'm Henry Stuart." He extended his hand. Lawrence took it and they shook hands, and man to man sought and held the other's eyes, sharing, after a moment, the briefest of nods. "I did leave someone behind in Idaho. Thank you for asking. I have two sons, Harvey and Thomas, there. And a dear friend, a preacher who worries for my unchurched soul."

Henry told Lawrence that there were many in the town he had left whom he counted friends, and when the attendant said it sounded to him like the makings for a sweet return someday—"all them good peoples back there waiting"—Henry only nodded. "You stay gone awhile and then dress up all pretty and go home struttin' so they wonders where you been and what you been up to." At the suggestion of getting dressed up for going home, Henry decided he did not want to ride another mile in his boots. Full of the moment, Henry asked Lawrence if he might remove his boots and socks and occupy his seat on the train as a barefoot sojourner for the balance of the trip.

"Hoowee, sir. That steel floor cold on a October night." Lawrence's grin was broad and full, his eyes dancing. "Ain't a rule, though, says you can't go without shoes if that's what you wants to do." Lawrence shook his head. "Lucinda be hitting me on the head I come home and drag off my old shoes. Tells me to get out on the porch with my nasty-smelling feet."

"Lucinda and Harvey, my son, would get on well. Harvey is terribly embarrassed of a shoeless father going about town, I'm afraid. I think he must have assimilated his very British grandfather's hidebound sense of decorum."

"You sound kind of English yourself," Lawrence said, and Henry allowed he had been born in England and lived there until he was ten. "Yep, I coulda told. I pick up stuff like that pretty good." He watched Henry preparing to remove his boots. "You go around your hometown barefooted?"

"I did, Lawrence. I did, and it was to me a complete delight."

"Then you get them boots off and be delighted on Lawrence's train." A woman in a seat three rows toward the rear of the car called out for the attendant and he drew himself up into a more official posture, lifted his hand to the bill of his cap and tugged it down tightly and begged Henry's leave.

"By all means, and thank you for your time," Henry said. "I hope I have not kept you overlong."

"Oh, no. Not to worry, sir. Just taking care of my passengers. Good night to you."

"One other thing. May I give you these boots of mine? I don't intend to wear them again."

"Aw, no, sir," Lawrence said without a second's hesitation, his voice lifted in pride, and Henry became embarrassed for having assumed such familiarity. The attendant, however, quickly added, a smile lifting his brown cheeks apple-round, "George love to have them shiny boots. He a porter about your size and them boots probably going to fit him fine. I send him back here directly when we pull into the station in Memphis. And he don't say thank you, I'll scob his knob."

Lawrence tipped his hat and turned quickly to go, then stopped and said over his shoulder, his eyes full and bright, "And I thank you, sir, for you to offer me them boots. They look like some good ones."

Henry turned to look out the window, hoping to see if the night sky yet revealed her stars. The last two nights and days had pressed down upon the earth holding this railroad track underneath a smooth and cloudy sky, a bowl heavy and hewn from gray marble. The darkness beyond the interior light of the passenger car transformed the window glass into a mirror and Henry saw only his reflection.

From the tiny platform between the connected cars he would be able to see the stars in the velvet night sky and breathe some fresh air into his singed lungs. But before standing, his boots side by side on the seat, he removed his socks. Lawrence was right, the floor was cold. A shiver ran up Henry's legs, coursing over the skin of his back to the nape of his neck. He mindfully relaxed his shoulders, which had instinctively drawn up against the shock of the chill, and let his breathing descend deeper into his chest. In a minute, a kind of distantly beheld warmth drew near and settled on Henry. He sat still.

Henry blinked when he was suddenly addressed by a loud, high-pitched voice that came at him from near his left shoulder. "Them the boots you getting rid of?" Henry had fallen asleep. And the train had pulled into the station in Memphis.

Henry turned to a bone-thin man, the porter George, already nervously extending his hand to accept the boots. Without saying a word, Henry passed the Wellingtons to the man, the perfumey scent of Harvey's polish still strong about them, the shiny leather holding and reflecting the nuances of light from the train car's side-mounted fixtures.

"Thank you, sir."

"You are welcome."

The porter moved away, his eyes locked on his prize. Henry turned on the seat and placed a hand on the back of the seat and stood. He looked around the car at the few other passengers, returned the nod from a well-dressed young man, a pretty woman at his side, and walked toward the door at the rear of the car. He thought he could feel the eyes of the young man registering his bare feet as he made his way for some fresh air. And Henry believed the day would come when his own mind's eye would be blind to such followings.

· TEN ·

In the dream, drawn deep into sleep that hummed like the rhythm of his train car on the rails, Henry is beckoned by his father to come nearer to the cloth-upholstered wingback chair where he sits, his left foot drawn up and resting atop his thigh. The old man drops his hand to his boot there, pulling back the pant cuff to reveal the boot's top. His long, thin fingers absentmindedly caress the fine leather. Henry has now approached and is standing before his father. The son waits to look into his father's eyes. He cannot see them because his father's head is tilted slightly downward, but Henry imagines that beneath the bushy white eyebrows, Walter James Stuart is studying the fine grain of the cowhide beneath his fingertips, appraising the stitching there, wondering, perhaps, how there came to be a nick near the heel. Minutes seem to pass and the decor of the room and arrangement of its walls, doors, and windows transforms to resemble houses Henry has lived in.

Though Henry's attention is intermittently drawn to the kaleidoscopic backdrop, his focus is upon his father. The old man still has not looked up. Henry stands, shuffling his feet—will that attract his father's notice?—and brings his hands around behind him and clasps them into the small of his back in a gesture of standing rest that Henry even yet assumes in wakefulness.

In an outer room a telegraph key begins clacking its staccato metallic call. Without raising his eyes to look at his son, the old man waves Henry off toward the telegraph machine, tapping now in earnest. Henry turns and walks through open double doors to the small rosewood desk that followed Henry's father from England, to every home in America, a dark and dainty piece of furniture, incongruous even in a dreamscape with the business of telegraphy, Henry's father's vocation. The machine is now pecking like an agitated toy bird frantically trying to accomplish some private purpose before the return of its overwatchful young master.

Then in the way of dreams, the telegraph instrument shifts its shape to a dark living thing, and from it issues the raspy cawing of the night-black crow that it has now become. Henry looks away in horror toward where his father is still seated; his father now looks up from beneath his shaggy brow and fixes upon Henry a warm and beautiful smile that is all that could be desired by a son, a smile so tender and loving that Henry moves his hands together, palms pressed together flat in front of his chest.

The telegraph machine has grown suddenly quiet and Henry looks to see that it is now changed into a dove, one eye cocked toward him and glistening like an ebony pearl. Its beak opens and a woman's voice sings words in Russian to him that Henry recognizes as Tolstoy's, from *A Calendar of Wisdom*: "The more you transform your life from the material to the spiritual domain, the less you become afraid of death." An overlarge month-and-day calendar page is tacked to a wall back of the rosewood desk, February 2. Henry's father appears at his side and removes the calendar page from the wall and gives it to Henry. They both stand together, facing each other, and Henry's father raises a hand to Henry's cheek.

It is warm. And when Henry awakens after a long-held echoing note from the *Twilight Limited*'s whistling call to the rolling night, Henry still feels upon his cheek the warmth of his father's hand.

• E L E V E N •

Henry watched the landscape outside the train window begin to unroll more slowly, the October sun stretching and softening the afternoon shadows. Had Henry been a blind man he would have known the train was slowing. The train's sounds and vibrations grew quieter and lost intensity. Sailors said of their ships' sounds when getting under way, "Now she's talking!" And this ship of the rails was hushing down. The change, Henry thought, was something like canoeing through churning rapids into waters still swift yet more placid, where the unbunching of muscles and nerves allowed steadier, deeper breathing.

October 16, 1925, 3:14 P.M. and right on time, coming up on half past three, just as Lawrence Washington had said they would, the Union Pacific *Twilight Limited* was approaching the station in Mobile, Alabama. The heat and humidity had come on last night, Henry even detecting a warming of the metal floor beneath his bare feet. At first Henry had thought a fever, like other fevers he'd had in the past three months, was setting in and chills would soon follow. But Henry had not felt the heat behind his eyes, which is where his fevers had burned him most, and quick as that, he knew he was feeling the ambient temperature of the air outside. He was at first mildly embarrassed, then just shook his head and smiled.

Henry reached into his shirt pocket, the fabric limp with perspiration, and removed a note he'd penned on a small white card from his book satchel:

George,

Please accept this my hat as a gift to go along with the boots. It is a new hat, and has spent less than ten minutes on my head. If you do not wear hats, perhaps you know someone who would take it. It should give many years of good service. Thank you.

—Henry Stuart

He held on to the ends of the card with the thumb and forefinger of each hand, lowering them to rest in his lap, holding the card as if he might wish to refer to it. Henry turned and looked out the window and knew the creeks and bayous of the Tensaw River swamplands were falling well behind the southbound train, its twin silver rails now spiked into oaken crossties laid on hard clay outlying the approaching city of Mobile. He'd studied for hours at his kitchen table in Nampa maps of Mobile and Mobile Bay and its eastern shore, rolled out flat there underneath warm yellow light where he and Molly had so often sat and read to each other.

Henry tucked the note card behind the hatband and put the hat back on the seat opposite him where it had spent most of its journey to Alabama. No one had sat there during this four-day trip. These four places on two facing benches had been Henry's hearth and home since leaving Idaho, the smart felt hat with its fashionable brown silk band his only traveling companion, and he nodded to it. A crooked grin brightened his face.

"Even though you are quite short, sir, I will miss you at times," Henry said to the hat. "We have traveled well together, and you have been most agreeable company. Not at all argumentative, and that is a rare, if sometimes boring, trait." Henry was vaguely aware over his left shoulder of someone watching him from a nearby seat, but finished his salutation to the hat. "My sincere best wishes for a continuing pleasant train ride and a good life with George."

And he bent forward and brushed a bit of lint from the brim, sat back and once more directed his attention out the window. Buildings, warehouses, cars and trucks, scattered people walking here and there, power lines strung in many directions, all stood in counterpoint to the rolling woods beyond, which were, however, receding rapidly. The *Twilight Limited* would soon be stopped at the Gulf, Mobile & Ohio terminal, the ornate building an architectural gem of Mobile, Alabama, and her waterfront.

Though the long train would soon be coming into the station, the steam-driven locomotive relaxing its pell-mell pull, an involuntary quickening of Henry's pulse stirred him to full attention, his eyes moving about more. He took up the book satchel from the seat beside him and placed it on his lap. He laid both hands palm-down on its canvas side as the picture out his window became entirely a city scene. The attendant Lawrence Washington entered the front of the train car and immediately made eye contact with Henry, but then acknowledged with a glance the other few passengers in the car, nodding to someone in a seat somewhere behind Henry.

"Mr. Stuart," the attendant said, touching his index finger to the shiny black bill of his cap. Henry nodded. "I reckon you be 'bout plum wore out. But you be getting off this old rattling thing soon now."

"I am a bit stiff, Mr. Washington," Henry said. "All in all, however, it has been an easy enough trip thanks to your kind service." Henry pulled his collar away from his neck. "It is a good deal warmer, I must say, than the land I left." Sweat shone upon Henry's forehead. "Is it usually this mild in October in Alabama?"

"Sometimes it is, sometimes it's not. You can't never tell how it's goin' to be down here by the water. It wouldn't surprise me one bit, Mr. Stuart, it don't be cold here in two days. Then, sure as the world, it get up hot again and you be rolling up your sleeves on Thanksgiving Day. It's bound to be that ocean down there that make the weather so crazy. You think that might be so?"

"I am afraid I don't know, Mr. Washington. But, if time permits—" Henry glanced away from the attendant, looked first at the satchel on his lap, then out the window, then back to the attendant. "If time permits I do look forward to getting to know all about this new country I've come to." Henry's words trailed off as he contemplated an omission he had made in his packing. The attendant begged

Henry's leave and walked away down the aisle. Henry was distracted and did not pay heed to the attendant's leaving. He was nonplussed that only now it had occurred to him that he'd left something behind in Idaho that he should certainly have brought along. He would correct his mistake, send a telegram to Thomas and bid him hire the railroad to ship his loom to him. Weaving a rug might be just the thing to add to his piney woods days a measure of contentment and a sense of accomplishment.

Henry tapped his fingers on the book satchel in his lap and recalled Henry David Thoreau's rejection of the gift of a rug while setting up house in his cabin in the Concord woods on the shores of Walden Pond. Thoreau sent the rolled rug right back with its courier and a message to its sender that he'd come to the woods endeavoring to reduce his distractions, that he already swept the stoop, that he did not wish to sweep the stoop and shake out a rug. Two things to do in place of one, writ large to the broader universe of a day's doings, would be considerations too many. The irony was not lost on Henry that the distraction of a rug would deepen the crimson of his own blood to a more animate hue.

Since Henry had left his teaching post at the college, weaving rugs had been his chief pastime. He had been inspired to give it a try after watching an old Navajo woman at work weaving a simple yet exquisitely beautiful rug at the Idaho State Fair. Henry had stood transfixed for most of a morning watching the dyed yarn growing into a multicolored, intricately patterned rug up the vertical strings of the loom. Henry watched the woman's long brown fingers, a fat turquoise and silver ring on the third finger of her left hand, and thought of someone playing a harp. Henry only stood and watched, saying nothing until more than two hours had passed. "You possess a special gift," Henry had then said to the quiet woman. For a long moment, she made no reply, nor looked at Henry, but finally turned her eyes upon him and said, "Whatever gift I have is borne of patience, only patience." And then she looked back at her work, and Henry had not spoken again, but watched her for another hour or more.

The talent for weaving was somehow oddly available to Henry

from his first effort, and he had won a blue ribbon at a later edition of that same state fair. It had surprised Henry that he found within himself the patience for the slow practice of rug weaving—more than a thousand feet of yarn went into a three-by-five-foot rug. The long hours were easily passed in preparation for dying his own yarn from vegetal pigment. It had surprised Henry too that he had no patience for displaying his rugs or for demonstrating the craft he was learning. So Henry never entered another of his rugs into a competition. His skill and artistry grew after he made a month-long trip south into Arizona and New Mexico to learn more from the Navajo weavers. Word of his rugs spread around Nampa, and as time passed, he was pleased to sell an occasional rug, but drew more pleasure from giving them away.

He could recall his delight when five years earlier he had paused while filling out his 1920 census form; he had been about to write in his profession, "college professor—retired," when he smiled and with histrionic flourish stabbed the pencil to the paper, marking down instead "weaver—rugs."

The train's wheels were now protesting the brakeman's work, the steel wheels and the steel rails setting a commotion to announce their arrival at the GM&O station. The attendant moved down the aisle to see to the needs of his passengers, gave a wink to Henry, and announced in his rich baritone voice, "Mobile! Mobile, Alabama, ladies and gentlemen. If you going to Mobile, you safe and sound at home."

Then Lawrence Washington stopped and looked back at Henry, just now standing to the center of the aisle, hitching up his satchel strap. He cried out to the passengers, "Got Mobile, and that big ol' Baldwin County across the bay. Fairhope! Welcome home to Fairhope!" Henry nodded and smiled, and the attendant touched his finger to the bill of his cap before turning and going on down the car.

TWELVE

The port city waterfront outside the GM&O station was abuzz in the long shadows of a mid-October late afternoon. For Henry, stepping off the *Twilight Limited* into this thrumming scene of a busy day at the docks was like coming out of a tunnel. At its entrance had been the backdrop of pastoral winter hills and valleys and purple mountains in Canyon County, Idaho, and at its exit this terminal, a gleaming white fairy tale castle presiding over the riverbank warehouses and buildings and the encroaching Mobile streets noisy with all manner of traffic, on foot and on wheels.

The rails he had been riding for miles through the fog-shrouded delta bottomlands cut across the silver ribbon of the Mobile River, which now bounded the eastern limits of the city and fed its keen appetite for commerce. Strung along here were cotton docks and passenger boat docks and banana docks and lumber docks and shipping docks and seafood docks. Men in hats, their sleeves rolled up, quickstepped here and there, calling out and answering. Bells and klaxons and whistles sang out above the din. The open-air market at Star Fish & Oyster Company had dozens of galvanized tubs of red snapper, and the oystermen's schooners sat with halyards slapping in the light wind while black-booted sailors talked about tomorrow morning's possibilities. Oyster shuckers and fish dressers babbled and pried and sliced. The blended copper-and-musk scent of fish and blood and the sea permeated the air and was more notable than even the smell of the train, with its oils and fires and steam and cargo.

"Hey you, old man!" a voice called from somewhere behind Henry. But Henry did not think he was being hailed, so he did not turn or look as he followed a thick-waisted black man who carried his heavy suitcase and someone else's small steamer trunk. This man, a porter with the bulk of a stevedore, had come into the GM&O crying out for passengers seeking to board the *Bay Queen* when she docked and would make her last run of the day across the bay to the piers of Daphne, Stedman's Landing, Fairhope, Battles Wharf, and Point Clear.

"You," the voice hailed again. "You old barefooted fool!" And Henry slowed and looked behind him, seeing a young man in baggy clothes and a flop hat who had been a passenger in his rail car. Henry remembered his boarding sometime yesterday and his sipping from a pocket flask while yet walking down the aisle. The young man jogged toward Henry, and Henry felt a bristling of the hairs on his neck, involuntary, like a dog's hackles rising. Henry turned back and continued following the porter, wondering what was about to ensue and feeling some apprehension for its outcome.

In a moment, the young man was at Henry's side. "Hey, you some kind of a nut or a drunk or what?" The young man wobbled in his step and smelled of alcohol. His hair was greasy and curled from underneath his dirty hat. "Not to say I don't like a drink good as the next man, you know, Pops. But I don't sit on no train talking to hats and giving my boots to no nigger." The young man tapped Henry on the shoulder. Henry kept walking, kept his eyes straight ahead. Henry tightened his jaw, found himself thinking of a brief poem by Thoreau, where some men are seen as hectoring bullies, and

Who can claim no nearer kinship with me
Than brotherhood by law.

Henry could think of no law, not even the kinship of species, that would bring him into brotherhood with a man so much a bully, so spiteful about another man's race. Henry noticed that the pace of the big black porter had slowed almost imperceptibly. He did not wish this man to risk the consequences of coming to his aid, of challenging a white man, and thought small talk might buy some levity.

"You are the chap who boarded the train just yesterday. Mississippi, was it?" Henry himself slowed a step to create more distance between the two of them and the man lugging the bags down the dock.

"Tennessee. And I ain't no *chap* and we don't like crazies." The young man tapped Henry's shoulder again. "We got our ways of dealing with people who get too friendly with the nigger help."

"I am sorry, sir, if I have offended you." Henry stopped and faced the young man. The porter stopped also, continuing, however, to face away from the pair. He made no move to set down either the suitcase or the steamer trunk. "If you will please grant me your pardon," Henry said, "I will take care to stay completely away from you."

"Or how's about I throw you in the river? You know how to swim, old man?"

"I know how to swim."

"You done got your boots off. Old goat like you ought to last all of two or three minutes in that cold water if I lighten you of that bag across your shoulder." He looked at Henry's book satchel. Henry laid a hand to its strap across his chest.

The porter turned slowly like a giant grizzly meaning to backtrack its path. The big man did not take a step nor move a muscle, only looked intensely at the young man. His face was as black and as broad as an iron skillet and his eyes shone like black fire. His face was pulled into such a scowl that the skin between his eyebrows looked like grooved obsidian. The fearsome effect of the porter's glare was exaggerated and rendered almost evil when he smiled, a gold cap on his front tooth. The other front tooth was missing.

The surly young man stumbled back a step. "I ain't scared of no nigger. And I can still throw you in that river, old man, and not even blink my eyes."

The young man's words reminded Henry of a Sufi parable, in which a tiny old monk was met on the lane by Genghis Khan, who wheeled his horse around to block the monk's way. "Do you know who I am?" demanded the warrior chieftain.

"You are the khan," said the monk flatly, at which show of little emotion Genghis Khan reared his horse and drew his giant sword with a flourish.

"Do you know, too, that I can cut off your head and not blink an eye?"

The monk lifted his face and looked directly at the khan and said, "And do you not know I can allow you to cut off my head and not blink an eye?"

When Genghis Khan beheld absolute serenity in the monk, whose words rang with absolute truth, he swung his sword in a huge flashing arc and returned it to its long scabbard. Taking his horse's reins into both hands, he briefly closed his eyes and nodded his head toward the monk and kicked his horse and rode on his way.

Henry wondered, *If the monk had conveyed even the slightest smirk, would his head have rolled?* He guessed that it would have. Henry realized, too, that he was not sufficiently enlightened to have said "throw me in and I'll not blink" without putting a twist at the end, likely just enough to inflame and provoke the worst response. But Henry was spared the temptation to give the Sufi priest's words a try when the porter did the only other thing he needed to do in order to chase away the thuggish young man. He dropped the bags and curled his hands into fists. Only that. And the young man back-pedaled, stumbled again, turned, and took several hurried steps in the other direction.

Henry shook his head, wondering at the flame of hatred flickering in men's hearts, requiring no breeze to bid it spread, only the fanning from private thoughts and prejudices. Newspapers of the summer had carried stories of forty thousand Ku Klux Klansmen marching on Washington, D.C.

He was about to thank the porter when the black man reached out his right hand, as big as a baseball glove, and roughly swept Henry aside. A jagged oyster shell the size of a tea saucer, but heavy and sharp-edged, sailed past where Henry would have been standing and struck the porter on his shoulder, bouncing off his canvas shirt and clattering to the boards at his feet.

"Sorry, sir. Thing coulda cut yo' ear off."

Henry whipped his head around to see the young man running away full tilt down the dock. The two men watched him go until he became lost in a crowd of oyster shuckers and fish cleaners. Henry reached to shake the porter's hand and was struck by the unusual size of it. His grip was strong, but not overly so, and his palm was rough and calloused, but warm. "Thank you," said Henry. The porter looked directly into Henry's eye, but said nothing. Henry's gaze went above the porter into the streaked clouds, tinted with the dying glow of an evening sun. Gray gulls and brown pelicans plied the air above the riverfront, now and again diving toward the water for a fish or a piece of a fish from the Star Fish & Oyster Company operations. But Henry was not distracted by the seabirds. His staring was intense, as if he were looking for something hidden there in the colored palette of sky.

Abruptly Henry said, "Honest intention is what saved the Sufi priest. That alone. I never saw it until now."

"Sir?"

"Oh, never mind," Henry said. "I won't trouble you with all of that. What is your name, if you don't mind? Mine is Henry Stuart."

"Folks calls me Mule."

"But what does your mother call you?"

"She don't. She dead." The porter looked sideways at Henry. "But you thinks I got some problem with Mule, I ain't. Lets peoples know they might get kicked, they mess with me." The porter cracked another gold-trimmed grin, this one, however, dancing with all that Henry so far found good about his arrival in Alabama. Then he told Henry he would like to make haste and get the bags down to the wharf where the *Bay Queen* was set to tie up any minute.

"Do you work for the steamship company?" Henry asked the porter lifting the bags.

"Naw, sir. I just come down here and tote stuff for folks. They gives me a little money, most the time."

"I see," said Henry. Then he asked how long the *Bay Queen* would be at dockside. The porter told Henry the steamer would continue to take on cargo and passengers for about an hour, that it would get under way across the bay at five thirty.

"The *Bay Queen* the last one of the day," Mule said. "She come and get peoples in the morning and dinnertime and suppertime. There she come up the river now. I got to get moving, sir. Got to quit this talking. I don't draw no pay for talking."

Henry apologized, but the porter said nothing, firmly set to his work now, striding away. Henry kept following his suitcase, hitched up his satchel to a more comfortable position. Henry came abreast of the loading brow, but stepped away, into the grassless black soil just back of the creosoted planks of the dock. He stood well back, watching the double-decker *Bay Queen*'s giant curved bow approach the dock, her paddle wheel churning a whitecapped brown froth on the surface of the river. Men on the deck of the boat called out loudly to other men dockside, all in an attitude of readiness to catch and throw and haul in lines.

The blunt thick single stack of the *Bay Queen* protruded high into the sky from amidships and poured black smoke into the descending twilight. Shouts from the deckhands and dock crew were drowned out by a percussive blast from the steam whistle mounted atop the captain's wheelhouse. Henry rubbed the soft white stubble on his chin and cheeks with the back of his hand. He watched the frantic bustle of getting a big boat docked, though he knew these men were simply about work they knew with precision, and that the frenzy was only in the eyes of onlookers.

And try as he might, Henry could not yet seem to break the feeling that he was just that, a watcher. Not even his bare feet upon the soil sustaining the foundation of this city could ground him to this place. For above the soil, the air was vibrating with such *intention* toward business—of making and getting and moving and saying— that all introspection was difficult or drowned out altogether. Henry had stepped off a train into an electrified circus fantasy, soiled from transport, its bolts dangerously loose.

A heavy sense of displacement had cloaked Henry almost from the moment he had departed the exquisite main hall of the GM&O

terminal, and the feeling closed on him more tightly with each step across the boards in the passenger area. As he had followed the big man's hard-soled boots banging heel and toe, heel and toe, down on the wharf, it was almost as if the encounter with the young man from Tennessee had been inevitable. Another trumpeting blast from the *Bay Queen's* whistle indicated she was docked and her afterbrow was down. Passengers who had been milling about began boarding, holding on to the hand rope sagging between brass-ball-topped stanchions. Henry removed his book satchel and sat down cross-legged on a thin patch of brown grass and watched, his mind and heart full of uncertainty.

· THIRTEEN ·

Henry had boarded the vessel at the last moment and now took up a spot portside and forward on the second deck of the *Bay Queen.* Just behind him and up a short ladder on yet a third deck, the captain was in his wheelhouse steering the vessel southeastward across Mobile Bay. Henry laid his hand atop the balustrade, gleaming slick spar-varnished mahogany running the circumference of the deck. The upright balusters were painted white and richly detailed. These steam-powered bayboats and their sister riverboats were spectacular in appearance, and Henry imagined them especially fond products of a naval architect's imagination.

The bayboat's deck vibrated beneath Henry's bare feet and the Mobile city skyline twinkled with pinpoints of soft yellow light as that horizon was passing astern. The sun had set behind the city twenty minutes earlier just as they got under way. A smoky orange glow billowed up from the skyline and stretched up and down the shoreline.

Whatever was the sound of the steamer's engine and its drive arms rotating through giant bearings was lost on the wind. Nor could Henry hear the sound of the side paddlewheel, its sloshing plunge into the brackish water. The apparent wind in his face and the *hushhhh, hushhhh, hushhhh* of waves meeting the dancing bow of the steamer were the only sounds in Henry's ear. He rubbed with the flat of his hand the softness of the short beard growing on his cheek. Thomas, his son, when a boy, had walked into the bathroom where Henry stood at the sink shaving, puffs of warm lather on his chin and cheeks.

"Why do you shave, Father?" the little boy had asked.

And Henry had answered that it was so his face would be smooth and clean. Now as Henry considered his stubble, he knew that in the boy's mind a new question would have formed: "But why do you wish a smooth face?" Indeed, from this evening's perspective, Henry could find no reason to have a smooth face. He would let his whiskers grow. Shaving was a bother at any rate.

The water was wine-colored, an iridescent plum hue reflecting the deepening palette of the cloudless twilight. First stars blinked on and a boyish giddiness washed over Henry. "Star light, star bright, first star I see tonight" came into his head. And what, Henry wondered, is the wish I would wish tonight? But he stopped himself and would not allow one to form in his mind and lean, as it would, toward an uncertain future. He cajoled himself to be here in this present moment. Here with these waves, these slow, fat ripples on the broad expanse of Mobile Bay and the *Bay Queen*'s easy motion, her pitch and yaw smooth like waltz steps. Henry's spirits swelled with each gentle lift of the bow. It was a fine, balmy night, Henry's first on a large boat since his Atlantic crossing from England in 1869, more than half a century ago. It was remarkable to Henry how utterly familiar this passage on the water seemed, how his mind had saved the feeling. He knew that this bay crossing would likewise be retained in his memory and treasured, partly because it was so quickly and effectively overcoming a little blooming of sadness.

"It's beautiful out this evening." A woman's voice right beside him startled Henry from his musings. "And you've chosen the best spot on the boat." The woman was in her thirties, attractive, with thick and wavy hair that caught the evening's dying light and shone like harvest wheat and was gathered and pinned loosely about her head. Her shoulders were draped in a colorful handwoven shawl of heavy wool that she drew up to her neck with one hand while she placed the other on the balustrade near Henry's. The temperature had dropped rapidly since sunset, though it felt good to Henry; he had not had a coughing spasm since midday and felt strong. Henry faced the woman at his side and bowed his head briefly, acknowledging that yes, this was a good spot.

"May I stand here and share this claim of yours?" Though the woman was addressing Henry, her gaze was fixed across the open water. Atop a twenty-foot staff rising from the center of the bow, the union jack fluttered and snapped madly in the wind.

"Certainly."

"My name is Kate Anderson," she said, extending her hand and taking Henry's firmly. Henry shook her hand and introduced himself. She proved to be lively and inquisitive and Henry found he rather liked her. She asked him a spate of questions. It seemed to Henry this woman was genuinely interested in his story, and he imagined she was like that with most people she met. She induced in Henry an openness and willingness to self-disclosure that surprised him. He marveled at how easily he had crossed a threshold of trust with her.

So Henry told her that he had moved from Idaho on the advice of his physician, that, never having been to Alabama before, he had chosen Fairhope and bought, sight unseen, ten acres of land, and that he was to be met within the hour at the dock at Stedman's Landing by one Peter Stedman, whom he knew only through their many letters exchanged. Kate said that she did not personally know Mr. Stedman, but that he was a man well regarded in the town.

When Kate asked Henry what would be his gainful endeavor, he answered that he would first off provide himself with shelter. She was surprised that his land had no house. "It makes for an adventure, you see," Henry said, and told her that once he could keep warm and dry upon his place, he would read and write some and walk a good deal, "as did my Mr. Thoreau." Then Henry described how Thoreau walked in the mornings and wrote in the afternoons; if something prevented his morning's walk, Thoreau claimed his afternoon's writing output suffered. "I have no books to write, but I love to walk. And I will weave my rugs."

"You weave rugs?" she asked.

"I did, yes, in Idaho," Henry said. "And I shall in Alabama as soon as my loom arrives."

"And what will you do with these rugs? Sell them?" Kate seemed more than curious. "I do appreciate hand woven items." She touched her shawl.

"I noticed the lovely wrap you have there." Henry paused. "I really have given no thought to how I will dispose of the rugs I weave." Henry lifted his chin and his eyes drifted to the horizon as he considered this, but briefly; then he turned his attention back to Kate. "Did you weave your shawl?"

"Oh, no. It was a gift," Kate said.

Kate had let her own attention wander, it seemed, for she was quiet a long moment and then blurted out, "I see that you are barefooted, Mr. Stuart." And Henry was surprised at the comment, and more surprised at his own quick retort.

"And I see that you are not." Henry smiled, and believing his remark might seem a bit flirtatious, fixed his face in a more serious expression as he made a show of standing back to look at her shoes with their pointed toes and high tops with crisscross laces. "There is an Oriental saying, 'Hell is a stylish shoe.' If that is true, it seems to me that, conversely, Heaven might be no shoes at all."

"*If* the first statement is true," Kate said. "That is the question, if." Kate shook her finger playfully. Henry flexed his toes. The boat's vibration felt good to his feet and legs. Though it was growing darker, the sky's color deepening to a mauve-tinged blue, Henry could still make out the flight of gulls as they came near the boat. What could be freer than flight? Henry thought and, without sharing his interior monologue, said, "And what could be more confining and irksome than tight shoes?" He turned toward the woman. "Some places in China I believe, it is still the custom to tightly bind a girl's feet to actually stunt their growth and keep them small and dainty."

"I guess if I stop to think about it, these shoes of mine are a bit tight. But my feet are not in the least dainty, at least to hear my mother tell it." Kate put her finger to her chin. "But you know, I rarely think of my shoes. I mean to say, I never think of my toes. They are just down there. And I think that even if they suffer some, we tell them to shush and just keep to their business of being down there in our shoes." Kate giggled.

The pair talked on, and Kate told Henry that she was a teacher. And then as quickly as that, Kate let go the rail and put her hands on her hips. "Did you see the headlines in the papers about those schools in Texas forbidding poor teachers to teach evolution? Can you believe that?"

"I'm sorry. I have not seen a paper." Henry's eyebrows pulled together into a frown. He knew that many people had followed with rabid interest the summer's great sideshow in Tennessee, becoming well known as the Scopes Monkey Trial. He said as much to Kate.

Kate shook her head and huffed out a big breath. "If Mr. Darrow and Mr. Bryan had not been such grandstanders shamelessly promoting their own reputations in the Tennessee trial," she said, "perhaps some important ground could have been gained against those who wield their Bibles like clubs." Kate said she had read in the newspaper of a remarkable new invention called a television and wondered to Henry if he thought this new thing, if it caught on, would help diminish ignorance. Henry replied that he feared ignorance would always be with us, then shifted the talk away from this topic that so inflamed his new friend.

"So have you been teaching long?" Henry asked.

"I've been teaching for almost six years," Kate said, and told Henry all about Marietta Johnson and her now-famous School of Organic Education. Kate became excited as she told him how their students had no homework and no examinations, and not one child was allowed to fail.

"John Dewey came all the way down here from New York to see our school," Kate said, gesturing with her hand. "He stayed for a nice long visit, then wrote about us in his book *Schools of Tomorrow*. He even put in a photograph of Mrs. Johnson that he himself took." Henry was encouraged to meet a teacher whose enthusiasm had not flagged. His own had dwindled as semesters accumulated. Kate grew more animated, saying, "Mr. Dewey's very own fourteen-year-old son attended my class and others for a week near Christmas. I still remember what a sweet young man he was."

Pointing at him, Kate asked Henry, "And do you want to know something truly special about my school? You are going to love this," she said before he could offer an answer.

"Apart from the fact that Kate Anderson is on the faculty, I can't imagine anything more special."

"You may remove your tongue from your cheek, Mr. Stuart," Kate said rather sharply, and Henry realized she believed he had spoken condescendingly. His face warmed. Kate tossed off the small affront and said, "The special thing to which I referred, Henry Stuart, is that our children are not required to wear shoes to school, and many do not."

"Really?" Henry was mildly astonished and completely delighted. "I do believe that I have never heard of such a thing in these modern times. I must meet this Marietta Johnson!"

At the handrail, Kate turned more directly toward Henry. "We have one student, Paul, who has a bet with his chums that he will not put shoes on the entire year."

Henry was looking at Kate, hanging on to her words, and entranced by the vision of a schoolyard filled with barefoot children. Kate started to say something else, but stopped speaking suddenly and gestured beyond the bow of the *Bay Queen*. "Ah, just look at that!" she breathed.

And Henry saw immediately what she meant. Above the black and ragged tree line marking the horizon way off in the distance to the east, there arose such a spectacular curve of yellow moon as Henry had never seen. It appeared huge and rose so fast that its emergence above the far shore was a visible motion. And this moon-rise was happening with the wash of sunset light not yet completely vanished from the western sky. Neither spoke a word for five full minutes as the harvest moon's golden face transformed to snowy silver as it ascended. Other passengers had come out to the balustrade. All was silent save the wind and waves and gentle thrum of the boat.

Kate drew Henry's attention to a reddish spot that resembled a painter's brushstroke applied there within the darker tree line along the eastern shore. It grew more illuminated, becoming, as they watched and as the moon's light set the shoreline alight, a pumpkin orange swath there on the horizon.

"What am I seeing, Miss Anderson?" Henry asked.

"Those are the red bluffs. Ecor Rouge on old mariner's charts." Kate explained that they were high bluffs of red clay so readily visible that the earthen wall had become the guiding landmark for sailors northbound into Mobile Bay. "Even Admiral Farragut, who damned the torpedoes in this very bay, relied upon Ecor Rouge to keep his bearings and avoid running aground." Then she told Henry that many people, particularly visitors from Maine, found it dubious that these red bluffs were the highest point on the U.S. coast from Maine to Texas. Henry could have guessed this woman was a teacher, so ingrained in her was the tendency to teach.

Henry stopped attending to Kate's pedagogy, and nestled down inside himself to meet a confusing mix of thoughts about dying and thoughts of the beauty of life in this moment. Only when the first other passenger to move away from the rail had walked past Henry and Kate did Henry speak again.

"How my spirit does soar, Kate Anderson, as from off those red bluffs." Henry shook his head and inhaled deeply, the breath finding this time a cool passage into his lungs. It seemed to him entirely unlikely that next year's October harvest moonrise would find him absent from this sphere of earth, that he would have ceased to exist upon this beauteous and sensual plane.

Again, jumping from his inner thoughts to outer expression,

Henry said, "But no matter, then. Only now, only this. Engulfed in these velvety breezes and bathed in this silver moonlight, I feel at one with this moment. At home here in this place."

Henry put his hand lightly on the woman's shoulder, risking the familiarity but deeply desiring that degree of rapport. "Yes, Miss Anderson, I feel I am being borne home over these calm waves." Then Henry fell silent. Nor did Kate speak. What was left unsaid was being spoken to them both in nature's own sweet silent language, and they were pleased to listen.

· FOURTEEN ·

Henry knew for certain it was Peter Stedman striding across the dock at the landing of the *Bay Queen*. A tall thin fellow about Henry's own age, his hair and beard thick and black, no streaks of gray prominent enough to be detected under the bare-bulb lights at Stedman's Landing. His sleeves were untidily rolled up, and his forearms were muscled and sinewy.

"I have no need to ask your name, Henry Stuart. I'm Peter Stedman." The man was smiling, his teeth even in the dim lights appearing starkly white within his bushy beard. He extended his hand in greeting. "Glad to have you for a neighbor. I believe I could've picked you out in a stampede. When I read your letters I saw a face to go with the voice I was hearing. Definitely your face, sir."

Peter made no bother to conceal his regard for Henry's bare feet. "I could've sworn, though, I saw a man with shoes on his feet. Somebody swipe your shoes, Mr. Stuart?"

"No. I gave them to the porter, George, on the train."

As Henry paused to consider what further information he should divulge, the matter was decided for him. Peter Stedman seemed to lose interest in Henry when he took note of the woman standing just behind Henry, obviously attending to their conversation. "And who is this lovely lady, Mr. Stuart?" Turning to Kate, he added, "I know I've seen you about town, but we've not been introduced."

Henry was a bit flustered by the rapid flow of talk upon this first meeting, but recomposed himself and said, "This is Kate Anderson, a teacher at your Fairhope Organic School, and I'm sorry that I failed to learn"—Henry glanced at Kate—"if it is Mrs. Anderson to her students, or Miss Anderson."

"I am Mrs. Anderson, Mr. Stuart," she said, her eyes moving from Henry to Peter Stedman. "Hello, Mr. Stedman." She looked back at Henry. "Mr. Stuart is without shoes so that he may keep out of hell, I believe, Mr. Stedman."

"Sounds like there's a longer story there. But it'll keep," Peter said. "My grandnephew is a student at the Organic School and reports he actually likes to attend. They've got some secret if that's so. I hated every day of school."

"Most children do, I'm afraid. But a school where children actually wish to be present, that is a place I certainly wish to visit if I may," added Henry. "Mrs. Anderson was kind enough to keep me company on my first bay crossing and told me a bit about her school." Henry looked toward Kate. "And if I may repay that kindness by visiting in your classroom, Mrs. Anderson, it would be an honor. Perhaps there is something of merit I could share with your students."

"That's sweet of you to offer, Mr. Stuart. And I will remember that, though it was my pleasure to stand with you." She turned to Peter Stedman. "He had the best spot along the rail." Kate clasped the shawl to her neck, patting her hair with her other hand. "Well, I'll just leave you two to get acquainted. And I'm sure you must be exhausted, Mr. Stuart. All that long way on a train, you'll need a good night's rest."

Kate bade the men good evening. She walked away down the dock, her hard, thin soles clop-clopping across the planks, to join a man in a dark suit and hat, tipped at a jaunty angle, who was about her age and had just come on the boards and waved to her. The man placed his arm about Kate's shoulders, and they merged into the darkness at the far end of the dock, outside the pool of yellow light pouring down from the occasional bulbs depending from cross arms on high poles. Mosquitoes and tiny moths swirled in the orbs of light.

Henry observed the darkened mass of land around the dock. The big shoulders of the bluff Henry had seen from the water rose up at either end of the landing, more abruptly to the north. As Henry lifted his eyes to the night sky, the full moon was dimmed by the electric lights. Henry turned quickly when he heard a loud *gronk* in the darkness low over the water behind the *Bay Queen* and asked Peter what it was.

Peter told him that it was a blue heron, "a big lanky fellow who hangs about the landing. Goes by the name of Solomon. Been here as long as I've operated the landing." Peter looked as if he'd say more about the bird, but seemed to think better of it, and said instead, "So welcome to Alabama, Henry Stuart. I know you'll feel right at home in no time." Peter said he'd get Henry's luggage, and Henry said there was only one additional suitcase.

"Traveling light, huh?" asked Peter, motioning for Henry to follow him to the spot on the dock where the *Bay Queen* passengers' luggage had been stacked and was watched by a porter. The bayboat rested alongside the dock, thin tendrils of smoke drifting up toward the pale stars from her stacks, her engine idling, her lines tight to thick pilings.

The crew stood ready to cast off the heavy lines when the last of the passengers had disembarked and all cargo for this stop had been off-loaded. The men smoked and talked among themselves and yet kept a watchful eye toward the wheelhouse forward on the upper deck for a signal or word from the skipper when to shove off for the next landing at Fairhope pier, three miles south. Peter had written Henry telling him to look for him at Stedman's Landing, that on second thought, the scenic arrival at the Fairhope pier would not be very dramatic in the dark, and that he'd not given proper thought to Henry's long train ride.

"My books"—Henry patted his satchel, a fixture at his side now for four days—"and enough clothes to wear. What more does a man need?"

"Well, shoes, perhaps." Peter grinned. "As we drive you'll have to tell me about heaven and hell and your bare feet, Mr. Stuart. I guess a man needs stuff such as the pile of hardware and supplies I've stacked into your barn."

"Ah, yes," Henry said, "there is that. And I do thank you for getting those items." Henry could actually feel a slight psychological or emotional weight being loaded into a corner of his mind as he was reminded of a list of belongings awaiting his use and care and sorting. Black Elk was right. He was reminded, too, of St. Francis's prohibition against owning property, that an owner must take up a weapon and defend the thing he owns; and therein is sown the seed of war.

But Henry could not believe the principle of right living must necessarily be founded upon total surrender of worldly goods. He had read that Tolstoy was still unhappy at eighty-two. Even after giving all his estate to his wife and children and working long hours in the fields with peasants, Tolstoy felt he had failed to live rightly.

Henry knew that, nonetheless, many were deeply influenced by Tolstoy's effort, and not too many years ago Henry had read that a prominent German, Ludwig Wittgenstein, after reading Tolstoy's *The Gospel in Brief* had come home from the war and disposed of his entire inherited fortune. Henry was himself mightily impressed with Leo Tolstoy, but the Tolstoyan movement Henry could not embrace. As a young divinity student Henry had gleaned something he thought profound in Matthew's gospel: "A rich man from Arimathea, named Joseph, who had himself become a disciple of Jesus," was so influential that when he went before Pilate and asked for the body of Jesus, it was given to him. So here was a rich man who followed Jesus but never renounced his wealth.

Henry came to believe it was one's unwillingness to give up possessions that was the true spiritual burden. A fellow seminarian had told Henry he believed he had found corroboration in the story of

Abraham and Isaac: All that God wanted from Abraham was his *willingness* to sacrifice his son, not the deed at all. Henry had argued with his fellow divinity students at Mount Union that a rich man willing to part with his riches might as well remain rich.

"It was not any trouble at all pulling together your list of supplies," Peter said, clapping Henry on the shoulder. "Fact of the matter, I rather enjoyed spending someone else's money. Now we'll get going to my place. My wife has the guest cottage warm and tidy and awaiting you, and I expect she's keeping some supper on the stove for you, too. Leddie is a wonderful cook."

"Do you suppose," Henry asked, "that we might take the time to go tonight to the property I purchased? I know it's a bit impulsive, and I do not wish to offend Mrs. Stedman. But I've been thinking a good deal on the train about my new place."

"I'm happy to oblige, Henry. I'm still myself sometimes like a kid at Christmas. Drives Leddie nuts. Anyway, it's only five minutes out of the way. Your place lies very near my home, which itself is ten minutes' drive in my truck. Just north of the landing here down the county road apiece." Peter hoisted Henry's suitcase and frowned. "Now, I don't know how well you'll be able to see to trudge around on the place."

"Thoreau said that to walk outside and gaze at the full moon is nothing," said Henry, "compared to walking along a path alight with the full moon's glow. The one is a taste, the other a feast."

"Then let's have you feast away, my friend. Mrs. Stedman will not mind a bit if we spend, oh, even another hour before getting home."

So Peter, walking ahead of Henry to a black high-topped Ford truck, a Model T, stepped onto its running board and tossed Henry's suitcase into the back. He reached for the strap of the book satchel to take it as well, but Henry said no, he would keep that on his lap. "I think I've come to rely on this bag as a counterweight, if not my anchor," Henry quipped, "and I'd surely fall over sideways or go adrift in the night if I were relieved of it."

Henry climbed into the cab of the truck and laid the book satchel on his knees. The leather seat covering was stiff. Peter cranked up and shifted gears with a grind on their ride up the short hill back of the landing. They bounced along south a short distance on a well-traveled two-lane shell road, then east on a dirt road that Peter called East Volanta Road. Peter pushed a knob and switched off his headlights while still rolling along the rutted lane at a good clip, swerving once to avoid a pothole.

"No risk it, no biscuit, as they say!" Peter laughed as all went black beyond the windscreen. Henry noticed the truck quickly slowing and a lowering of the whine of the four-cylinder engine. Then in seconds their eyes adjusted to the moon's pale illumination of the landscape and the dirt roadway sprang into ghostly form and soft focus ahead of the truck. Peter accelerated and laughed again. "This is the way to enjoy a night's drive. By the light of the moon."

A joyride in a Ford Model T pickup was not what Henry had had in mind, but he could not prevent himself from smiling broadly into the dark of the truck cab. Henry glanced sideways at his good-natured host. Peter Stedman was a good man. Henry had no doubt of it. In moments, Peter switched the headlights back on, attempting to locate a suitable parking spot. When he had pulled the truck onto a wide shoulder area of red dirt, nuzzling into a bristle of brown broom sage, he killed the engine. He put both hands on the steering wheel and did not move. He paused until the silence of the night wrapped the automobile and light from the full moon silvered the trees rising up all around them.

Tall, straight pines were all Henry could see. He turned to the driver. "May I?"

"Be my guest," Peter said, gesturing with his left hand out the open window of his truck to the susurrous forest gathered around them in the night. "Your property is bounded by this Volanta Road. It's off to the left, starting back behind the truck fifty yards or so. You've got ten acres, so the line goes a ways farther down ahead of us, then cuts back up over that rise and runs for several hundred yards. Pretty much rectangular in layout, you'll remember from my maps."

"Yes," Henry said. "I have one of your maps in this shirt pocket right now." Henry told Peter he would leave his book satchel in the truck and take a brief walk up over the rise. "I just want to feel this piece of Alabama in my feet. I want to breathe in some of the air stirring up from the soil. You don't mind if I do this alone, do you, Mr. Stedman?"

"Not at all. But you've got to call me Peter, Henry. I'll just stand outside and lean up against the fender and smoke my pipe." He lifted his hand. "You hear that whippoorwill?"

"I did hear its call. Lonesome sound, isn't it?" Henry became quiet and said nothing more, nor moved. Both men waited for the night bird to sing again, but no sound came except for the softest of sighs where the wind played high in the pine boughs.

"I'll return shortly then, Peter." Henry twisted the metal handle and stepped out onto the running board. He leaned over and looked back into the cab of the truck. "Thank you for this," Henry said, patting the metal doorframe.

With both feet on the ground, and standing unencumbered by his book bag for the first time since leaving Idaho, Henry immediately felt something like a current of energy entering the soles of his bare feet and, for the second time in an hour, was confirmed in his mind that he was at home in this place. The whippoorwill called again, and a third time before Henry took a step. Such a lonesome trill, Henry thought. "It's good that I will be here to give you company," Henry said aloud, but quietly. He bent forward slightly to balance his steps up the little incline before him.

As he cleared the hill, Henry's breath began to burn, and he knew his lungs would rebel. He wished to get outside the range of Peter Stedman's hearing before he bowed to the hacking that would wring his windpipe and blur his vision. Henry reached out and took hold of a pine sapling not much bigger around than a shovel handle, and bowed his shoulders and head when the first cough arose in his chest. The air went out of Henry with each spasm. He was near doubled over before he began to sense the passing of the worst of it. He spat on the ground, though he hated to spit onto this ground that offered its living warmth to him. And in seeming answer to his thought, there was an immediate surge of heat tingling the bottoms of Henry's feet, as if it accepted his blood and saliva. Chief Seattle's eloquence arose like a voice in his mind: "And the very dust upon which you now stand responds more lovingly to their footsteps than yours, because it is rich with the blood of our ancestors, and our bare feet are conscious of the sympathetic touch." His coughing quickly abated to a soft moan, such as a large dog might make when curling down before a flickering hearth.

"Will you help me then?" Henry asked the land, his face down, the moon's pale light helping his eyes to see. He let go of the sapling and dropped to his knees. He put both hands on the ground covered by springy pine needles. With his fingertips he parted the brown straw, brushed it aside to expose the moist, loamy soil, and continued his work until a circle the sweep of his arms' reach had been bared. Henry put his palms down, widespread so that he might bring his chest down between them to the earth, and he lowered his head, turning his face to put his cheek on the cool dark ground. He breathed with purpose, very slowly and deeply, and the musky scent of the soil filled Henry's nose. He closed his eyes and breathed out, oh so slowly, then in. The earth's bouquet became a warm pink swirling fog behind his eyes, and the words of Chief Seattle came again to him: *We are part of the earth and it is part of us. We love this earth as a newborn loves his mother's heartbeat.*

"I sense that the land would give me its strength." Henry's voice was hardly more than a whisper, but full and certain. He was willing to accept in gratitude whatever would be offered. The peace he sought for meeting death, that it could be helped by the earth waiting to open and receive his body, was to Henry a beautiful proposition. Seattle knew that the wind that gave his grandfather his first breath was born of the fires and ice of the earth over which it blew, and said, too, that the same wind would receive his grandfather's last eye.

The stirring of a sleeping bird in the branches above him caused Henry to think of Peter and his wife Leddie, and, not wishing to keep them any longer from their night's rest, he arose and walked back in the direction of the parked truck. He was greeted from quite a distance by the sweet smoky aroma from Peter's pipe. As he drew nearer to his new friend he stepped more briskly among the moon shadows falling in bright relief between the trees.

· FIFTEEN ·

Henry was awake before dawn, and well rested, having slept deeply without dreaming or even turning over on the cushiony feather mattress dressed in clean, soft sheets that smelled to Henry like an autumn afternoon. The guest cottage behind of Peter's house was tiny, a single narrow room with a high ceiling. It was furnished with only a bed, a chifforobe, a washstand with a pitcher and basin, and a small desk and chair.

Without need of a lantern under the moon, Peter had carried Henry's satchel and suitcase from the truck directly to the cottage, stepping confidently down the winding path between dense leafy bushes as Henry followed. Inside on the simple pine desk a glass-chimneyed lamp lighted the room, a low flame guttering above a short wick that dangled into a base filled with amber coal oil.

Henry looked around his quarters. An oil painting of a horse, the pigment darkened on the canvas, hung on the wall in a simple frame. On the desktop beside the lamp, in a standing metal frame, a small watercolor of vibrant hues unusual to the medium depicted a broken tree in silhouette at the water's edge, backlit by a setting sun across the bay. Henry guessed this was the work of a local artist. Turning, he noted two windows in the front of the cottage, one on either side of the door. Both had their shades pulled all the way down.

"I think," Peter had said, putting down the suitcase and satchel near the bed, "it's going to be best to meet Mrs. Stedman in the morning. Do you mind, Henry?" Peter rubbed his forehead and eyebrows with his open hand, then pushed his fingers through his thick hair, disheveling it so that it pointed in all directions.

"No, of course not. I've kept us late." Henry apologized, but Peter would hear nothing of it, saying that he had an easy agreement with Leddie about coming home of an evening. "If she's still up and in a mood to chat, she leaves on the parlor light. If it's off, like tonight, I know she's retired to read or gone to bed." Peter said he would make a quick return trip from the kitchen with a biscuit and some milk, maybe a piece of salt meat.

"Thank you, Peter," Henry said. "The milk and biscuit will be enough. No need to bring meat." He patted his shirtfront at his waist. "It might lie heavy on my sleeping stomach and cause me to dream of trains and boats." Both men laughed, and later in the dark, as Henry was falling asleep, Henry was grateful for the good humor of his host. With a certain liberty of thought, his reception to Baldwin County could feel like a homecoming, were it not for the poignancy of his departure from Idaho. He knew he was laying his head to sleep in a place where his sons would never walk, where Will Webb would never raise an argument with him. Henry knew too, however, that they would not watch the tuberculosis steal his life away in visible degrees, not stand helplessly by as the sickness overtook him. For that he was grateful.

And even if it was true that death is the order of life, Henry's time to die had not yet come. In this moment he was alive. Only the past was dead, and he would live day by day without fear or regret.

It was still dark outside when Henry pulled on his trousers. He found matches in the desk drawer and lit the lamp. By its flickering light he poured water from the ceramic pitcher into the basin and washed up with the cloth and bar of soap on the washstand. He finished dressing and sat down at the desk with his copy of Tolstoy's *A Calendar of Wisdom* and read in Russian the entry for today's date, October 17. There were four small paragraphs of the author's reflections on religion. Henry reread the page slowly, then closed the book and continued to sit, wondering if man's place in the universe and the nature of his creation is truly "becoming more clear and easily understood with the passage of time"? Henry was about to retrieve his journal from within his satchel and write some lines about church and matters of the spirit and how they were not necessarily mutually inclusive when there came a knock on the door behind him.

"You awake in there, Henry?" Peter called out.

Before rising from the desk chair Henry answered that he was, then went to open the door. The pine planks under his feet were swept clean and were cool and creaked at some of his footfalls. Henry turned the knob and swung the door back on its hinges, standing back for Peter to enter. The moon had long since set and the morning was still and dark.

"I won't come in. I saw your lamp on and thought you must be up and stirring." Peter's breath frosted the air when he spoke. "Just come on over to the house when you're ready. We'll have some breakfast and then go and see about your place in the full light of day. And you might want to bring your coat; the temperature must've dropped twenty degrees last night." Peter puffed his breath out to make a vapor plume as if to corroborate his statement. "Feels good, though. I was raised Up East, Massachusetts and Connecticut, and I still miss a real change of seasons. You don't get that down here on the coast." Peter tapped the doorjamb with his knuckles as an exit from that topic. "Well, enough of that. Just come on over in a bit. Leddie's got breakfast going and coffee brewing."

"I'll follow you now, if I may," Henry said. "May I leave my book open on the desk?"

"Sure, sure. The cottage is yours," Peter said. Henry had not yet told Peter that he planned to move onto his land immediately and sleep in a corner of the barn until he could decide on what in the longer run would suit his requirements for shelter. He also wished to go there right away this morning and make some improvements to the barn to make it more livable. Still, he would not be discourteous to his hosts and appear anxious to part with them.

Henry followed Peter up the path to the house, where a light shone in two windows on the back corner. They mounted the steps onto a broad back porch running the entire length of the house, and

Henry remembered there was another like it in the front. While details of the home were not visible in the dark, Henry knew it was large and handsome. Peter held the door for Henry to enter the warm and spacious kitchen, smelling of bread and coffee brewing and breakfast cooking on a gas stove. Peter's wife Leddie turned from the stove and greeted her husband and visitor with a smile. She seemed shy and did not look long at Henry, though Henry saw her look at his bare feet. But she exhibited neither disdain nor much interest, and turned back to work at the stove.

Leddie seemed to Henry a quiet woman. She was broad and stout and had a pleasant round face. Her kitchen was painted a pale yellow with tall white cupboards and blue-and-white-checked curtains on the windows. The beaded-board ceilings looked at least fourteen feet high, and a simple chandelier hung from its center directly over a round claw-foot oak table set with heavy plain white china.

Through the meal Leddie asked no questions of Henry, seemingly content to follow along with Peter's casual interview. In one of Henry's letters to Peter he had said the move to Alabama was advised by his physician, but had given no further details. Peter did not ask about Henry's health this morning.

Leddie served the men scrambled eggs and fried ham and kept their coffee cups full. When Henry asked about the warm white mush, Leddie became a bit more animated and asked Henry if he did not know it was grits. She sat next to Peter, looking briefly at her husband with an expression conveying incredulity and a slight smile. She fixed her gaze on Henry, who said that he had never eaten grits, but that he found them quite good. Peter explained that grits are made from coarsely ground corn that becomes hot cereal when boiled in water.

"Add salt and pepper and butter and it's a real gourmet delight," said Peter with a wink. "When I was a Yankee, we had farina. But if you're going to live in Alabama, you are going to eat grits for breakfast."

"Would you like more, Mr. Stuart?" Leddie asked.

"Oh, no, I'm quite full." Henry thanked her for preparing his breakfast, then, taking a chance that he might be correct in his guess that Leddie was the artist who painted the watercolor in his cottage, asked her if she painted. She blushed and paused, stealing a glance at Peter, who answered, "Does she paint? You ought to just see! Later today when the sun's up, we'll come back here and she can show you her work. She's got a studio full of things."

"And the watercolor in the cottage?" Henry asked. "Did you paint that?"

"Yes I did, Mr. Stuart." Her eyes reflected the pleasure she felt from the notice the painting drew from this visitor.

"I quite like that," Henry said.

"Well, thank you for saying that," Leddie said, now smiling, eyes bright. "I too like that little piece. Others in my class were not so impressed and did not think it as good as some of my other things. That's why I have it in the cottage, I suppose. It isn't framed very well, either." Leddie dabbed the corner of her napkin to her mouth, then placed the white cloth on the table as she rose to get the coffee-pot.

"Go ahead and tell Mr. Stuart what that writer fellow said about that particular scene."

"It's just that Sherwood Anderson, whose *Winesburg, Ohio* I have read twice all the way through, and pieces of it frequently—well, he lived in Fairhope about five years ago for a few months and enrolled in the watercolor class I attended. I finished that piece in class and he saw it and said it was the precise *emotion* of a bayfront sunset."

"The fellow goes to one class and never comes back," Peter added. "Sounds like something I'd do." Peter raised his eyebrows. "Except he paid a full tuition and walked away from that. Now me, I'd have got some of my money back."

Henry remembered something in one of the Fairhope brochures he had received in Idaho about Sherwood Anderson, but assumed he had only visited, and did not know that the writer had lived in Fairhope.

"Five years ago?" Henry mused. "That would have been, I believe, about the time *Winesburg, Ohio* was first published."

"That's right," Leddie said. "I talked to him only a few times around the town. He walked the beach a good deal, and I talked with him on our beach one day for quite a long time."

"It's not *our* beach, dear," Peter corrected.

"I know, Peter. It's just a way of saying something."

"Waterfront land like ours and anybody else's," Peter said, directing his remarks toward Henry, "is titled to the mean high tide mark. Beyond that it's in the public domain."

"At any rate, on the beach in front of our home, I encountered Mr. Anderson one morning. I found him quite friendly and a good conversationalist."

"I am not sure that all writers are," Henry said.

"That's the day," Peter tossed in, "that he told Leddie he thought the so-called single-tax reformers of Fairhope were just a bunch of middle-class eccentrics."

"Oh, he wasn't all *that* abrasive, Peter. He just said that the world was in quite a mess and people here all snug in their cozy bayfront cottages did not seem to know or care much about it."

"And so what was Mr. Anderson doing about the state of the world?" Peter asked snidely. "Typing it into a proper order?"

"No, dear. Edith Barnhill did his typing for him, as a matter of fact." Leddie's face was becoming flushed, and Henry thought perhaps she was growing irritated with her husband, who seemed jealous of Leddie's regard for the author. He did not wish to interfere, but neither did Henry desire to witness an argument.

"Peter, I wonder if we could go soon to my property? I mean, in case you might have planned to give me a tour of the town this morning," Henry said, hoping to change the subject. "I have a fancy about sleeping there tonight and would like as much time as possible today to get a corner of the barn cozy."

Peter and Leddie both looked wide-eyed at Henry.

"You mean to sleep in that barn?" Peter asked.

"Does it have walls and a roof?" Henry asked.

"Well, yes, but—" Peter answered.

"Then I should think a barefoot traveler from Idaho can manage there quite well," Henry said with enthusiasm. "Shall we go and have a look?"

This information had the effect of charging Peter with a mission of discovery and adventure, it seemed to Henry, for he jumped up from the table right away and said, "This ought to be good! Let's go and see what a couple of old fellows can get done in a day." Peter strode over to his wife, placed his hands on her shoulders, and kissed her cheek. "Thank you for breakfast, honey. We'll come back here at noon for a little lunch and let Henry have a look at your paintings." Peter turned back to Henry, just pushing his chair back from the table. "Well, let's go then, man. We've got work to do!"

"Thank you for your kindness and hospitality, Mrs. Stedman," Henry said.

"It's our pleasure to have your company," Leddie answered, gathering the cups from the table. "Peter has spoken of little else since we knew you were moving here." She put the cups on the counter near the sink.

"You will dine with us at our table this evening," Peter said with certainty. He winked at Leddie. "And Leddie and I agree there's no way we're going to let you sleep tonight in that barn."

Henry smiled and said nothing more. He turned and nodded to Leddie when he reached the back door, where Peter waited. She said, "I do hope your first day in Baldwin County is pleasant and productive."

Peter added, "Mr. Stuart gave away his shoes on the train ride here as a means to the salvation of his soul. Or something like that." He held the door open for Henry and clapped him on the shoulder as he passed through the doorway. "I keep forgetting to get the full story."

When they turned onto East Volanta Road, drawing near to Henry's land, in front of the windscreen the sun was rising above the tree line into a cloudless sky, a chilly breeze curling into the cab of the truck. Henry and Peter had their windows down and their elbows propped on the door ledge. Peter slowed and turned off the narrow lane and drove his truck up and over the hill, between trees and around stumps. Henry saw out his window the place where he had lain on the ground last night, the brown pine straw still bunched up. He was anxious to get out of the automobile and put his feet on the ground, and found himself thinking *my ground,* despite knowing that the earth and sky cannot belong to man, that it is more appropriate to believe that man belongs to the earth. Again, however, for Henry the illusion of ownership wasn't a malignant proposition if it lacked a crazed attachment. Henry had been able to give away his land in Idaho, and he believed he could, if he must, let this land go, too.

Peter drove skillfully, twisting the big steering wheel, bouncing along at a good clip until he parked alongside the barn underneath a giant live oak that presided over piney woods all around. There were some few other hardwoods scattered here and there, mostly hollies and sweet gums, and one big dogwood with bare gray branches spreading low and wide.

"The structure certainly appears solid," Henry said, taking in the barn from where he stood beside the running board of Peter's truck. Still holding the door handle, he let his gaze shift from the barn to the gently undulating land. The topographic maps Peter had sent to Henry in Idaho had shown that the land on the eastern shore of Mobile Bay from the mouth of the delta to the north and for fifteen or twenty miles to the south was bunched up at the water's edge and unusually rolling, with knolls and hills and creeks coursing through ravines and gullies and stretches of sheer bluffs standing over sandy beaches. Henry's ten acres were on one of the highest hilltops on the map, hence the *mont* in Montrose, the village of homes and a post office just to the north.

"Oh, she's a good, solid barn all right," Peter said. "Foot-wide, five-quarter cypress planks, nailed up board on board to stout rough-sawed horizontal framing. You'll not find a sturdier barn. Good size, too. What? Thirty by forty?"

"That looks accurate," Henry said. "Some of the roofing has come loose in places, I see. Some sheets are quite rusty. Those should be replaced altogether, I believe. Do you agree, Peter?"

Peter said that he did agree, and would go tomorrow into Fairhope and bring back pieces of corrugated tin the right length and some lead-head nails. In the middle of Peter's continued talk about the supplies and tools they would need, Henry lost the thread of what Peter was saying as a kind of warmth began to radiate upward from the ground into his feet. The sensation was not nearly as intense as last night, but it was strong enough to distract Henry. He found himself wondering whether this was some symptom of the consumption, but could not reconcile that with the way in which the tingling and warmth energized him.

"Hey, you better listen up there, Henry." Peter laughed. "I'm regaling you with masterful building tips, and you're daydreaming." Henry apologized and asked Peter what plan of action they should follow. Peter told Henry that if he actually intended to take up residence in the place, the southeast corner of the barn would lend itself best to a bit of renovation.

"There'd only be two interior walls to cover," Peter said with authority. "The outer walls on this corner are plumb and square and solid. The roof's pretty good." Peter led the way to the barn and inside through a big double door midway down the west wall. One of the hinges was broken and that door leaned against the building. Peter pointed to the corner of the barn he thought they should work on.

"The floor's mostly solid," Peter said. "This corner used to be the corncrib." Morning sunlight streaked through loosened or bent-back pieces of tin on the roof and into the dim spaces in the barn. Dust motes swirled in the chilly draft. "We can frame in a couple of windows and a door, lay a ceiling over those exposed joists, and you'll be snug as a bug in a rug. In about a week. If we work hard."

"Then, mister foreman, let's get to it!" Henry said, rubbing his hands together, curling them into fists, wondering if the arthritis in his knuckles would flare up with the work of hammering. "Tell me what to do first."

Peter said first they would get the tools they needed, inventory their materials, draw a rough plan—he calculated the finished room would be fifteen feet square—and get to work within the hour. Peter said he was looking forward to some manual labor, and it was interesting to Henry how Peter's prattle abated when they got busy with their project of drying-in this corner room. When he was working, Peter, like Henry, became single-minded and focused on the task at hand. Henry knew working with this man would be good, and he was glad for the necessity and opportunity to get out of his head and into his hands for a spell.

· SIXTEEN ·

In a short time, before the sun was three hours high in the sky, the two men had fallen into a natural and easy working rhythm, a complementary push-pull, accomplishing their task like a well-sharpened Disston handsaw cutting through a two-by-six heartpine plank. Each anticipated the other's next move—what tool to hand, what measurement to take, when to steady a board, where to lay a hand in support—and what would be needed, and each stood ready to provide it. Henry kept working right through lunch while Peter dashed home to bring back some cornbread, some black-eyed peas in a Mason jar, an onion, two small baked sweet potatoes, and another quart jar of sweet tea. The afternoon was going by quickly. Henry knew that Leddie would be disappointed that he did not come to see her work, but he would visit her studio tomorrow, in the morning before the work of the day began.

Henry had known last night upon first meeting this man who labored by his side today that theirs would be an easy fit. Then meeting Leddie had deepened his conviction that this place was right and his decision to come here had been a good one. Soon he would write to Will, saying how place is important. And if Will was feeling frisky, he would take Henry to task, reminding him how Henry liked to quote Emerson's position on the "intoxication of travel." Emerson said that no matter where you go, you find no one other than yourself and all of your ghosts there waiting to greet you. And given a lazy afternoon with Will, Henry would agree, but add that a lion and a bee and a rattlesnake will each claim a place to call their own. Then Will might allow that yes, Jesus seemed to stake a spiritual claim to Jerusalem. The two men might agree, as they parted company before evening, that there was a validity in the premise of the importance of place. Some are great and good places that feed the soul, and others are benumbing and tiring.

Henry stopped swinging the hammer once the head of the nail he was driving was flush with the soft silver grain of the cypress plank. Some rough carpenters might deliver another whack to set the nail into the wood, but that left a dimple encircling the nailhead and marked the board with evidence of amateurish cobbling.

He would rest for a spell, and when the shank of his hammer handle was snug in the string of his nail apron, Henry stood up straight and turned from the wall and looked away toward Mobile Bay, a mile and more west from this hill that was his new home. He could not see the bay itself, but perceived a shroud of soft light reflected upward from it into the moist blue air beneath the afternoon sun. Henry wiped his brow with the sleeve of his shirt, and it left a slight stinging. The coastal Alabama sun, even in November, quickly took its reddening pinch on the skin, especially on fair-skinned men just moved in from Idaho.

Henry's eye was caught by a movement, and he looked and saw a large brown oak leaf twirling downward toward the ground. He watched it land, catching upon its points and withered stem. Arching there like a creature in a defensive posture, it trembled in a breeze that teased across the hill. Then the leaf got caught up and tumbled away by a puff of wind, and the little drama caused Henry to visualize a hardshell crab knocked over and rolled to the surf's edge by a bullying tern. Still in all, it seemed a kind of resurrection for the oak leaf. In Henry's daydream, it had become a crusty, skittering brother of the sea. Henry wondered whether he, after quitting this world, would find himself a player in someone's musing, and would his spirit perchance answer in an afterworld dance of joy and gratitude?

"Are you trying to go slack on me there, Henry?" Peter rounded the corner of the barn, brushing sawdust from the front of his shirt. "I've got a stack of one-bys cut and ready to nail up on that east wall. We give it a good push and we'll have you a dried-in room by sunset." Peter gazed up at the sun. "But let's have a drink of cold water before we get back to it."

Peter went to the well and let down the gallon tin bucket on the cotton rope that unwound off a slick eight-inch-thick poplar log set crosswise over the well shaft. The section of log turned on a metal axle that ran through its center. The ends of the axle were inserted into upright timbers at either side of the stone surround. The timbers supported a small gabled roof. One end of the log's metal axle was bent into an L-shape and formed a winding handle. Peter applied pressure with the flat of his palm to slow the turning log as the bucket neared the water at the bottom of the well.

"Come get yourself a drink, old man," Peter called out.

Henry walked over, and while Peter busied himself winding up the filled water bucket, Henry took the drinking bucket from its heavy spike protruding from one of the uprights, removed the dipper from which all and anyone drank, swirled the water and dashed it onto the ground a few feet from the well. He walked back over to the well and held the bucket while Peter filled it with fresh, sweet, cold water drawn up from a reservoir forty feet down in the earth. Henry handed the dipper to Peter so that he could drink first.

"Thank you," Peter said. He filled the dipper and lifted it to his lips and drank deeply. "Ahhhh," he said in relish. "God, that's good water!"

"Mind if a girl has a sip?" Both men quickly turned their heads to see Kate Anderson walking up, a young girl of perhaps three on her hip, and the man from the dock last night walking beside the little girl. Kate had on a simple cotton dress, a solid warm brown the color of autumn leaves, and underneath a white blouse. She looked to Henry like a pioneer wife, self-reliant in her bearing, though not hard in aspect by any means. Henry thought her lovely with her cheeks reddened by the walk and the chilly breeze. Her hair was loose and hung at her shoulders.

Henry noticed too that Kate's shoes were more practical than the fashionable ones she'd worn on the bay crossing. These were of soft black leather with a wider squarish toe and almost flat heels. The little girl had on a plaid dress of the same earthy tone. Both dresses seemed to have been chosen for a complementary effect. The man, his face open and friendly, had on the same dark suit and hat as last night. He lifted a finger to his hat brim and nodded.

"I had no students stay after school," Kate said, "so when I went to my brother's dry goods store to pick up my daughter, I asked him to bring me and Anna Pearl out here to find your place. I am completely intrigued to learn how you'll live here with no house on your land."

"It looks as though these two men are busily constructing a home of some sort," the brother said. "I hope you don't mind, sir, that I've brought my sister here. She is so insistent sometimes."

"Have your drink, Mrs. Anderson, and then you might as well get the tour of the hard work Henry and I have accomplished just since a little after daybreak today," Peter said, handing the dipper to Kate. Peter had explained to Henry this morning when they had drawn their first bucket of drinking water that it was customary in these parts to equip a well with a drinking bucket and a single dipper for everyone's use. "Kate, let's not keep these men from their work," the brother said, then added, "Begging my sister's pardon, how are you this afternoon, Mr. Stedman?" He shook hands with Peter, who introduced Henry.

"I was in your store last week, Wesley," Peter said. "I bought some work gloves, but you were busy in the back. Seems I'm always on the run when I stop into your store."

"You got what you needed, I trust, Mr. Stedman," Wesley said.

"As always, Wesley," Peter said.

"Do you have tin drinking cups, Mr. Ingle?" Henry asked.

"Matter of fact, I do," he answered.

"Then I'll be a customer soon," Henry said, indicating that he and Peter had decided on a trip into Fairhope for supplies in two days.

"And I'll give you a nickel tour of the town, if I can keep the two cents change." Peter laughed. "But you're the lord of this manor, Henry, if you want to show your guests around."

"There isn't much to see, Mrs. Anderson, Mr. Ingle. But I'm happy to show you what Mr. Stedman and I have done today and tell you what more we plan to do."

"Mama, the man forgot to wear his shoes," Anna Pearl announced. Everyone looked at Henry's bare feet. Kate looked back at Henry. "Anna Pearl!" Kate's brother scolded.

The uncle's admonition was discomfiting to Henry, and he thought to lighten the moment. He rocked back on his heels and gave an exaggerated wiggle of his toes, smiling.

"Could you not find them?" the little girl asked. Henry laughed aloud, and the others followed suit. Anna Pearl was not amused and put her balled fists onto her hips. "Well?"

Then Kate answered for Henry. "He gave them away to a poor person who badly needed shoes. Isn't that right, Mr. Stuart?"

"I must not tell a lie, Anna Pearl," Henry said, his face serious now. "I was escaping an angry orangutan whose banana I borrowed and I ran so fast I ran right out of my shoes."

All waited to see how this would strike the little girl, and with only a slight hesitation, Anna Pearl said, "But you got his banana, and he gets to keep your shoes."

Henry and Peter and Kate and Wesley might otherwise have laughed, but all thought better of it and ventured only guarded smiles. "And that is only fair," Henry said, his eyebrows raised high.

"Yes. But you should give back his banana." Then she asked her mother, "Can we go, Mama?" Kate and Wesley agreed they should get along, and promised to come back on a day when there was not so much work to be done.

"You are welcome to visit any time you like, Mr. Ingle, Mrs. Anderson," Henry said. The little girl was tugging on her mother's hand. Henry thought to extend his invitation to Mr. Anderson as well, but quickly decided that would be too presumptuous and familiar. Henry could not stop himself from wondering why Kate had made no mention of him. "And thank you for coming, too, Anna Pearl."

"Okay," the little girl said, smiling at Henry and stealing another look at his bare feet.

"If I can be helpful, Mr. Stuart, please just tell me what I can do," Kate's brother said.

"Thank you, Mr. Ingle," Henry said.

Then Kate added that she too could be counted upon for help, such as she could offer. "And again, Henry, welcome to Fairhope," she said, her face warm and her eyes lively. Kate smiled when she said, "And if we should meet a big orange monkey with your shoes, we'll certainly try to recover them for you." Anna Pearl nodded her serious assent.

Wesley lifted Anna Pearl into his arms and Kate placed her open hand in the small of her daughter's back as they walked. When they had gone a few steps, Kate, without stopping, turned and looked over her shoulder at Henry. He raised his hand and she smiled. Peter stood quietly at Henry's shoulder until the guests were disappearing down the hill and into the trees, then he said, "What tall tales you tell, Henry. Angry orangutans, indeed! Now, if only you had that long-armed monkey to swing your hammer for you, we'd soon have lodging for you here on Mount Henry."

Two days later, on Wednesday morning, Henry and Peter drove into Fairhope, along the main street, Section Street, a hard-packed oiled dirt lane dividing the town into east and west sides of about equal proportions, the western part extending a half mile or so to the piney woods bluff overlooking the beach and waters of Mobile Bay. East of Section Street the town finally dwindled into broad expanses of flat farmland. Fairhope Avenue began at the center of town and took off eastward into the potato and cotton fields and pastures and pecan groves, rolling westward downhill past giant gnarled magnolias and live oaks draped with Spanish moss, under the shade of twisted junipers and shaggy cedars to the bay shore. At its foot the city's heavy plank and piling pier stretched nearly a quarter mile out over the water. The city of Mobile sprouted low and gray on the horizon in the distance off to the northwest.

Henry found the town pretty much as he expected, appearing a great deal like other towns across the country, wood frame architecture mostly, homes more impressive nearer the bluff with its bay view. Fairly large two-story masonry buildings dominated the corners of Section Street and Fairhope Avenue. Peter was proud of the Masonic Hall on South Section, built of blocks about fifteen years earlier. The town's personality seemed pleasant, open, and inviting, also as Henry had anticipated. Henry was given to consider, however, the apathy and disdain that grow from familiarity, and how much more acutely aware he was of his surroundings here along Mobile Bay than he had been in Idaho, noticing closely this land and its particular coastal complexity, its trees and grasses and lush vegetation. Pilgrimages open one's eyes, he thought.

For one thing, Henry was totally surprised at the resort-like feel of the Fairhope bayfront. Out there at the end of the wharf, Henry saw from their vantage point atop the bluff two huge triple-decker steamboats, one of them the *Bay Queen,* the other a larger vessel. Peter told him, as they stepped from the truck, the big one was the *Fairhope,* owned by the Single Tax Colony. There must have been twenty automobiles parked in front of the cluster of buildings nestled in the shadow of the bluff. Half a dozen people walked out or back on the boards of the pier, wide enough to drive a car upon.

"Is that a railroad track I see running out to the end of the city pier?" Henry asked, propping his bare foot on the running board of the truck. Peter said that it was indeed, and was known as the People's Railway. "Mules tow small wagons for fetching and delivering things from and to the boats," Peter added. When Henry allowed that there seemed to be quite a lot of fetching and delivering going on this morning, Peter said, "It's busy all the time." Then after a moment's pause, his hands in his pockets, a wistful gaze in his eye,

"It has the look of a harbor town Up East, don't you think?" Henry said that it did, and then they just stood for several minutes in silence and watched the busy scene before them. From where they stood, gulls and brown pelicans looked like insects buzzing over the water.

Later Peter went up this street and down that avenue—Church and Mobile, Magnolia and Fels—encountering only a few other vehicles rolling about. Peter made sure he did not leave anything off Henry's tour. When Peter announced, "Well, that's Fairhope," Henry thanked him and asked for a telegraph office, from where he sent a message to Thomas to ship his loom to Alabama at his earliest convenience. Then they picked up some things at McKean's Hardware and Building Supply. Henry had forgotten to have Peter purchase for him a long galvanized tub for an occasional full bath, and when he inquired of the storekeeper the availability of such, Peter interrupted and said, "I'd use one of the deep holes in Rock Creek. Those few times this winter when a hot sponging from the washbasin doesn't satisfy you, a dip in that cold water down at the creek will wake you up." Henry agreed that he would do just that, and begged the clerk's pardon, saying he would not need the tub after all.

They walked out together and went back to Henry's barn, where they worked the rest of the day until dusk. Five days later, on Monday afternoon, they finished the room in the corner of the barn. They had spent most of the morning on the final day of their project installing the flue for Henry's Chicago Foundry No. 14 cast-iron potbelly stove, which they had set in the corner of the room nearest the door. They turned the stove in such a manner that the stovepipe from the back of it went out and up the gable-end wall; then they positioned it on the floor in the center of a square sheet of asbestos-backed tin, forty by forty inches. There was not much chance a spark from the firebox could jump beyond it and catch the wooden floor afire.

Just before quitting time, Henry suggested they burn a fire in the potbelly stove to make sure it drew well. It performed perfectly, probably because they had extended the last section of stovepipe to a height two feet above the roofline. The small stove, a five-stick fire blazing within it, did not smoke back into the room at all.

· SEVENTEEN ·

It was morning, and the sun was backlighting a silvered sky, darkening to heavy gray where it encircled the horizon above a ragged tree line. Henry was washing his breakfast bowl in a white porcelain-coated metal bucket when he heard an automobile approaching. A gusting wind blew a dust plume down the road ahead of the car, and Henry stood up from his task, wondering who it might be.

Henry lifted the bowl from the water in the bucket and slung droplets from it onto the ground. He reached a small white cotton towel down from where it hung on a holly branch near the well, dried the bowl, and returned the towel. He took the clean spoon from his pants pocket and placed it inside the bowl and was taking steps toward the barn to put the dish away when the nose of Peter's truck drew up over the little rise, rolling slowly, the engine almost at an idle.

Then the Ford coughed to a stop and Peter Stedman got out, slowly straightening his lanky frame, brushing imaginary dust from his shirtfront. He looked back inside the car as if to make sure he'd not forgotten something. Satisfied, it seemed, he approached Henry, who held the spoon in the bowl with his thumb, wiped his other hand on his pants and extended it in greeting when Peter stepped up.

"Good morning to you, Peter," Henry said, nodding.

"How're you this morning, Henry?" Peter asked, shaking Henry's hand. Henry said that he was fine, thank you, and asked his visitor if he would like a cup of hot tea or some water.

"No, I've had my coffee already this morning," he said, looking around. "I see you got all your supplies put away," Peter continued, referring to the miscellaneous hardware items from the list Peter had gathered and delivered onto the property two weeks earlier, things the two men had not used in completing the construction of a dry and tight corner room in the barn, a room Henry now called home. They had left the buckets of paint, the iron wheelbarrow wheel, a big coil of manila rope, a hoe and shovel and rake, and other things stacked outside the barn in a neat pile. Then they had kept the whole cache of supplies dry underneath a huge dark green canvas tarpaulin secured at the corners with pieces of wood.

"I found a place for everything in the barn," Henry said.

"And what about your place in the barn, Henry? You feeling at home yet? Looks kind of homey around here."

At this Henry brightened. He put the bowl down on a log and reached out to put his hand on the shoulder of his new friend. "Come here, please, Peter. I want to show you something," Henry said, already taking a step. The two men walked past the Ford, its cast-iron engine block still clicking rhythmically as it cooled, a light rubbery odor of steam following them for several steps.

"Just down here," Henry said. He pointed to a copse of thick-middled pines just to the right of where Peter had tracked up the hill, his comings and goings of the last three weeks beginning to show as twin tire paths pressed into the soil and sparse grass.

"Did you notice this as you drove up?" Henry asked.

"What?"

"My sign."

"Where?" Peter looked left and right.

"Just there," Henry answered, pointing to where a three-foot-long white-painted board, ten inches wide, was nailed to a slender pine. The breeze lifted abruptly, with surprising strength, and the pines hissed above them as their needles and branches were mightily disturbed. The two men were seeing the sign's back from an oblique angle, and no letters were visible.

"No, can't say as I saw that, Henry. I expect I was trying to see out past the hood of my truck coming up your incline there. What's it say?"

"Come. Let me show you." Henry's determined and quick pace reflected his enthusiasm for what he was about to reveal to Peter. When they had rounded the tree and were at an angle to see clearly, Henry smiled and lifted his left hand, palm up, in the direction of the sign.

Peter's dark eyebrows pulled together in a studious frown. "Tolstoy Park?"

"I have followed the custom of your bayfront neighbors who hang signs by the road naming their places, and have named my Alabama estate," Henry said, folding his arms, a smile on his lips, eyes on the sign. Then he looked at Peter.

"Well?" Henry lifted his eyebrows.

"Well," said Peter, "it says Tolstoy Park. That I can see. And a nice job of lettering you've done, Henry. But I guess I'm wondering why it says Tolstoy Park."

"He's a Russian author."

Peter pinched his brows more tightly together and snapped his head around to face Henry. "I damn well know that. People down here in Alabama do read, you know. I've read some of the man. I even know what he looked like, and if you let your whiskers keep growing, well—"

"Of course, Peter. I'm sorry. You asked why, not who. And the why of my sign is that I find in the ideas of this man Tolstoy a source of great light for our world."

Peter let this go without comment and Henry didn't know what to make of the silence. Peter Stedman seemed to Henry a contemplative man, from many things said while bending and working together on Henry's room in the barn. As they sawed and nailed, ideas chased about by them both made Henry believe that Peter's personal philosophy followed a line of thinking laid down with broad margins. But Henry would give this time, and was certain his new friend would bring up Tolstoy again and that avenues of discussion would be available to them then. Sometimes the considerate pause before a word, Henry thought, was as important as the word itself.

Peter gestured toward the sign. "I'm not like some I read about who're crazy to make this Russian writer over into a new messiah."

"You misunderstand me, Peter, if you think I regard him in that way. He himself told Maksim Gorky that heroes are a lie and an invention, that there are only people, people and nothing else. I might revise that and say there are ideas, only ideas. No people. His ideas intrigue me. His name is absolutely incidental to the veracity of his thinking, his practical recommendations for living."

Henry paused to pick up a fat pinecone at his feet, squatted there while examining its woody needle-tipped scales. Peter put his hands into his pockets and stepped closer to Henry's sign, as though scrutinizing the lettering job. When Henry stood up, the cone still in the curl of his hand, he added, "Likewise, you would never find me in search of the historical Jesus. Who cares to fix a dusty man upon a map or within a day of the week, or smelling of sweat on his way to the toilet, when what has issued from his mouth is that we must love one another as our very selves."

Henry had become agitated, and Peter was in something of a retreat from this as-yet-unseen side of Henry when, as if suddenly remembering why he'd come to see Henry in the first place, he said, "Oh, I've come to tell you there's a storm coming our way. Not like one you might've seen in your travels back of the salt line, I fear." Peter waited for Henry's follow-up.

"I'm sorry. You said 'back of the salt line'?" Henry glanced at the sky, then back at Peter, who was clearly pleased by the opportunity to explain, and also relieved to be delivered from further scolding. Henry felt repentant for his anger with Peter, and noted that some of his aggravation might've come from the touch of embarrassment he'd felt that his sign perhaps had been perceived as a little silly. Henry had been so excited to think of the name, he had not stopped to consider how others might view it. But he would not take down the sign or change the name.

Peter charged ahead, telling Henry that once the sea had covered a great deal more of the land than now. "Some say all of the earth was at one time underwater, 'without form,' as you Bible-men have it."

"I'm not a Bible-man," Henry said, and laughed.

"You were in the seminary, you said. Right?"

"Yes, but—"

"Well, there you have it," Peter said. Henry felt somewhat like he thought Leddie must have felt as she had talked about her author acquaintance at the breakfast table. "Anyway, and then the water receded, but not to where it is now. It took a big long pause"—Peter lifted his arms theatrically and spread them wide—"like it rested while making up its mind how far to draw back."

And Peter explained that men of knowledge knew where the surf's edge had been during that great pause, that shark's teeth and the fossils of fish and shelled creatures were easily found well inland by men shoveling foundations for buildings and while plowing their fields or digging wells.

"The ocean reached up to a hundred, hundred and twenty-five miles north of here," Peter said, admitting at the same time that he did not know where the line lay on the East and West Coasts, but that wherever it was to be found, it was the *salt line*.

"Ohio and Idaho and such places as you've lived are back of the salt line. Hereabouts we say north of the salt line and south of the salt line." Peter then offered that opinions and sentiments and behavior were more 'monkey-like' south of the salt line, a little less predictable, and unlike, say, what may be expected of slow-eyed cows.

"So too can our weather along the coast get mighty monkey-like, and what's coming this way could be about like a bull gorilla," Peter said, his eyes twinkling. He told Henry that the shrimpers and fishermen at the Fly Creek docks were forecasting bad weather. "Those men who work out there on the water know the weather better than anybody, and they say it might get rough with this storm."

Henry listened attentively, looking at the wind tossing the treetops, listening to its occasional whistle. When Peter asked if Henry wanted to go with him, to stay at his home or in the cottage until it was over, Henry thanked him but declined his invitation.

"Whatever's coming, Henry, could arrive onshore by nightfall," Peter said. "Maybe it's something tropical building out in the Gulf, though not likely a full-bore hurricane this late in the season. That calendar runs from mid-June to mid-November." Peter rubbed his head in thought. "This is already November sixth, but you've got to be careful, Henry Stuart. I'd speculate you've not seen anything like what might visit us."

Peter emphasized that a hurricane was not impossible, mind you, but the autumnal cooling of the Gulf of Mexico waters would pull the teeth of a big storm, rob it of its fierceness and strength. But when Peter had offered a last few words of caution and driven away in his stake-bodied Model T truck, and as the afternoon clocked away and the weather continued to build, Henry began to believe that this wind had fangs enough for a good bite. As Peter had suggested, it was unlike the funneled winds of the tornadoes Henry had seen three times in his life. This wind grew broad and heavy and wet and by late afternoon lay upon the land like a smothering thing.

As Henry looked around his barn, double-checking for items that might become airborne and catapulted to God knows where, the sky took on an odd metallic cast, like hammered lead. And beneath that strange light scattered clouds flew low and fast, becoming elongated, shredded, slate gray and blue-bottomed. The wind's whoosh at times prickled the hairs on Henry's neck when it lifted up some polyphonic moan that sounded like a chorus of ghosts from fairytale legend. Henry carried two long boards toward the toolroom in the barn and long strands of cottony hair on Henry's head were whipped about as if he rode in an open motorcar. There was as yet no rainfall and the air temperature dropped rapidly in the gusts. A loose flap of tin on his barn roof banged the two-by-four purlins, raising an insistent ruckus.

Storm birds, like torn and dirty scraps of paper, spun defiantly higher and higher. And on their insistent, plaintive voices—all but lost in the din—there also came to Henry the voice of Maksim Gorky's "Song of the Storm Petrel" and lines of particular beauty:

And the petrel in the cloud-heights,
The one rival of the lightning,
Scatters down his splendid crying,
Drawing from the very danger
Urge and will to cry forever.

And there was in Henry something of growing kinship to the urge and will to cry forever, drawn from the very danger of the fire in his lungs. Would that I, he thought, could bend back this consumptive illness and break its will to destroy me. The pulse of blood through Henry's veins gained intensity, synchronizing with the swirling wind and rising with adrenaline, drawn from the very danger of this gathering storm to fill his ears with an internal roar, his own claim to life forever.

And then the rains came so hard that the drops were like pellets, flying horizontally and stinging his flesh and causing him to squint against the blinding spray. The wind tore loose a board from his barn, one at the corner on the front existing wall. He and Peter had found several boards with nails almost pulled out and he thought they had renailed them all. They had missed at least one, and when it pulled free and went flying and shattered against the broad trunk of a live oak not forty steps to his right, splintered daggers were set sailing.

Henry did not even flinch.

Trees were bending in supplication to the sheer force of the wind and rain, snapping upward comically in the brief lulls like prairie dogs checking to see if the coast was clear after the thunderous passing of a bison herd.

Henry had to lean more aggressively into the blow to maintain his balance. And even though he was somehow curiously enlivened by this uncertainty, his senses keen and sharp, he knew that he should move immediately to shelter. He realized the danger. Henry knew it would be folly to challenge such a formidable opponent.

But he believed that to hole up in the barn was the worst thing he could do. And as if to corroborate his assessment another gust ripped loose a piece of tin and sent it flapping madly out of sight into the swirling gray mist.

Henry knew he must act quickly. On a small knoll to his left was an empty block-walled cistern once used for irrigation and watering livestock, six feet around and perhaps three feet tall, several cracks at its base on one side preventing the accumulation of water inside.

There was a big sweet bay tree right beside the cistern and it was being thrashed about and could be flung down, but Henry believed the round concrete wall would hold it off him if he sat on the bottom and put his back toward the windward side. Henry had examined the old catch basin on his first day in Tolstoy Park, figuring to repair it and put it back into service providing him a constant supply of water for irrigation. He knew that on the ground inside the structure were three wide pieces of scrap plank that could be put to use as a makeshift covering from the rain.

Henry crouched low and struggled uphill toward the round concrete structure. Somehow it all seemed funny to Henry, an old man alone in the woods trotting along in a tear of wind, and he found himself chuckling as he grabbed the edge of the cistern. It was beneath waist height, and with a small effort he was able to swing himself around and up and over the curving wall. Henry fell with a guttural *umph* and hit the earthen floor on his hip and elbow, but the soggy earth cushioned the blow and prevented a broken bone. Henry had always been nimble and strong, with good bones, and the consumption had not so far diminished his strength and agility. He wagged his head and smiled, thinking, *Foolish old man.*

He rolled onto his side, pushed himself up to a sitting position, and scissored backwards to the edge of the cistern. He drew up his knees, tucking them tightly by wrapping his arms around them. He flexed his bare toes on the cold wet grass. This will do, he thought, hunkered down in the shallow well, though he would really rather be up and looking about to properly regard this awesome atmospheric display, his first hurricane.

Henry was about to grab the planks to prop over his head in a kind of lean-to when, with a loud and strong complaint, the wind pushed hard and there came a loud crack directly above him. A huge branch as thick as a man's middle came crashing down and landed across the cistern, spiking the ground inside with smaller limbs, one of them grazing Henry's shoulder, ripping his shirt, and scraping the flesh of his upper arm. Henry lifted his arm and moved the torn fabric and saw that he was not cut badly, more of an abrasion, but with blood already trickling and a burning pain radiating into his shoulder and chest and forearm. He folded the cloth back over to cover the cut and gave it a light rub, then pressed down to stanch the blood.

Now, with the fallen branch creating something of a roof, his hiding place seemed more a shelter. The space was darker and the wind muffled slightly. He bent forward and pulled a board up and tilted it against the concrete wall, then another in the same manner, and the third until he had a little diagonal roof pushing up against the stray branches.

Henry crawled underneath, finding enough room at the wall's edge to sit up. Henry would not call his cistern cozy, but it was not in the open weather and was his best choice for riding out this storm. He put his head back against the concave concrete wall. When he rolled his head to the side, a weariness tugging at him, he saw a silvery fibrous mass on the ground beneath a branch that at first he thought was an animal, an opossum or raccoon. He blinked to clear his vision and squinted.

It was not a living furry ball, but a bird's nest, a circle of silver-gray twigs and straw as big around as a broad hat brim and two inches thick. It was round and solid. He leaned in the direction of the nest, but began to feel the familiar rustling and burning tingle in his chest that presaged a coughing spell. He closed his eyes. He did not hold his breath, but slowed it and became single-mindedly focused on the inflow of air into his nostrils, its passage down into his lungs. He could feel the air expanding his chest, slowly, slowly. He willed the warmed air deeper into his chest, down to his diaphragm, and felt his belly moving outward. He was glad right now not to be constricted about the waist with a leather belt, and he was pleased to have given himself permission to refrain from them after Molly died. Nowadays he only wore loose suspenders and large-waisted breeches.

Instead of blowing his breath out, he likewise followed it upward in a controlled exhalation. This process of mindful breathing through several cycles subdued the spasm he had felt coming. He kept his eyes shut and listened to the wind, less cacophonous now, more musical, like an organ's trembling bass chord within an empty church.

And when some time in the night the sonorous roll was finally passing away to the east, the great wind in retreat, its noise abating, Henry had become settled and nearly overcome with fatigue. Sleep caressed his brow and he yielded without even so much as rising for a peek. It was far too black to see, at any rate, and he would have all of tomorrow to assess the damages to his barn and property.

Henry curled into a ball and found something of the warmth a dog enjoys in such a position. Without effort he fell into a slumber colored by dream images lacking a story line. As he spiraled deeper into sleep, one by one the array of faces and places and situations in his mind's eye faded and were replaced by a pastoral dreamscape of simple sense and hue.

In Henry's dream, a seabird swoops low across the wave tops and glides to a stop on a white sand beach scattered about here and there with long pieces of straw. The bird, a hook-beaked osprey with fierce yellow eyes, selects a golden stem and flies with it to a juniper sapling growing up from the sand. The diligent bird builds its nest, straw by straw, trip after trip, circle after circle woven together. When the nest is complete, the osprey serenely perches on its rim, and with its beak plucks a feather from underneath its wing.

The feather is long and elegant and bathed in pearlescent light, reflecting colors like an oil sheen on water. The seabird vanishes and the feather falls onto the sand beneath the juniper. A hand appears to retrieve the feather and Henry knows it is the hand of Black Elk. The medicine man stands and weaves the feather into the bird's nest. Then he bends and scoops sand into his cupped hands, spitting into the sand and stirring it and shaping it with his finger to fashion a loose block that transforms into a stone loaf that Black Elk offers to the dreamer. And Black Elk folds his arms across his chest and looks with eyes as black and shining as a crow's wing into Henry's soul and a single voice arises in a melodious chant as darkness descends upon Henry's sleeping mind.

· EIGHTEEN ·

Henry awakened in the quiet dark, his back still curved against the wall of the cistern and the boards still leaned in place, concealing the sky above the fallen tree. He lay there for several minutes, not moving, recalling with complete clarity the dream he had had, and understanding its symbolism, Henry became full of certainty and purpose. He would build for himself a cottage, round like a bird's nest, and of concrete like the cistern that had given him shelter from the previous night's storm, round like the hogans he had seen in the desert Southwest.

Still lying in the damp grass, but not chilled or hurting, Henry remembered many of the words Black Elk had spoken at the Nez Percé lodge so many years ago: "The Power of the World always works in a circle, and everything tries to be round. The sky is round, and I have heard that the earth is round like a ball. And so are all the stars. The wind in its greatest power whirls. Birds make their nests in a circle, for theirs is the same religion as ours."

Henry slowly pushed himself up to sitting. He rubbed his shoulders, his neck, his head. He rubbed his knees, his feet. To an observer it might appear that Henry was examining himself for injury. Instead, he was calling life back into those places, summoning strength and intelligence, conjuring his will to do this thing. What would Peter think of him beginning a new home right on the tail of constructing the corner room? What would Peter think of a home that was more a hut than a house? More like the dwelling place of a Navajo warrior than an expatriate English rug weaver? So certain was Henry, however, that he had been directed in a dream to do this thing, that finally—though it would not be easy—it could not matter what Peter would think.

Henry believed that people's minds speak with many voices, and among them are voices that cannot be trusted. A wise man develops a steward who keeps mental order and bids some voices keep quiet. Was this dream-talker one of the demented ones who was getting the floor because Henry's disease had weakened his steward? He sat with the idea for a long time, and decided that building a round concrete home was not harmful to anyone, and if the project were dementia-induced, a little craziness should be allowed to a dying man.

All right then, Henry thought. So where to begin? At the beginning, of course. But there was no rush at all, and so he would sit and think, formulating his building plan.

A Navajo winter hogan with its nine supporting posts and eight sides was close to round. Henry did not know a great deal about their actual construction, nor would he attempt to imitate a hogan too closely, but it provided a better basis for thought and direction than the bird's nest in his dream. For instance, Henry knew that a hogan is begun with a circle dug down into the earth. The soil a foot or more deep along the Alabama Gulf Coast would hold a temperature of close to sixty degrees year-round, Henry thought. So that's where he would begin. He would dig.

But where?

Henry considered the terrain and layout of his ten acres, and it became apparent that there would be no better spot than right here on the site of the cistern. It was the highest knoll in Tolstoy Park. There was already—what would Henry call it?—*circular intent* in the soil, an imprint of the cistern. There were no tree roots to cut through in the digging down a foot and a half or so. And he could also discern because of the lush grasses growing within and around the cistern that the soil here was not hard packed, more dark sandy loam than red clay. He would have to pour a concrete floor to support the weight of the block walls, but a slab would still allow him the benefit of a constant ground temperature. Yes, this would be his spot. He would even dismantle the cistern blocks carefully so that they could possibly be reused.

And what size hut? Henry's thoughts flew along. His corner room was fourteen feet, which was a reasonable size, and without corners to catch and collect this and that, it would be more than adequate for a lone resident. With thoughts of the adequacy of the shelter, he was suddenly nonplussed. Why would his dreaming mind believe he would derive much benefit from the effort of constructing such a heavy and durable cottage? Henry did not expect to live out another year. And yet Black Elk's visit to his dreamscape bore authority. His symbolic intent was clear: Build a house round like a bird's, but of cement blocks like the cistern. But why?

Henry focused his thinking, slowed it. He combed through the dream images. He heard again the phrases of the medicine man and, like a man lost in the deep forest, kept returning to the same place, to this: *Their religion is like ours.* The religion of the birds is like Black Elk's. Henry's religion had for years been intensely private and singular in purposeful reading and careful study and now he only wanted to find peace for dying. Was Black Elk trying to point the way for Henry? He cast about for some understanding.

He straightened his back against the cistern wall and closed his eyes. And quickly they flew open. Henry had experienced an epiphany. Birds do not read and study and argue high ideas into the depths of commiseration. Birds build nests. And curl their thin yellow talons around gray branches and blink their eyes and eat and fly. Henry would search for his peace with his back bent in the labor of building a house, from that and nothing more, save his hands curled around the handle of a shovel or trowel, and closing his eyes when he grew tired and eating when he was hungry.

With growing excitement, Henry recalled one of the most interesting of his teachers at Mount Union Seminary. Brother O'Neal had been a thick-chested and hairy-armed man, bald, with a resonant, incongruously soft-spoken voice. He was a former Trappist monk from the Abbey of Gethsemani in Kentucky who looked like a lumber-jack. Henry would never forget his opening remarks that semester: "By invoking the Holy Name of Jesus, the dean has given me permission to conduct an experiment in this class. Basically, the thesis we will explore is founded on the questions 'Why did Jesus choose a fisherman to see to it that his teachings outlived him?' And similarly, 'Why not pick a learned churchman for the task?' "

Then Brother O'Neal reminded them that he was no longer a brother and that they might call him Mr. O'Neal, though none of the students accepted the invitation. Henry believed they found him more mysterious as *Brother* O'Neal. And Brother O'Neal reminded them that his theology was his own, and he demanded that each student also have his own theology. "So what we shall do in this class for the duration of this semester is to work with our hands. In total and complete silence. We will open no books. We will discuss no theology. We will dig with shovels. But while we work, we will dig deep into our minds and hearts. There is something of powerful spiritual force to be gained from hard work. Jesus saw a rock when he looked at Peter, and clasped his calloused hands." Brother O'Neal's eyes were like burnished copper and danced with a curious light when he declared, "We will wear the shoes of the fisherman." Brother O'Neal's class had been the best of Henry's four years' study at Mount Union.

The prospect of self-reliant work immediately took on special significance to Henry. As he contemplated the possibilities and yet confronted his physical limitations, the pure challenge animated him. Henry decided that it mattered so entirely to his philosophical purpose that he would have to refuse all help in the construction of his round house. God, that would be tough! And maybe even more difficult, he would put down his reading. He would put down his writing. Brother O'Neal had said that opening day, "What did Lao-Tzu say? Educated people cannot be sufficiently wise. Was that why Jesus chose the fisherman? Tolstoy has said that we should read less and study less, but think more. [Henry had become right then a more willing participant in the experiment.] And Thoreau opined that only when we forget what we were taught can we find real knowledge."

Henry would reach back to the lessons of Brother O'Neal's class and make an oath to work as hard as his bones and muscles would let him. He would build a house of blocks in a circle, while disassembling the burdensome blocks of his learning. What was to be gained, he believed without equivocation, was some peace for dying.

Henry's thoughts, like yellow leaves dropping into a fast-running and foam-flecked stream, spun and dipped and leaped. What had Peter said? *Like a kid at Christmas.* He would mix sand and cement in a long wooden box. He would take a sharpened stick and scratch a date into each block. If he died tomorrow, today's block would be the journal entry of his last day.

Its wisdom would be easily read: Today I worked.

And the wise would interpret the intrinsic value of work that exceeds the accomplishment of the task. No work is wasted. Not even a dying old man's labor to build a house in which he might never sleep. Henry's contemplation would reach no higher than the correct mix of sand and cement, proper stirring, accurate dates, right alignment, plumb stacking. So lost was Henry in the excitement of his plan he did not hear Peter Stedman's truck drive up.

Ahh-oogah! blared the klaxon on the Model T. Henry jumped and banged his head on one of the heavy boards of his lean-to roof within the cistern. "Henry Stuart! It's Peter Stedman. You in there?"

Henry twisted sideways onto his hands and knees, crawled from underneath the boards, found a clearing in the branches of the fallen sweet bay tree, and stood up. He put a hand on the rim of the cistern and slowly raised his leg to step over.

"Here," Henry called to Peter, some steps away standing beside his truck, its big headlights throwing a bright light on the boards of his barn. Henry saw that the door he and Peter had framed in was standing ajar. The window beside it was broken, all the panes of glass shattered, the framework wrenched loose and hanging in splinters. Tiny tree branches and leaves littered the ground, and there were some larger limbs here and there, on the ground and dangling from trees.

What could be seen in the spread of lights before the truck was a confusion of damaged vegetation. But the morning dark was quiet. Little wind stirred, nor did birds chitter their tentative waking notes. Peter let Henry take in the scene without speaking.

"You okay?" Peter asked, coming around the front of his truck toward Henry. His hair was ruffled and his shirt open several buttons. "I told Leddie I had to get right over here. She said I should never have let you ride out a hurricane alone. But I knew a practical Englishman would survive the night. That was a smart call crawling into that cistern." He grinned and pointed at the structure behind Henry.

"I fared quite well, I do believe," Henry said, becoming conscious of some stiffness in his joints and an ache in his shoulder. "That limb scraped my shoulder when it came down, but it's mostly a surface abrasion, I'm sure. It appears to have been quite the blustery night."

"You could say that." Peter laughed. "My anemometer hit eighty-five miles an hour in some gusts just at midnight. Remarkable, too, how quickly it died down." Peter frowned. "We'd better take a look at that shoulder. Let's go back to my place and get Leddie to see what you've done there."

"I'm all right, thank you, Peter." He began moving toward the barn. "Let me just get a lamp going in here. See what kind of mess I have." Henry wiped his hands on his pants, then rubbed the top of his head, a little center of pain from bumping the board.

"You sure about that, Henry? Leddie'll be bothered with me if you don't come and let us see you in the light."

"Oh, no, thank you. I'm fine, really. It's kind of you to worry so, Peter, and to come and see about me like this."

"Well, as hurricanes go, it wasn't much of a storm. But still, winds up above sixty, seventy, can fling some stuff around and knock a man's head off."

"Yes. I saw a piece of tin go flying off my roof before dark came and the worst of the storm had arrived."

"Here, I've got another lantern in the cab. Let me light it and we'll see how much work we've got to do on this place. See what got messed up."

"You had better switch off your headlamps, Peter," Henry offered. "The battery will go quickly."

"Yeah, and I don't want to hand-crank this old gal. Best thing that ever happened was getting a battery into these things and electrics. Last truck I had, what was it? A '20 model, had those contrary carbide lights, and every start-up could break a shoulder." Peter went to the cab and opened the door to retrieve his lamp and matches, and in a moment had it burning. He dropped the globe and adjusted the wick for a sharp flame without much smoke. "Hey, hold up there, Henry. I'm going to cut off these lights. Don't stumble. I've got my lantern going, just wait a second." Henry stopped just short of the open door to the barn.

"I'll wait just here, Peter. I have another lantern like that," Henry said, gesturing toward the one Peter was holding up as he approached the barn. "Did you bring your matches? I expect mine are wet."

"Got the matches," Peter said, patting his shirt pocket.

With Peter leading the way, the two men stepped through the doorway and onto the wet board floor of Henry's room. The planks felt cool and soft under Henry's bare feet. Paper and books were blown about, and the twigs and leaves were everywhere inside, just as they were outside on the ground. Rolled into the corner was a section of stovepipe, a piece of the flue from Henry's cast-iron stove. Peter swung the lantern around to find the entire flue come loose, other sections of the stovepipe still attached, but pitched at crazy angles. Water had gone down the pipe sections and into the stove, which had seen only half a dozen fires on those few cold days since Henry arrived. But the supply of ashes was sufficient to have flooded with the water onto the floor, making a thick black mess. A puddle spread over half the wooden floor.

Several sheets of paper and Henry's books floated there. Shards of glass from the broken windowpanes and the chimney of Henry's desk lamp were strewn about the room. The base of the lamp was tipped over and the coal oil had spilled onto the desktop.

"Sure you don't want to ride to my place and have a hot breakfast and some coffee, or tea—Leddie can make tea—before getting this work detail going?" Peter asked, bending over to retrieve a wet map page from the floor.

"This is quite the scene of disorder, isn't it?" Henry said, heaviness and irritation in his voice. He had tacked Molly's kitchen rug to the wall and it was down on the floor in a wet heap.

"Yep, a shambles, you might say," Peter replied. "One that'll still be here an hour from now when the sun is casting some light on the subject."

"You are right, of course, and you and Leddie are so kind to continue to extend your hospitality to me, Peter," Henry said, sagging a bit in his demeanor and comportment. "But I think that I'll stand by here. I believe I would find it more frustrating to leave it and come back to it."

"I can see that, old man," Peter agreed. "Well, let me have a look at that cut on your arm. Then we'll get your lantern lit and get a jump on the day."

Henry began to think he would rather have had Peter go, leaving him alone to take in this little tragedy, to sort out his thoughts and get past the aggravation of this delay. He wanted to decide on how to go about the cleanup and to survey other damages, likely to the roof. But he would not decline Peter's generosity twice, and so, after bending over to lift Molly's rug into the crook of his arm, he turned his torso, presenting his shoulder and torn shirt to Peter. Henry attended to the disarray in his home, the holes in the barn room, his eyes moving around the floor bathed in the yellow lamplight, over the debris.

Henry's appraisal failed to note the moccasin curled near Peter's right foot. Neither man saw the strike, but both heard the thump when its nose and fangs met Peter's calf just above his boot, and they heard the thin splash as it fell back, ready to spring again if the intruder did not retreat. The pain came instantly to Peter, and just as quickly came Henry's awareness of what had happened. Then he saw on the floor the fat gray-brown coil of snake. Henry snatched Peter by the shirtsleeve and pulled him roughly away from the moccasin, taking the lantern, all in a single rapid gesture.

"Damn, damn, damn!" Peter said, his jaw tight, his teeth clenched as a searing firebrand heat spread up his leg. "How could I be so stupid? Warm spell like we've had. This storm. Gets all the snakes moving again. I didn't even look around on the floor!" Peter was shaking his head.

Henry threw the rug down on the desktop, and spun around the straight-backed desk chair, and shoved Peter into it. "Hold on, Peter!" Henry took two quick steps to the corner of the room and grabbed a hoe. Henry had honed its blade shining sharp just yesterday morning. Still holding the lantern in his left hand and gripping the hoe handle at its middle for balance and heft, Henry swung the hoe down onto the snake's back with such force that it was cut into two writhing pieces. The snake's mouth was open wide and Henry flipped the hoe blade over and brought the blunt arm of it down fiercely, smashing the snake's head.

"Let's get you to a doctor," Henry said. "Now!"

Henry tossed the hoe toward the corner. "Now I'm the one giving thanks that your Ford has a battery," Henry said, his eyes darting around the room in the dim light.

"Here," Peter said, knowing that Henry was looking for something to use as a tourniquet and handing him a red bandana from his back pocket. It was just barely long enough for Henry to get a knot in it when he pulled it tight around Peter's leg just below his knee. "Wonder the bastard didn't go for your bare ankles, huh?" Peter shook his head, his lips drawn thin against the pain.

"Shall we get a move on, Peter?"

"Can you drive an automobile?" Peter asked, genuinely concerned as they approached the truck. Henry opened the passenger door.

"Well enough for our purposes this morning, I do believe," Henry said. Peter swung his legs into the cab. "Here, Peter. Let me remove your boot. No need to cut it off when your leg swells. Come on, man, be quick about it!" Henry had to pull hard to get the boot off. Peter's leg was already swelling.

Henry went quickly around the front of the truck, its radiator still hot and smelling of steam. He lifted the bail on the lantern and blew out the flame, and with a minimum of fumbling about got the

Model T started and into gear, driving a big arc between the trees and toward the rutted lane of Peter's making, bouncing and jarring their way on down to East Volanta Road.

"Where will we find a doctor, Peter?" Henry asked. Peter's head was rocked back and resting against the rear window, his mouth slightly open. Peter mumbled something. "Speak up, Peter. Give me directions!" But Peter gestured feebly with his hand, pointing straight ahead. At the intersection with Bayview Road, the road that ran north and south along the bluff from Daphne to Point Clear, Peter held up his arm and flopped his hand to the left. Henry guessed they were heading to Fairhope. In minutes, just within the town limits, Peter instructed Henry to turn in to a driveway to a home situated near the street and set underneath two of the largest live oak trees Henry had ever seen, heavily draped in long gray beards of thick Spanish moss.

Without waiting for further instructions, Henry jumped from the truck and ran up onto the veranda, jerking back the screen door and rapping with his knuckles on the glass in the top half of the door. "Doctor!" Henry called, then again and a third time, knocking all the while. A light came on in the parlor, then a porch light, and the door opened. Without waiting for introductions, Henry blurted out to the dark-haired young man in striped pajamas and house slippers that Peter Stedman had been bitten by a moccasin ten minutes ago.

"Let's get him in here right away," said the doctor, a blue shadow of beard stubbling his face. The two men ran across the yard to the truck to fetch the patient. Halfway between the truck and the house, Henry began coughing so violently that he had to step away and turn his back. Henry bent and placed his hands on his knees and hacked and coughed until his eyes watered, and the breaths between the coughs were loud and wheezing gasps for air. "I'll see you next, sir," the doctor said firmly. "Come inside when you're okay. I'll get busy with Mr. Stedman."

When Henry had regained control of his breathing and could stand erect again, the sun was coming up. The sky above the dense line of trees out across the road grew lighter by the minute. Henry looked at Peter's truck, grateful he had not crashed. His driving skills were rudimentary at best, and untried now in months. Thomas, who had given him some basic lessons behind the wheel, would be proud, Henry thought. He was then overcome with such a palpable urge to get in the truck and drive back to Tolstoy Park that he actually took some steps toward the Model T, stopping only when a woman, presumably the physician's wife, called out to him to please come inside. Henry turned to face her. "Thank you," he answered to her. "But I will take a seat on your porch, if I may. Is Peter going to be all right?"

"I think so," she said. "Thanks to you. But you'll have to ask the doctor. I will tell him you're on the porch." She paused, looking at the sun's first light breaking through the trees. Her shoulder-length brown hair was brushed and she had on a plain dress and shoes. You could not tell she had just been awakened by strangers. Henry thought perhaps this happened often, some emergency in the night. "It was like this the last hurricane," she said. "It came ashore in the night and the next day was clear and lovely, if you could look past all the mess on the ground. There wasn't much real damage last storm." She walked out onto the veranda and stood at its edge, looking at the sky and around at what she could see on the ground. "Do you think this one tore things up? It didn't seem so bad as we listened to it barge through last night."

Henry was about to answer that he thought it had not been especially destructive, judging by what he could see as they drove along here, but then he came to believe she did not really care one way or the other for a reply, so he made none. The lady turned and disappeared back into her house. Henry took a seat on the front steps, waiting for news of Peter, prepared to tell the doctor that he himself was fine and needed no turn in the clinic. And Henry flexed his toes on the wet ground beside the broad steps and watched the sun climb higher into the coming morning.

NINETEEN

Henry bent and picked up the two pieces of the moccasin's body, one piece in each hand, and was surprised at the thickness and weight of the larger piece. He walked outside and dropped the snake into a hole he had dug a few feet off the northwest corner of the barn. It was just deeper than the head of the shovel and broad as the brim of a hat, easily dug into the damp black soil. The hurricane had soaked the ground, but it was drying quickly as the day continued warm and bright underneath the November sun. Henry used his foot to push the mound of dirt into the hole and cover the dead snake.

The doctor had suggested that Henry leave Peter with him and his wife for the morning and come back to get him in the afternoon. Henry had taken the truck to Leddie. When he told her Peter had been bitten by a snake, she drew in her breath sharply and put her hand on the door frame to steady herself. Henry told her that Peter would recover completely in a few days. He did not tell her that the doctor had asked to examine him as well as Peter, to at least put his stethoscope to his chest, and that he had refused. He hoped the doctor would not voice his concern and possible diagnosis to either of the Stedmans. Henry had avoided all such talk in his letters to Peter, and did not now want his health to become a topic for sidewalk speculation here in Fairhope.

He asked Leddie whether he would be needed to fetch Peter home in the afternoon, but she said that she would take the truck and go to the doctor's home now and wait for him. Henry declined the offer of a ride to Tolstoy Park and said that he wanted to walk, to see what the hurricane had done in the woods. The half-hour walk had revealed no great damage beyond a ravaging of the trees. The one other house on East Volanta Road was set back too far for Henry to know if it had suffered mightily in the storm.

When Henry arrived at his barn, he had begun digging the hole in which to bury the viper he killed. *Thou shalt not kill.* But better wisdom, Henry thought, would be: *Do not kill unless you must.* Henry had not hesitated to swing the hoe blade down on the back of the moccasin, but neither did he believe he was avenging an act of malice. Lore had it that a cottonmouth moccasin, alone among snakes, would seek out and attack humans. Henry didn't believe it. This moccasin that had bitten Peter had simply been afraid of the human stomping around nearby.

Despite our terrible hunger for some comprehension of the nature of God, Henry believed, knowledge of God's workings would always remain unattainable. But we might get closer to divine understanding, he thought with a wry smile, if we could figure out why we kill snakes, why we behold them with such loathing. For Henry, without remorse, it had been a strike for a strike. The snake's strike was motivated by fear, he was sure. Was his own strike out of fear? Henry's strike had been precise, calm, purposeful, and without question, retaliatory. But why? He had not recalled fear or anger when he raised the hoe.

Henry remembered a tale about a samurai warrior who went to vindicate the death of his master. In battle with the one who had slain his master, the samurai was victorious, and when he was about to run the other through with his sword, the fallen man spat into his eye. And as anger rose in the samurai, he sheathed his sword. "My mission cannot be accomplished in anger," he said. "Another day, then."

Anger or no, the snake was dead and in two pieces. The end was the same, was it not? He hoped in his time remaining he would not face a day when he must kill a man, for he feared that he would do it. Or that he would not kill, and find the inability to do so a worse consequence. Thankfully, combat seemed the province of young men. Henry was lost in these thoughts as he dragged the last of the dirt into the hole with the side of his foot. He used his toes and the balls of his feet to tamp down the tiny earthen mound. He walked back to begin cleaning, organizing, and repairing his room. Out of his head and into his hands.

Henry began with the floor. He picked up the ruined books and papers and piled them in a heap on the small desk to the side of Molly's rug. He took the rug and hung it over the back of the desk chair. He swept up the ashes and glass. There was adequate light in the room to see well what he was about, and Henry guessed he had about two hours left of sunlight. Tomorrow the sun would set a minute or so earlier, and the next day, and the next and the next, until it started back the other way on December 22. Henry wanted to get right to work on his round cottage, and the more he thought about that good work, the more his enthusiasm for straightening out the mess in the barn room waned.

Henry decided with a small bubble of joy to allow himself to paint on a different part of the canvas. It was, after all, his own life that he was rendering here. So he walked out of the barn room, picked up the shovel again, and carried it over to the cistern. He dragged away the broken limb and stepped over inside and tossed out the planks that had kept him dry through last night's storm.

With his face lifted to the sky, and in a histrionically deep voice, Henry said, "Here on this spot is the hut-circle." He grasped the handle of the shovel with both hands and raised it high in front of his chest, then grinned at his silliness. "This ring of ancient stones marks the place where shall stand the sacred shelter of King Henry the Last. The dwelling shall be raised up out of this holy ground," Henry said, maintaining his affected deeply resonant voice, turning slowly, slowly around inside the cistern. "Right here!" Henry said with a shout, and he pierced the point of the shovel blade into the grass and soil at his feet. Henry let the shovel stand and lifted both hands to the sky in an attitude of worship. He lifted his face and closed his eyes, and suddenly, without warning, tears flowed from the corners of his tightly shut lids. He did not lower his chin, nor did he try to blink back the tears. He kept his eyes closed and said, "Oh, Molly! How I do miss you." He stood that way for long minutes. Finally

Henry opened his eyes and asked aloud, "How has it come to this? That I am here and you are not?"

Henry reached out and took the shovel by the handle again, and this time pointed the blunt end of the hickory handle at one of the blocks in the cistern wall and poked it forcefully. A hairline crack appeared along its mortar joint, and he struck it again. And again, and the block began to jar loose. Henry set aside the shovel and tried to pry the block loose. It would not come free. Henry turned to the next block in the top row and banged on it with the shovel handle. It did not respond as well as the other had.

So he leaned the shovel against the low wall and stepped over. He went to the rick of stovewood and brought back a heavy piece of split oak to use as a small battering ram. He banged several times until the block came loose. Then Henry picked up the shovel and inserted its blade point into the crack in the mortar joint and pried downward on the handle. The block popped loose and toppled over outside the cistern. The first one he had worked on came out easily then. He moved to the next block, and it was easier work than the other two had been. When it got too dark for Henry to see well what he was doing, he had removed all the blocks in the cistern walls except the bottom course. In that course some blocks were broken, and he expected it to go well when he attacked it at first light tomorrow.

He was completely satisfied with his labor of the afternoon, and with sweat dampening his shirt in the coming dark, Henry went to his corner room in the barn and lighted his lantern. By that soft glow he finished cleaning his floor. He tacked a woolen blanket over the broken window, though the evening still held the day's warmth. He opened a big round-top chest of wood and painted tin and brass. It was quite old, with leather hinges, its interior paper-lined with a fleur-de-lis pattern. Peter had given it to him and Henry had put his traveling luggage into the room on the side of the barn with his tools. Henry lifted out the top tray of the trunk, and from underneath brought out clean and dry bedding for his cot.

He took the lantern and went to the well and got a bucket of fresh water. He heard an owl hooting down the hollow toward Rock Creek, and an answering call from somewhere back of the barn. Henry came inside and closed the door. He sat at his desk and slowly ate an apple and had a cup of water. In the morning he would start a fire in his stove and have hot cereal of oats and cornmeal and a slice of sourdough bread from the tin on the shelf and a cup of black tea. Within the hour Henry was sleeping soundly, cradled in the dreamless dark.

· TWENTY ·

At noon the next day, Leddie came in the truck to say Peter was at home and resting and that he sent her to inquire after him. Henry was on the roof of the barn nailing down a sheet of tin that had blown loose on the corner. Leddie was holding a basket filled with something covered over by a white towel. "I brought some fresh oat raisin bread and a wedge of cheddar for you," she said. "I'm sorry you're having to work alone, Mr. Stuart."

"Please, Leddie, think nothing of it," Henry said, backing down the ladder. "I'm almost finished with the repairs and cleaning. It really wasn't the task it seemed to be when I first looked over the place in the daylight."

"Yes," she said, looking about, but in a cursory way. "Mr. Stuart, I . . ." Leddie said nervously. "I don't like to do this, but Peter insisted. I feel it's none of our business unless you choose for it to be."

"Mrs. Stedman, Leddie, please, ask what you will," Henry said. He knew where this was going. The doctor had most likely said something to Peter or Leddie or both about his coughing fit yesterday morning.

"It's just that Dr. Anderson said he was concerned about you. He told Peter and me that he has reason to believe you should schedule a visit with him for an examination. Lord knows on what he bases his opinion, for he would say no more than that." Leddie seemed quite distressed to be saying these things, and Henry believed Peter must have emphatically requested she take up the matter with him. "It's just that he placed a burden on us when he said we should encourage you to come around to his clinic."

"Leddie, I'm sorry. The doctor—did you say Anderson?" Henry wondered if there was a family connection to Kate Anderson, the schoolteacher and mother of Anna Pearl.

"Yes, Dr. Anderson," she said. "His family has been in Fairhope since before we came thirteen years ago. He moved here with his new bride and opened his clinic only two years ago. Why do you ask?"

"Oh, I met a schoolteacher on the bayboat ride here whose name is Anderson. Kate Anderson," Henry said. Leddie said yes, Kate was the doctor's sister-in-law.

"At any rate, the good doctor's youthful initiative overcomes decorum here," Henry said, gesturing with his hand. "It's not a thing a doctor should do, to make a community matter of his concerns for someone's health." Henry frowned. "Especially when such concern is entirely speculative."

In the way only a woman can do, Leddie seemed to pass through all hesitation with Henry. She drew one eyebrow downward and said, "*Is* it a speculation, Henry?" She placed her free hand on top of the one holding the basket handle and lifted her chin. Henry was reminded of a schoolmarm waiting for a student to repeat why he had not turned in his homework paper with the rest of the class. Henry could not help but smile.

"Leddie, you and Peter have been more than kind to me. I'll not lie to you now that you have asked me a direct question," Henry said, his smile fading. "But I do not wish to hold my health and well-being up for public scrutiny and inquiry. I'm sure you can appreciate my feelings."

Leddie would not let it go. "Is there something wrong, Henry? Are you not well?"

"If I am to tell you this, it seems Peter should hear it as well. But since he is abed himself, and you are here asking me, I will answer and let you tell him what I have said to you." Henry motioned toward one of the neat stacks of blocks he had made with what he had removed from the cistern. Leddie hesitated, but when Henry himself sat down on another of the chair-high stacks, she too took a seat, shifting the basket to her lap.

"Leddie, my doctor in Idaho suggested a change of climate would be beneficial to me," Henry said. He paused, sitting slightly forward and putting his hands on his knees. Henry looked Leddie straight in the eye. "I moved here to make it easier to manage the tuberculosis I have. It is noncontagious. It is in advanced stages. It is terminal."

"Terminal?" Leddie shook her head, honestly unfamiliar, it seemed, with the term. Her eyes were wide and locked on Henry's. There was nothing to do but tell her the truth. "My doctor said I haven't long to live. Perhaps a year."

Leddie put her hands to her mouth so rapidly that she dropped the basket from her lap. The small loaf rolled from underneath the cloth as the basket tumbled upside down. Nor did she move to pick it up. "Oh, my God, Henry! That's terrible news. I cannot believe it." Leddie might have stumbled on with her small exclamations of denial, but seemed to catch herself and stopped speaking entirely. She simply looked at Henry. He was glad she did not weep. He didn't know her well enough to meet that just now.

"But, Henry, you seem so, so—"

"And that is indeed a curiosity, Leddie. I feel so well, so often. Only sometimes am I even aware that I have consumption. The doctor said it will follow its own course, present its own 'personality,' if you will. But generally, it will get worse soon. Then it will progress rather exponentially, according to Dr. Belton in Nampa."

"Oh, Henry. Why did you not tell us?" Then Leddie recognized that her question was inappropriate. "I'm sorry. That is neither fair nor proper, Henry." They both sat in total silence for a full minute. "Is there anything we can do for you? Should you be doing this work?"

"No, Leddie, there is nothing that I need. Thank you. And yes, I absolutely should do whatever I wish that is not forbidden by the law or common decency." At that Henry smiled, attempting levity. His visitor responded to it with her own slight smile. But then Leddie's face became serious.

"So Dr. Anderson was right. But how did he guess?" Leddie asked, somewhat bewildered.

"I fell into a coughing jag on his front lawn when I drove Peter there with the snakebite yesterday." Henry seemed to think through the scenario. "I suppose the better doctors have a strong intuition for differential diagnosis." Then Henry expressed to Leddie his sincere hope that the young doctor did not talk to others up and down the Eastern Shore.

"Our Dr. Anderson, I'm afraid, Henry, is quite the gossip. Some of the ladies I know, well, they're no longer patients of his." Leddie's face flushed with the candor of her comment, and she looked as though she wished she had refrained from sharing that news with Henry.

Henry too was at a bit of a loss to add anything sensible to her revelation, and so in a minute said, "This warm spell seems to be hanging on quite a long time." He wiped the sheen of sweat from his forehead with the back of his hand. "Are you not allowed a winter's respite here in Alabama?" But Henry did not really care to talk about the promise of a cold front. His thoughts returned to the name Henry Stuart hanging out like the laundry over Fairhope's morning coffee. It was to Henry deeply disconcerting. Even imagining someone in town saying, "There's that man who is dying" as they indicated his presence on the sidewalk with a careful nod—or worse, a pointed finger—filled him with dread.

In Nampa most of his social intercourse had been limited to his sons, Harvey and Thomas, Jeremiah in the post office, and Will, who was like a brother to him. How many times had Harvey rebuked him for not attending church with a barb like "Father, there will never be a church congregation of two or three." And while that was not his reason for staying out of church after Molly died, avoiding the press of people could have been enough by itself to keep him home of a Sunday morning.

In retrospect, Henry was quite surprised at how easily he had of late spoken to porters and strangers on boats, but had attributed it to the holiday mood that accompanies travel. Emerson had written of the intoxication of travel, and indeed, in the manner of wine breaking loose men's tongues and spirits, Henry had felt a definite lowering of his guard. Kate Anderson, upon this brief moment's reflection, was a beguiling soul who might have broken through Henry's defenses in any case. But now here was this looming prospect of—how many?—*dozens* of people becoming familiar with him, wanting to know his story.

And in truth, Henry knew there was nothing he could do. And besides, what did it matter? Tolstoy Park was remote enough to afford him all the privacy he could want. The hard part would be resisting the companionship of Leddie and Peter, and perhaps Kate, as he worked to build his round house in the manner of silence and solitude that he would adopt from Brother O'Neal's class. Henry wondered if Jesus did not long for company when he spent his forty days in the desert. It was clear to Henry that his too was a spiritual exercise, for as a practical matter, a dying man building a round house of concrete made no sense at all. This construction, Henry now believed, might—in the way of Brother O'Neal's teaching regarding the value of handwork for the building up of one's soul—strengthen his own soul so that he might pass into death more easily.

And here was Leddie, dear wife of Peter and a good woman with a generous spirit, who, it seemed, with her gifts would teach Henry something of the nature of a "gracious receiver," a term Will Webb had often used. Leddie asked Henry to take the watercolor sunset scene from the guest cottage, the piece Sherwood Anderson had told her he liked. It was hanging now in his barn room. How would he tell her he was about to become monastic? Admitting to her he was sick was one thing, a fact of sorry luck over which he had no control. Putting off his friends was a choice that seemed at complete odds with the needs of a sick old man. He looked up at Leddie. She was staring at him.

"I know you're busy with your repairs," she said, "and have things to do. I won't keep you, Henry." As she stood up from her block seat, he could see that she was uncertain what to do with the bread. "I do so hate to throw away food, but I suppose—"

"I would not allow that," Henry offered quickly, extending his hand to take the loaf and the basket. She smiled warmly as Henry said, "An old bird like me needs a little sand in his craw."

"Oh, I do hope it is edible, Henry." Leddie brushed off the seat of her dress and clasped her hands together. "Well, I'll tell Peter that you are faring well. It's all that I can do to keep him in the bed, woozy as he is. And his leg, it is twice its size and the most violent purples, blues, and yellows." Leddie grimaced, and after a pensive moment added, "I should think it would be a challenge to illustrate a medical text in those colors."

Henry agreed, becoming thoughtful himself as he considered how true it is that life is seen through a lens of remarkably personal grinding and polish. Here was Leddie considering her husband's predicament and appraising it in terms of pigment and hue, seeing Peter's wounds as a challenge for a watercolorist. Henry escorted Leddie to the cab of the truck and closed the door when she was seated behind the wheel. Henry hesitated, battling briefly with himself, then said, "Leddie, this news of my health that you will take to Peter, it is my sincere desire that neither he nor you be vexed to worry over it." Henry looked away over the treetops, then back at Leddie. "It's my own burden to bear, and if I'm not at peace with the reality I face, I am at least on practical terms with it." Leddie nodded slowly, looking closely at Henry as if to detect the veracity of his words. She seemed satisfied and said that Peter would be around as soon as he was able.

"He thinks it is funny that you call your place Tolstoy Park, but he admitted that he much prefers it to the names of the places on either side of us, Cozy Pines and Gull's Roost. He shudders each time we pass their mailboxes." Leddie laughed, and her eyes told how she loved her husband, as Molly had loved him and embraced his own peculiar view of things. She ground the gears into reverse, and through her open window said, "Peter said for me to tell you to save some work for him. He so enjoyed working beside you on your barn."

As Leddie made her wide turn and bounced forward across a rut Henry lifted his hand to wave good-bye, but she was not looking. There were many trees and bushes to dodge, and Leddie kept her eyes forward. And Henry knew there would be no dodging the dread of telling Peter that he would not accept his help.

TWENTY-ONE

Henry decided to stay with the roof repair, since that would all but finish his hurricane recovery operation, and went back up the ladder to finish nailing down loose sheets of tin, taking lead-headed nails from the cotton nail apron tied around his waist and, from a squatting position, pounding them down with his hickory-handled sixteen-ounce hammer. At times he had to squint against the sun's reflections off the metal and be careful not to fall from the roof. After an hour's work, he was satisfied that he had completed his task on the barn roof, and climbed down the ladder.

When his feet were pressing on the cool damp earth, he stood a moment, holding onto the ladder, listening to the nearby *skree* of an osprey. He listened again, cocking his head, detecting not one bird but two, a call and an answer. Where were they? A shadow passed over him and he stepped back from the ladder and looked up.

He saw the pair of ospreys overhead kiting through the blue, slow steady spirals on an updraft. The larger of the two was the female. Their shrill calls to each other would carry with ease for a mile or more. The male drew near, then fell away. Some courtship ritual,

Henry thought. And their appearance was his signal to get things moving with this project.

Henry stood and watched the playful, gliding flirtation until they disappeared behind the thin foliage of a pin oak. He went into his toolroom in the barn and took a large file from the shelf. He reached his shovel from the corner and went back outside and sat on the stacked blocks knocked loose from the cistern, just where he had sat talking to Leddie. Henry worked with precise long and rhythmic strokes of the file sharpening the blade of the shovel. He would answer the great fish hawks' wheeling circle with a circle of his own, digging a round hole about a foot and a half deep in the earth in the manner of a Navajo starting construction of a hogan.

With a fine and shining sharp edge on the shovel blade, he walked to the center of where the cistern had been, his hut-circle, to the very point where he had previously thrust down the shovel blade, and did so again. This time he held on to the handle and put his bare foot on the edge of the blade and pushed downward. The soles of his feet were toughened, but not enough to overcome the pain of digging barefoot with a shovel. Now this was a problem. Henry owned no shoes.

He immediately sorted through a mental checklist of solutions. Henry had always drawn pleasure from puzzling over how to fix this and that thing. Once, before meeting Molly, he had spent a year working in Washington, D.C., as an "assistant engineer" at a hotel there. He was a handyman and was frequently called upon to find clever ways to resolve problems, and he loved the work. It occurred to Henry that a wide block of wood somehow attached to the shoulder of the shovel blade would do the trick. But then how to attach it so that it would stay put for the work? Or he could attach the block to his foot by means of makeshift straps of leather. He was about to head for the toolroom when he spied Peter's boot on the ground. Henry could not stop the laugh that rose up in him, a belly laugh like he had not enjoyed in some time. How in the name of God could that boot have not made it into the cab of the truck this morning when Henry removed it from Peter's foot? The coincidence of his need and the boot's availability struck Henry with incredulity so sharp that he gave another laugh and shook his head.

"But I could never put another man's boot onto my rather dirty foot," Henry said aloud. An answer came into his head that was so plain and clear it seemed almost an audible hallucination: You have clean socks among your things in the barn. "Well, by Jove! If the shoe fits wear it, as they say," Henry said, grinning like a schoolboy about to dip pigtails into his inkwell. Henry took the boot from the ground and looked inside the cuff of it, where it was clearly stamped size 10. Henry's size, of course. Peter would, he hoped, get as much of a laugh from this as he. Henry went straight inside and opened his footlocker and took out a pair of clean socks, chose one and stuck his foot into it while standing, purposefully testing his balance and flexibility, and without putting his foot on the floor put on Peter's boot. It went on easily and felt good. Never had a boot or shoe felt so good, he thought.

Henry walked out of the barn, a kind of *ffff-pahh, ffff-pahh, ffff-pahh* rhythm filling his ear, but more felt than heard, as he went barefoot-boot, barefoot-boot, barefoot-boot across the grassy hill.

· T W E N T Y - T W O ·

When Leddie came at noon the next day, sent by Peter to ask after his boot, Henry told her that he would have to purchase new ones for Peter. "For I have borrowed the fallen comrade," Henry said, still delighted with the gift of the boot in answer to his needs yesterday. By now, Henry had dug down in the grass, into the dark rich soil where the cistern had been, had made an excavation six inches deep in a fourteen-foot circle. Leddie's mouth was open, her eyes wide, as she walked up to Henry's work site.

"I see that you are indeed, putting Peter's boots . . . ah, *boot* to hard labor." Leddie had her fingertips to her cheeks, her eyebrows raised. "What are you doing, Henry?"

"I am digging the foundation for a cottage."

"A round cottage?"

"Quite round," Henry answered. "I thought to build a home for myself without corners where rubbish might collect." Henry looked to either side of himself, at the dirt circle in which he stood. He looked over his shoulder. "Well, strictly speaking, not completely round, since I will use rectangular blocks of cement. Like those you sat on over there. Slightly longer. But by using twenty-two or twenty-three straight sides, it will become quite round."

"But why, Henry? Why, with what you told me yesterday, why would you undertake to build such a, a *heavy* little house? Or, what did you call it, a hut?"

"Actually, I referred to what I shall build as a cottage." Henry rubbed the short whiskers on his chin, adopting a contemplative gaze. "But hut is acceptable, if we delete the implications of the temporary nature of a hut per se. Since all in this temporal world of illusions is short-lived, why not? A hut it is, then, Leddie! And as to why now, I am reminded that Socrates was found studying a new language on the night before the morning of his death. A pupil came to see him, and in surprise asked, 'Why do you now study a new language?' And Socrates answered, 'If not now, when?' If I don't build my hut now, dear Leddie, then when shall I ever build a hut?"

"Are you sure, Henry," she said, "that it was not you who was bitten by the snake, and that some fever has not taken hold of you?"

"No fever yet."

"Oh, I am so sorry, Henry." Leddie's face was flushed, and she dipped her head. "I am sorry."

"Don't worry yourself, Leddie," Henry said. "One must have something of a sense of humor regarding such somber things. Balance is required, especially now. Do you agree?"

"I do agree," Leddie said, fidgeting. She was clearly uncomfortable now. "Well, Henry, I think Peter will be happy that you have rid him of this boot, and the other like it at home. He never liked them, and only wore them because of his contrary nature regarding the waste of money." Henry remembered what Peter had said about Sherwood Anderson walking away from the art class tuition. "I will tell him that you need his help more than ever now, what with your new project." Leddie said she would bring the other boot, and Henry started to tell her he only required the one, but he thought better of it and said nothing. When Leddie left Henry, it seemed to him she was driving much more deliberately than yesterday, as though on a mission to tell Peter of Henry's fall into dementia. As the Model T disappeared from view down the hill, two questions came to Henry's mind: What could he do to keep the round house in Tolstoy Park from becoming a tourist attraction? And would the hardware store in town deliver sand and gravel to him?

Regarding the former question, he had no appetite to answer questions about what he was doing here on this ten acres. It was hard, he found, even to field Leddie's queries. Such a great deal of energy would be required to defend the effort of a dying man to build a round concrete house. And Henry believed he didn't have the luxury of energy to spare. He could not risk its dissipation in talk that would sound to sane ears like so much silly prattle from a goofy old man. Henry thought how Noah must have felt building a big boat on dry land among gawking neighbors. Answering questions of curiosity seekers could be literally painful for Henry.

What could he do? A NO TRESPASSING sign would violate Henry's sense of community. He would have to think about some method for fending off his good neighbors without offending them terribly and implement that measure soon. With a twinkle in his eye and a nod of his head, he thought that perhaps he could just send word through Kate to her talkative doctor brother-in-law that his consumption was the "catching kind." That would keep everybody away. But no, that would be the mean-spirited resort of a curmudgeonly old coot, *which of course,* Henry thought, *I am not.* Could it be enough to simply make an honest request for, what would he call it, spiritual quarantine? There were plenty enough models for that in history and sacred literature. Oh, well, something would present itself as the right course of action.

Now, regarding the latter question. He would walk to Fairhope in the morning and find out if he could order sand and gravel delivered. If the answer should be yes, Henry would place an immediate order for enough sand and gravel and Portland cement to mix and pour a slab of concrete in the bottom of the hole. In all his rush to get things going with the digging, Henry had overlooked the procurement of raw materials for his slab. He would also buy a large metal mixing tub of some description for stirring together the three ingredients that would transform magically into stonelike concrete.

Enough lollygagging, thought Henry, and he got back to digging in earnest. He had worked with a ditchdigger once who taught him to work at his own pace, that slow digging was not bad digging as long as it was steady. The ditchdigger told Henry to find his rhythm and keep it like a heartbeat and a hole would happen all by itself. "Man don't dig no hole," the digger said, "he just move a shovelful of dirt, and another shovelful of dirt, and one more shovelful of dirt, and keep on till the hole say stop."

So Henry dug. One foot sweated in a boot. One foot balanced him on cool damp dirt. Henry believed Peter would be pleased with the contribution of his boot to the job, a tool as important to Henry now as the digging blade. "Diddle diddle dumpling, my son John, went to bed with his breeches on, one shoe off and one shoe on, diddle diddle dumpling, my son John." Perhaps, thought Henry, tonight he should sleep with his trousers on, and he poured another blade of black earth onto the grass outside his deepening circle.

Henry thought about pouring a concrete slab fourteen feet in diameter and four inches thick, of sufficient strength to bear the load of all that masonry. He ran the math in his head, while continuing to dig. A radius of 7 feet, squared, equals 49, then times 3.14, or about 150. That got the area of the circle. Now, if he poured his slab 4 inches thick, that would be a third of a foot. So the area in feet times the thickness in feet would equal the cubic volume of concrete Henry would have to pour. One third of 150 would be 50. Henry was going to have to stir up by hand about 50 cubic feet of a mixture of sand and gravel and concrete and water.

He figured too that he could handle the mixing of about 10 cubic feet per batch. That would take five or so batches. He would have to work fast so that the different pourings would adhere well one to another and therefore keep the integrity of the slab strong. So the mixing and the pouring needed to happen as near the hole as possible.

What if he built a mixing box made of planks with a sheet of tin for the bottom? And what if, Henry thought, he put hinges on the board at the end? By dangling the end of the mixing box over the hole, he could let down the gated end and quickly push the batch of wet cement into the hole. Then do another as fast as possible. And another. It would be a physical test for him in his condition. He would have to do all the mixing and pouring in a single day, and on a day without rain or freezing, though Henry had little concern about prospects of temperatures falling that low. Back in Nampa, in mid-November, nighttime lows would already be running at freezing and below. The train attendant had been right. Coastal weather was fluky—generally cool, but sometimes downright warm, and so far not at all cold.

Henry figured the three-mile walk to and from town to order the sand and gravel and concrete would take him about three hours. If he made that journey in the morning and got back to his digging tomorrow afternoon, by Thursday morning he could be ready to mix and pour concrete. With his plan fixed in his mind, Henry settled into his work with the shovel and purposely resisted abstract thoughts. He was practicing a kind of meditation wherein the mind looks at only what is in front of it. If you are washing clothes, wash clothes; if you are cold, be cold; if you are digging in the dirt, dig in the dirt. Henry didn't believe it would work to deny abstract thoughts from entering his mind. Such outright repression could backfire and blur his mind even worse. Instead, Henry would train his perception on the physical world in Tolstoy Park. "What is the sense of this work?" Henry would exchange the thought for: "What is the weight of this shovel?" When he drifted to consideration of the worth of his life lived so far, he would think of how many hours of sunlight he had left to dig today. When Molly's voice entered his head, he would listen for the song of the whippoorwill that called down the evening.

If he went about the work of building his round house in what he believed would be the right manner of single-minded, self-reliant work that he kept willfully grounded in the very present moment, its benefit to Henry could be enormous, even soul-perfecting in the way that Brother O'Neal had tried to teach him so many years ago. On the other side of the coin, there could be a price to pay for turning away Peter's offer of help. No amount of reasons for doing so would satisfy Peter, Henry was afraid. When it came down to it, he could only ask for Peter's trust.

· TWENTY-THREE ·

Henry's room was silent and dark when he awakened. He lay still on the cot, blinking. As the sleep left his head, he began to make out shapes in the room, the cast-iron stove, his round-topped tin and oak chest, the desk with books opened so the still-damp pages could continue drying, though he held out small hope for their salvage. When he could see well enough, he got up and pulled on his trousers and shirt, tugging the suspenders over his shoulders. He rotated his shoulders and arched his back, which ached rather badly, worse than in a long time. He lifted his arms and stretched, and after a few minutes of flexing, he felt the pain subsiding.

Henry started a small fire in the stove, and soon had hot water to mix with the cold water in the basin for washing up. He did not empty all of the steaming water from the kettle, saving some for a cup of tea. He was not very hungry, so he ate only an apple and a small piece of bread.

He sat for a while at the desk, listening to the birds awakening in the low branches outside the barn. He twisted the wick key on the oil lamp and raised the flame. The light grew brighter, but the flame was too high and began smoking the globe. Henry adjusted the wick's height so that the flame burned cleanly and bright and in that soft light he wrote letters to Harvey and Thomas, and another to Will. His sons had written him twice, and Will three times. Henry had written each of them once, telling them of the lush coastal landscape, and how Canyon County's arid and rocky, rolling terrain with its backdrop of gray mountains seemed a thing of some dream he had once had, so close and overpowering was the damp green of this place. He described Tolstoy Park for them, and told Will that he might have guessed Tolstoy would have a place, so to speak, with him in Alabama.

He missed them, he'd written, but he knew he had made the right decision to come to Alabama. In each of those first letters back to Nampa, he'd included postcards he purchased from Kate's brother's store. There had been in Ingle's Dry Goods a countertop rack of Fairhope scenes depicted on photo postcards, and Henry had bought an even dozen. He mailed one of the postcards to Jeremiah, selecting for him another bayfront scene, a different angle on the Fairhope pier and the sailboats and steamboats and swimmers and strollers that Henry knew the postman would enjoy.

In the letters Henry composed this morning, he wrote that he enjoyed the companionship and hospitality of his new neighbors, that his health was holding strong so far, that he was busy with a new building project. He hesitated before writing: "I am building a round house of concrete for myself, something of a cross between an igloo and a hogan and a beehive. If I'm able to see out its completion, I will have a photographer make a postcard of it for you." Then, to cut short further explanation about the building of his hut, he'd told them of the moderate hurricane he had lived through and that his barn had suffered significant damages and this would be his hurricane hideout. Henry expected they might still think him going a bit daft, but once again, further understanding of his plan would probably not be possible no matter how long a letter he wrote. So he would not try. He closed the last letter, the one to Will, and sealed the flap. He put the three letters in his trousers pocket and would mail them in Fairhope this morning.

When the dark began to fade to the pale blue light of dawn, Henry arose and washed his cup and brushed away the bread crumbs from the white china plate. He opened the door and stepped outside and flung the apple core over behind a thicket of wild huckleberry bushes, where he expected a raccoon to soon finish off the morsel. He looked around at the land and trees and sky. He could see no stars and imagined sunrise would be above a cloud cover. He thought perhaps the stiffness in his bones foretold a coming rain and maybe cold weather.

After making sure he had taken enough money from the cash box in the bottom of his trunk to pay for a yard and a half of sand, an equal amount of gravel, and several bags of concrete, and with a clean handkerchief stuffed into his shirt pocket, Henry walked away from the barn, angling to the south and a little west across Tolstoy Park, heading for Fairhope. The terrain fell gently but steadily toward Fly Creek, probably a half mile down the hollow. Henry picked up the narrow draw he had previously noted, its shallow sag into the earth a watercourse for runoff from the hills above the creek and an excellent trail for trekking to the creek, free of almost all understory growth. The downhill walk was easy and the going fast, if quite a zigzag down the draw through the forest of tall pines and a scattering of hardwoods. Henry could feel a gathering moisture in the cool air, and the dampness in the wind muted his footfalls and softened the springy carpet of leaves and pine needles under his bare feet.

The morning's light was now full and gray. He paused and listened. The land had become a flat shelf populated with wide-butted cypresses and extremely tall hickory trees, and he knew the creek must be nearby. He heard first the skittering of small birds on the ground and the louder going of a squirrel, then the creek burbling not far ahead, probably just behind the tangle of dry saw briars and thick bushes there past those sweet gums.

Taking up a fallen stick the thickness of his wrist and as long as himself, Henry knocked back the vines and tiny branches and stepped through the opening onto the sandy bank of Fly Creek. He might have been stepping into a scene from an ancient jungle, so verdant and dark was the foliage overhanging the creek. A silver log, all its bark worn off by rain-swollen rushing torrents in years past, was pitched diagonally across the creek. The log functioned as a partial dam and formed a pool twenty feet across. The water was slow-moving now and so clear that Henry could see the white sand bottom four or five feet below as though it were underneath glass. A gray-brown mass of waterborne debris trapped by the log had sprung new plant life, and even in late November, green was shooting up from there.

In fact, unlike the bare and gray winter hills and valleys of an Idaho November, perhaps with snow falling already, these Alabama woods were remarkably green in winter. The magnolias had their leaves, the sweet bay and holly trees had their leaves; some of the varieties of oak were deciduous, but most of the oaks had their leaves, and the willows, the pines, and cedars were green. Much of the understory vegetation, honeysuckle and briar and privet, was thick with leafy jade. If Henry were a painter, he would set up his easel here. He would cover canvas after canvas with pigment. He would try to awaken an image reflecting the light falling here upon this immense green world. Henry could only stand in reverent awe.

When he shuffled his foot in the sand, he dislodged a fat acorn and it tumbled down to the water's edge. The acorn might have been a piece of wise man's gold, so captivated was Henry by it. He fumbled in his shirt pocket for the small daybook he had brought from his desk drawer in Idaho. He had a piece of pencil in his trousers pocket. He sat on the sand with the journal on his knee and the pencil poised above a clean page. There in the acorn's fall was his own life. He wrote, and for the sheer fun of it, angled the words down the page:

Down the hill
        The
                Acorn
                        Rolled
Until it struck a stone.
Stock-still it lay then,
                Quite surprised
To find itself at home.

Then Henry went back to the top of the page and put a title, "Finding Home." This tiny brown-capped scion of a bossy oak had, for Henry, just borne witness to the truth and circumstance of his own predicament: No matter where he landed when all these days were said and done, he would be at home. How could it be otherwise?

Henry held the book and pencil between his folded hands, draped between his bony knees. Indeed, he thought, as Jesus had suggested, the stones—and acorns—do sing. If only we will listen, they have our lives to tell. Henry sat for minutes longer, letting his eyes glean nuances of beauty and serenity from these surroundings. Though the muscles in his temples were beginning to tighten against the first pain of a headache, he smiled when he remembered the language in the brochure that had initially attracted his attention to Baldwin County. It was not the factual telling of how this county was almost as large as Rhode Island, with more miles of coastline, but the promise of health benefits. Henry had read the paragraph enough times sitting in his study in Nampa to have it almost memorized: "No climate is more favorable to health than the Gulf Coast, as evidenced by natives and residents of Baldwin County. Hundreds of delicate visitors, or invalids, slowly recover from wasting or nervous diseases, and return to their homes with renewed energy, and that exquisite feeling and sensation of youth." Here was all but a written promise of a drink from Ponce de León's fountain.

These woods were private and quiet, a good half mile from the shell road that became Section Street, an oiled dirt road entering town. Henry thought he would take a plunge here in this pool on his return, but further thought of the cold creek water gave Henry a brief shiver, and he wondered if he might have a slight fever. Henry stood up and put his pencil and journal in his shirt pocket. Looking about, he thought it best to make his way along the creek bank, where the foliage was less dense. He made good progress, able to alter his course only a little now and then and still keep close by the easy moving flow of clear water. Now and again he would stop to examine a fallen pine, the coffee-colored wood soft and moist where the bark was peeled off, or look closely at some green sprig of new growth he didn't recognize. Sketching and identifying and naming such would come later, when his cottage was complete.

And if his health failed and he could not finish it, that would not matter. This building endeavor was his to do, Henry knew, and his hut would be a suitable enough charge to see him to his last day. His mind had plenty of data stored away, he knew many things, and if it was his choice to add more learning, to study another language, he would postpone it deliberately until his hut was done. Repeating that long ago spiritual exercise Brother O'Neal had taught him would be difficult for Henry, so thirsty at all times was he for reading and study. *But that's the point, young man. A kind of Lenten denial of your cravings. If you cannot see its value, then you will especially benefit!* "Yes, yes, good monk," Henry said aloud to the quiet woods, enfolding him in a primal embrace. "And if my store of days is sufficient to raise my little house, it shall be the curiosity and amazement of the neighbors for miles around."

Through the trees up ahead Henry could see a grassy berm. He had veered some several steps away from the creek to have a closer look at a huge dogwood tree standing alone in a copse of tall pines. It seemed to Henry so forlorn, its leafless web of whitened branches a gentle geisha's fan. He looked now toward the embankment and knew it marked the shoulder of the county road. The bridge over Fly Creek would be to the left and not far. Henry experienced something like reluctance as he stepped from the woods and into the weeds and grass onto the shell road, leaving behind his temple of trees.

The road dipped down toward the bridge, and soon after its crossing went uphill and curved gently to the right, where it took up a course without curves due south to the center of town. The shells gave way to oiled sand and clay, brown and hard-packed. A white sign with dark blue letters and gold trim was affixed to a square post and read "Welcome to Fairhope." Henry was feeling some better, though his energy was low, and he walked with longer strides. He would get his materials ordered out to Tolstoy Park and return home right away and get back to work digging his foundation. There he seemed to find renewed strength.

Though the sun was obscured behind a galvanized sky, low clouds of mottled gray and white, and Henry did not have the benefit of shadows to aid his reckoning, he knew it must be about two hours since he left the barn, somewhere around eight o'clock in the morning. Stores were open, some people were going about here and there, walking and motoring, though it seemed a rather sleepy morning in the town.

As he drew near the main intersection, where on its southeast corner he would find McKean's Hardware and Building Supply, he heard a bell tolling somewhere in the direction he was heading. Before stepping onto the long gallery in front of the store, he paused to listen more closely to another sound from farther down Fairhope Avenue. Children's voices became more distinct and sounded to Henry happy, as if from a playground or park, and he knew it had been the ringing of a school bell that he'd heard moments earlier. Peter had pointed out the lovely campus of the Organic School; in fact he'd stopped the truck on the street in front of what appeared to be the administration office.

"That's the Bell Building," Peter had informed Henry. Then he pointed to another small building. "If you ever come calling here, Mrs. Johnson's office is in there. She would direct you to your friend Kate's classroom." The bell atop the Bell Building had, no doubt, just called the children off the yard and into their classrooms.

Henry went into the hardware store and found the man who had helped him when he and Peter had been here before. "Carl," he said when Henry asked his name. "Carl Black."

Henry told Carl that he wished to order a quantity of sand and gravel, and some bags of cement, that he was constructing a slab of some two to three cubic yards.

"You might as well," said Carl, "go ahead and get more than enough. Leastwise on the sand and gravel. We don't always have the gravel in good supply." Carl reminded Henry that there was plenty of sand available, but gravel had to be trucked down from the middle part of the state. "Sand and gravel is not what I'd call expensive anyway."

Henry and Carl together computed again the amount of material needed to do the job. The order was given and paid for, and delivery promised the following morning. Henry bade Carl good day and was about to walk out the door when Carl called out, "Mr. Stuart, will you be needing some help with your work? Somebody's always in here asking where they might get some work. I know Mr. Stedman is laid up with his snakebite and a man in your condition—"

Henry winced and his face grew warm. "I don't require any assistance, Carl." Henry turned completely around to face the man. He was about to say something about not needing either his health and affairs worried over about the town, but stopped himself.

"Sorry, sir. Just thought, you know, you might be needing a hand on your place. I didn't mean to pry."

Henry shook his head. The look in Carl's eyes reminded Henry of a loving dog that has been scolded. "Never mind. It's nothing, Carl," Henry said. His face, he hoped, conveyed to Carl there was no harm done. Henry had in fact experienced a brief swelling of anger, completely misplaced. In anger, truly the harm is to oneself, Henry believed, and our body's cells are like children who shrink at the argument of the parents. Thoreau said the body is the first student of the soul, and if the soul is stirred in anger, the body learns to throw tantrums. Henry's father had always cautioned him that if he became angry, count to ten, and if still angry, count to a hundred, and if still angry, count to a thousand.

Henry turned to leave. "Thank you for your help," he said, then "And for your concern, Carl." He stepped aside to let another man enter, and left the store.

Once again, immediately outside the store, Henry's feet still treading the broad pine planks of the porch, the voices of children at play fell on Henry's ear. Their unbridled gaiety, their merry chatter punctuated by shouts and laughter, helped to ease Henry's mind. He could hardly believe the talk had already commenced, though Henry imagined that a small town's appetite for distraction could drive them to home in on the progress of his illness, the deterioration of his condition.

Suddenly, above the children's playful babble there arose such a shrill scream that it spun Henry around and sent him running in its direction almost involuntarily, a response of the father in him. He was down the porch and onto the dirt street running full tilt before the piercing cry was interrupted for an inhaling breath. One of the children had been injured. Henry covered the two or so blocks to the Organic School campus and arrived at the cluster of children ringed around a boy sitting on the ground holding his left foot, blood from between his toes pumping a puddle onto the brown grass. Henry immediately removed his shirt and wound it into a thick bandage. He had to forcibly remove the boy's hands from his foot to determine that the wound was a deep cut right underneath the big toe. He wrapped the shirt around the foot and applied enough pressure directly over the gash to stanch the blood flow, all the while attempting to soothe the child.

"I have the bleeding stopped," Henry said evenly but strongly. "I won't let go until we get you to someone who can clean and stitch this cut." The boy, a red-haired fellow of about ten with wide blue eyes and a scattering of freckles over his nose and cheeks, let out another wail when Henry said "clean and stitch." Then Henry asked the young man what his name was. "Inman," he said, still sobbing. He clenched his teeth tightly and rolled his head back with his eyes closed.

"What'd I step on?" he asked.

Henry turned to the circle of children. "Someone, please, what has Master Inman stepped on to cut his foot?"

"This," said a dark-haired girl, dropping a sardine can onto the ground beside Henry. The lid was turned back, the little key still inserted into the loosely curled flap of jagged metal. One sharp edge of the lid had a tiny smear of bright red blood on it. Seeing this, Inman howled again. Henry believed another question might have a calming effect, so he asked, "Can you tell me what happened?"

The boy began to settle himself and explained how they had been playing the game of "Annie Over," telling Henry you threw a ball over the building and somebody on the other side caught it and ran to the side from which it had been thrown. If the player got there without getting tagged, he or she got to take a prisoner back to the other side, and so on, until everyone was captured or the bell rang them inside.

The boy was just finishing his explanation when the teacher trotted up to the gathering. It was Kate Anderson. She looked at Henry, her eyes wide in surprise. His face must have registered similar surprise, for she reacted to him then with a tentative smile that quickly faded in deference to the wounded child. By now in the telling Inman had stopped crying and was breathing more easily. Inman then told Henry and his teacher how he caught the ball and took off running for the other side of the building and stepped on the leavings from someone's lunch of yesterday.

Henry turned to Kate and said, "I've had a careful look at the laceration to the bottom of Master Inman's foot, and it'll surely require stitches because of its proximity to the crease where the toe flexes."

When Inman yelled again, but without the weeping, more a howl of anger, Kate said, "I suppose, Mr. Stuart, sometimes it's just hell to run around without shoes on." The other children gasped to hear this language coming from their teacher. They giggled and looked at each other. Henry could not prevent his look of utter appreciation for how these tables had been turned upon him, and for Kate's quick wit and her clever pun.

"Touché, Mrs. Anderson" was all Henry could think to say.

"Well, enough of that, Mr. Stuart," Kate said, expressing her satisfaction and a desire to move on to the business at hand and see to the boy's doctoring needs. "I'll get Freddie. He's our janitor. He will drive us to the doctor's office. But first, I will deliver my students to someone else. Mr. Stuart, if you will be so kind as to stay and wait with Inman."

"Certainly," Henry said, winking at Inman. "How could I let this man down?" But Henry's thoughts had run away from the boy. He felt the dread of another encounter with Kate's brother-in-law, and yet Henry knew he must confront Dr. Anderson. In so doing, in bluntly asking the physician to respect his rights to freedom from intrusion, there would be something gained toward recapturing his privacy at Tolstoy Park.

Henry watched Inman squint his eyes against the pain spreading from his foot, and wondered to what degree the mind could resist sensations of pain. Or not resist it and instead accept physical hurt. What if we focus all our concentration on the center of pain, hold it up to the light of intense examination? Would it possibly yield to such scrutiny and retreat at least a little? But then as Henry became quite chilled, goose bumps spread quickly over him and he could not warm himself. He gave a mild shudder, and drew himself up tighter in his squatting position. He reminded himself: If you are cold, be cold. Allow it to be so. Henry mused, *And what else could I be?* That was the intelligence of it.

Henry did not see Kate walk up beside him. She removed her heavy shawl, the one she had been wearing on the bay crossing his first night in Alabama, and draped it over Henry's shoulders, patting his arms as she did so. Before Henry could protest, she was walking away and addressing her flock, "Come along, students, let's see if Mrs. Johnson can think of something to do with your young minds while I go see what to do about a young foot."

With one hand Henry held his shirt bandage to Inman's foot, with the other he closed the shawl at his neck in a gesture much like Kate's on the deck of the *Bay Queen*. A fever was beginning its slow burn, and Henry's energy to resist was low. The walk to town, his bother with Carl, and the excitement of Inman's injury had exhausted him. The fever would take him, would put him into his cot, he feared. His digging and pouring would be delayed. And just now, Henry's eyes hot behind the lids, his temples in a tightening vise, he did not care.

"You okay, mister?" Young Inman looked directly into Henry's face.

"No," Henry said. "I don't feel well, Master Inman."

"Maybe you could have my place in line at the doctor's."

This brought a smile to Henry and a little lift. Seeing Kate for a bit would also help. She reminded him of Molly thirty years ago. Not so much the way Kate looked, but more her optimism and feisty manner.

· TWENTY-FOUR ·

By the time Freddie brought around the school's black sedan, a dented and unwashed Chevrolet with a loose, rattling front bumper, Henry was quite sick. Yet he still held pressure to the boy's injured foot as the janitor drove Henry and Kate and Inman to Dr. Anderson's clinic, and relinquished his post only when the doctor's wife took over from him in the outer room of the office.

"The doctor is with another patient," Mrs. Anderson said.

"Henry stopped the bleeding and ruined his shirt," Kate said, and then put her hand on the woven wrap across Henry's shoulders. "The shawl is quite nice, though, don't you think, Virginia?" Henry couldn't even muster a smile as he plopped down onto a bench. Kate's sister-in-law seemed embarrassed and said nothing, looking intently at the folded white gauze she was pressing against the bottom of the boy's foot. She spoke to a large black woman who entered the room. "Ida, would you see about the gentleman's shirt. Since the blood is still damp, if we drop it into the sink for a good soak, it might not be stained."

Ida picked up the bloodied shirt off the floor near the boy's feet. Henry made no move to surrender the wrap. The chill from the fever caused him to tense his shoulders, and the pain pulled at his neck and face muscles. He felt quite sleepy and robbed of his energy, and his eyes burned. Kate stepped across the small waiting room and sat down beside Henry. "Henry, Lord! You look terrible." She put her hand to his forehead. "And you're burning up!"

"What's the matter with the man, Mama?" Kate's daughter had stolen silently into the room, carrying a doll by its arm. "Do you want to use my stepascope?" The little girl had a toy stethoscope around her neck and a toy hypodermic needle in her hand.

"Oh, Anna Pearl, honey. You aren't supposed to wander into the waiting room." Kate looked quickly to her sister-in-law to determine whether her daughter was in trouble.

"But I heard you talking, Mama. Is it time to go home?" the little girl asked hopefully.

"No, honey. Mother has to go back to the school for a bit when this young fellow here is taken care of." She pointed to Inman, who was not saying a word, as if his silence might render him invisible to the doctor when he came out to stitch and give shots. Anna Pearl looked at her aunt holding the bandage, saw the white cloth tinged with red, and made a face, wrinkling her nose.

"He's bleeding," she said. Then, directing her attention to Henry, said, "It's that man who got the gorilla's banana, Mama. Is he cut, too?"

"Missy Anna, you jus' full of questions," Ida said, attempting to take the little girl's hand. Anna Pearl snatched it away. "Folks up in here are sick," Ida said with a frown. "We got to go back to your play-room so the doctor can make them well. Come on, girl. Ida will play with you a spell."

"Virginia, I don't mean for her to get in the way here," Kate said. "I so appreciate your help with her. I'll—"

"Anna Pearl is wonderful company and no bother at all, Kate.

But"—and Virginia turned and bent down to Anna Pearl—"you must let us see to these people. I will come back and see about your dollies as soon as we get caught up out here, honey."

"Here, let me go back with her and get her settled," Kate said, scooping up her daughter. "Henry, will you be all right for a moment?" But Henry did not answer. He looked at her, but was leaning to the side on the bench and was feeling worse by degrees. The busy waiting room was becoming more than he could handle. He tried to rise, but was unsteady and weak. He shook his head and closed his eyes, trying to breathe some strength back into his muscles. When he opened his eyes the doctor was beside him.

"Mr. Stuart?" Henry focused on the young doctor's face, his brown eyes hard and flat. "I need to know, sir. Are you diagnosed with tuberculosis?" Henry continued to look at Dr. Anderson, but gave no answer to the question. The doctor told his wife to take the boy back to the examination room and clean his foot. He turned back to Henry. He was shivering with the fever, clutching Kate's shawl.

"Do you have TB, Mr. Stuart?"

Henry nodded.

"Is it the contagious strain?"

Henry shook his head.

"May I contact your physician in Idaho to confirm what you are telling me?"

Henry took a long slow breath, and slowly said in a whisper, "His name is Dr. Patrick Belton in Nampa." Then Henry, in halting words and phrases, gave the physician an address where he might get the information he wanted. Henry tried to rise again.

The doctor put his hand on Henry's shoulder. "Please, sir. I have a bed for you in the back."

Henry shook his head. "No." The pain in Henry's lower back was like a fire in his bones.

"Mr. Stuart, I must insist that you be practical. I can give you an injection that will help you." Dr. Anderson put his hand underneath Henry's arm to help him to his feet. Henry accepted the assistance, but then pulled back from the doctor. He removed Kate's shawl and placed it on the bench and stood there in his thin undershirt. Collecting all his strength, Henry said, "It's very important, Doctor, that you abandon your mission to tend my health. I accept this illness as a condition of my life, and if it is to be the circumstance of my death, then so be it." Henry hesitated and simply looked at the doctor for a long moment; finally he extended his hand to the doctor, a gesture that seemed to confuse the man. The doctor slowly lifted his hand as if to shake with Henry.

"You can help me, Dr. Anderson." The young physician raised his shoulders as if to say, *But how?* Henry started to speak, but the pain in his head and body stopped him. In a moment, with the doctor clearly becoming uncomfortable caught in the handshake stance, Henry let go the doctor's hand and said, "I've chosen a path here, Doctor, and I know it's difficult to understand . . ." Henry turned his head and coughed, and it was answered with a pain in his temples like a nail had been driven into his skull. "But what I most need is my privacy, sir."

"Mr. Stuart," the doctor said, "I assure you—"

"No, please, Doctor. I know I don't have long to live. I left two sons and my best friend at the other side of this country because solitude is important to me now." Anna Pearl's sobbing drifted down the corridor, and Henry looked in the direction of the door leading to the back of the doctor's office. Kate stood there. Her eyes were wet with tears and Henry realized she had been listening. He looked at her when he said to the doctor, "It's the path I've chosen," and then returned his gaze to Dr. Anderson. "On a journey to a place where I alone can go." He looked down the hall toward Kate, back at the doctor, and then turned and walked out the door of the clinic into a slow drizzle falling from a gray sky and into his own dark night of the soul. He was deeply sorry that Kate had learned in that way that he was dying.

The windblown mist grew heavier, though it was not yet a rainfall, and Section Street going north was slick and muddy. The oil used to keep down dust and resist the rain's penetration, minimizing erosion and road repairs, was wicked to the surface of the street and bore a thin odor of petroleum. Henry's feet slid beneath him, mud now covering the bottoms of his trouser legs to his knees. He could hardly focus, and his whole body shook with chills and there were knots of pain in his back and legs. His lungs felt raw and burned with each breath. He wanted only to be at Tolstoy Park. It seemed now on the back side of the moon.

Henry followed the curve of the road as it became a crushed oyster-shell base that crunched under his hardened bare soles as he went. He faltered and waited until the wheezing abated. On again, his eyes holding to the ground, and downhill he went to the bridge and crossed over Fly Creek. He stumbled as he stepped from the road-way onto the shoulder. He caught himself, stood stock-still a moment to regain his balance, then set off into the woods, wading down the road embankment through the long grass and weeds into the perime-ter stand of tall pines.

He held to the creek bank as he lurched along through the woods. The going was easier along the sandy shoulders bordering the creek. Smaller bushes and vines were sparse, and the larger trees were spaced farther apart. Henry could not seem to focus. A thin whiplike huckle-berry branch caught him across the face and stung his cheek where it cut into the soft flesh above the line of his whiskers. He lifted the back of his hand to the spot and pulled it away with a smudge of bright blood from his wrist to his knuckles.

An effort to clear his throat turned into a spell of dry coughing. He stopped where he walked and stood leaning against the rough bark of a pine until his breathing came easier. The spasm had not found the claws to reach into his lungs and bring up the blood. When he began walking again, Henry's foot plunged into a shallow stump hole and he fell headlong into the narrow gulley that marked the beginning of the draw he would follow to the top of the hill and Tolstoy Park. Henry struck the ground and rolled onto his side. He lay there a moment and became angry at this halting and wretched hike, frustrated with himself, tired of the illness that plagued him. Like snatching off a broken fingernail to get on past that part of the situation to whatever bleeding or salving must come, Henry knotted his muscles and stood up. He tightened his jaw and took to the hill with renewed resolve and even greater strength, it seemed.

When Henry arrived at the site of his shallow dig, the drizzle had stopped. He passed by the hole only for the purpose of retrieving his one Peter Stedman boot from the barn room. In five minutes he was pressing his boot sole down hard on the shoulder of the shovel blade and it was biting easily into the soft, wet soil. Standing in the center of the broad round hole in the ground, Henry hefted and turned and spilt the shovelful of dirt onto a mound growing just outside of his circle. He would not of his own free will lie down for this consumption. It would have to take him standing up or knock him down. Henry kept digging. By the end of the day he was sweating and bone-tired, but the fever had left him and his head had stopped throbbing. He had finished digging a hole sixteen inches deep and fourteen feet across.

The late afternoon sun found brief freedom as it slipped beneath the woolly rug of clouds being dragged away from the horizon. A freshening breeze was moving the whole messy overcast quickly eastward, and Henry felt that the sickness in his chest was for the moment pulled away from him. Henry put away his shovel and boot and walked back down to the creek for a bath, carrying clean, dry clothes in a cotton sack over his shoulder. He stripped naked and waded into the cold water, going farther and deeper until he could lower himself and be covered to the neck in the creek. He did not move until he stopped shivering from the chill of the water. He had not brought soap, but briskly rubbed his skin underneath the water and ducked his head, massaging his hair and beard in the flowing creek. He felt strength returning slowly into his muscles and clarity into his head.

Henry eased out of the creek and swiped away the water from his skin with the flat of his hands. He took the dry clothes from the sack and put them on his damp body, gathering his other trousers and shirt and putting them into the sack. Henry hiked up the hill, believing his work would truly be a medicine-way for him. If it would not heal his body, it would at least make it stronger, and a strong man dies easier than a weak man. And he knew from the experience of Brother O'Neal's class those many years ago in Ohio that the work would absolutely help clear his mind, and a clearheaded man dies better than a befuddled man.

Later, after the oil lamp's yellow light seeped from the room in the barn, Henry lay in his cot listening to whippoorwills calling to each other across the hills and hollows of Tolstoy Park. He had not read at all. Henry had decided now was the right time to begin his reading fast. He fed his imagination instead by picturing the whippoorwills, fat like robins and gray-brown, with a great wide beak for scooping mosquitoes on the wing, and nestled down into their hidey-holes in the grass and leaves singing up desperately at the night. And as two whippoorwills crossed their songs in the hollies and sweet bays down toward Rock Creek, a baby's dreamless sleep gathered around Henry's head.

· T W E N T Y - F I V E ·

On this day Henry felt stronger and more agile. He breathed easily and dug with a strong back and strong arms. Before the McKean's truck came from Fairhope with sand and gravel and concrete, Henry had dug another small three-foot circle, its edge touching the perimeter of the larger one, lying at the due west 270-degree mark on the compass, and six inches deeper than the main floor bottom. This smaller circle would be the floor of a recessed stoop at the threshold of the entrance to his hut.

Henry heard the delivery truck whining in low gear up the hill from East Volanta Road, finding its way along a rutted course laid down by Peter's coming and going over the past month. The driver got out of the truck slowly, as if to put off for a bit longer the work ahead of him. He was a burly, wiry-haired man with a bushy mustache. He asked Henry, "Where you want us to put this stuff?" When Henry had shown them just where, two Negro helpers crawled down from the bed of the truck, and the three of them unloaded first the bags of Portland cement, then the sand and gravel, shoveling it into two mounds near the hole as Henry had so directed them.

While they did their work, Henry finished constructing a mixing box, two feet wide and eight feet long, with one-by-ten sides and a piece of roofing tin tacked on for the bottom. The box was upside down on two sawhorses. He screwed the last of three butt hinges onto an endmost board so that it could be let down like a flap.

Henry stood beside the box in the middle and hefted it gently off the sawhorses and onto the ground, holding it by one side so that it would not fall. He dragged his new mixing box to the edge of the foundation hole, near the piles of sand and gravel, with the hinged end hanging over the hole. He would work from the east side to the west, pouring his stoop last.

As Henry walked away to retrieve from the barn his hoe and trowels and screed board, he heard the men laughing. When he came back with his tools and laid them alongside the mixing box, the driver cut his eyes left and right at the two men helping him, as if ascertaining from them permission to speak. They grinned at the driver, but quickly looked back at the shovel blades they were working into the heap of sand in the bed of their truck.

"We got shoes for sale back at the store, mister, you want us to bring you a pair next time we come out here," the driver said, hardly able to stifle a laugh. His helpers could not, and they laughed aloud. Henry had forgotten to remove the one boot at the completion of his digging, and was foot-booting it about the work site. He looked down at his feet, as if unsure what the driver meant.

Without so much as turning up the corner of his mouth, Henry said, "No, but thank you. I've discovered that if I wear out one boot completely, then switch and wear the other until it's used up, a pair of boots lasts twice as long." This comment brought looks of serious consideration to the faces of all three men, and sidewise glances at each other. "You will perhaps wish to try it with your next pair of new boots or shoes," Henry said professorially.

He went back to the barn, more to enjoy a private grin than for any other reason, though he did return with a pair of leather work gloves squeezed into his right fist, slapping them against his trousers as he came along. The men soon finished their unloading and left Tolstoy Park, the driver alone in the cab and the two Negroes bouncing in the back of the truck with the shovels. Henry sat down and removed his one boot and arranged it near the other tools of the morning.

He had awakened before dawn with a keen appetite and had a large bowl of mush that he made himself from ground cornmeal and wheat stirred together in boiling water on his stovetop. He had poured in honey and eaten his fill. A hot cup of tea and a slice of bread had finished his meal. That good breakfast was still with him, and he stepped over to his well and drew up a fresh bucket of drinking water. Henry slaked his thirst and was set now to work without interruption through the rest of the morning.

Henry pulled on his gloves and took a wide stance, shovel in hand, and began to count shovelfuls of sand, ten of them, and gravel, seventeen, dumped into the mixing box. With the point of his shovel he cut into a bag of cement, scooped out and added five shovelfuls to the mix. He put down the shovel and took up his hoe. He pulled the ingredients, chop by chop with the hoe, toward the end of the box, mixing as he did so. With one end of the box cleared, Henry shoveled into that end another round of raw materials in the same ratio, called a five-sack mix, correct for foundations. He then stirred the new batch in its end. Then he pulled the dry mix all together into a heap at the middle of the box. When Henry was satisfied with the blending, he stopped and put down the hoe.

From an oaken barrel nearby he slopped in water, bucket by bucket, about four gallons, until he believed he had enough to wet his boxful of well-stirred sand and gravel and cement. He would have to mix with the hoe perhaps ten batches of this quantity of concrete, and in quick succession. A batch would have to be poured and quickly followed by another few cubic feet of wet concrete so that each pouring adhered well to the previous pouring.

Henry jumped into the foundation hole, careful to step around the evenly distributed stobs protruding precisely four inches from the ground. Wet concrete poured to a depth flush with the tops of the stobs and screeded level would give him a good flat slab of consistent thickness. He removed the pin from the hinged end of the box, flipped it down, and with the hoe pulled gobs of concrete into the hole with him. Henry pulled and pushed the batch of concrete with his hoe until it was close to level, then finished the job with his screed board.

The lightness of his body as he sprang from the hole was so remarkable that Henry wondered where the sickness was hiding. He stopped and looked at the gray-green mass of concrete puddled in the hole, thankful for the deep shade of his trees in Tolstoy Park so that the slab would dry more slowly. He moved his box to a new spot on the circle and fell to his work in earnest, shoveling faster. In less time he accomplished the same process to make another box of concrete. He would work as rapidly as he could while maintaining a rhythm that he could sustain all day. He tossed away his gloves. With sweat in his eyes and dirt on his hands Henry dodged thoughts of dying. How could one possibly fathom the unfathomable depths for which no human had the reach? Henry spun to his work, comfortable that he could completely plumb the depths of a concrete slab.

Henry pulled the new batch of concrete into the hole and screeded and leveled it. From a bucket of water, he splashed the growing slab to retard its drying, keeping it green while he worked and poured the next round of concrete. And the next. Again and again as fast as he could work, until the foundation was poured.

Henry then quickly plopped two short sections of board onto the green slab, dropped onto his knees on the first board, and began floating a smooth surface there with his wooden trowel. This was work he had not done in twenty years, since building his home in

Nampa, but he had a sure hand with it, and the slab was acquiring a hard, flat, polished sheen. He was working backward toward the stoop, backing from one kneeboard to the next as he troweled.

"Hello!" A woman's voice called out. "Mr. Stuart, hello?" It was Kate. He kept working. She was approaching on foot from toward the road. Anna Pearl was walking beside her, and they were holding hands. "Henry," she called again. He backed up onto the second kneeboard, still bent over the slab, using the trowel to steady himself. Then Henry crept back another two feet into the smaller circle for the stoop, still with its dirt floor at this point. Leaving his trowel in the hole, he stood up and wiped his hands on his trousers. Henry looked back at the slick surface of the wet slab. He had worked it well. It was smooth as placid water. Kate and Anna Pearl walked right up to his hole in the ground.

"Oh, I want to make a footprint!" Anna Pearl sang. She was bouncing on her tiptoes, clapping her hands in front of her face, green eyes wide above a radiant smile. Henry looked at Kate. She shrugged as if to say it was all up to Henry, that she didn't care if he did not mind. But then Kate's face transformed from the frivolous business of her daughter, and she looked intensely at Henry, a careful appraising look. He believed her scrutiny was for ascertaining that he was okay. He found he could not return her gaze and changed the subject, as it were, by rubbing his hands across his shirtfront to clean them of cement and going to the only other topic at hand. "If your mother thinks it's proper," Henry said, talking to the child but expecting Kate to answer. "It would be an honor to have you make footprints on my new concrete." Henry pointed to the slab.

Henry found he was nervous about this surprise visit. He was unsettled about the prospects of revisiting the exchange between himself and Dr. Anderson..Kate had been upset, that had been easy to see, and she was entitled to further discussion. But Henry simply didn't know how to talk about it further with Kate. He was fond of her, that was true, but their friendship was still so new and his struggle with tuberculosis so intensely personal.

"Now, Miss Anna Pearl, you must be very still," he said, the frown loosening on his face. Henry reached for the little girl, who fairly leapt into his grasp. He hoped that she wouldn't kick about. He wouldn't have much time to rework the slab, which was beginning to set. "I think I shall turn you around, young lady, so that your shoe print is pointing inward." He sat her back down on the grass outside the circle and coaxed her to turn facing away, then reached to lift her again. "This way I'll always have someone entering the room with me. Is that all right with you?"

She nodded vigorously and then suddenly asked, "What room? Is this a room? But it's round. Is this a nursery rhyme house?" She twisted her shoulders and head to look at Henry. "Are these little walls made of dirt? Where are the windows? Will you put on a roof? Can Mama and I—"

"Anna Pearl, honey! Poor Mr. Stuart can't talk that fast," Kate said. "Let's do the footprints and then maybe Mr. Stuart will tell us about his house."

"But I want my toes in the mud," she cried. "I want my shoes off like Mr. Stuart. Can I, Mama? Take them off, please." Anna Pearl reached for her mother, nodding as if the matter were absolutely decided. Kate took her, shaking her head. "I'm sorry, Henry," she said.

"Oh, no. In fact, I quite like the thought of . . ." and Henry became contemplative for a moment, "It will have special meaning for me to cross my threshold in company with these young soles." Then Henry gave a big smile. "There is a pun there. Do you detect it?"

"No, it went right over my silly girlish head," Kate said, wagging her head about and putting her fingers to her cheek. Then, pursing her lips in mock disdain, she said, "Of course I got it!" She shook her finger at Henry. He smiled and looked away, pretending to survey his concrete work. Kate knelt down and removed the tiny black shoes and white socks from Anna Pearl's feet. She giggled when she stepped down barefoot on the cool grass. The little girl's glee was infectious, and Henry found himself feeling much lighter, and completely attentive to Anna Pearl. She reminded Henry of Thomas for some reason, perhaps the mischievous sparkle in her green eyes. They were the color of an oak leaf in late summer.

Molly had deeply wanted their second child to be a girl, and had been so certain that it would be that she could not hide from Henry her disappointment when Thomas was born. A friend of Molly's had dangled a needle on a thread over Molly's swollen belly, and it had spun in a manner that, the friend said, meant surely that a daughter was coming into the Stuart home. Henry too had looked forward to raising a daughter at Harvey's side and to indulging himself in a father-daughter bond like the one his own father had had with Henry's sister, Helen. When Helen had later met and married an English fellow she met in Ohio and moved back to London, it had broken his father's heart. He seemed afterwards to never quite mend his despair.

Henry knew that Kate was pleased with this moment between him and her daughter. She stood to the side of the hole near a dark mound of soil from the excavation effort. He looked briefly at Kate, her eyes bright and her arms crossed, as he raised Anna Pearl to lower her bare feet onto the wet slab. It completely surprised Henry when Kate promptly took a seat on the dirt pile, without apparent regard for her clean dress. She dropped her canvas tote at her feet.

"I've brought you something, Henry," Kate said. Henry, not knowing just how to acknowledge what she had said, said nothing, but directed his attention to Anna Pearl. Kate said, "When you've finished there, I'll give it to you."

Henry addressed Anna Pearl happily. "So are you ready there? We must do this before I drop you and you get completely stuck in the mud."

"You better not," she said, her eyes growing wide. "My mama will be mad at you. And then she might not give you her poem."

Henry glanced at Kate as he set Anna Pearl onto the green slab just inside the spot that would become the threshold. He was attending to this event with as much focus as he could, in view of Kate's nearness. Henry reined in his wandering thoughts and said to Anna Pearl, "There now. Just be as heavy as you can, but do not wiggle your toes or feet. We want a very clear impression of your little feet."

"Yes, because you have big feet," Anna Pearl said with finality, as though tiny feet were the obvious preference. "Am I doing it right?" She looked at Henry and at her mother. "Is that good enough? This mud is cold."

"That is perfect," Henry said, lifting her onto the grass. Kate did not get up. Anna Pearl scrubbed her feet on the brown blades of grass. Henry stepped up beside her and went for his water bucket and the piece of cloth he had been using for slinging water onto the slab. He wet it and brought it to Kate, now cuddling Anna Pearl in her lap. Kate took the cloth and began cleaning her daughter's toes and feet. Henry went back to inspect the artful handiwork. Two tiny footprints pointed toward the center of the circle, with toes and pads and heels perfectly visible, and not a grain of sand otherwise disturbed in the foundation.

Henry must have been admiring with great affection what he saw, for Kate spoke up, "Ah, the taciturn Henry Stuart is pleased with his big mud pie!"

"Yes to both," Henry answered, smiling. "I'm known to be somewhat taciturn at times, and I am delighted with this wonderful mud pie."

"My brother, Wesley," Kate said as she pulled a sock onto Anna Pearl's foot, "asked me to tell you that things are slow in his store this time of year, and he really would be happy to take some time in the afternoons to give you a hand."

"No." Henry's response was so swift and at such a volume that it surprised him and Kate equally. "I'm sorry, Kate. That was more than taciturn."

"More like the Billy Goat Gruff!" Kate said.

"Who's that trip, trip, tripping on my bridge?" Anna Pearl said with her chin low and her voice as deep as she could make it. "Mama read that to me."

Henry ignored Anna Pearl. "It's just that I must do this alone, Kate, for reasons I'm not sure anyone would understand. There seem to be so many who want to help. And I know it looks like I need all the help I can get."

"That I can't say, Henry. I don't know how much help you need. I see a perfectly lovely circle of concrete sunken into the ground. Beyond that I don't know what your plan is." Henry looked at Kate, and she briefly looked away. "Well, Leddie did say you're going to build a house. A round house. And of concrete. But that doesn't sound right, Henry."

"See, Kate," said Henry, his voice conveying something of exasperation and defeat. "*That doesn't sound right.* Of course it doesn't sound right." Henry's voice softened and his eyes now reflected something of the plea that came into his voice when he said, "Kate, please, I don't know how to express my wish to do this work alone, to not explain myself again and again, and to not seem rude. But I must ask the kind people of Fairhope to leave me to my woes and fortunes. I wish to be left alone here in Tolstoy Park." Henry clasped his hands behind his back and turned slightly away from Kate, following with his eyes the slope of the land as it fell gently away in all directions. "This hill . . ." Henry said, and paused, not certain how he would express to Kate what this place had come to mean to him, how his plan of solitary work was for him a near desperate need.

Kate quickly filled the silence. "Is what? Your sacred burial ground? And we of unclean spirit may not enter here?"

"Kate."

"No, I must say this." Anna Pearl placed her hand to her mother's lips as if to quiet the unrest in her mother's voice. Kate brushed her daughter's hand away, with the admonition to play on the pile of dirt. Anna Pearl obviously found no reproach in her mother's instructions, reacting as if she had been invited to a birthday party, quickly crawling up and over the dirt mound. "There is something in your eyes, Henry Stuart, that no one could have prepared me for. When I saw you here in the daylight the next afternoon following our bay crossing, I was unable to look away from your eyes."

Henry was astonished and embarrassed for Kate to speak like this, but if his reaction was written on his face, it offered no deterrent to Kate, who continued. "I have not seen such brilliant blue eyes since my late husband's sweet gaze." With the news that Kate was a widow, Henry had difficulty listening to the rest of what she said. "But more than their familiar color, there is something of exceeding under-standing and intelligence in your eyes." Kate went on. "If you were a preacher man, Henry Stuart, you would have a congregation as big as all outdoors. If you were a mesmerist, you would have access to the queen's court."

"Kate, this is all rather—"

"Rather what?" Kate stood up quickly. "An affront to your incon-gruous wish to be martyred in the town's imagination out here in Tolstoy Park? Did you know that Henry George, whose followers founded Fairhope, exchanged letters with Leo Tolstoy? It's gone all around town that a mysterious philosopher who is a friend to both Henry George and Leo Tolstoy has moved here. But what smart man refuses a doctor's help?"

Kate reached her bag, taking from it something the size of a book and wrapped in brown paper and string. "Here, this says it, which is of course why I did it." When Kate saw Henry's look of reluctance and confusion, she added, "It's a poem that I lettered and put into a frame for your wall. The poet has said all that I feel, Henry."

Henry was coming out of his stupor, drawn inexorably to know what poem. How like himself to make such a gesture: to fix the lens of poetry upon life's best and worst and inscrutable and insightful moments. He knew he would accept this gift from Kate. He asked her quietly, "Will you tell me what poem you have chosen?"

"Open it," she fairly commanded, and with some excitement, Henry did so. Underneath the glass and framed in carved wood over-laid with gold leaf were sixteen exquisitely lettered lines in flowing black ink. Henry read the title, "Stopping by Woods on a Snowy Evening," and the four quatrains. For him, two lines always made palpable the loneliness in those woods.

The only other sound's the sweep
Of easy wind and downy flake.

Henry knew that Kate was waiting for him to finish reading and wanted him to say something. When he did not, she said, "I find it irreconcilable the light I see in your eyes with your unwillingness to fend off for a little while the journey into those dark woods. Let the doctor help you, Henry. For God's sake, let Peter and others help you with this, this—" She pointed to the round hole.

Henry surprised himself by saying, "But the woods, Kate, are seductive. Heroes and thrill seekers are titillated and tempted at every turn to look beyond the veil. And albeit morbid, there is an almost universal fascination with the 'sweep of easy wind and downy flake.' The void is a vamp, dear Kate."

"Anna Pearl! Let's go." Kate brushed dirt from her hands, as though brushing away Henry's words. When Anna Pearl did not answer her mother's call, Kate scolded her and said to come immediately. "I will not allow my daughter in earshot of such empty-headed pedantic nonsense, Henry Stuart. I don't even know that Mr. Frost was writing about man's existential woe-is-me loneliness, but I know that there can be miles ahead of you traversed through beautiful country. Or you can wallow in your mud pie like a self-absorbed pig."

Kate snatched Anna Pearl's hand and strode off down the hill toward East Volanta Road, swinging the canvas bag in tight, jerking arcs. Henry watched her disappear through the pines, hardly making sense of all that had just occurred. Still, he found no enthusiasm for launching into a well-reasoned, carefully articulated defense of his mind in this matter of building his hut alone. A soft wind off Mobile Bay brought trills of laughter from royal terns and seagulls winging high above the darkening water, and Henry wondered if it was he they mocked as their voices floated away into the twilight.

TWENTY-SIX

Henry took Kate's calligraphy into his barn room and hung the frame on the wall near the window. He stood back, resting his hand on the cold iron of his round stovetop, and read the lines again and thought, what if this poet was indulging himself in a masterful dance with the felicities of language and intended no exhortation to plow on through life's deep snows.

In an obscure little book of poetry published perhaps two years earlier, something called *Harmonium* by Wallace Stevens, Henry had found a disturbing phrase. The poet had written, "Death is the mother of beauty; hence from her, alone, shall come fulfilment to our dreams. . . ." Molly had been dead just a year when he read that line in "Sunday Morning," and many nights in sleepless frustration Henry had reread the poem, hoping for some insight into its illumination of the truth of death. Only in these last several weeks, faced with the fact that it would be his eyes alone closing forever against the light of this world, did he think he'd made real progress. Kate couldn't possibly understand why he needed to work by himself on his hut. How could she or anyone look at this through his eyes? His own sons couldn't even reconcile his leaving Idaho.

Henry straightened the Robert Frost poem on its nail and went outside knowing, however, that the off-kilter complexities of human relationships could not be evened up as easily. He walked over to his water well and drew a bucket of fresh water and had a long, slow drink, deciding to spend the balance of the afternoon building five forms into which he would pour his concrete building blocks. So he sawed boards and nailed together small boxes eight inches wide, six inches high, and about two feet long. By the time he had nailed the last of the boxes together, the sun was setting. Henry lined up his boxes near the pile of sand, and tomorrow would experiment with a run of blocks. He knew the mixing recipe for mortar, and for a foundation, but Henry did not know the right proportions of sand and cement for blocks. He would try five slightly different batches and see which set strongest and hardest. For now he would join the birds and head off to roost in his barn, crawl onto his cot and wait for sleep to give him rest from thinking.

The weather turned cold in the night, and the next morning Henry was moving stiffly, tending his business with pain in his joints. His right knee was swollen, and his knuckles felt as if they had been cracked with a hammer and burned in hot oil. But his father had always counseled him that if you stop working when pain and illness come, then you grant those conditions power over human will. So he worked constructing a wooden form at the threshold to his round room, designing the threshold piece with a raised angle that would keep most of the rainwater falling on his stoop from running inside onto his floor. He mixed a small batch and poured the concrete into the threshold form.

He would let that set and harden for the rest of the day, since the drying would be retarded in the cold air. Tomorrow he would pour the stoop and build up around it a low retaining wall with pieces of broken bricks he had discovered in the hollow by Rock Creek on the north of his property. Steps to the stoop would come at the very end of construction, should his time last that long.

Peter had told Henry of a pre–Civil War brick foundry that had operated on Rock Creek. It was long gone now, but had left behind a scattering of tons of bricks and pieces of bricks free for the taking. Henry had gone there with a sack slung over his shoulder and easily found the site of the old foundry. Some of the huge foundation beams were still lying solidly on the ground at the creek's edge. And Rock Creek, in many ways, was to Henry prettier and even more private than Fly Creek to the south. The walk down the hill to Rock Creek took a few minutes longer, but the going was easier, with fewer trees and bushes and briars and vines. The path would easily accommodate a barrow, and should he discover more uses for the bricks in his building project, he could wheel them back up the hill in considerably greater numbers than could be borne in the sack across his back.

Henry tried a sand-and-cement mixture and poured it into his block forms, varying the ratio slightly from one to the next. In the afternoon when the first five had been drying for several hours, enough time, he discovered, to hold together when carefully broken free of the form, he mixed and poured five more blocks. Again he experimented with the ratio of sand and water and cement, writing down the ten different recipes, so to speak, assigning each different blend a number of its own. He sharpened a stick with his pocketknife and carved the identifying recipe numbers into the drying blocks. And Henry scratched into each block a date, using numbers three inches high. On the very first block he marked *11-11-25*.

By the time the shadows of evening began to stretch across his work area near the circle foundation, he had fifteen blocks numbered and drying on the grass at the circle's perimeter. He had at first thought to set the blocks to dry on planks laid out on the ground, but then decided he wanted the blocks to "communicate" with the moisture in the soil and find their own right drying time.

And Henry had found his own right way to silence the tongue in his head, set to wagging yesterday by Kate Anderson. Brother O'Neal's technique of *being here now* with the physical properties of the work at hand, of mindfulness of sights and sounds and weights and odors, of sensation of the air temperature, of the pain in his body and the stinging of the breath entering his lungs, each had prevented all but the briefest thoughts of Kate and Anna Pearl. It was also a means by which Henry was helped to overcome the considerable craving for his books and paper. His only writing would be letters to Will, and Thomas and Harvey, and those he would limit in number and length.

Henry cleaned his tools and put them away to finish the day and went to his room, shutting out the cold dusk. He lit a lantern and built a small fire and heated an iron kettle of water, mixing it with cold water poured from the pitcher on the washstand into the ceramic basin. He removed his clothes and took a bar of soap and a square of cloth and washed himself and put on clean long johns. His appetite was not keen, so he did not eat. He cast a longing look at his shelf of books, warped, wrinkled, and discolored from their dunking in last week's hurricane. Some were still damp. But he had made a pact, and he would honor his self-imposed moratorium on reading until work on the round hut was finished. Nor would he write in his journal. Brother O'Neal had argued: *Books and writing are agents for the accumulation of ideas and your minds are overfull.* Many of the Bible-quoting students at Mount Union had an intense dislike for Brother O'Neal. How dare he disparage their reading? But Henry's mind *was* overfull, and like corners in a house, squared off by all the notions in his head. Clutter tends to gather in corners. Fully focused work with one's hands rounds off the corners in one's mind.

So Henry sat bent forward, forearms resting on his thighs, his fingers laced, and the flickering lamplight played on the walls of his room, and he watched the shadows dance there until his eyes grew heavy with sleep. He smiled when he recalled his last meeting with Brother O'Neal, helping him sort and put away the shovels and tools in the shed near the plot of ground where the students had worked during the semester. "Your books, Henry Stuart," Brother O'Neal had said, swabbing sweat from his forehead with the back of his hairy hand, "are your most valuable possessions and your most powerful tools." Then he had smiled broadly and winked at Henry, whose own eyes must have been big as saucers.

When Henry lay on his side on his cot, his woolen blanket covering him to his chin, a thin headache stretching between his temples, the only sound was the snap and pop of the cast-iron belly of his stove cooling from the dying fire. Sleep rolled over Henry like fog over the marshes at the headwaters of Mobile Bay, and his mind was still and quiet as the silver mist under a windless sickle of moon and the arcing of the stars in Leo.

B y noon the next day Henry had poured his stoop and five more blocks. By nightfall, his stockpile of numbered and dated concrete building blocks was thirty-five. That night he answered letters from Thomas and Will. Harvey had not written in some time. In Will's letter, Henry explained that he was conducting a spiritual exercise of solitary work on his crazy concrete house. "The notion seems sheer folly," Henry wrote, "when I consider the weight of these blocks I'm pouring for the construction of my hut. What old man would resist help to raise an eighty-pound block into place on a growing wall? But so far I've declined the offer of help from the brother of my schoolteacher friend, Kate Anderson, and the man at the hardware store said some men in town wish a job with me. I can tell you, dear Will, and you will understand, I believe, I pray, that it is not a hut I'm building. In truth it is my soul I'm building. How can one man help another with that task?" Henry looked forward to Will's reply. He wrote to Will and Thomas that they should not expect more than one letter each few weeks while he worked on his hut.

In the morning the wind blew cold across the hillside, arousing a hiss from the tops of the wagging pines, but Tolstoy Park was blanketed with sunshine and Henry worked easily and with good strength in his arms and back and legs.

When darkness came on his fourth day of hard labor he slept soundly, but awakened to a fit of coughing and could not eat although he was hungry. A cup of tea made from steaming water out of his kettle helped him settle down and warmed his lungs as he swallowed. He sat by the fire crackling in his stove for a much longer time than usual; the sun was breaking the top of the tree line when he went out to work.

Henry would not, no matter how his body ached, refrain from working. He simply moved somewhat slower as he mortared down a course of bricks. He laid them following the circle of his stoop, from two o'clock on a watch face to ten o'clock, the two points where the stoop met the larger foundation slab. He felt a bit feverish, and the afterburn of the predawn coughing spell compromised his stamina. Nevertheless, he put down another course of bricks around the stoop's semicircle. The next courses he laid in two short sections on either side of a two-foot open space where, last thing, he would put in his steps. He was tired. Still, he refused to stop, working as nearly as he could at the good steady rhythm of the past few days.

Because I could not stop for death—he kindly stopped for me . . . Henry found comfort in Emily Dickinson's poem rendering death as a civil gentleman inviting her to join him in his carriage where centuries passed feeling shorter than a day. If there was all that eternity stretched out there, then neither would he stop these short moments to rush into forever's arms. He would lift a heavy concrete block and mortar it into place. Would that dark-cloaked and kindly gentleman atone for his rude interruption and stay awhile, lift a block into place on Henry's circular walls? Henry was becoming lonely in Tolstoy Park and wished for the company of a workmate. "Here, before we go," Henry said aloud with a smile, and pointing with his trowel, "heft that one just there and set it just here, Old Man."

"I reckon we ought to discuss a fair wage before I lay into this brute work!" Peter Stedman's voice behind him startled Henry, and he was perplexed at having been caught talking to thin air. But Peter believed Henry had been talking to him, for he asked, "How did you see me when I was behind you? And creeping," Peter barked, "to the degree that a man with a stump for a foot and leg can creep."

"Hello, Peter," Henry said, grinning, amused at the coincidence of Peter's appearance on the shoulder of his thought for company. "I was quite expecting you, though I wasn't sure on what day." Henry inquired how his healing after the snakebite had progressed. Peter's leg was swollen, his breeches leg slit to the knee, and he had on only a heavy sock. Peter said it had hurt like all get-out, and he had been quite addle-brained these last five days, but encouraged by the prospects of getting back to work in Tolstoy Park. Henry tensed, for this would be harder than talking to Kate. Peter had been so kind and helpful and generous to him reaching back to before the two men actually met. But Henry knew that, no matter, he could not reconsider his decision to work alone out here. He had already compromised Brother O'Neal's exhortation to silence.

"Tell me the plan, Henry," Peter said, wide-eyed and looking all about at the pile of test blocks and the excavated circular foundation. He lifted both palms. "What in God's name have you got going here?"

Henry was certain Leddie had told Peter that he was fighting the tuberculosis. He expected Peter was too uneasy about the subject to bring it up. Henry would speak of it himself at the right moment. "Well, my night spent in the cistern hiding from the storm caused me to believe a man could no better construct a dwelling than to have his walls go around in a circle. I supposed the birds must be on to something. So here you have my bird's nest."

"You've gone completely mad in Tolstoy Park," Peter said, shaking his head. "You are a bird all right—birdbrained, barefooted, and shaggy-whiskered, Henry Stuart. How in Sam Hill have you got all this done by yourself? When Leddie first told me you were building a little round house for yourself, I thought it was the snake juice talking. Now I see it with my own eyes and I still don't believe it." But then Peter became intrigued with Henry's project.

Henry told Peter how he was experimenting with different ratios of sand and water and cement, that today he would test the blocks and make many more examples of the strongest. But that he would pour in a day only the number of blocks he could lay the next, figuring maybe five or six, since the mornings would be spent barrowing sand from the beach a mile away down Volanta Road and across a piece of woods. He would mix and pour in the afternoon.

"My foundation is fourteen feet across, and I've decided I'll make it fourteen feet high to the topmost part of a domed roof."

"A domed roof?" Peter was incredulous. "Just how will you accomplish that engineering feat?"

Henry pointed to the circular retaining wall where his stoop would be. "As I laid those pieces of bricks there, it occurred to me that I could replicate that pattern in smaller and smaller concentric circles until the circles close in tight enough to pour a small vented cap for the very top." Henry was pleased with the modification to his original plan of having a roof of teepee'd poles like a hogan. Peter looked like someone had just described to him the workings of a spaceship to the moon. "There are thousands of bricks down the hill by Rock Creek, not a half mile there." He pointed with his trowel. "Then I shall plaster over the entire dome with a coat of mortar mix."

"So you'll have a door there," Peter said, indicating the stoop.

"The Navajo hogan, something like my hut, has its door facing east to greet the rising sun. I've given in to a bit of old-age melodrama, and look to the setting sun." Henry waited for Peter's reaction, but Peter let it go by.

"What about windows?" Peter asked.

"Six of them, spaced equidistant from the door. Seven openings should provide ample ventilation and cooling in your Alabama summers. With my windows hinged at the top and propped open at the bottom, I'll get a slight updraft of air off a fifty-eight-degree floor and out the roof through two vent openings. I should be quite comfortable. In the winter, of course, such as you have here, the floor at that constant temperature will be a kind of warmer."

"Amazing," said Peter. "Just amazing." Then Peter's face clouded and he shifted his stance, shuffling his feet where he stood. "I've got to ask you this, Henry. You're talking about living through summers and winters, but, well—Leddie tells me you are a mighty sick man, Henry. Has she got her story straight? Said you told her yourself."

"It's true, Peter. I am supposed to die."

"Well, hell, I reckon so! Me, too."

"My doctor in Idaho said a year or so, Peter," Henry said, stepping out of the foundation excavation and walking over to stand near his friend, but not facing him. They were more shoulder to shoulder, and looking away across the hill like two mariners watching the weather build off the coast. Henry fidgeted with the trowel as he talked. "Dr. Belton could not determine a date, but he was quite certain that the consumption from which I suffer will shorten my life, and do so sooner than later. Who knows how much of this work I'll finish? A count of months, not years, I'm afraid, Peter."

"Maybe he's a quack," said Peter.

"A similar sentiment was expressed by my youngest son," said Henry, a crooked smile upon his lips. "But the doctor let me read over his shoulder the pages from his medical texts. The symptoms present in a way consistent with his prognosis, Peter." Henry told Peter that on many days he felt strong, and Peter raised his eyebrows and tilted his head in the direction of Henry's big stack of blocks. "I guess so," Peter said. "I would not have figured a seminarian capable of the masonry trade."

Henry let that comment go by, thinking how if only Peter could know that his greatest sense of life's accomplishment was the variety of things that he could do, his self-reliance, and the labors that he was willing to attempt.

"Yes. If there was not this, this feeling in my body." Henry hesitated. "Something like a strong intuition of something present inside me that quite simply does not belong there. Even on days when I feel well and strong, that sensation is there. Unmistakably consistent. Like the sound of Gentry Creek that I could always hear from my study window in Nampa. Sometimes I would forget about it while reading or writing. Then I would hear it again." Henry stopped, and they stood in silence for half a minute. "But I've decided, Peter, I'll be there when death comes. But I won't be complicit beyond that. Only to be there. Does that make sense to you, Peter?"

"No." Peter shook his head. He bent and massaged his leg below the knee, wincing when he found tenderness and pain in the swelling. When he stood up, Henry continued speaking.

"I will not face away. I will not hide, nor shall I cringe. But I won't step one step to meet my death. I will be here working when death comes, or I will be sleeping when death comes." As Henry spoke, with the flat of his trowel, he slapped his thigh rhythmically for emphasis. "I will not have the sheets pulled over my face when death comes. I will not reconcile the possibilities of my future with death."

There was then another space of heavy silence. Peter dreaded what he was about to say. He was near nauseated with anxiety. "Does it make sense to you, Peter, that I can't let you help me with my work on this little house?"

"No, Henry, it does not."

"Can you look at this as my solitary walk into the desert, my forty days alone with God?"

"Henry, I hate to break it to you, but you are not Jesus."

"Nor do I plan to teach the world how to save itself," said Henry, anger riding to the surface of his emotions. If there was only love and only fear, then his fear was the loss of Peter, and his anger was therein born. He tossed down his trowel, the point driving deeply into the soil, like a knife-thrower's dagger. "But I can learn in solitude how to save myself."

"What's to save? You told me you were born a Baptist and baptized and went to seminary?" Peter turned to face Henry. "Not going to church won't count that strong against you."

"You misunderstand me, Peter," Henry answered brusquely. This was going as he worried it would. "A man has only to save himself from himself, from his own fear. Fear is the only hell we face." Henry spoke firmly, without equivocation, and his tone was authoritative enough to supplant, for the moment, argument from Peter. "If I tremble when death comes, then I have not met God in his likeness, and I will have still miles more to go before I sleep in eternity." Here was Henry's "Everybody Gets to Heaven" theology that Will would have recognized at once, but for which Peter would brook no quarter.

Peter said, "Well, this sounds like so much horse patucky to me, Henry." And then Peter clapped Henry on the back, which surprised Henry. "But you know what, old man? If I were in your shoes, I wouldn't rightly give a care what people to the left and people to the right thought it sounded like. So I'm going to leave you alone, friend. I'm not ten minutes from here. I'll come if you change your mind and need a hand. Or I'll come and sit a spell and shoot the breeze if you get lonesome. And I expect you'd want me to bring your loom when it comes. Right?"

"I would appreciate that, Peter." There was nothing more that Henry should say to Peter, and he sought in his friend's eyes only some confirmation that he understood. But Henry could not read Peter. He bent and retrieved his trowel from the soil.

"One more thing before I go, Henry. If it's a walk in the desert you want, you'll want to get your groceries and such at Miss Nellie's store in Montrose. She's not far from that little post office. And you might want to switch your mail to come there. You'd not encounter as many people up that way as in Fairhope." Peter tested his weight gingerly on the swollen leg and quickly rocked back to the other leg, then tried it again. Peter's face showed the pain he felt.

"Anyhow, Miss Nellie Graham has got about anything you'll want except hardware," Peter said. "She takes a liking to you, she'll get you those things, too. Order them in and have them to you in a few days or by the next week easy." Peter told Henry that while he would let him have his head in this, he would also take the liberty of checking in with him every week or so. "Leddie will pitch a hissy fit," Peter added, "if you turn down a meal delivered out here every now and then."

Henry could tell that Peter had misgivings and frustrations with him for fending off his offer of help. It seemed to Henry hypocritical for him to accept the offer of food. "You can please tell Leddie that cooking for me isn't necessary," Henry said.

"Nobody said it was," said Peter, and hobbled to his truck and drove away.

As the quiet descended once again on Tolstoy Park, Henry felt as he thought Parsifal must have felt when he finally found the Holy Grail. Something like, *so what?* Here was Henry at the point where his life in facing death could come to some deeper meaning. And what other chance would he have? Like Socrates again, if not now, when? On the other hand, humanity is a collective principle, so what is a life lived absent the company of others?

Henry had often debated back at Mount Union that the way of the monk was not fully functional. In the abbey a monk was shielded from the taxman and the landlord. He was saved the trouble of compromise with a wife, spared the doubt of raising a son. Is it not more meaningful to find peace in the storm rather than to hide out from the storm? Was he creating a monk's circular cell in Tolstoy Park? But what gain would it be to win the whole world's company and lose one's soul in the bargain?

Oddly, it seemed to be Kate's voice in his ear that would correct the path of his thoughts, for he was bound off in a direction that would surely have brought him past this very spot again and again. But Henry tried to shake off the image of Kate, tried to turn his ear away from her voice that chided, "But, brave knight, while you were hunting the Holy Grail your mother died and you didn't even attend her funeral." Was this holy order of solitude he was commanding the worst and most dangerous symptom of his consumption?

With these ten thousand questions, a throbbing crept into Henry's head, almost as if the tail-chasing of ideas brought a tightening of the vessels in his brain. He squeezed the handle of the trowel, raised it in front of his face. With his fingers and the heel of his palm Henry rubbed at the dried flecks of mortar there on the blade. Shifting his thoughts from the ephemeral and existential to the close at hand and practical brought a small measure of instant relief from his headache, or at least he forgot it to some degree.

With that little lifting of the fog in his head, Henry took quick advantage to gather headway in the manner he had come to trust: he listened and heard the angry caws of two crows down the hollow and the merry steam whistle of a bayboat wavering on the light wind and an insistent dog barking somewhere. He looked and saw his neat gray blocks in a stack and the crushed brown grass and a diligent beetle wrestling home its prize. He felt the cool soil on the soles of his feet and the wrinkle of his shirt cuffs at his wrist and the warm sun on his scalp. He closed his eyes and inhaled and smelled woodsmoke and pine needles, the mound of damp earth, the brackish bay water and her countless crabs and mullet.

He stood and remembered being taught by a Shoshoni woman in Idaho to chew one raisin slowly, and to swallow it even more slowly. Henry opened his eyes and lifted his arms, testing his shoulder joints. He walked to his three stacks of blocks, chose one and another, and pecked on them with his trowel blade. Some chipped and crumbled more easily than others. He thunked them with a length of stove wood. Finally he chose recipe number three. Those blocks were far less crumbly, and with only two days drying time, it took ten blows upon the center to break off a chunk.

Gathering some sense of ceremony Henry lifted the second of the number three blocks and walked around to the other side of the circle and placed it on the grass just outside the foundation. It was heavy, weighing around eighty pounds, and he had bent at the knees to put it down. It pressed into the soft grass. He moved ten more of his huge blocks, creating a stony ring around the grassy perimeter of the slab. He hopped down onto the concrete floor, and found himself experiencing a brief elation to think of this sunken concrete mandala as a floor.

In a washtub, Henry mixed sand and cement into a batch of wet mortar and dragged it to the edge of the circle. He laid down a bed of the mortar in a line four inches wide following the curve of the foundation for about six feet, enough to set three blocks. He lifted the first block, holding it against his midriff, and set it down atop the mortar bed. It settled down to within an inch of the floor, squeezing out mortar at its edges. Henry tapped the block with the blunt end of the trowel's wooden handle until it showed a half-inch mortar joint at the bottom. He took another block from its grassy spot and balanced it on its end on the floor while he "buttered" the end of the block with mortar. Then he set this one into place and tapped it down level with the first. He repeated the process with the third block and then scraped away the excess mortar with his trowel, adding the mortar back to the washtub.

In two hours he had set all of the first eleven blocks, the beginning of a wall that curved almost halfway around the floor. Henry measured and calculated it would take twenty-two of the full-size blocks and a make-up block sixteen inches long. Henry's veins pulsed with the adrenaline of excitement. A wall was taking shape. His hut was coming out of the ground! With a little sunlight left, and feeling energized from the afternoon's progress, he poured three more blocks and a make-up block in a new form he knocked together. He had enough sand left in the pile to finish this course and once more all the way around the circle, then he would have to make a wheelbarrow pilgrimage to the beach at the foot of Volanta Road. He would bring back two washtubs full each morning and that would be his day's supply, perhaps enough for four or five blocks.

As dusky dark was blown in on a freshening breeze and the temperature dropped steadily, so that Henry could see his breath like smoke before his face, he walked into the center of the floor of his hut and sat down cross-legged, straightening his spine and holding his head erect. He steadied his breathing and closed his eyes and offered a prayer of gratefulness, offering in prayer, as he believed he should offer, to remember in all things to yield his will to Universal Will. It was the only prayer Henry ever raised, and discernment of Universal Will his only and great confusion.

· T W E N T Y - E I G H T ·

On through Thanksgiving and Christmas and into spring Henry worked raising his walls. Some days he was sick. Other days he was strong. Most days were somewhere in between the extremes of wellness and illness, but always there was an echo of pain in his back and in his lungs. Always there was the ache of loneliness. Letters from Harvey and Thomas and Will had all but stopped. But he could not falter in his resolve to mine the treasures of solitude. Moses had gone up alone on Mount Sinai. A Sioux warrior goes alone into the sweat lodge. Alone, Henry would find himself and lose his uncertainty of spirit. Alone he would meet God. Everyone dies alone.

One day in early February he had been so weak that he could not arise to work, and as such things sometimes go, it was a day that Kate and Anna Pearl came for a visit, the first since Kate had left Tolstoy Park in anger. He could offer neither welcome nor resistance. He could not even speak, he was so weak. When she left, Henry cried. He thought she had gone away again in anger. But she soon returned with a crock of warm chicken soup. Anna Pearl stood right beside his cot and asked if she might call him Poppy Stuart.

When Henry had awakened feeling better the next day, he could only dimly recall the most general aspects of the visit from the Andersons. The details, things that might have been said, the passage of time while Kate and Anna Pearl were in his barn room, were all absent from his memory. Henry felt that was probably best, because his mind was unsettled about Kate and there was no need to layer on more confusion.

Henry's rate of progress in raising the walls had slowed considerably when he ran out of the sand he purchased from McKean's Hardware. But he had not even the slightest inclination to hurry toward completion. The twice-daily trips to fetch sand from the shore of the bay allowed him four blocks on most days. Some days he got five poured. What need was there to rush?

He was in his sixth calendar month of work, his sixth month without cracking open a book or writing a page in his journal or a poem, his sixth month of relative solitude. He had not had a letter from Idaho for two months. His withdrawal from reading and writing was manifested in discomfiting periods of free-floating anger. During those spells, he would sometimes curse a block if it lay askance when placed in its mortar bed, curse the water if it poured too freely from his bucket into the sand and cement mix. Henry cursed a stone in the path of his wheelbarrow that caused him to drop the handles and spill his load of sand. On those days there seemed to come an answering reaction from his tools and materials. A piece might break off a block along some invisible hairline crack. The water bucket would turn over and pour out its water when set down, the axle come loose on the barrow.

Henry remembered how Tolstoy advised, "Very often people are made proud by their control over their own desires, and by the force with which they master them. What a strange delusion!" Henry knew that when one thing is pushed down by force, another pops up with equal force. He saw that he had to apply great force to control himself and stay to this lonely course. For Henry had no desire that exceeded his yearning for Peter to come and work with him. Yes, he wanted so badly to read, but at this time his work was primary. If one of the points of fasting is to recognize the craving from which you have retreated, this fasting was working. Still, even without Peter's help his block walls grew upward. He would press on and hold this course. What was the biblical injunction? No man, once his hand is laid to the plow, is fit for Heaven if he looks back, and Heaven or no, he would not look back.

When he began the lintel course it was late April. The lintels were the longer blocks above the door and the six windows. Black Elk's reverence for the Six Grandfathers was imagined when he decided on a count of windows: North, South, East, and West, and Earth and Sky. Henry was careful to turn down and make visible the dates he had with precise lettering carved into the lintel blocks: *4-3-26*, above the door; *4-19-26, 4-21-26*, and *4-22-26* above the first three windows; *4-27-26, 4-28-26*, and *4-29-26* above the last three windows.

Above the lintel course, Henry ran two additional courses of blocks. In the first course above the lintels he put in a clay sleeve for the flue from his cast-iron stove. Above that, a single cap of a thinner but wider block that extended three inches outward past the plane of the exterior wall, creating a narrow overhang that pitched most rain flow away from the walls and windows. From this point on up to the top, where he would construct a vented roof cap, also of concrete, Henry would use salvaged half bricks for the concentric circles of the roof dome.

When, in the second week in May, Henry began mortaring the brick pieces into place, he had gone three weeks without a coughing spell, and had had only occasional mild headaches of short duration. He drank plenty of water and ate fruit and vegetables, such as he could acquire from Miss Nellie, and grain, and bread with tea. His muscles knotted and bulged when he lifted and mortared. Sweat flowed freely from his pores. He slept well at night and awakened each morning before dawn, never later than four, he guessed. He bathed weekly in a secluded pool at a bend in Rock Creek. Twice he had received brief letters from Kate, and a scribble from Anna Pearl at Christmas, but he had answered neither. Henry only worked and ate and slept, like a sleek raccoon or a furry opossum or a black-winged crow.

In the early spring from atop his hill in Tolstoy Park, he had watched an osprey flying with gathered twigs and branches. She seemed to Henry so authoritative and aloof. On a trek to the beach he discovered the tall dead cypress in which she had laced her sticks into a bulky three-foot-round nest. She had also used cornstalks and seaweed and driftwood. Henry sat on the sand and watched her mate fly in from the north with animal bones, ribs that shone like needle-sharp teeth through a mustache when he stuffed them in among all the brown debris. The female of the pair was bigger, with a wingspan of six feet. But the male was a fierce hunter, and Henry watched him fall into a dive and come up with a fat mullet twice in the hour. With each catch, when he was on the wing he would turn the fish head first into the wind to cut down on resistance. Henry thought the pair of ospreys beautiful and elegant, and he made pencil sketches of the birds in his journal. He was disappointed that they took not a whit's notice of him. His loneliness burned his chest.

Every now and then curious callers had come up the hill into Tolstoy Park. Henry felt no desire or obligation to greet strangers, for that could have invited questions and longer stays. He did not even lift his hand in greeting. A pair of teenage boys had sat for most of an afternoon, watching, not speaking even to each other, and wandered away in silence about the supper hour. But Peter did not come. He hoped Peter's absence was not abandonment of their friendship. If only, Henry thought, I can live to finish this hut, finish my semester of solitude, keep to my dreamquest, get back and find my friends still waiting at the campfire.

When Henry was setting up his ladder one morning in early May, an old man in dungaree overalls had come right up to the side of his hut and stood feet apart and arms crossed for twenty minutes. Henry kept working, spreading the legs of his ladder on the foundation floor so that from inside the hut he could work the circles of bricks in the dome. He had sewn broad straps onto a canvas bag to sling over his shoulder. He would take a dozen or more half bricks up the ladder in his bag, fishing out one brick at a time, mortaring it into place by intuition and dead reckoning, and retrieving the next. He completed a whole circle before moving to the next course of bricks, a much slower approach with frequent moves of his ladder, but it prevented the requirement for complex bracing. Henry laid into place an entire bag of bricks before the old man spoke.

"Never saw me such a damn thing," the old man said, scratching his head one minute and pawing his chest inside the bib of his overalls the next. "You missin' a chance there, feller, you don't sell tickets to this sideshow. What in tarnation's a Tolstoy Park anyhow? A hideout for loonies?"

He stood for a few more minutes until Henry had gone back up his ladder with another load of bricks, and, stopping, Henry said to the intruder, in words after the poet Frost, his eyes wildly alight, "Something there is that doesn't love a wall, that is sure and certain, but 'tis true also that good fences make good neighbors."

"You some kiney crazy old poet?" The old man harrumphed and added, "It beats a gobblin' goose, it does! Well, keep at it, son. You gone need a good hard place like that to hide in time folks gets wind of this beehive foolishness you buildin'. They'll all come to see and you'll want a damn fence. Be like trying to fence out ants, though. Everybody's goin' to come see the poet of Tolstoy Park. *Heeeee!*" The gnome-like old man screeched, an absurd cross between a hyena's laugh and a scream of pain.

"I suppose . . ." called Henry to his visitor, "I suppose I might sim-

ply ask uninvited persons to take their leave, and give me my peace."
Henry stared at the man, who seemed to take little notice that he'd
been asked obliquely to leave. The old man in fact drew closer and
looked intently at the brickwork Henry had accomplished. The man
was gnarled and bald with a hooked nose. The teeth still holding in
his gums were yellow and crooked. He was quite short and bent forward at the waist.

"I've got just the idea, for you, mister," said the old man, his
hand laid flat on his head. "Down in Fairhope we got us a sun-
worshipping nudie. Except for his bare butt, he's a right respectable
fellow. But I tell you this, nobody wants to see old Franklin's naked
behind. I don't know a soul who'd even think of dropping in on old
Franklin for fear he'll be skinning the wind in his yard."

"And you are proposing, I take it," said Henry, the corners of his
eyes and mouth working hard against a smile, "that I could publicize
about town that I am a *nudie,* and that would staunch the flow of curiosity seekers to my loony bin?"

"I can just about guarantee it," said the man. "I am just telling you
what I know about the dearth of callers at E. O. Franklin's place."

Henry nodded and placed his finger to his head, indicating a salutation, adding, "I will give the matter serious consideration." As
quickly as a shift in a breeze on the broad waters of Mobile Bay,
Henry became perturbed at the interruption and was about to plainly
ask the man to leave him to his work when the little man spoke
again.

"I 'spect you ought to think up something. Ain't much that'll stop
rubberneckin' fools from overrunning your place here." The man
lifted his palms. "Look at me, I'm here, and I am not what you call
curious. Though I did wait till I was right sure that consumption you
got ain't the catching kind. Doctor put it out around town not to
worry."

Henry could feel the heat rising up his neck. If anger could be
read on Henry's face, the old man was oblivious. "People said you
wasn't taking no help with your work on account of you didn't want
to get anybody else sick."

Henry came down the ladder, dropped his sack onto the ground, but held on to the trowel. He approached the man and could not relax the military tightness in his shoulders. Henry stopped only several steps in front of him.

"Get off my land, sir!" Henry said from low in his chest, aware even so of the futility of counting to ten or even to one hundred. "Take a message to the citizens of Fairhope that I wish no further intrusions into my privacy. Wag your tongues until they are loosened at the hinge. But do it out of my earshot. Now go at once!" Henry took a step closer to the man in overalls that Henry could now see were quite dirty. The trespasser hardly blinked, laying his hand back on the top of his head, some few long and stringy hairs above his large ears floating wildly about in the wind.

"Gen'ly I got better stuff to do," the little man croaked, "than go traipsin' about of an afternoon." Then he wagged a finger in the direction of Henry's hut. "Still and all, a round house is not a common sight." The old man put both hands in his baggy back pockets and without another word turned to go. Henry watched him hobble out of sight down the hill, saw the old codger looking back and shaking his head when he passed the sign that read "Tolstoy Park."

Henry turned and picked up his sack and went straightaway to load it with pieces of brick. He paused at the top of his ladder with the heavy sack on his shoulder and wished for an actual fence around his place.

But Henry directed his attention back to the work at hand, contemplated the structure of his hut so far. It was at that moment, from that high vantage point, that it occurred to Henry that the floor area was ample while bare, but would begin to close in quickly when furnishings were added, however few and small they might be. In a flash of inventive insight, he devised a plan for suspending his bed above the floor. He would go see Miss Nellie in the morning and ask her to order in for him some four-inch lengths of female three-quarter-inch threaded stock. He would embed them in mortar joints the very next course. He would screw eyebolts into them and tie a bed frame to them, and his bed would hang a good seven feet off the floor. He would crawl into bed of a night by way of a ladder affixed to the wall.

Henry beamed at his clever idea, quickly laid the bricks in his bag, and went down and got more bricks to finish this course. Then he would take a break for the balance of the afternoon and walk to the beach by his path along the banks of Rock Creek. He would take clean clothes and a bar of soap and get a bath on the way. Today, perhaps, now that he had made an important advance in the design of his own nest, the osprey pair would acknowledge him, their earthbound brother.

· TWENTY-NINE ·

In mid-September, his beehive-shaped brick roof nearly complete, his hut all but built, Henry looked down toward East Volanta Road and saw Peter driving up for the first time in several weeks. The truck stopped and Henry could see that Leddie was with Peter. She got out of the truck with a basket. Peter cried out, "Hey, old man, got some good home cooking here. Got cornbread, stewed squash, and purple hull peas, and two fat red ripe tomatoes picked from Leddie's own garden." Henry stopped work and washed up at the well. He had not yet said anything to his visitors, had only nodded as he walked past them. Henry was lost, did not know how to behave. He was like a sojourner who pines for home, but cannot find a comfortable place to sit in his own parlor when he returns. He was hungry, that much was easy, and Henry would not refuse Leddie's meal. He took the basket like a skittish kitten, looking at the ground as she handed it to him. He turned back the cloth covering and removed the food onto an upturned washtub. Henry could not think of anything to say to Peter and Leddie. He felt awkward with the Stedmans standing there side by side watching him. Nor did they seem to have anything to say, so Henry excused himself and went into the barn for a spoon and a fork. When he came back he asked them if they would join him. This seemed to break the tension and Peter and Leddie both answered at the same time that they had already eaten. Henry saw them exchange glances.

"Is there something wrong?" Henry asked, taking a seat cross-legged on the grass before the washtub table.

"It's none of our business really, but . . ." Leddie paused, seeming uncertain whether or not to continue. The look of doubt and the frown that came upon Peter's face lasted but briefly, then he blurted out, "Your loom's come, Henry. I got the message from the dock freight office in Mobile, and I had 'em send it over. It's on the back of my truck."

"Peter!" Leddie seemed clearly annoyed that whatever had been on her mind was diverted down this new pathway, and going now in a headlong rush. Henry leapt from sitting and shoved the rest of a piece of uneaten cornbread into his mouth.

"It's here?" Henry's words were muffled and barely discernible around his mouthful of food. Henry reached the flatbed of Peter's Model T truck before Peter. In a large wooden crate with slats and braces and corner supports was Henry's loom. Stenciled onto the side was: MOBILE, ALABAMA GM&O TERMINAL—HENRY JAMES STUART, C/O PETER STEDMAN, MONTROSE, ALABAMA—BALDWIN COUNTY. Thomas had obviously disassembled the H-loom down to its basic component parts for easier shipping, for the crate was not nearly as bulky as Henry had imagined in his fantasies of the loom's arrival. He had visualized two or three stevedores wrestling it onto the deck of a bayboat bound for the Eastern Shore, and that many on this side of the bay cursing and struggling to set it on the People's Railway wagon for the ride up the bluff to the cargo depot in Fairhope. This crate he and Peter would be able to handle with ease. He remembered that the loom was not especially heavy, having slid it across the floor of his shop in Nampa to reposition it for more light through a window.

"That's the most animated I've seen you since you stepped off the *Bay Queen*," said Peter, coming to stand beside Henry at the truck. When Peter laid a hand on Henry's shoulder, Henry braced slightly, as if remembering his resolve to be alone in Tolstoy Park, recognizing that his loom could, if he was not careful, become like a Trojan horse and allow social intrusion into the life he had jealously molded over the last several months.

"Yes, well, I am grateful that you have brought this to me. I shall pay you whatever you feel is fair for the effort and transport," Henry said to Peter, addressing him in a formal tone. Peter exploded, cursing aimlessly for a time while stomping around his truck.

"Leddie, get your basket and stuff. Leave the food. Soon's I get this box on the ground we're getting out of here." Peter marched to the back of his truck and let down the tailgate. Without even waiting for Henry he took hold of the corner of the crate and spun it toward himself with surprising strength. "Get ahold of one side, Stuart. Lead the way."

Henry realized as he lifted one side of the crate that Peter was terribly offended for his act of friendship and generosity to have been translated to something akin to mere drayage. Henry could hardly refrain from apology, but refused for the greater gain of probable estrangement from the Stedmans. They were almost the only ones to come onto his property anymore, though recently less and less. This effrontery to Peter, though it had not been intended, would, Henry believed, bring an end to their visits. When Henry stepped past Leddie, he could see that she too was incensed. She spat her words at Henry as she gathered her things from near the washtub. "Kate Anderson told me in town this morning that her daughter was ill and asked would I get word to you. The little girl is asking for you, *Poppy!* And I am furious to think that you'll not go to that child."

Henry was stung. He almost stumbled as he neared the barn, his words faltering. "Is she—"

"Oh, don't you worry, Henry Stuart," Leddie said, her words venomous. "Her uncle's a doctor. She'll get the right medicine. It is too bad there is not a prescription for compassion."

At the broad X-braced plank door to Henry's toolroom, Peter dropped his end of the crate. "Drag it inside yourself," Peter said. "Or leave it out here to rot. I don't give a damn, my friend." And in less time than Henry could assimilate all that had just happened, he was alone in Tolstoy Park. He could not pry his thoughts from the image of Anna Pearl outstretched on a bed, her arm lifted, her hand open to take his. And he would not be there. He would not go. It was just as well. He hardly knew the child.

• THIRTY •

The day's heat was full-born even at dawn; the soaking humidity had lain heavily like a wet towel on Henry's back, and since noon he had been feeling progressively worse. The weather turned bad, and a summer drizzle settled in underneath a sky that dropped low and became smooth gray. After working for the past two hours on the roof's uppermost courses of handmade blocks, he was beset by a tingling numbness and beginning to crave a dip in Rock Creek. He could barely trowel wet mortar on another piece of brick. But he would not quit early. And when at the shank of day he at last laid down his trowel and mortarboard and climbed down from the domed roof, his legs were shaking, and he could feel a fever climbing up his back from whatever mysterious places in the body's wet dark crevices such maladies hide out. He had for a week or more felt but denied the lurking signs of a strong relapse of the consumption. Now it felt turned loose like dogs set on a deer in plain sight. Henry did not even take time to gather clean clothes into his sack before setting out down the hill for his bathing pool.

By the time Henry picked up the sandy creek bank, tall gray-barked hardwoods were his companions. A dull thumb of blunt pain pressed down on him and made it hard for him to walk. A wind-swirled mist chased between these lonely trees, but no birds or animals were seen, no calls were heard. Thunder rumbled up in the darkening flat of clouds that hovered ever lower, the tremulous note rolling toward him from some starting point far off in the west toward Mobile.

It felt to Henry like his insides had been lacerated and like something molten was leaking into his chest and belly, so badly was he hurting. He stepped over a log and tripped, falling on his hands and knees, and began to vomit. A question knifed into his head. *What if this spell was psychosomatic, arising from disgust at his unwillingness to answer Anna Pearl's call, his refusal to respond to Kate's wish for him to see about her daughter?* With bile burning his throat and his mouth befouled and stinging, for the first time since removing his boots in front of Dr. Belton's office in Nampa, Henry began to think that he might die, not far off on some other page of the calendar, some other date, but on this day. Today, the eighteenth of August, 1926. At this hour of early evening. Barefooted, shirtless, with blood on his pants from where he had earlier dropped a brick while reaching it up above his head. It had fallen and slashed his forehead at his eyebrow. His beard almost a year long and cotton white. In Baldwin County, Alabama, with no next of kin to claim his body, he was dying.

Even in this maudlin moment of reckoning, Henry knew that this was as good as any day, these circumstances as right and fit as any for a man to lie down and die. What could make it better? Sunshine? It would not follow him into the darkness. Warmth? It would stay behind. Better health? The last rattling gasping breath would stop as certainly as one sweet and silent. Companions? They could not go with him. No, this was a day well suited for dying. So when Henry's foot caught in a bramble of honeysuckle vines and he fell and rolled into the shallow cold water, clear and quietly parting around his outstretched legs, his bare elbows pointing down into the mud, he did not attempt to rise. A fever burned in him, and his breath caught and pumped little plumes of heat before his face. The longer he lay in the water, the warmer it became. He ceased to shiver. A numbness and tingling flickered over his skin, his bare arms and neck, his bare feet, his hollow belly.

Odd, Henry thought, how desperately he wished now to be back up the hill in his barn room. There was no one there to welcome him in, no one was there with a meal set in anticipation of his return, no one would hold out to him a cup of steaming tea. There would be no one there to pull the woolen blanket around his chin when he lay stretched out cold on a hot summer day and trembled on his cot. And yet there was nowhere in the world that Henry would rather be. His legs would not take him, however, and his eyes would not find for him the way home to his Tolstoy Park.

Henry could almost hear the coursing of the blood in his veins, like turbulent water through a sluice, a needle of hot pain in his inner ear. His breathing seemed fixed in the topmost part of his lungs. His vision was blurry, his mouth was dry. He relaxed deeper into the slowly moving creek, so that by turning his head to the side, his mouth found water to drink, and he swallowed deeply, as if to put out a fire inside himself. A fallen length of pine tree situated at an angle into the water served as a rest for Henry's head when he had scooted over beside it. He drew up one knee, the stream curling underneath his buttocks and back, one leg down in the water. Something like sleep was dragging him into darkness fringed with a low-cycle humming sound that Henry could also feel. The chill was going out of him, and he grew warmer, and he could feel it as a source point, almost as if he were lying on a hearth in front of a cabin's blazing fire.

Henry suddenly believed that when he closed his eyes he would die, and he resisted that submission. His eyelids fluttered, and his mind became suddenly illuminated with a silvery image of his mother, down on one knee in the grass and holding him hard to her breast and smiling for a camera. They were in a park in London that floated indistinct in Henry's memory. It was a pleasant place, but Henry was frowning and had his tiny arm stiff and extended, pushing away from her. And still she smiled for the camera, one of those tall-legged heavy-clicking black-cloth-covered affairs waiting for a flash of powder in its tray. Henry blinked and the image disappeared.

Into his head came a voice, perhaps his own when a child, "Now I lay me down to sleep, I pray dear God—" And then there was the camera again, now in front of him on its spindly legs, a triangular tray of gunpowder poised above it, held aloft by an unseen hand. A brilliant and blinding explosion of light that was at once from the hallucinated camera and likewise from the bunched heavy-weather clouds above the wooded hollow through which Rock Creek found its way to Mobile Bay. The light's latter source was, however, verified when such a boom of thunder echoed down the hollow that it struck Henry where he lay on the ground as a physical jolt. And where Henry had been near to giving in and closing his eyes, they were now open and alive and focused. The tall hickory trees, tightly balled bright green shells dotting the branches, small punctuation marks distributed randomly across a luminous gray page of sky. They reached their heavy limbs upward. Inviting. Who?

It was then that Henry spied the huge speckled osprey drifting down on wings spread so wide and broad they looked unnatural. And when the bird of prey curled its mighty wings into scoops against the wind for slowing its flight, and extended its razored talons toward a fat horizontal hickory limb, its frightening beauty arrested Henry as no art or music or poem or paragraph ever had, as no landscape or beautiful woman ever had, as nothing ever could.

Alight on the branch, its wings now tightly tucked, the fish hawk cocked its head and burned its fierce yellow eye into Henry's pupils, parting its carnivorous beak slightly. The osprey offered itself to Henry as a terrifying threat and a golden promise, and taken on either proposition later, it now, in this very present moment, was a defiant protector. And as if he were being drawn nearer to his mother's sweet soft lullaby, Henry knew suddenly that he could sleep right where he lay and that he would not die awash in this creek, nor would he die in the January winter or in the kite-flying spring or in the wet tropical summer. Henry James Stuart was not a name to be carved on an Alabama tombstone, and he now knew that. He did not know where his passing would be written. As Paul had written to the Thessalonians, "Now, brothers, about times and dates we do not need to write to you, for you know very well that the day of the Lord will come like a thief in the night." So let it be written to him, let his thief come in the night unannounced, blotting out any doctor's mistaken writ.

THIRTY-ONE

For an hour, in soothing silent darkness Henry slept, his body half in and half out of Rock Creek. Had he come loose and floated on the current like a silver-bottomed poplar leaf, he would have meandered around curves and bends and down short straight passages underneath a heavy canopy of tree branches until in a mile he reached the narrowly bounded shoreline within Bayou Volanta. Bobbing and eddying for just a short time, still drifting westerly, Henry would meet the low waves of Mobile Bay. He would drift southward on the clear green water for another mile or so and bump into the black-tarred pilings of Fairhope's big pier, algae and spiky white barnacles marking high tides. He would awaken there to the afternoon's burble of voices, the *Bay Queen* and the *Eastern Shore* unloading passengers and cargo, perhaps for a late summer's week-end stay at the bay house. But wait. The stevedores were struggling with a plywood crate. It was marked for delivery to Henry James Stuart, c/o Peter Stedman. Henry jumped in his sleep as though disturbed by a loud noise. Peter and Leddie came down the wharf and Kate behind them. They walked up to the crate, where a doorknob had appeared. Leddie grasped it and turned it, and the side of the crate opened like a door on hinges. Inside was an empty cradle and Kate screamed and Henry awakened as if doused in ice water.

His body was prone in the water, his head pillowed on a fallen tree. He willed his body to rise, but it would not, as if it demanded a full accounting of the circumstances of this moment before entering into complicity.

The sky lay confused and roiling; tearing through the treetops and the drizzle was a blinding sidewise spray. It was cooler by degrees, with night coming on in a wind that screamed down the hollow. In an instant Henry knew a monstrous hurricane was clawing up Mobile Bay, its deceitful eye surveying this inland shoreline of Baldwin County. Storm or no, Henry was bent on finding Kate and Anna Pearl. Furious intention injected his bones and body. There was no chill shaking Henry, no ache in his head. He sat erect. He remembered the broad-winged osprey and looked up to the tree limb where it had perched before he slipped into the void. It was not there, and Henry wondered if it had ever been there. That he could not know.

High up on the hillsides sloping up and away from the creek where the wind had an open shot, huge trees were twisting and falling, popping like small cannon shots when they gave up to the ripping wind. Henry had no idea how to negotiate his way through the woods in such a maelstrom. Tolstoy had suggested that the lonelier a person is, the more clearly he can hear the voice of God. He had been swaddled in loneliness these many months of masonry work and had heard nothing. Nor did he hear him now when he needed direction. He felt like Moses when God said he was not allowed to look upon the face of Yahweh and instead turned his "hinder parts" to him. But if Henry felt God's backside to him and was being subjected to His sepulchral silence, he heard loudly and clearly his own inner voice: "This storm is a killer. Get up and go help someone." This was a call, a command, to abandon self-absorption. This was an entreaty to regard his fellows above himself.

He felt strong and clearheaded. Not so much as a trace or an echo remained in him of the symptoms he had experienced in the schoolyard and at the doctor's office and on that dreamlike day in the barn room. Nor were there present the shadow pains, as Henry had come to think of them, that followed him and lay at the ready to crawl up his body and into his organs and bones and tissue and flare into some fit of coughing or some cloak of pain to be endured for an unknown short or long time.

Henry marveled at the certitude and energy he felt sitting half in and half out of a creek that was rising and swirling more fiercely by the minute. Henry knew that he would not fail to reach Kate's house. Something of a mysterious nature had been worked upon him, and short of medical knowledge that did not exist, he could not conclude a single thing about it. And he would not spoil what he had been given by carving into it intellectually, even later when these winds would be working their way north into Pennsylvania. When your breakfast plate is set with warm fresh bread, you do not try to divide it into its flour and eggs and butter and milk.

Like a boxer about to enter the center of the ring, Henry drew a nervous breath and stood upright into a wind pushing with such force it seemed like a moving wall, solid and vertical. Creek water drained down his body and clothes. He felt wrapped in new skin, buttressed by new muscles, framed with new bones. His mind was cleared, as if the insistent wind had blown away a chalky shroud. With a moment's mental preparation—he would make his way in great haste to Peter and Leddie and they would tell him how to find Kate's home—he bowed his back and his bare toes found purchase in the muddy bank and he scampered up it with the sure footing of a squirrel. Limbs and branches stung his cheeks and scratched his arms, and once his whiskers became entangled in a spiny huckleberry switch that snatched his head around with such force that it tripped him and he fell hard on his side. Last week he would have kept still where he lay, waiting for the pain to subside. On this day he rolled onto his knees and got up right away, moving fast toward where Rock Creek met Bayview Road. Peter's house sat overlooking the bay on the bluff north of the creek. He needed to get there before dark.

As Henry ran, he could not prevent his thoughts from also chasing an intense curiosity about the worth of a life and why one would be given back to someone set and ready to lose it. He was as certain of his reprieve from death as he was certain that day would dawn tomorrow. "With gratitude overflowing, I accept this," he said aloud to the wind. Henry believed his recovery was an arcane endorsement of the building of his round hut. And this storm, a trumpeting from Gabriel to go out of Tolstoy Park and see what he could do to help other people. Though he did not hear a word, no hurricane-induced auditory hallucinations to trick him, he felt there was something expected of him in exchange for a life extended. In what seemed to Henry counterpoint to the buffeting rain and wind and gathering dark, he extended his finger toward the sky and said, "I shall this say only once: if this is an ark I have built, I must remind the architect that it will not float." Then his comic mood, crashing like a wave on the shore, was followed by a sighing retreat. The great ocean into which he fell back seemed mocking and ominous, and each wave meeting him was a curled lip, a sneering taunt, each echoing the others: "You, Henry Stuart? There is not enough in a thousand of you to repay a life given back."

Saul of Tarsus, on the road to Damascus in the time after the death of Jesus, was interrupted in his mission to seek out and slaughter the crucified teacher's disciples. He was struck blind. In three days he was given, literally, new sight. He became Paul and began to preach the teachings of Jesus, rallying new churches far and wide. If this strange remission of tuberculosis was for Henry his Damascus-road experience, what would he see differently?

With his body seemingly renewed in strength and health, perhaps his mind was the weakness that he would have to fight. Henry would silence this chorus. He must not gain madness for the loss of consumption. The book, he believed, would always be open on what had happened to him, lines on the page slowly written, dubious faith in designs unknown.

Henry reached the roadside shoulder and grabbed a thin sapling and pulled himself against the wind onto Bayview Road. He crossed the wooden bridge over Rock Creek, brown water boiling down the middle of the stream, carrying all manner of woody debris. Henry saw a dead skunk floating under the bridge, and a raccoon shooting downstream clutching a piece of rotten log, so waterlogged it was hardly buoyant. The raccoon's eyes clearly telegraphed its terror. Up the road on the left he could see the corner of the Stedman house. No lights burned in the windows. Henry hoped they were home. Otherwise, he did not know where to find Kate and Anna Pearl.

He thought of the poem he had composed in his mind on a day soon after her bedside visit to him. He would commit it to paper now that he could abandon his moratorium on writing. He would offer it to her as a gift in kind for her hand-lettered Robert Frost poem. It was bleak and pessimistic, but he would tender it as an apology for his behavior. He would title it "The Navigator," an ironic testament to his loss of way:

> *The oar, the rudder, and the sail*
> *Are at once to no avail*
> *When white near blue with green I have seen;*
> *Yet near, then far, now cold.*
> *At the fancy of my soul, or the shadowbox.*
> *Perhaps a loud ticking and a tock.*
> *Their anchor chain, your key and my lock, wasted*
> *When the shore, it seems, lies broken on my dreams,*
> *And the compass points adrift.*

Henry's clothes were soaked through and dripping water and the rain blew into his eyes. He fell into long strides, bounding up the hill. Twice on his way he thought a shadow had crossed him and looked up, but saw nothing. Henry's heart pumped strongly, and his lungs filled deeply with cool damp air. No resistance arose in him for the uphill hike. His eyesight was keen and his hearing sharp and he felt enlivened and animated as though bathed in adrenaline. With even greater conviction he knew there had been, he knew without doubt, some strange and remarkable rejuvenation in his body. The moaning of the hurricane winds made his incongruous calm well-being all the more real.

His fellow divinity students at Mount Union College had argued whether such cases as they had studied were true miracles, or a spontaneous healing with an obscure medical explanation. The effect by either designation was the same. The former, however, was the product of divine intervention, the latter a realized physiological possibility. Henry must force himself to let that debate go, for ultimately, he knew, a debate was all it could amount to. There could be no knowledge, only hypothesis. There could be no answer, for there was as yet only a dimly formed question.

THIRTY-TWO

Henry flew up onto the Stedman front porch, the wide veranda so slippery from the rain it might as well not have had a roof. Huge ferns spilling from hanging pots slung about on their short chains. Henry banged on the door, and almost immediately Peter stood there, his eyes wide, a lantern bail looped over his fingers, and a yellow flame arced over the wick behind the smoky glass globe.

"Henry, what the—"

"Peter." Henry held his friend's eyes in an intense gaze, and almost immediately all that had gone wrong between the two of them was made right. "Peter, I am sorry. Leddie and you are—"

"Okay, none of your sermons, preacher." Peter let go the door and reached to catch Henry's shoulder. Henry stepped back a step. "This is going to be one whale of a blow before she tracks out of here in the morning. Get inside, man!"

"No, Peter. Tell me how to find Kate and Anna Pearl."

"Are you insane?"

"Quite. And still I require directions."

Leddie appeared at Peter's side. Henry was about to repeat his apology, but Leddie raised her hand in a gesture that told Henry nothing more need be spoken on the matter. Her eyes conveyed annoyance. "You cannot go there tonight, Henry," she said evenly. "Driving is out of the question and walking's no safer. She would certainly be at her brother-in-law's clinic and that's a half hour's—"

"Of course!" Henry said, and grabbed for Peter's hand that held open the door. The door was banged back by the wind, but Peter left Leddie to take care of it while he shook his friend's hand.

"I'd go with you, Henry." Peter cut his eyes at his wife. Leddie shook her head, her face a mixture of puzzlement and bemused resignation. Henry knew that Peter would love the adventure and would not hesitate to strike out with him, but he would not leave his wife.

"Stay in the road, old man. At least that way in the open you might possibly see the milk cow before it falls on your head." To emphasize his humorous comment, Peter put his fist to Henry's shoulder and gave a small shove. Becoming suddenly serious, he said to Henry, "Take this lantern. I've got four more fired up in there. This one's got a full tank of coal oil and a good wind-tight globe. She'll lay with you the whole way."

"Tomorrow," Henry said. "We will get right to work on repair and cleanup operations here at your place."

"This house has seen hurricanes before. We'll start in Tolstoy Park."

"My hut is all but complete. Only the very top is open and it is in no danger at all. The barn, well . . ." Henry began backing away, the lantern in his hand. "We will do what we must." Henry pointed to the ferns tossing around. "You should take those down. They might wind up at my place."

"Here, Leddie. Hang on to the door!" Peter said. "Let me grab these plants down." There were four hanging pots, one between each set of columns across the front of the porch. Peter flipped up his collar and dashed to the left. Henry took care of the two ferns to the right, setting them by the door for Peter and Leddie to take inside. And with that, Henry ran down the steps and jogged across the yard, the wind at his back now, blowing him along at a good clip. When he reached the road he stayed to its middle and set a long-legged quick-striding pace that he believed he could sustain for the whole of the muddy walk before him. His toes curled to grip the road surface, crushed oyster shells and sand that would have torn a tender foot to shreds. The lantern was not that much help with visibility, but Henry was pleased to accept its loan from Peter. The wind whistled and moaned in his ear and Henry kept his head down, finding the little pool of light around his feet quite a comfort in the nightmarish barrage of sound and flickering lightning.

As he struggled on through the inhospitable night, Henry found himself arriving once again on the periphery of the echoing question: What is it to say a life has been given back? Death still expects us, will not be denied, is waiting at the end of some measure of time. What then is gained in the reprieve? All the existential hand-wringing over life's meaning probably comes to rest in whether or not we think that life ends at death. And if it does not, then surely this now must be a stage of development. A baby lies in the crib, toddles, walks, and grows up to run. But then there is the backsliding to an old man's crib.

If there is a way off the wheel, it is accomplished in the advancement of the mind. Henry knew of some dying eighty-year-olds whose intellect retained the resilience of youth. Tennyson at fourscore years had written a poem he himself placed on a par with any he had composed, and indeed, insisted that it evermore afterwards be included in all anthologies of his work, placed at the very end. Ah, those exquisite lines:

> And may there be no moaning of the bar,
> When I put out to sea,

And there it was, Lord Tennyson hoping to keep his mortal eyesight on some immortal plane so he could see his Pilot face to face. And Henry found something off-center about it, the more he wobbled the notion around in his head, to the degree he was able to focus his mind, beset as he was by such a beastly wind. He believed it was more likely the Buddhist monks had it right: Keep your eye on what's for supper. Henry had read that the highest position of reverence in certain Buddhist monasteries was that of the *tenzo,* who was essentially the gardener and cook, who delighted in preparing and serving meals to others.

A tree snapped and crashed to the ground somewhere very nearby, just up ahead off to the left of the road, and whipped Henry's attention back to the present moment. He crossed Fly Creek bridge, approaching the rise and curve in Bayview Road that merged into the straight-arrow due south run of Section Street. Henry could scarcely believe the transformation of the water flow underneath the bridge. The waist-deep stream that he had forded barefoot so many times was now shown by the near steady tremble of lightning to be a growling, hissing torrent, a sluice of such intensity that any living thing caught in its sucking rage would drown in half a minute.

Henry did not know how long he had been traveling through the dark and stormy night, but it seemed to him soon enough that he reached the driveway he recognized as leading to the Anderson clinic. Where Peter's house had been dark and quiet when he had approached it, Dr. Anderson's place was lit up like a desert valley town in the evening of a black velvet night. There were three automobiles and two trucks parked out front. Rain struck Henry with such force that he had to squeeze shut his eyes at intervals, instead of blinking, to clear his vision, and what he was seeing made his pulse quicken. People were hurt, he was sure. The unbelievable sound of the wind had acquired the tonal range and complexity of a voice, and it mocked the ear with an evil, slow, and mirthful *hunnnh, hunnnh, hunnnh,* like an idiot's laugh. Henry picked up the pace, then ran full out. When he crossed the porch to the door, he did not even knock, such was the anticipation of activity inside the doctor's office.

The first person he saw was Kate, who saw him at the same time. She blinked back tears that welled up immediately. With both hands she was pressing a folded bandage to the neck of an obese woman whose eyes were shut, her mouth moving as though she were speaking, and Henry guessed she was praying. There were perhaps half a dozen other patients in this front reception area. Most were bleeding from various cuts. One woman was sitting beside a man, leaning her head against his chest. Her face was swollen, with one eye bruised black and puffy. She made mewling kittenish sounds and wept with shaking shoulders. Through a side door, in an anteroom, more people were sitting in chairs waiting. This hurricane had its teeth bared, growling and snapping as it came, sinking fangs into all foolish enough to engage it in the open.

"Anna Pearl?" Henry fairly shouted, exposing the first fringes of panic that had lain benignly in a far corner of his mind as he had slogged along, negotiating his way to this place.

It was Ida who answered and said, "That baby's fine." Ida was wrapping gauze around the forearm of a thin man who remained standing while his wound was being attended. He reminded Henry of a great blue heron, his neck curved forward, his eyes holding no expression. Blood soaked through each ply of the gauze until Ida had wrapped it so thickly that the pressure was great enough to block the flow. Ida turned back to Henry and tilted her head down to look over her glasses at him. "She sho kep' askin' fer Pappy Stuart while her belly all tore up with the flu."

"Poppy," corrected Kate. "Not Pappy. Poppy."

"Same difference, ain't it?" Ida offered no disguise for her indignation. "He didn't show up, now did he?"

"Ida!" Kate scolded, a dark frown upon her face.

"Sorry, ma'am." Ida secured her bandage on the skinny man's arm and asked him to take a seat in the waiting area, saying that Dr. Anderson was treating an emergency and would see him as soon as he could. The man said nothing and walked straight past Henry and out the door. When he opened the heavy varnished six-panel door, the intrusion of wind noise into the room was so great that all were forced to look out at the wild night. He looked back briefly at Ida and nodded his thanks, then stepped outside, closing the door on the racket. "Folks gone do what folks gone do," Ida said, shaking her head.

Kate lifted the pudgy hand of the woman she was helping and placed her dainty but chubby fingers on the bandage, applying pressure with her own hand until she was satisfied the lady would keep the bandage tightly pressed to the wound on her neck, then gave the woman's fingers a pat and left her side to walk over to Henry. Without hesitation, she put her hands on Henry's shoulders, looking into his face, then pulled him into an embrace, laying the side of her face against his chest. Henry put his hands lightly on Kate's shoulders.

"Kate, I am sorry that I have been so, well . . . wrong in my judgment," he said softly.

"I'm not at all sure that you have been, Henry," she said, fixing him with a contemplative gaze. Henry wondered whether she and Leddie and Peter were so easily forgiving because they thought he was dying. She stepped back and looked him up and down. He was sopping wet. Kate's cheek glistened from his wet shirt. Her hair was disheveled and there were spots of blood on the front of her dress, but her hazel eyes were bright. "How in the world did you manage to get here in this storm without getting your head knocked off?"

"I dodged about a bit and kept moving," Henry said. "The hurricane that greeted me soon after my arrival seems like kite-flying weather compared to this."

"Oh, this place has been heaving since I got here with Anna Pearl. So many people have been hurt. My brother was afraid for Anna Pearl and me and brought us here just before dark. She's in the back with my niece and her mother."

Looking around at the injured people, Henry believed there were none whom he might help, and satisfied of this, he wished to see Anna Pearl. "May I say hello to her?"

"Of course. She's just down the hall. I'll walk back there with you. I need to get that man over there something for pain. I'm sure he's broken his wrist and Douglas will need to put on a cast. He's hurting terribly." Kate pointed out a middle-aged man wearing a stiff-collared white shirt with the sleeves rolled up. He had a huge walrus mustache and wore wire-rimmed spectacles. Kate said as they walked down the hall she believed him to be a lawyer from Mobile, and that he owned a bay house near the Stedmans. Her small talk seemed nervous.

"Well, you're lucky, Henry," Kate said. "Being outside is how most people are getting hurt." She shook her head. "I guess maybe they just have to step outside for a quick look, then something flying through the air or falling down knocks them silly. It's quite a mess. And I fear the worst is still to come."

"Will the houses stand?" Henry asked. Here he was now, making small talk.

"Oh, most will, don't you think?"

"Trees will crush some."

"And people living in the low-lying areas south toward Point Clear are at a higher risk, Douglas says. If we get a storm tide, some-one will surely drown."

"It must also be very dangerous for the local fishermen," Henry said. Kate became alarmed and asked did he not think most would be weather-wise and safe in the harbor before the storm came into the bay. "Oh, I expect so. But then most will not leave their boats un-guarded. The lines will need tending as the tide rises. And I cannot think of a worse place to greet a hurricane than at dockside," Henry said, talking as they walked down the hall.

"And your brother?" Henry asked. "Is he not here?"

"Wesley decided to stay with his store."

"Hmm," said Henry. Kate was opening a door into a small room at the back of the house.

"Hmm, indeed," said Kate. "That's not what Wesley's wife said! Sometimes he is quite reckless." Kate opened the door wide. There was Anna Pearl sitting cross-legged on the floor with another little girl about the same age. An assortment of small toy dolls and crayons and paper and a toy cup and saucer were on the floor between the girls, but neither attended in the slightest to the toys. They were clearly frightened. Anna Pearl's cousin had been crying. Her eyes were red and swollen. Kate's sister-in-law sat on a three-legged stool drawn up close to the children.

"Henry, this is my brother's wife, Claudia Ingle. This is her daughter, Maria." Claudia was quite shy, made only the briefest nod, and herself became wide-eyed as the wind kicked against the shutters that were tightly closed and latched over the one tall window in the room. Anna Pearl leaped to her feet. "Poppy! You did not forget us!" She stopped suddenly. "But why did you not come when my tummy was sick?"

"I was not able, dear child," Henry said, going down on one knee. Anna Pearl came near him but made no move to go to him, nor did Henry extend his arms. "My tummy was sick too. But now, it seems, we are both better. Is that right?" Anna Pearl put her hand on her midsection as if to determine an answer.

"Yes," she said. "I am all better now."

"And you, Henry? How are you feeling?" Kate asked, concern drawing her eyebrows together.

"I am all better, too," he said. "Though I cannot quite—"

Ida's yell for help from the front of the clinic started both little girls crying immediately. Claudia dropped onto her knees and grabbed them and hugged them to her. Anna Pearl struggled to reach for her mother. "Stay here, honey! Mother has to go help." Henry was already at the door and Kate flew past him, pushing loose strands of hair behind her ears as though they would hinder whatever she would have to do up front. Henry, as he was closing the door to the small room, spoke firmly to the three huddled in the middle of the floor. "You will be okay here. Kate will be back as soon as she can."

"But, Poppy!" Anna Pearl was wide-eyed and crying around her fists as she bit down on the knuckles of both hands. Henry put a finger to his lips. "You are safe," he said softly. "This is a good place for hiding. The storm cannot find you here. I promise." Henry shut the door gently and rushed to the front, where he found Dr. Anderson on his knees over a young man's limp body stretched out on the floor just inside the front door. A broad puddle of water had drained onto the floor around the body from clothes and boots that were soaked and muddy. Henry could see that the young man's face was pale blue, his lips purple. The doctor was trying to resuscitate him with artificial respiration. Kate and Ida and the doctor's wife were greeting two men in shining wet yellow slickers who were dragging in another body, also drenched and flaccid, the head lolling to the side.

One of the two men was babbling about how a fishing dock had given way down at the foot of the hill in Bayou Volanta at the mouth of Fly Creek. "Waves just kept crashin' and crashin' and one minute they's four men bent to their lines and the next they're all in the water. Just all in the water. Water comin' from everywhere. Boards twistin' and nails pullin' out like they's made of straw. Two men still in the water. We got these two. Two more still down there. Somebody might could get 'em."

Henry knew that the road down to the fishing docks was only a few hundred yards south on Section Street and he knew that he would go. "Can either of you men drive us back there?" Henry asked.

"Naw, or we'd be on our way back. Truck drownded out on the road back there."

"Henry!" said Kate. "You can't go out in this, in your—"

But Henry was already pushing past the man at the door and for the second time in less than an hour found himself slogging through a night unlike any he had ever lived through. He had known men in Idaho home from the war in Europe who spoke of the terror of nights in muddy trenches with blinding bombs lighting up the sky and twisted bodies strewn about like cast-off clothing. This was not that, for tomorrow this hurricane would wobble farther inland, becoming tornadoes and monsoon rains, devolving finally into thunderstorms and showers. In three days, here, the sun would burn dry the soggy ground and summer breezes tease white cotton curtains at open windows.

But tonight it was for Henry like a war zone. There was danger and threat in all that he saw, heard, and felt as he ran down Section Street toward West Volanta Road. At least two men were fighting for their lives in a slosh of nasty brown water curling and hissing its way toward Mobile Bay. Or they were drowned and some mother or brother or father or wife was left to sing funeral songs on an August afternoon.

Henry's feet slipped out from underneath him twice as he went careering headlong down West Volanta to the town fishing docks. The first time he fell hard on his backside, and the second he plowed nose first into half a foot of yellow-brown slop. Lightning overhead was a continuous flicker and helped him find his way. It must have taken twenty minutes to reach the bottom of the hill, and Henry feared no one could have fought a raging creek for that long.

He was right. Several men were gathered around a body being dragged back from the collapsed dock. One lion-headed fisherman, a thick broad-backed man six and a half feet tall, was still bound about the waist with a heavy hawser, the long end of it dragging behind him. Henry guessed the man had gone into the creek attempting to rescue the drowning man, had got hold of him, but was pulled back to the dock hanging on to a dead man. The big man himself, who was crying like a child, confirmed the story. But his crying was not like the panic-flooded hysteria of Anna Pearl and her cousin; he wept like a boy who'd lost a puppy. "When I got him by the shirt he was alive, boys," the fisherman said, talking loudly to be heard above the wind. "Alive like us! Weak but fighting. Then he went limber on me. I guess I lost him."

And the big fisherman bowed his head and sat down on the ground while two of his friends gathered the drowned man up by the legs and arms and carted him to an automobile. Henry reckoned they would take him to the doctor's office. Other men surrounded the fisherman, attempting to console him. Henry asked one of the men, one who had kept an eye on Henry as he approached the group, "What of the other man? Some at the clinic said two men were still in the creek."

"He got tangled in a big cypress that came down on him. It twisted him under, then him and the whole tree sailed out into the bay. He's lost. The rest are accounted for." The man speaking then asked, "You come down from the clinic?"

"I left there a half hour ago coming here," Henry said, wiping at the rain slashing his face.

"What do you know about Robbie and Jeff?" The fellow was almost shouting. "The ones that got hauled up there. They make it?"

"I cannot say," Henry answered. "They were both unconscious when I saw them."

"Well, those fellows will be taking Albert's body up to Doc Anderson. No need in you staying out in this mess, mister. You ought to ride on back with them." The man turned to join the group of men at the side of the fisherman. He turned back and shouted to Henry, "Nothing you could've done, mister. But thanks is due just the same." Then he merged with the half-dozen fishermen who tightened into a knot around the big man, untied the rope from his waist, and escorted him into the block bait house, where a swinging lantern lighted their sadness.

THIRTY-THREE

The Alabama Gulf Coast—and Florida's and Mississippi's—gave up two hundred forty-three souls to the hurricane. The newspapers carried the stories for several days as the body count grew, harking back to the big storm of 1906, when more than 350 people died. This hurricane clocked wind speeds of a hundred fifty miles per hour, and the storm surge running before those winds climbed to fifteen feet above high tide.

Henry and Peter worked together with saws and axes and a rope and a block and tackle to cut away fallen trees and hoist them off houses; with hammers and nails they nailed back siding and roofs. They loaded and unloaded Peter's truck, carting in supplies and carting out debris. They went from one neighbor to the next in Montrose and Fairhope, calling at more than thirty homes, serving as volunteers in an army of Eastern Shore residents for nine solid days from pewter dawn to lantern-lit night.

Many women worked alongside the men and Henry saw Kate frequently. Twice they took their meals together away from the others, and when she asked how his health was, he told her that his consumption was in remission. When she asked him how he knew, he said that he knew in the same manner as a woman knows she is with child. He told her about a conversation he had had with Peter about the autonomic responses of the body to a big storm. How animals go crazy and human illness is provoked or subsides as a consequence, perhaps, of the atmospheric pressure on the water content of cells and tissue—in the brain, the organs, the blood, the fluids coursing throughout the endocrine system, indeed the marrow of our bones. "Maybe," Henry said, "the hurricane pumped something loose in me that forced the disease to retreat."

Kate said that she was completely puzzled and fascinated by the likelihood of such a far-fetched explanation. Henry told Kate that he too was perplexed and his curiosity was stirred, but that he did not have time to "tend the pot just now." Kate laughed aloud at Henry's turn of phrase and said, "Oh, Henry, you are such a silly and delightful man. If I were twenty years older, I would be knocking on your door and bringing you my best baking, tempting you to a lonely-heart solution for a widow and a widower."

There it was. Just like that, an amorphous notion of a special bond with Kate, and Henry's undeniable warm affection for her was suddenly held up to a light. And something about Kate's free-spirited admission of interest in him, delivered in the same laughing breath alongside a notice of caveat for their near three decades' difference in age, was at once a kind of relief and at the same time a kind of hurt. Though Molly was dead, he still harbored a devotion to her memory that would be awkward at best to reconcile in a relationship with another woman. Molly's ghost was surely with Henry, and he found the haunting pleasant and a comfort. He believed he required nothing more than sincere and close friendship with women such as Leddie and Kate. On the other hand, Kate's company animated and enlivened Henry unlike that of anyone else since Molly's passing. And Henry actually found himself fending off mild jealousy and experiencing some distress when Kate flirted with a young lawyer from Point Clear. The interest the two of them exhibited in each other followed a rapidly rising level, and Henry's emotions were put to the test when Kate came to him and asked him, "What is love like, Henry?"

She sat down on the stump beside him where he and another man had just sawn down a broken pine tree. When Henry cautioned Kate about pine sap getting on her clothes, she waved her hand. Henry's fellow sawyer shouldered the long crosscut saw and said he would go see whether somebody else could take a turn with him. "So's the two of ye can talk a spell," he said with a wink.

"It seems so awfully complicated and not at all straightforward," opined Kate. "I love you one way, Henry, and I loved my husband another, and I feel something unlike either for Walter. What is love like, Henry?"

There was not an iota of hesitation as Henry sat on another stump and began to quote a poem he had written for Thomas when Thomas had asked the same question of his father after his first serious relationship went on the rocks. "Love is like itself: undivided, outside of time; the sense behind the seasons, whose circle needs no line." Then he paused to say what it was he was reciting. "I wrote this for my son. May I continue?"

"Yes, please do, Henry," Kate said, sounding a bit desperate. "Start again. Will you?"

Henry recited:

> Love is like itself:
> Undivided, outside of time;
> The sense behind the seasons,
> Whose circle needs no line.
>
> Love is like itself:
> Counting one as all;
> Each moment in eternity
> Rising upon the fall.
>
> Love is like itself:
> Without degrees or kind;
> Unknown to "this, not that"
> And seeing all while blind.
>
> Love is like itself:
> True without polarity;
> A pointer on its balance staff
> In perfect singularity.

Kate sat and stared at Henry as though a bird had flown down and sat upon his head. Henry looked at the ground, at his dirty toes, and found tears brimming in his eyes. He would not look up when she got up and came to stand in front of him. She bent and kissed his bare head, a light touch of her lips like the caress of soft wind from a bird's wing taking flight. Kate walked away, and Henry did not move for a long time until the sawyer found his way back and said, "They'll break yer heart in a thousand pieces, won't they, old man?"

"They will," Henry said. "And it is indeed a rare privilege. Once is not enough."

Henry set off ahead of his workmate, leaving him to ponder. But soon the two were pulling the crosscut to free a twisted and heavy live oak branch from where it lay propped against a corner post on a back porch. Sawdust flew and the oak limb groaned as pressure on it was released so it could be shoved away from the house. Henry and the others worked relentlessly, and the weather in the aftermath of the killer storm held good, and repairs and cleanup got done in fair time. After a good lunch with all the crew on the ninth day of work, everyone went home. Some were missing family or friends. Everybody knew somebody who had died.

Henry went to Tolstoy Park and poured blocks to finish his domed roof. Peter offered to come and help, but Henry asked him if he would forgive him his desire to complete his hut alone. Peter said he would not begrudge him the little home stretch run, but that he would be around next week to help set up Henry's loom. Henry smiled and thanked Peter and set off with the sun at his back, going barefoot through the woods along Rock Creek toward his hilltop hut.

Henry had been in the company of so many people, working so constantly, going to bed so tired and sleeping so soundly in Peter's guest cottage, that he had taken only brief and shallow dips into the pool of unknowing that formed in the hollow of what happened to him the day the hurricane struck. His and Peter's conjecture about autonomic reaction was as deep as he had gone. In the solitude of Tolstoy Park he would plunge more deeply there and try to come up with answers. But he would move with extreme care, exercise due diligence, and refuse to hurry. He could trust work. His mind was a trickster. Henry would therefore work a great deal and think a small amount.

Henry was excited to get back to his work site. His last blocks were still in the wooden forms, poured the day before the hurricane hit. The carefully lettered date, *9-17-26,* numbers two inches high, looked up at him from each hard-dried concrete block in the row. He bent to the task of breaking them free of their forms, stacked them near the perimeter wall of the hut, and mixed concrete to pour the final blocks. He sharpened a new stick and precisely carved *9-27-26* into the tops of each new block. When this batch of blocks was set and ready, he would lay the final course in the roof of his hut. It would be round and odd and neighbors would come from miles around just to see it. It would be finished. It would be his home.

By the time Henry had cleaned and put away his tools, collected clean clothes in his sack, and walked to the creek for his evening bath, the scattered cloud cover of the morning and midday had coalesced into a woolly rug of mottled gray.

"The sky is the daily bread of the eye," said Emerson, and another day's worth of proof was being prepared overhead, a moment of theatrical presentation for the sun. The carpet of clouds broke away from the western horizon, as though being tugged rather quickly to the east, and the sun, furious with its brief afternoon's confinement above the clouds, dropped into the slit between earth and sky and set afire the bottoms of the clouds. The contrast of the spectacular warm oranges and yellows and reds blazing across cool blues and blacks and grays at the base of the uneven and scattered cumulus was unlike anything Henry had ever seen. And he had been surveying wondrous skyscapes for half a century.

Henry stopped walking. At a clearing in the trees on a hillside just above Rock Creek, he swung his sack around off his shoulder and dropped it beside him on the brown leaves. He took a wide-footed stance and clasped his hands behind his back, his eyes lifted toward the sky to the west, where the colors were swirling and changing by the moment. The cloud bottoms seemed stirred in a volcanic pool of light. In reverent awe Henry said in a full voice, "Such beauty!" And in swift response a voice inside Henry's head said, "I have worlds far lovelier than this."

Henry was overcome with something like fear. An electrical charge spun around his body, spiraling upward from his feet and into his legs and groin and belly, into his chest and neck, his face tingling like it had been slapped on both cheeks. His hair felt alive and wind-blown though no breeze stirred. And Henry dropped to his knees, his bare toes finding the damp soil underneath the pine needles and leaves. He remained in that position for a quarter hour, unmoving, breathing slowly and deeply, watching the sky. Listening. The silent edge of dusk spread across the hillside. The fire in the clouds went out without complaint and they continued to slide back to the east. A luminous dark blue and purple void appeared to welcome the first star.

Henry stood up bemusedly and gathered his sack of clothes and found his way to a deep pool at a bend in the creek. He disallowed any speculation, employing the technique of mindfulness he had practiced for years. He felt beneath his feet the cool sandy loam sloping toward the stream, then the shocking chill of the water. He heard an owl hooting. He smelled the damp woods and the bar of soap in his hand. The water began to feel warmer as Henry remained in it, submerging himself to his neck, rinsing away the soap. More stars came out. Skittering animal sounds whispered from the forest floor.

Henry went below the surface of the creek with his eyes open to the liquid dark. He looked into the emptiness until his lungs insisted on a breath. Henry rose out of the water and waded to the bank. He opened the sack and took out his dry clothes. He used the sack to dry his body, then stuffed his damp, dirty clothes into the bottom of it, and twisted a knot in its top. Tomorrow he would come back to this same spot in the creek to wash his clothes.

He got dressed and took up his sack and walked home through the night woods with Tolstoy's counsel whispered to his listening ear: "There is simplicity of nature, and there is simplicity of wisdom. Both of them evoke love and respect." And Henry, with loving respect for things he did not know, for unknown worlds in a grain of sand, for what Cicero had called the unseen force that guides the body and guides the world, yielded to an that unknown and unknowable force. He would rest in this pool of unknowing for as long a time as he was granted.

Henry sat on a huge driftwood log, its entire bottom side settled deeply into the brown sand. For the last two months, since the hurricane had paid its angry visit, there had been more logs and planks and seaweed thrown up onto the beach by the waves, more debris awash in the tidal drift all up and down the shoreline. The old dead cypress that had held the osprey nest was blown down, and Henry missed its stark silhouette against the sky, but more, he wondered about the pair of ospreys. He knew that a bad storm would claim among its victims birds and animals, and he could only hope to find them returning someday soon to this stretch of shoreline.

Henry watched the sunset across the bay, as had become his near-daily habit. He would make the late-afternoon walk from Tolstoy Park, following Rock Creek to the bay, and sit in a seat-like crook of his driftwood log while the evening sky above the western horizon became a flood of colors. Pigments of autumn, the fiery golds and rusty oranges, were brighter than the pinks and mauves, and the display against the shaded blue background seemed a watercolorist's celebration of the coming October night, though Leddie said her art teacher had told her never to try to paint a sunset. It is an affront to God, the teacher said, and the artist is doomed to fail. The most skillfully accomplished piece is an embarrassment when compared to its subject.

A long year of masonry toiling was done. Yesterday he had mortared into place the last of the blocks, finishing the three steps down onto the circular dugout stoop in front of his door. Henry had worked the blocks from the lowest step to the highest step, then come back and put in the middle step. The date scratched into the middle and last step was *10-26-26.* A work that had begun in earnest on the ninth of November last year had taken Henry three hundred and fifty-one days to finish. And somehow in the digging and lifting and mortaring, a life had been reclaimed.

It was interesting to Henry in retrospect, how the storm on the one hand had rent the fabric of so many lives, and on the other had helped him to mend his own. Struggling to make his way through the explosion of debris and torn and fallen trees, hearing voices on that surreal morning after as they had called out for help from unknown places, he had heard Tolstoy's words as clearly as if he had been reading. A man facing death, Tolstoy had written, if he knows that death is coming in one minute, in that one minute he will wish to console an abused person or help an old person stand up or put a bandage on someone's injury or repair a toy for a child.

For Henry, the loss of concern for himself was like a summer day's cool drink of water. Not until the hurricane had he fully apprehended the heaviness of keeping his privacy, defending his solitude, looking away from a hand held out in his direction. But now he could see, in an honest look back at the last fifty years, that he had often been stingy with his time and affection. His sons had certainly not had all of him they'd wanted. But now he better felt the intimate connection between all people, and most important, a common mortality. If there was any way at all to feel deep inside some kinship with the strangers who constitute humanity, it would have to be accomplished in the singular knowledge that we will all die. Above Mobile Bay's distant western shoreline, only one sun was setting for the many who watched. All who joined Henry in viewing the close of this day would also join him across the great divide. All would sing their hero's death song, then make that brave leap.

But for now, this hero's home was on a knoll in Tolstoy Park on this side of the great divide. And a goodly walk distant from the beach for a mortal man with some stiffness in his bones. But the walk would limber him up after his sit-down with the sunset. He rose up from his log, scanned the sky for the fish hawks, as he did each day, and brushed the sand from the seat of his trousers. It would be full dark by the time he got to his round house. Henry had come to relish this trek home in the shank of the evening as his eyes adjusted to the closing darkness. He had read that an owl needs only the light from a single small candle to survey three acres of ground on a moonless night. It was quite amazing to Henry how well he could see the path before him through the woods and along the bank of Rock Creek, a mile and a half to home.

Walking up the hill from the creek bank, Henry was greeted each return trip from the bay with the fact that his barn had been shattered. The curtain walls and roof system had been bashed to the ground. The vicious wind, in cahoots with whatever thing it could lift up and spew before it, had left Henry a tangled pile of construction materials. One interior wall had been left oddly unharmed, probably because the roof and rafters had closed down over that wall like a mother hen's wings over her biddies. What had been kept safe in this enfoldment were Henry's chest of clothes and his cot on the interior side of the wall, and on the exterior side, his precious loom in its crate. And a long-ago product of that loom: Molly's kitchen rug.

Henry had moved the cot, his big oak and tin chest, and whatever other of his scattered belongings he could locate over an acre immediately into his round hut. He had hung Molly's rug on the concave concrete block wall by securing it to a long dowel he whittled from a sapling and suspended with wire. Henry stood back. "There now, dear Molly. No puff of wind will reach inside this little pig's house of stone to ever again blow down our rug."

When Peter had come around to help him move and put together the loom, he argued good-naturedly with Henry about his decision to set it up in the center of the floor of his hut.

"I figure you must get lots of enjoyment out of your weaving, but in the middle of this little round room? We can build you a little workshop in no time flat, Henry. You've got planks and framing and roofing," said Peter. "This thing is going to get in the way sooner or later." Peter had shaken his head, his hands on his hips, as they finished building a frame for his hanging bed and had stretched and tacked onto it a canvas hammock of sorts. "You believe you've had a remission of the consumption. I believe it too if you say so, and I hope you outlive me, friend. So leave some damn room in this hut of yours for a man to come home and relax! Some room for a friend"—he hooked his thumb at his chest—"to come and sit a spell."

"We'll sit outside," Henry had answered. "And that way there will be less chance someone will stay overlong." Though Henry laughed when he said this, there was a measure of comfort in the prospect of shorter rather than longer visits. Nurturing his interest in the neighbors' affairs didn't have to mean an obsessive interest that precluded his solitary pursuits, especially now that he was back to his reading and writing. He had actually purchased a new typewriter from Wesley Ingle's store. Henry had to order in what he wanted, a Remington, and Kate had brought it out to him when it came. The loom was about five feet wide and four feet deep on the floor, so that there was five feet behind it to the wall, and on that wall Henry had put a narrow desk made from pine boards salvaged from the barn. Peter had given him a small straight-back mahogany chair that fit the space and desk perfectly. With room for a glass oil lamp and the typewriter and a book, it was a good writing desk and suited the space ideally.

To the left of the door into the hut, Henry put the small potbelly cast-iron stove, which the hurricane winds had turned over and rolled underneath a pile of boards and tin roofing. Most of the flue pipes were completely lost or crushed. But Henry ordered more from McKean's, and Carl Black brought them to him.

Henry had constructed a tall, skinny bookcase to stand against one of the narrow wall spaces between windows. Next to the bookcase, Henry set the chest with his clothing. Above the chest, he had books on some single shelves bracketed to the curving concrete wall. Whitman's *Leaves of Grass* stood right beside his tiny volumes, Maksim Gorky's *Reminiscences of Leo Nikolaevich Tolstoy,* Tolstoy's *What Men Live By* and *What Shall It Profit a Man?* And his Russian-language edition of Tolstoy's *Calendar of Wisdom.* These four books had been in the chest and had not been ruined in the storm. Henry would acquire other books in due course. For now, he could go an entire day thinking on the brief daily readings from the *Calendar of Wisdom.*

And in fact, as his footfalls drew nearer his darkened hut, he was lost in starlit contemplation of a passage he'd read there last week, where a Chinese proverb wondered how it is that a bird knows her purpose in life, how and when and where to build her nest, but man, who is the wisest among all creatures, doesn't know his purpose in life. Perhaps in the morning when Henry arose, he would type the passage into a letter to Will, and put some thoughts in response. Henry had written to Harvey, Thomas, Will, and Jeremiah to share his elation that he'd finished his year-long work on his hut, that it had withstood a brutal hurricane, and that he was well, and, he believed, healed.

His news of good health raised the question, Would he be returning to Idaho? At first he'd thought to avoid the matter, but it would be so conspicuous left out. *Alabama is my home now,* Henry had written. *Tolstoy Park is my ten acres of Heaven. I will not be coming back to Nampa. I know that ten days' round-trip travel and even a short visit here would take half a month and therefore how unlikely it is that I will see you again. But I can only hope that you will someday partake of the adventure and come to Dixie. My love for you is undiminished and I hold you as close as my breathing.* All had, sooner or later, answered his letters. Only Thomas was angry with him. And that was what Henry had expected. In their responses, Will had been philosophical, Jeremiah had been frivolous and gay, Harvey matter-of-fact, and Thomas boiling mad. And, Henry knew, if any one of the four of them should ever pass across the threshold of his round hut, it would be Thomas. There was the irony and the sadness, for Henry believed none from Nampa would ever come to Fairhope. And for that loss, sorrow would be the offbeat of his heart as long as he would live.

But the onbeat would be crimson joy. Henry had never in his life slept so well, awakened so animated. His toes wiggled and his bare feet tingled and his white whiskers blew in the Gulf breezes and he was happy in Tolstoy Park. He drew up the hill, almost home, and emotion rolled over him when he was greeted by the sight of his domed hut. These nighttime returns from the beach made Henry believe he knew how the cavemen felt when they came home to their dwellings of an evening. No king loved his castle more. And it occurred to Henry on this cool autumn night, as he crossed the threshold and went inside, as he crossed over the tiny footprints of Anna

Pearl, as he stepped beside his loom with a nearly finished rug hanging on its crossbar, as he carefully mounted his seven-foot ladder so he could crawl up and over into his ceiling-hung hammock, that the very construction of this simple round and domed hut of his might be the single most subliminal act in which he would ever participate. His purpose in life was here laid out round like a bird's nest, and raised up in concrete.

· T H I R T Y - F O U R ·

Somewhere over Kate's turkey for Thanksgiving and Leddie's ham at Christmas, Henry decided he would give up eating meat. Tolstoy had said that it might be written in some books that it's not a sin to kill and eat animals, but he himself called it a rude and terrible habit. Kate's new friend the lawyer had made quite a show of telling all gathered for the repast how the very tender, moist, and juicy turkey breast upon which he carved was only the day before proudly feathered and strutting over his barnyard.

The writer Henry Beston had called for a wiser and more mystical concept of animals, Henry remembered, in his *The Outermost House:* "We patronize them for their incompleteness, for their tragic fate of having taken form so far below ourselves. And therein we err, and greatly err. . . . They are not brethren, they are not underlings; they are other nations caught with ourselves in the net of life and time, fellow prisoners of the splendour and travail of the earth."

Henry did not even think about dragging out a soapbox from which to proclaim himself a vegetarian; instead he quietly went back to work constructing, this time using the leftover blocks that had failed to meet his standards for use in the hut, what amounted to long, waist-high planters, four of them that would stretch away over the grassy slope behind his hut like so many store counters. In these he would grow his food; everything that he wished to eat that could be grown in this subtropical climate, he would plant and grow and harvest—or he would not eat it.

In cold January, Kate and Peter came to work with Henry on the planter boxes. Henry was that day awake before dawn. It was now an automatic event that he was up before four A.M. each day and setting fire in his cookstove for warmth and tea and his breakfast mush. Not two hours of daylight had gone by when his helpers had come to Tolstoy Park. Anna Pearl came too, and Leddie to watch the child. Henry was glad Kate's lawyer friend had not come to help. Peter brought his leather work gloves and mortared and set blocks. Kate—and Leddie to the degree that she could spare the distraction from the busy Anna Pearl—barrowed over from behind the barn site shovelfuls of dark, rich topsoil enriched by cow manure in years gone by. These wheelbarrow-loads of dirt went straight into the three-foot-tall, nine-foot-long planter boxes.

"The strawberries alone you'll be able to raise and harvest from these boxes," said Kate, "make the work worthwhile. For my wages, I expect an early boxful for making preserves." Her remark was the signal for them to stop for a simple lunch of fruit and bread and cheese with sweet chilled water from the well for drinking. The sun was bright and chased the frosty nip from the air, so that Anna Pearl and Leddie were outside the hut more than inside, where they had been reading and drawing and fiddling some with the loom. Henry knew the little girl would find it a magical contraption.

By late afternoon they had all put in a good day's work building the planter boxes, finishing two of them and getting a third well started. They had even raked through the soil removing twigs and roots. His helpers were packing up to leave when Kate said, "Oh, I almost forgot, Henry." And she drew from her wide dress pocket a newspaper clipping, saying, "Mrs. Johnson has secured Mr. Clarence Darrow, that lawyer we spoke of when I first met you, for a lecture date at our school. Isn't that something!" She held the clipping before her, teasing. "And guess what he has chosen for a lecture topic?" Kate was beaming.

"Railroads in America?" Henry answered with a smile, lifting his shoulders in a questioning way.

"Well, of course not! Just you look here, sir!" she said and handed over the newspaper item scissored from the *Fairhope Courier* of January 28, 1927. Henry took it, and Kate's surprise was given away immediately in the headline CLARENCE DARROW TO LECTURE ON TOLSTOY. The piece read: "Clarence Darrow, noted lawyer of Chicago, will given a lecture on 'Tolstoy' at Fairhope on Sunday, Feb. 20. It will be given at Comings Hall on the Organic School campus and a small admission will be charged to benefit the Marietta Johnson School of Organic Education. It is hoped that those from outside of Fairhope who are interested will take this occasion to drive over. There are plenty of seats and a few seats in the front will be reserved."

Henry could not conceal his interest and enthusiasm. "Well, I'll surely be in attendance. This is most exciting news, Kate. This rabble-rousing lawyer just might be a fellow Tolstoyan."

"It gets even better, Henry," Kate said. Leddie was smiling and shaking her head at the piecemeal way in which Kate was letting out her information about the lawyer's visit. "One of those reserved seats down front is for you."

"Does that make you happy, Poppy Stuart?" Anna Pearl was leaning into the center of things, tapping Henry on his shirtfront to ensure his attention as she asked her question. "Mother said it would make you very happy to see the man come to talk."

"And your mother could not be more right." Henry paused, and looked toward his hut in contemplation. "Perhaps I'll finish that small rug for Mr. Darrow. I believe I can do that in three weeks." Henry began immediately to consider the task. He became lost in the daydream of creating this gift of a little rug. He had been thinking more and more that his Navajo-style rugs could provide an income upon which he might live here in Tolstoy Park when the money he had brought with him was spent, since he would never recant the bequest of his property and money. His weaving would most certainly become his livelihood, such little as he would need, but it was a deeper joy by far for Henry to make a gift of one of his rugs.

The first rug off his loom had been one for Anna Pearl, all the fibers colored with plant and vegetable dyes that approximated the palette of the Mobile Bay sunsets that so awed him. For boiling into dye on his stovetop, Henry had gone out gathering wild holly berries for a dusty rose color, juniper berries for a dull blue; brown onions gave him a rich gold, and he got a dirty yellow from goldenrod. Lichens taken from scrub oak yielded a soft red. Prickly pear cactus was transformed in the steaming pot to a royal purple dye. Henry was even able to get some summer wild blackberries put up by Leddie in a Mason jar, though the sugar in the preserves gave the lavender a deeper grayish tone.

All the shades of Henry's plant dyes were a soft pastel obtained from a dyeing process he had been using for years in Nampa that was quite simple. He would boil the wool in alum salts and water as a mordant, and then dip it directly into the dye bath. In the fall and spring, Henry would usually leave the wool in the dye bath for several days in the sun's heat for darker and steadier colors. At other times Henry would reheat the wool in the dye bath to just short of boiling, let it cool for one night, and rinse the fibers the following day. For Anna Pearl's rug, small sunflowers he had taken in hot August before the awful storm struck provided the dominant hue, a warm caramel that, along with the pattern colors, he obtained by the first method.

Anna Pearl didn't have to speak a word of what the rug meant to her. When he unfolded it and held it out in front of himself to present to her, her eyes sang their delight. Her tiny fingers had ruffled the fringe across the bottom. In order to allow the good spirits of the blanket to escape and permit him to make another good blanket, Henry had given the blanket a border with a spirit trail, a *chinde*, a single-color strand from the interior leading to the outside by way of the fringe.

When Henry wove a rug, he wove from the depths of his spirit and from the fullness of his heart, and with the careful eye of a focused mind. Directly across from his upright loom, at eye level on the concave wall of the hut, Henry had lettered a small sign for his own inspiration: BY THEIR WORKS YE SHALL KNOW THEM. And more, it was a reminder that his remission from consumption, he believed, had come as a consequence of work with his hands. Work for him was the very stuff of salvation and healing. For that reason, from now on, whenever he should write or type or spell the word *work* for any reason, he would use an uppercase W at its beginning.

Kate and Leddie began gathering things in preparation to leave. Peter knocked dirt from his gloves onto his trouser legs. "I have worked like a mule here today, old man. I'll not leave this hill without a promise of strawberries for your underpaid, underfed workers," he said, feigning irritation. "That old lawyer's not the only one deserving of a prize here. If it's Tolstoy that gets you generous, I'll tell you stories about the Roosky and do a Cossack dance at the same time."

"Oh, Peter," said Leddie. "You are such a humorist." She began fumbling in the canvas bag hanging from a strap on her shoulder. She had brought in it certain supplies for Anna Pearl's comfort and entertainment during the day. "I have something for you too, Henry." Henry thought how this blind groping inside a bag was peculiarly the way of a woman, while he believed a man would put the bag down and either open it and peer inside to spot his prey, or dump out the contents and in that manner get what he was after. A woman's way, however, Henry admitted, worked well enough.

Leddie produced a small booklet with leather covers and a string tie. She handed it to Henry, blinking her eyes and looking away. Henry discovered the book was filled with blank pages, and he at first thought it was a journal and thanked her for such, but Leddie corrected him, saying, "It's a guest register. I thought perhaps you'd like to ask those who come to visit you to sign their names and put down a date. It would be a nice keepsake, I think," she said a bit shyly, for she looked as though she thought Henry did not share her wish to keep such a record. But Henry quickly thanked her.

"I have now a person or two each day who wanders up my little hill to have a look at my home. And, I'm beginning to think, to have a look at me." Henry knew that he must present quite an interesting sight, barefooted, with baggy pants and suspenders, white hair and beard. Even Henry was surprised at how very bright white his hair had become. Both his beard and the hair on his head were quite thin and silky, so the wind moved them into whatever coiffures it chose. "I'll keep this just inside on the bookshelf and bring it out for signing when someone comes calling." He took the book in both hands and held it to his chest. "It'll be a signal to them that I'm not the curmudgeon of legend."

"I doubt that'll be enough to convince them, Henry," said Peter, assuming a grave face.

"Oh, you're still looking for the strawberry pledge, Peter," said Henry, waving him off. "Thank you, both of you, for the gifts you have given me today."

Peter poked out his lips in the way a child might and said he was always being left out, and he reckoned the only thing he could give Henry was a sip of his good Tennessee whiskey. When he reached his hand behind to his back pocket as if to take out a bottle, Leddie shot her eyes first at her husband, then at Anna Pearl, and back to him, saying sternly, "Peter!" When what came up in his hand was a red and gold tin of pipe tobacco, she scolded him again. "Peter Stedman, you should not even joke about such things in front of this child."

"You're right, honey," Peter said. "My flask is my serious companion and I have left it behind."

Henry and Kate chuckled, and Anna Pearl looked from one adult to the other, at a loss for the reason for their laughter, but then herself joined them in an exaggerated and histrionic tiny burst of laughter. Leddie was won over to the moment and shook her head.

Returning the tobacco tin to his pocket, Peter said, "You know, speaking of souls lost to the vicissitudes of drink, how's about on the Sunday of the lawyer's lecture you come and go to the church with Leddie and me, Henry?" Peter apologized to Henry for his rudeness in not offering sooner to bring him to their church as a guest. "You being a seminarian, you probably enjoy a good church every now and then," Peter added, grinning.

"Thank you, Peter, for the offer. I'll walk to town that day if you don't mind. It clears my head." Henry looked at Peter, and with some hesitation, added, "I will decline your invitation to go to church. I haven't been to church since my wife died some four years ago." Henry put his hand into the loamy rich soil heaped into one of the planters, then brushed the surface with his extended fingers, smoothing and patting there.

"Well, Henry," said Kate, "it's been a wonderful day on your hilltop. Not nearly as cold as I feared when we set out this morning. Now, it's all up to you to grow bushels of good things to eat." Henry told them he would finish the third and a fourth planter and get his seeds into the ground by Easter. Kate gave Henry a hug, followed by Anna Pearl, and with a handshake from Leddie the women went on to the truck and crowded onto the seat in the cab.

"Peter," said Henry, "it might come up again to invite me to church with you. And I do thank you. But I don't have much use for the institutional church. The God I know doesn't come into this world through the rafters of a church building. I worship a God who is everywhere present, in his temple of trees and bushes no less than underneath the spire of steeples."

"Now, how'd I know you'd have something like that to say, Henry Stuart?" Peter asked, bothered but not actually angry, if his face was reading true. "Though I'd have also thought you'd be a little more ready to go to church, what with this healing you seem to have found."

"If I'm healed, it was a divine gift. But I can't, Peter, believe it was tendered like so much fishing bait, with a sharp and curved hook hiding inside."

"I'm not talking about fishing, friend Henry. Church is just good people out trying to find God," Peter said. "Now I reckon you could liken that to casting here and there to find the Big One." Peter gave a loud guffaw that Henry met with a smile.

"But we don't need to fish for God, Peter. He's got a line on us. Always."

"You're a hardheaded fellow, Henry," Peter said.

"My friend back in Nampa," Henry said, "Will Webb, who is a preacher, made such a declaration on many occasions. I have to believe that you are both right."

THIRTY-FIVE

Morning was flying around the world, but had not yet arrived in Tolstoy Park. Birds roosting in the fat cedar near Henry's hut were just beginning to shake the sleep from their wings, their small voices like a gaggle of children whispering too loudly, and now and again one would find some note of its daytime song and be answered from a nearby tree. Henry sat at his narrow desk, and for the third time read by lamplight a letter that had come two days ago from Thomas. He was still angry and wanted to know again whether Henry would come back to Nampa if indeed his illness was in remission. Harvey and Will, each in separate letters arriving within the last week, had admitted to second thoughts on his decision to stay in Alabama and had made the same query: *Why won't you come back home?*

Henry knew this must be difficult at best for them to understand. And quite frankly, Henry was at a loss how to express it differently or more clearly, that he *was* at home. He could write that he had died and had been reborn and this was certainly, therefore, home. But that would be read as churlish and his attempted levity would be lost, and worse harm done. All he knew to do was write to tell them again that he would not return to Nampa, that his days, however many or few he had remaining, would be spent on the Eastern Shore at his round hut in Tolstoy Park.

Thomas had, at least in one paragraph of his letter, taken an interest in accounts from Henry detailing the concrete construction and circular design of his hut. Will and Harvey had made only cursory mention of the round house. Harvey taking him to task for expending such effort to create a curiosity of cramped quarters when the same work might have produced a better and more traditional dwelling. Thomas's tone, by the end of his letter, was less strident, and dropped the announcement that he was getting married and that would probably prevent any travel in the near future. Henry had been mentally composing his reply to his sons and friend in Idaho since walking home from yesterday's Tolstoy lecture, choosing his words more carefully with each mental iteration so as to not disrespect their love and concern for him while at the same time holding steadfastly to his choice to be here in Alabama, not there in Idaho.

Mr. Darrow had spoken yesterday of Tolstoy's flight from home in Yasnaya Polyana, from his wife and children there, finally, at the age of eighty-two, and how he had died in a railroad stationmaster's house not fifty miles away, not a month gone. The lawyer had shared a sentiment of Henry's that fifty miles or five thousand miles, a month or a decade, degrees of time and distance could not minimize Tolstoy's act of leaving, the actualization of a long-simmering craving to fly away. Henry too had flown, nor would he return.

Some three hundred people, two thirds of them from homes on the Eastern Shore, had filled Sunday's seats in Comings Hall on the Organic School campus to hear the lawyer from Chicago who defended a Tennessee teacher's right to teach evolution. Henry heard no facts of Tolstoy's life that he did not already know, except to hear an actual reading of a piece of a letter between Leo Tolstoy and Henry George, the man whose followers had founded Fairhope. Clarence Darrow's lecture on Leo Nikolaevich Tolstoy focused more on his biography than on his philosophy, noting, however, that the events in a man's life, the dynamics of his family and those personal experiences with other members of his larger human family, form the basis of philosophical insight for an individual. Mr. Darrow had spoken of Tolstoy's journals and how entries in them addressed his unhappy later marriage to Sonya, and of his distress over their divergent worldviews.

Henry knew that, though sadness for loss of their company would never leave him, he would not grieve the separation from his sons and friend. He had come home in a certain larger and more spiritual sense. He thought of lines from a Rilke poem, of the dove who flew away and returned, knowing what serenity was, for she had "felt her wings pass through all distance and fear in the course of her wanderings." Rilke said the dove, in her venturing out, in her flying far from the dovecote, had arched her very being over the vast abyss, and was ultimately free through all she had given up. Henry would not deny his own belief that he had gained his life by giving it up. Now he would not cover his new life with the stones of family and history; instead, from those rocks he would rise up and fly.

Finally, as the day was dawning outside, Henry rolled a sheet of paper into his typewriter and wrote letters to Harvey and Thomas and Will. He told them simply that he was happy now, happier than he had ever been, and that he would not come back to Nampa. He ended the letters telling them they would always be welcome in his round home. In the middle of the morning Henry walked to the post office to post the letters, and made a trip down to the mouth of Rock Creek at the bay shore before returning home to find Clarence Darrow sitting on one of his planter box walls, sleepily kicking his feet and looking off down the hill opposite the direction from which Henry came. Henry spoke first. "Good day, Mr. Darrow."

"Oh, there you are!" the lawyer said, jerking his head around with a start. Henry guessed his visitor was his own age, or close. He had a stern and rugged countenance, and a growly voice that, for the lawyer on the other bench, must have been terribly disconcerting. "I hope I'm not intruding, Mr. Stuart. I did so want to drive out and see your place. You said I should pay you a visit, and I wanted to thank you for the rug. It's a work of art and I know just where in my study I'll hang it."

"I'm not sure it's art," Henry said. "I'm sure you remember how our friend Tolstoy preached that art is vulgarized and ceases to be art when money becomes involved."

"Ah, you sly old coot! You wanted to have me out here so you could dun me. Maybe try to sell me another?" The man hopped down, grinning broadly.

"And whatever you believe a fair amount, sir, please double it so

that I may know for sure and certain that I am not practicing art."
Henry joined his visitor, extending his hand with a smile. The lawyer
grabbed his hand, but didn't give it the knuckle-cracking squeeze
Henry thought such a blustery man might use in first meetings.
Clarence Darrow's hand was warm and conveyed a great, good spirit.

Right away the two men fell into step walking toward Henry's
hut, talking as easily as if they had known each other for years. When
Henry explained to Clarence that the rug was most certainly a gift,
but that he might begin selling his rugs soon as a means of income,
the lawyer asked how someone as clearly learned as himself came to
find himself alone, barefooted, and broke in the Alabama woods living in a concrete igloo, for Heaven's sake. Though he kept his story
as succinct as possible, the telling of his circumstances still took Henry
ten minutes, which time passed with the lawyer locked in concen-
trated attentiveness.

"I remember reading a while ago a statement of Anatole France,"
Clarence added as Henry was opening the door to his hut and standing aside for his guest to enter. "He said that the chief business of life
is killing time. And so it is. This hilltop of yours looks like a great
place for doing that."

Henry declared that no, he had to keep busy, and that he loved almost any work that fell to him. "My father quoted Immanuel Kant
to me as a boy: *The strong desire for a pleasant and ideal life is a child's
worst misfortune. It is crucial that children should know how to work
from an early age.* I'm certain Anatole France was also right. In any
case, I had no choice. My father insisted that I work. I'm of a mind,
even, that it was this work of building my hut that chased from me
the illness the doctor said would kill me."

"Oh, doctors! What the hell do they know?" Clarence boomed as
he went inside Henry's hut. During the brief roundabout tour inside,
Clarence expressed utter disbelief that Henry would crawl up a ladder and into bed each night, when he himself had trouble with his
rheumatism just getting into and out of a regular bed.

"A fellow can get used to most anything, I believe," Henry answered. The two men came back out into the sunshine, and sat on

two of five cement pilasters Henry had constructed low to the ground just for the purpose of sitting.

"If you are bound to work and can't avoid it," Clarence said, "and can be lost in the work, Henry, it's the most tolerable life one can have. You've got your gardens going over there." He stretched his neck up for a better view. "Looks like you've got it rigged so you don't have to bend and stoop," he said, still looking at the raised planter boxes. Then the lawyer cocked his eye toward Henry. "The Talmud says it's nobler to grow your own food than to be religious, a statement I always admired coming out of a religious book."

Clarence rocked back and tilted his face to the February sun, rubbing his hair briskly, continuing, "Now, I never was industrious. I could prove that by a number of people. Still, I have always worked, Mr. Stuart. Some task is always waiting for me and someone always calling to me. And I've never figured out how to avoid the task or ignore the call. So these seventy years of my life have slipped by, and I have scarcely seen them going."

"I guessed us about the same age. I've lived out sixty-nine years now, though I have been aware of their passing. Most particularly these last two," Henry said. "Chiefly I've wondered why I spent so much time filling my head with things of questionable worth."

"Questionable! You know good and well, Mr. Stuart, it's worthless." Clarence laced his fingers and held up his knee so that his foot was free to swing again as it had when he sat on the planter box wall. "What's the difference if we gather all the facts of the universe into our brains for the worms to eat? Might give the worms indigestion."

"It has occurred to me," said Henry, picking up a pine stick and doodling in the dirt between his bare feet, "that the more we think we know, the more we tend to think we matter. We become obsessed with our own cleverness. How and when we might ply our cleverness." Henry pitched the stick into the grass. "I think we have a constant desire to prove that we matter."

"You've nailed it, Mr. Stuart," added Clarence. "One can imagine nothing more tiresome and profitless than sitting down and thinking of oneself."

"Especially, I might add," said Henry, "when for not thinking of oneself we are repaid with room in our heads to think of others. That way, I believe, leads to love." Clarence fidgeted and seemed to Henry uncomfortable on a path of conversation that struck out over nebulous terrain foggy with words like *love*. Henry liked this man's company and reveled in the good conversation, and for the sake of keeping it longer into the evening, aimed for solid ground. He waited a long moment, and asked, "What of Sonya's attempt to stop Tolstoy from abandoning his literary copyrights? I suppose intellectual property is community property in a marriage, like so much real estate."

"Why, of course it is. You see that, Mr. Stuart. His writing, his books, have value measured in actual money," said Clarence. "Royalties. It's a mother's duty to feather the nest. She bore Leo thirteen children, man! Tolstoy was born into wealth. I'm not saying, mind you, he didn't work. But my father always told me that a thing easily gained is a thing easily tossed off."

"I suppose I was thinking," said Henry, "about the deep spiritual restlessness that motivated him and having a mate who did not share that. That must have been painful for him." Both men sat in silence. Henry wiggled his toes in the dirt and then picked up another pine branch to scratch a spot on his back. "What about you, Mr. Darrow? What I read of you, about the cases you take, makes me believe there's something more than money that drives you."

"Put it this way, I don't know the meaning of the word *success* in an ordinary sense. To some—perhaps to most—it means money. But I never cared much for it, Mr. Stuart, nor tried very hard to get much of it, or in truth, ever had a great deal of money." Clarence stood, brushing off the seat of his trousers. "But still, most of my life I've had what I needed." He suggested they walk over by the remains of Henry's barn and perhaps draw up a little drinking water from the well over there. And so in an easy manner, on into the afternoon and into the dusky dark, the two men talked. When the February stars overhead finally caught their attention and both men were silenced by the sheer number and brightness of them, like a scattering of sun-fired dewdrops on black velvet, it broke the spell of their amiable chatter. The lawyer stretched and said he was ready for a good night's sleep at the Colonial Inn in Fairhope. "Then I'll hit the road tomorrow. Back to Chicago," Clarence said, and told Henry how much he'd enjoyed his visit to Tolstoy Park. "I'll be back if you'll let me come."

"It would be my pleasure, sir. Indeed. Please come again, Clarence." And as he bade good night to Clarence when he got into his automobile to leave, Henry felt better about his letters to Thomas and Harvey and Will. Each was more than a letter, of course; it was a writ that he would never see his sons again, but according to a far different proposition than the prospect of his imminent death. This was a statement of a choice to live out his life without seeing them ever again. And that had nothing to do with how much he loved them.

• THIRTY-SIX •

And so Henry's days and nights became a pattern of months and years of work and rest, of walks slow and rambling, into town and down to the beach, of sketching plants and insects and sea creatures into his journal, of long visits with frequent visitors to his Tolstoy Park, of spirited talks with townspeople about religion and philosophy and Henry George's single-tax colony and Leo Tolstoy, of occasional lectures at the town hall, of gardening and learning to eat little but well from a variety of foods almost exclusively prepared by himself, of delightful lessons in weaving for the students of the Organic School.

Among the humorous anecdotes now woven into his life—Henry still smiled to recall it—he had been going to one of his Sunday afternoon lectures in the big open meeting room on the second floor above the hardware store in Fairhope, and he huffed up the small hill along North Church Street. It was August, he remembered, maybe

1935, 1936, and the subtropical sun baked down on a breezeless, humid day. Henry was sweating. He had become distracted looking for his handkerchief in order to swab his wet forehead, not finding it in his shirt pocket where he usually kept it. As he looked down, patting his trousers pockets, he bumped into a little old woman, who immediately struck at him with her thin hand, swatting his sleeved forearm as though she might be aiming to kill a mosquito alight there.

"See here, you, look where you are going!"

"I am most sorry, dear lady. I surely must pay attention," Henry replied.

"Well, you certainly must—" And then the old woman apprehended that this man might be going to the same lecture that she was going to. The Sunday streets were mostly deserted, except for pedestrians on their way to hear the address. She drew in her breath. "You cannot be planning to attend the talk on Robert Frost." It was a statement that came out like a question. Her eyes were piercing. Henry had not time to say a word. "See here, you are not only shabbily dressed, but you are sweating and I should think bear an odor, though I am not sufficiently near enough to tell." Henry stood and looked into the old woman's eyes for a brief moment before turning to walk away, back down the hill to an alley that allowed him to come to the hardware store's back stairs.

He was a bit late, and mounted the stairs, went straightaway into the meeting room, and directly to the lectern. By now, Henry had found his handkerchief, and patted his brow with the folded cloth. When he had spread his damp notes on America's bard across the angled oaken board atop the lectern, and looked out upon his audience of fifty or so people, Henry looked squarely into the face of the old woman from down on the sidewalk. She sat in the front row. Her mouth fell open and her face tilted forward, and the waxy skin flooded crimson beneath her powdered hair. Henry feared the old woman would leave, but she did not, nor did she look up from her hands gravely composed into the folds of her linen dress in her lap. Without preface, Henry recited:

Two roads diverged in a wood, and I—
I took the one less traveled by . . .

Henry stopped speaking, kept his eyes down on his papers, and without comment passed on to his lecture on the Pulitzer Prize–winning Frost. That had been all Henry had said, its import shared only by him and the old woman, by way of admission of his own "unique" appearance. Henry never saw the old woman in Fairhope again, and guessed she had come over from Mobile.

For nearly two decades Henry had lived in his round house in Tolstoy Park, and now Thomas and Harvey had taken up again their insistence that Henry return to Idaho, their letters coming more frequently this past year, the tone of them varying week to week from scolding to beseeching to reasoning to worrying, and Henry had answered each. He repeated to his sons, responding to their separate letters, that he was not lonely, as they suggested. His reply was consistent: "I am well and happy," he wrote, "and this is my home."

Henry told them of sitting in a dogwood blossom breeze on a bed of pine needles on the high bluff where Rock Creek gurgled its little contribution to the brackish waters of Mobile Bay and the remarkable colors spilled into the western sky south of Mobile at sunset. Henry penned descriptions of the belly-gliding shadow of the brown pelican so near the wave tips that ripples fell onto the water from the brush of air stirring beneath the huge wings. He described his intense joy at sighting the return of a pair of ospreys—could they be the two beautiful birds he had once observed?—to build their new nest in an old dead juniper that stood defiantly on a narrow strip of beach beneath the bluff. "And what need of more would a man with eighty-six years on God's earth have?"

But then this letter had come. Folded and tucked into the same envelope with a brief note from Harvey, written in neat curving script on a tiny sheet of floral-trimmed notepaper. It was a single page, in an old man's trembling hand, from William Webb, the man who had married Henry to Molly and then later had buried her, the man who pointed the way to Tolstoy Park.

My Dear Henry,

    Can it be ten years or more since I posted a letter to you? Indeed, can it be twenty years that you have lived in Alabama? Tom and Harvey would have me believe, too, that you still own no shoes! And I wonder that an old man's toes can abide the sting of frost on a February morning, the slather of soupy mud in April spreading them out. The soles of your feet must be as tough as the calluses of Jesus, John, and James combined. But not as tough, I think, as the task I have set for myself here in this scribbly note. Henry, I want you to come home to Idaho. And though I know of Tom's and Harvey's pleas of a like manner, my request bears no complicity with your sons' and is borne to you on an entirely selfish wind. I want so badly to see you, Henry, my dear brother, before I die. I have been abed now since spring, and the doctor tells me the summer will take me. Perhaps you yourself are not well or cannot otherwise easily travel, and I am mightily ashamed to place so boldly my own wishes before whatever yours to the contrary might be. But I damn well want to see you one last time, Henry, and if you will consent to grant me this one last request, then I will take up once again, firsthand with God Almighty Himself, as soon as I get there, the begging for your soul to be spared the fires of Hell. Will you come?

                                  Most Sincerely,
                                    Will

Now Henry sat on a stump near his garden and reread the letter. The sun was warm on his neck, and it felt good warming the shirt across his shoulders. It was harder these days to hold the heat inside his body, though the heat was still inside his mind, alight with the turning of the modern world—its radio broadcasts, its airplane travel—and on fire with anger at the early blindness of world leaders to the threat this Adolf Hitler had become; and warmed, on the other hand, in optimism that we seemed to have pulled through the Great Depression. Henry knew he was an old man, filled to overflowing with the life that had come his way, now become willing to let that be enough.

He continued to hold up the page in his right hand, and in his left hand the note and envelope. He let his eyes slide past the out-held page toward the open door of his home, to its low round wall and its open windows. Without taking a step nearer, he could smell the piney springtime wind mixing there inside his hut with the pungent ash and woodsmoke of two decades of winter fires and teapots every dawn. Breezes would waft and curl about his circular space seeking escape through the high twin vents in the top of the dome, but not before coaxing away some kerosene essence from his typewriter ribbon, not before brushing the earthen floor for a hint of its dusty aroma, not before filtering through the musty cotton canvas of his hanging cot.

And Henry knew that like this June morning's wind, soon he would leave his house. And he would not return. The death that had been put off so strangely those many years ago would make a renewed call for him and he would answer without alarm or regret, without hand-wringing or weeping. He had heard the *skree* of an osprey yesterday. He had raised his eyes to the sky but had seen nothing there. Then he had heard the cry again from directly overhead where he was looking, but still he saw nothing. And he came to believe his death song was being raised by the fish hawk. So yes, he would go back to Idaho. And he would see Will again. He would see his sons again. And if there was some need, he would meet Thomas and Harvey in dialogue over this long and purposeful absence from their lives. At least there was the possibility, if not the likelihood, that some understanding would be forthcoming for them. And such might grant them a measure of the peace that Henry had known every day since his healing at Rock Creek. At least there was that possibility.

Henry did not sleep well that night; the rheumatism in his bones seemed intent on making some gain while he was giving in to throbs of melancholia. Neither malady had successfully beset him these last many years, but now it seemed his fires were low and smoldering and not holding back the outer dark. The hut seemed empty, though it was only the loom that had so far been taken away. The janitor and some of the older boys and girls had come yesterday to take his small bequest back to Organic School. Now the students would have two looms on which to learn rug weaving. How many of those barefoot young people had Henry taught to weave a rug, each with at least one rug to take home? He could not count them.

It was well before daylight, and even earlier than usual for Henry to be up. In the soft yellow light of the kerosene lamp with its tall smoky glass chimney, Henry opened his pocketknife and with its fine steel edge carefully sharpened a point onto his No. 2 lead pencil, creating a small pile of red cedar shavings on his desktop. He put the knife and pencil aside and took down his flimsy leather New Testament and read the Gospel of John, his favorite book in the Bible. He read slowly: "In the beginning was the word . . ." and felt the old stirring of excitement that the most holy emanation was sound, not light. Painters painted light, but they could not paint sound, so it was halos and radiant beams depicting religious mysteries, and light had silently become for people the stuff of creation. But Henry believed it was sound. And he waited for the familiar sounds outside his round room in the soft blue light of predawn; how he loved those first birds who came off the roost, raising their small chuckling voices.

Henry put away the New Testament and took up his knife and the pencil and carved away another tiny sliver of wood. He thought of the art professor at Mount Union College who had so many years ago told his sketching class that a mechanical pencil sharpener was an abomination and a devilish device invented by the pencil companies to sell more pencils, and Henry smiled that he had absentmindedly cut away more wood than was necessary to expose a graphite tip. With the calloused edge of his palm he raked the cedar trimmings into a small empty wire-banded wooden nail keg that he used as a trash receptacle.

He opened his journal and wrote with the pencil at the top of a clean page: "June 11, 1944. Today after sunup Thomas will come from his hotel. Nineteen years in Alabama. Today I am going back to Idaho. Today I am leaving home." He looked up from the desk to the vacant spot on the curving wall where that quatrain from the James Russell Lowell poem had hung. Kate had lettered "A Stanza on Freedom," the lines that went, *They are slaves who fear to speak for the fallen and the weak* . . . He had given that framed poem to Peter last week when he signed the conveyance of his property called Tolstoy Park to Peter and Leddie Stedman. And he had pried loose from a pine tree the sign that read TOLSTOY PARK, the same one he had painted and nailed up some two decades ago, eleven times repainted, and had given that to Peter.

A hard damp wind blew from the south, sweeping the air into every crack and crevice in Henry's hut, bringing to his nose the scent of the sea from thirty-five miles down the bay. The sun was two hours high when Henry heard Thomas's automobile pulling up the hill. Thomas had been here for three days, coming and going from the Colonial Inn in Fairhope, doing some few things each day in preparation for Henry's leaving Tolstoy Park. Thomas had said right away upon his arrival that he would stay in town, and Henry had not insisted otherwise. It was remarkable to Henry how so quickly, after the initial awkwardness that each of them had blinked their way through following a tentative embrace, how quickly it had become matter-of-fact and businesslike between father and son. And now the only unfinished business was to leave this place. Henry went outside to greet Thomas, who walked up to Henry carrying a shoebox.

Henry took the unmarked brown cardboard box from Thomas and lifted it as high as his chest. His fingers trembled slightly, though Thomas would not have noticed had he looked. Henry extended the package away from himself. It was bound about with jute twine, tied in a loose bow at the top. He let his eyes rest on the shoebox. He might have been looking through a window, for Henry didn't see what he held there in his hands, but a swirling of years cascading back to a muddy slog down Rainier Street in Nampa, leaving the doctor's office with an invitation to die called to him over his shoulder. Near twenty years ago. Now he was eighty-six.

Henry set the box on the long green grass at his feet, among a heavy scattering of brown pine needles, and almost immediately a tiny beetle, a ladybug, landed there to explore in circles briefly before bending its silken wings out from underneath the rough red and black casements on its back and flying away, lifted on a light breeze that had sprung up.

"One of the last sermons I heard Will preach, Father, was also among the best I'd heard him preach," Thomas said, coming out of Henry's hut with the very same two pieces of luggage Henry had come to Alabama with. Thomas stopped, facing his father from ten feet away. Henry stood up from studying the grass. "At the outset," said Thomas, "he posed a question to the congregation, to the mothers and fathers in the pews: 'If you knew that tonight you would lie down and die into the arms of Jesus, what would you wish to teach your children on this your last day with them? What word would you wish to say to your wife or husband? What wisdom would you wish to leave with your friends?' "

Thomas walked over and stood shoulder to shoulder beside Henry, looking down the low rise toward a huge clump of pampas grass higher than a man's head and broader than a farm gate that had begun fifteen years ago in a small pot given to Henry by Kate. The sun's light upon the leafy ground chased cloud shadows as they slid along among the trees upon this hill in Tolstoy Park.

"And what would I teach you, Thomas, if I knew that I would die tonight? Is that what you'd like to know? If I could distill my years in these Alabama woods into a sermon, what would my message be?"

Thomas nodded.

Henry looked downward, and pushed at the shoebox with the toes on his right foot. "In your own way"—and then Henry turned his face to stare into his son's blue eyes, so much the color of his own—"learn to die in peace. That's what I think is important, Thomas. My own lessons for that have come from how I treat other people, from what things I give value, but mostly from understanding that in every instance fear is of my own making."

Thomas was silent, but nodded almost imperceptibly. Henry bent and picked up the shoebox and without looking back at his hut or at his son went to the waiting automobile.

THIRTY-SEVEN

Somewhere west of Memphis, the train angled to the north, and Henry had a view of the distant plains horizon rolling upward to meet the orange sun. He put his head against the glass. Even in the dawning summer the window was cold to Henry, and the chill and the steely vibration of the wheels over the rails tingled his forehead.

Here has one life been lived, a rhythmic rocking along like the *Twilight Limited* on a round-trip run from birth to death, reborn in mind, a new life in spirit. "Let your minds be remade, and your whole nature thus transformed," Paul had written to the Romans.

Henry knew that they were wrong, the philosophers and sages and saints, those who would have us believe that to realize our dreams is the worst that can come to us, a belief that our dreams' eye is not set upon matters of the spirit. Those crying such wisdom from their towers in the dark were wrong. Henry's faith proclaimed to him in both sunlight and sleep that we are all come from spirit and to spirit all shall return, no matter if the interim course runs on rails laid through wealth or poverty, through weakness or strength, through joy or sadness, through intelligence or ignorance.

What delight and help had Henry found those many years ago when first he read Emerson's line that fame and shame are the same, what insight into the nature of our real relationship, creator and created! How did those two lines go in that hymn of the Brahmin?

> *The vanished gods to me appear,*
> *And one to me are fame and shame.*

Henry looked across the seat at Thomas, himself now a silver-hair, and he became suddenly and deeply tired, but not weary as from exhaustion, more like the warm willingness to lie down and sleep at the end of a day bent to hard work. His feet were cold. Henry knew his feet would never again feel the fire in the earth. This buzzing in the train floor would fade and stop. Perhaps Tolstoy as he lay dying in a train station felt the rumbling of a distant train. This train would arrive where Henry had boarded it in Idaho, and Thomas would lift him from his seat by the window.

"You need a hand there, mister?"

And Thomas would say, "No, he's my father and he is sleeping." And his son would take him home and lay him in the room where he and Molly had slept together. Harvey would have put clean sheets on the bed and turned back the covers. The doctor would be summoned, and perhaps a preacher, but not Will Webb. He no longer waited for Henry. Thirty miles back Henry had felt Will leave him. But not for long.

He fumbled his small daybook from his shirt pocket and, taking out a fountain pen, opened to a clean page. Henry closed his eyes and let the darkness grow light with the sweet face of Kate, saw her hazel eyes wet and her cheeks traced with tears, her face troubled and searching as he had sat with her to tell her good-bye. She would miss him deeply, that he knew. He had been thinking what he might say to her, what thing he could tell her for her to know he was at peace with this last step, and that he hoped her grief could be for their separation, not that he was dying.

Kate and her Anna Pearl too would die someday, and Henry prayed that they would come to their moment of passing and find grace to meet that day in strength and calm. What could he give her by way of instruction? Behind his closed eyelids, a small voice, perhaps his own, perhaps not: *There is only one thing to know: Walk a path along which you can live your life in concert with others, if not being outright helpful, at least not causing harm. That learned, a life thus lived, allows one to die well.*

And Henry opened his eyes and blinked until the little journal's parchment-colored sheet was fully focused, then wrote, "A Poem for Kate and Anna Pearl," and before he slept, he reached back down the years and found the voice he had used for telling Anna Pearl stories when she was a little girl, and in a slow hand wrote:

When the Wind awakened
And moved across the still face of the water,
A tiny Wave was born, not much more than a ripple.
The wind pushed down harder upon the Sea,
Rolling the water before her, bunching it up,
And the ripple became a Wave in full.
And it grew until its head curled mightily upward,
Rolling onward, surging with great strength forward,
Rising higher and higher.
And now the Wave could see a great distance,
And he shuddered in fear when he saw
Those ahead of him, ceaselessly, one after another,
Crashing onto the sand
And dying with great pitiful roaring.
So the Wave cried to the Wind, begging her to be still.
But she would not.
And so he asked her, "Why are you doing this?"
The Wind asked, "What is it you think I do?"
"You are pushing me to my death!" the Wave exclaimed.
"And if I stop pushing?"
"The Sea will receive me back into itself," said the Wave.
"And if I keep pushing?" the Wind asked.
"I will crash—" and the Wave paused,
"and the Sea will receive me back into itself."
And the Wave,
Water before he was born,
And water evermore,
Laughed a great roar, and rolled mightily onward.

It was a Sunday afternoon in late June and Fairhope Avenue and Church Street were crowded with more cars and people than downtown Fairhope had seen in a long time. There was palpable excitement that the D-day invasion two weeks earlier by 150,000 Allied troops on the beaches of Normandy could help bring a sooner end to the war.

At the hardware store on the corner, on the second floor in a large town meeting hall, sat Peter Stedman. A tall window overlooking the street was open, and he sat with his simple wooden chair drawn up to the window for the benefit of any breeze at play and the sun's light so that he might see more clearly the words he was reading. The *Birmingham News-Age Herald* newspaper page was yellowing and becoming brittle, so he handled it carefully.

It would probably be an hour before the first of the others began arriving and he wanted this time alone to reminisce about Henry while reading again the reporter's story of a visit to Tolstoy Park. He adjusted the glasses on his nose, and bent his face closer to the page held open across his lap. He read: "Reporter Discovers a Modern Thoreau Living in Baldwin County." Peter found himself skimming down the article, his attention catching here and there: at the reporter's admission that he couldn't resist buying one of Henry's rugs, at a cataloguing of some of the titles on Henry's bookshelves, at the quotes from Henry—Peter didn't think the words sounded much like his friend.

Only the last paragraph evoked in Peter something of the sense of Henry. The reporter wrote, "When I left him at twilight, and cast one last look at the old man, I was reminded of Whitman's poem 'Maud Muller' and how the judge must have felt when he looked back down the lane and saw Maud Muller standing in the midst of the hayfield, barefoot, looking in his direction." And so, Peter thought our Henry Stuart stands, looking in the direction of us all.

Peter held the last sentence in his mind, looked up slowly and out the window. The street was busier now than when he had begun reading. Peter's hair and mustache were thin and gray, and gold wire-rimmed spectacles pinched his nose. He was wearing a starched white shirt and a black vest. He stood, and his back gave him pain. His right foot was asleep and he waited for the circulation to return before walking over to the small library table at the side of the room and returning the newspaper article to his folder there. Peter sorted through the sheets of paper in the folder until he found a single page, and took it out and held it as he walked back to the window. He bent down, and leaning slightly out the window, cried in a loud voice, "Anybody else coming up here best be making haste."

Peter unbuttoned his shirtsleeves and rolled them up, then sat back down to read from the page a poem Henry had written for his wife Molly. Henry had written out a copy of the poem and brought it to Peter the next time they were together after Peter had complained to Henry that it was not easy being a married man. That must have been twenty years ago. The poem was called "Together" and the lines had a remarkable effect on Peter each time he read them. Peter believed the simple words actually had propped up his marriage to Leddie.

Henry had written:

When the two shall become as one, / the one is still the two: / sound and silence together thrill the flute— / each note must have its space or the melody will not move. / Each heart must have its mind or the circle is not true. / When the One has seen the Other— / a voice not his, a passion not hers— / together in God they are now, as such, / written on a single page in lines not made to touch.

Peter looked up at the room as people filed in. Leddie walked down the center aisle and sat on the front row in the chair nearest the side desk. While others settled themselves along the back and side walls, Peter slowly got up and walked over to his wife. He gazed at

Leddie, bent and kissed her on the cheek, and handed her the page from which he had just read. "Here, Henry gave this to us." He gave her a big wink and a grin. "I've been holding out on you, honey," he said, patting her shoulder.

Leddie took the paper, glanced at it and then at the woman and man seated to her left. She folded the page along the old creases. "I'll read this later," Leddie said. "I'm sure Henry doesn't mind if I wait."

"Nope," answered Peter, "I don't expect he would mind at all."

Peter walked back to his chair, sat and and surveyed the room one last time before getting things started here. A man in the fourth row indicated there was an empty seat beside him, prompting two others to follow suit and announce vacant chairs on their rows. Peter got up and scraped the lectern back across the floor, sliding it back toward the open window. He released the top button on his shirt collar.

"You fellows want to open those other two windows back there?" Peter said, pointing to the far corner of the room. Heavy black ceiling fans paddled the warm, musty air, and several handheld paper fans waved in the audience. Conversation droned and chair legs knocked and complained against the pine plank floor. Peter reached into his trousers pocket and withdrew a penknife and rapped it on the wooden lectern, calling for the attention of the room. He looked at the face of his vest-pocket watch.

"It's hot in here, and I promise this won't take long," Peter said, when the people had grown quiet. "Our good friend and neighbor Henry James Stuart died two weeks ago on a train bound for Idaho. He was eighty-six. He lived up the road in his round concrete hut for almost twenty years, making a liar of his doctor who told him he'd be dead within a year or two of coming here." Peter filled his chest with air and hooked his thumbs in his vest pockets, peering over his glasses at the rows of people. "I've made it to eighty-four over all kinds of predictions, and I think Henry'd say let's just live until we die." Peter paused and walked over to the small table to his right and picked up a fan for himself, waving it in front of his face as he walked back to the center of the room.

"How many times did Henry Stuart stand right here where I'm

standing and give good talks on all manner of topics?" Peter told the story of a well-dressed woman waiting on the sidewalk to come upstairs and hear a lecture on Robert Frost.

"I got it from an eyewitness that this lady wrinkled her nose at this old bewhiskered barefoot man approaching her in baggy clothes. She told the old man he wouldn't be welcome to attend the lecture attired so shabbily, and asked him to go away. I'd have given a gold mullet to see the look on her face when that same old man came up by the back stairs to give his talk to the room where this very lady sat," said Peter, with a mischievous grin.

Peter let the laughter die down and then went on. "Newspaper stories, and there have been plenty about Henry Stuart in the last twenty years, frequently called him 'The Hermit of Tolstoy Park.' " Peter walked over to the small table again and opened a bag and took out a handful of notebooks. "I wound up with some of Henry's things, these among them. In here"—and Peter shook the fistful of books in the air over his head—"are the signatures of one thousand, one hundred and thirty-nine people, numbered and dated. It's a roll of names, a veritable herd of people who visited at Henry's round hut these last few years. That man was no hermit!" When the hubbub subsided, Peter added, "And Clarence Darrow's name's in here six times!"

Peter took a clean folded handkerchief from his back pocket and wiped sweat from his forehead. Kate Anderson stood up. "Peter, if I may say something."

"Of course," Peter said, lifting his hand as if in invitation to speak.

Kate turned to face the room, with the easy air of a teacher. She was lovely, her full hair was pinned up in loose waves, and she wore an elegant but simply cut dark dress. Her voice was even. "Without limit, he gave his time and his talent to the students at my school. He loved the children and taught them to weave rugs and how to read and appreciate poems. Some even became inspired to try their own hand at writing because of Henry's encouragement." Kate told how they made several field trips to his hut, and that he took entire days with her students. "I remember the children were just amazed that he climbed a ladder to get into his hanging bed each night," Kate said.

Anna Pearl stood up beside her mother.

"I was a little girl, and don't even remember asking to be allowed to call Mr. Stuart 'Poppy.'" Anna Pearl spoke softly, tentatively, as though not at all certain to continue with her private feelings. "And the word *Poppy* sounds funny coming out of my mouth now that I'm a woman about to be married." Anna Pearl said she would also like to read a poem that she had cut from the newspaper fourteen years ago when she was a student at Organic School. "I brought the poem to school to tease Poppy that he had a secret admirer, and I'll never forget how he asked me read it to him while he stood at the loom," Anna Pearl said. "It's called, 'To HJS, the Sage of Tolstoy Park' and it's by someone, Miss V.V. I won't read all of it, but it goes like this:

When I looked into his eyes,
(Never, I think, shall I see again such eyes as yours!)
I felt little and frightened and awed.
(They had not prepared me for this—
They never mentioned your eyes.)

"I read the poem to Poppy in a silly singsong voice. I wanted to tease him about having a girlfriend. But when I was quite finished, Poppy only looked at me, not a word, only his kind and tender glance. And it was as though I myself saw his eyes for the very first time. I too now think that none of us will ever again see eyes like his." Anna Pearl sat down and bowed her head. Kate sat down beside her and draped her arm across her daughter's shoulder, and turned her face to Anna Pearl. There was cool silence as strong as a presence in the hot, crowded room.

A man in a rumpled seersucker suit fanning himself with his hat, who had accompanied his wife to the eulogy, but perhaps begrudgingly, said, "I had to sit through a long-winded preaching this morning, and damn near swooned with heat prostration. Can we say good-bye to the old weaver and get outside before we're called to join him? Lord, it's hot in here, Peter!"

"You're right, Brother Ben. Then let's get outside where it's cooler," Peter said, and quite a din arose as the room began to empty. Only

Leddie kept her seat. She was reading Henry's poem, and Peter watched her face.

"He got this wrong, you know," she said, tapping the paper with her finger.

"What?" Peter asked.

"This *lines not made to touch*." Leddie stood up and Peter offered her his hand. She folded the paper and tucked the poem into her purse. Peter knew she would be its keeper from now on. Leddie placed her hand in Peter's, turned to face him, and said, "I should think a weaver would have known better."

Sonny Brewer owns Over the Transom Bookshop in Fairhope, Alabama, and is the founder of the nonprofit Fairhope Center for the Writing Arts. He is the former editor in chief of *Mobile Bay Monthly;* he also published and edited *Eastern Shore Quarterly* magazine, edited *Red Bluff Review,* and was founding associate editor of the weekly *West Alabama Gazette.* Brewer is the editor of the acclaimed, annual three-volume anthology of Southern writing, *Stories from the Blue Moon Café.*

This book was set in Garamond, a typeface originally designed by the Parisian type cutter Claude Garamond (1480–1561). This version of Garamond was modeled on a 1592 specimen sheet from the Egenolff-Berner foundry, which was produced from types assumed to have been brought to Frankfurt by the punch cutter Jacques Sabon (d. 1580).

Claude Garamond's distinguished romans and italics first appeared in *Opera Ciceronis* in 1543–44. The Garamond types are clear, open and elegant.